The Avlem Burden

A Fragments novel

Kell Willsen

S.F. Stories

For content advisory, see https://rb.gy/mpthr3

———◆◆◆———

To all my patient teachers

ACT ONE: THE TRAGEDY OF BRINNESHA TYNAR

Being a cautionary tale of hubris in the
face of wisdom

I

Brinnesha Tynar loved stories. True stories about her grandparents' journeying from Avlenia and founding their town of Perayen; made-up stories about brave heroes and strange adventures: Brinnesha loved them all. She used to wonder, before her Talent manifested, if she would one day create her own stories. Even once it became clear that she was a Finder, Brinnesha devoted herself to Finding and writing down as many stories as possible. Something that, right now, would be much easier if her maid would stop trying to dress her.

"I'll put my gown on when *I'm* ready, Alra, not when my sister tells you I am. You can do my hair, if you must, but don't get in my way."

"Yes, Miss Brinnesha."

Brinnesha wrote on, losing herself in the memory of that morning. She'd gone down to the Elemental village not more than an hour after sunrise, keen to witness the village waking up. Spring was well under-way, and the dew-flecked grass was springy under-foot. Everything was bright and fresh and delicious.

Wouldn't the Elementals be surprised to see her so early! They probably expected her to be lazy and selfish like other Avlem, even though she'd been visiting the village regularly for ages now.

Brinnesha entered the village beside the chief's hut, a little larger and better-maintained than the rest, though just as quaint. His wife, or perhaps his sister, came out as Brinnesha passed. The woman had a basket on one hip and a child in a little sack against the other.

Brinnesha waved, but the woman only turned away towards the fields. The blacksmith was making his forge hot, and didn't return her greeting. Brinnesha gave him the benefit of the doubt and decided that he hadn't heard her – just as the fishermen heading north to the river hadn't seen her on the road. From another Avlem Brinnesha would have taken these as deliberate slights, at best, but she could be patient. It must be hard for Elementals to overcome their dislike of her race. She had to give them time to see her as more than a child of their oppressors.

Not that *her* parents were oppressors, of course. They were wonderfully kind to everyone, up to and including their Elemental servants. This brought Brinnesha back up to the present and she thought of her own maid, now busy with Brinnesha's second layer of plaits.

"Alra, what do you think of this? It's a story about a fire Elemental who re-kindled the sun." Brinnesha regaled her maid at length with the new folktale of the mythic hero who travelled to the end of the world to bring back summer. She talked quickly, so caught up in the story that she could hardly keep still under Alra's hands.

Alra herself didn't enter into Brinnesha's enthusiasm at all, poor thing, but Brinnesha had at least made the effort. She ended by saying, "The storyteller in the village translated it for me this afternoon. Well, he told it to me and I put it into proper Sidrean. Did you like it?"

"Yes, Miss Brinnesha, I always used to like that story," said Alra, flatly. "The storyteller is my uncle."

Brinnesha was delighted. "Is he? Yes, I suppose he would be, wouldn't he? All you Elementals are so connected to each other – it's marvellous, really. Whereas all we poor Avlem have are the few relations that settled us here. Well, I suppose I've got all kinds of distant cousins back in Avlenia, but I don't think they count, do you? You can't really call people family when you never see them, can you?"

"Indeed, Miss Brinnesha."

The maid sounded almost resentful, which Brinnesha didn't understand. After all, Alra had three half-days off every month to visit her family if she wanted to. But perhaps she just was tired? All the same...

"Not so tight with those plaits, Alra, if you don't mind."

"Sorry, Miss Brinnesha."

That tone again. Brinnesha decided to let Alra go upstairs to bed early, and not wait up for her to come home from the party that night.

She said as much to her maid, who only replied, "Very good, Miss Brinnesha," and continued working on the complicated arrangement of her mistress's braids. And if she looked rather hard at the back of that mistress's head, it didn't hurt the braids.

Brinnesha's pencil scratched on for a few more lines, finishing the story she'd shared with her unappreciative maid. Then she stood up and held out her arms for her over-gown.

Alra dutifully wrapped the gown around her and tied the fastenings. Brinnesha put on her own necklet and stepped into her shoes at the exact moment that her sister called for her to hurry up.

Alra followed Brinnesha closely down the stairs, settling the cloak around Brinnesha's shoulders as they descended. Brinnesha fastened the front as she reached the last step, then nodded a dismissal to her maid. She smirked triumphantly at her sister, who was still waiting for her outdoor shoes and her cloak.

"See, Eris?" she said. "I don't need to hurry, because I know where all my things are."

"And because Alra's a treasure," said Eris. "Won't you let me poach her from you, just for a year or two? If she can manage you, she'll be perfect for helping me keep track of the children. I can barely deal with one toddler, and this time next year I'll have two of them!"

"You say that like it's my fault you got married early," Brinnesha replied. "And I wouldn't part with Alra for anything. She *is* a gem, isn't she? But I suppose you can ask her to help you during the day – I'm always out then."

Her sister replied only with a small smile, and abruptly changed the subject.

"Never mind that for now," she said. "I want you on your best behaviour tonight. You're seventeen, Little Sister. Nearly an adult. You have to start acting like one."

Brinnesha sighed at this well-worn refrain, and displayed her maturity by very deliberately not rolling her eyes.

"What's wrong with my behaviour? I don't do anything that you don't. Well, except Finding stories to preserve, of course." She made a slightly less mature smirk; her Talent was valuable and she knew it. More importantly, her oldest sister knew it.

"I'm not talking about your Finding. I'm talking about your blatant attempts to keep socialising with the Elementals. I don't think you really understand our position here."

"Merizat spends more time with Elementals than I do. She's out in the water meadows with them all day, almost every day."

"Our sister is training her Irrigation Talent, and you know it. That's study, not leisure. And she stays separate from the Water Elementals working there. Whereas you go down to the village whenever the mood takes you. Some people are saying you've got a lover, or worse."

Brinnesha scowled. "And by 'some people', I suppose you mean the awful old gossips who stand around in Brother's shop. I thought you knew better than to listen to people like that."

"I didn't say I believed them, Little Sister. But you don't understand the damage you're doing. To your own reputation, the family's – even the whole Perayen Community."

"I'm not doing anything to harm the Community!" Brinnesha snapped. "I use my Talent to help people, and I talk respectfully to the town elders... or as respectfully as I can, anyway. How am I hurting Perayen?"

Eris closed her eyes and Brinnesha could almost hear her keeping her temper.

"It's not just about how you behave inside Perayen itself – it's about how others see us. All of us. You're too young to remember, but Mother and Father worked hard for their good reputation; and your wild behaviour is putting it in danger."

This time Brinnesha gave in to the urge and did roll her eyes.

"Whatever you say," she said. "Let's go to this party, where I promise not to scandalise the Community."

It was a pleasantly cool twilight walk to the house where the Founders' Day party was being held. As they entered, though, the heat and noise washed over Brinnesha in a smothering wave. The main room was even worse. Glittering, glaring candles and the shimmering expanses of jewellery turned the whole space into one formless mass of bright, brittle chatter.

Brinnesha blessed her Talent as it led her to Talemar, the one person who could make this heaving pit bearable. But as she got close enough to see her, Brinnesha thought for one horrible moment that her Talent had made a mistake. She barely recognised her best friend in the sad voice that greeted her. Only the relentlessly twitching fingers remained. Even her normally bright eyes were dull and withdrawn.

Brinnesha walked beside this shell of her friend through the throng until they reached a quiet place near the windows where it was possible to have a conversation.

"How are you, Brinnesha? I hope your family are keeping well," said Talemar, from the shelter of a potted fern.

"Never mind the small talk, Talemar! What's wrong?"

Brinnesha felt rather than heard her best friend calm herself.

"I didn't get the apprenticeship," she said.

Brinnesha was momentarily speechless. But only momentarily. "What? But you're obviously the best person for it! Why would... oh, no. It's not because of me, is it? Because we're friends, and Mother thought it would look like favouritism or something silly like that?"

Talemar frowned for a moment, then shook her head.

"No, nothing like that," she said. "I got passed over because another candidate had 'a more appropriate Talent'."

"Oh, Talemar..." said Brinnesha. "How could anyone say that about your Talent? Why, you're..."

"I'm a Weaver," cut in Talemar. "My Talent is with threads on a loom, not ink on paper. Archivist Tynar's new apprentice is Olvar Harreal. He has a Talent with ink, and there's an end to it. I'm to go back to my shuttle."

Talemar sounded like she was going to cry. Brinnesha patted her shoulder rather helplessly.

"Why couldn't I have your Talent, Brinnesha? Why did I have to get stupid Weaving?"

Brinnesha froze, mid-pat, and Talemar blanched at her own blasphemy.

"I didn't mean that," she said, quickly. "I don't really hate my Talent."

"Of course not," Brinnesha murmured.

"It's just that I'm good at administration too," Talemar continued. "I know I am."

"I know you are too. And so should Mother. Ink indeed! Not that there's anything wrong with a Talent with ink," amended Brinnesha.

"Of course not."

"But your Talent for seeing patterns and keeping threads organised is obviously better. What is Mother thinking?"

Brinnesha stood up, then bent to give Talemar one last, comforting pat on the shoulder.

"Don't you worry. I'm going to talk to her about this."

"It's not... wait, where are you going?"

"To talk to Mother."

"Right now? Brinnesha..!"

But Brinnesha was already moving purposefully towards where her Talent told her she would Find her mother. Talemar's protestations faded into the hubbub of the party.

<hr>

Brinnesha was not surprised to Find her mother at the centre of the largest glittery group. Up close the sparkle was less blinding, but no less vulgar. Men and women talked with too many smiles, and smiled with too many teeth, and laughed without a trace of joy. Brinnesha cut through them and their conversations like the vapid illusions they were.

"Mother! I need to talk to you."

Pabiran Tynar turned towards her youngest daughter without disruption to either her smile or her manner.

"Now, dear? Can't it wait?"

"Right now, Mother, if you please. It's about your new apprentice."

"Ah, the bright young man you were telling us about, Archivist Tynar," cut in one of the glittering smilers. Brinnesha scowled at her and turned back to her mother.

"Yes, that person. Did you not get my friend's application, Mother? Why have you taken on some stranger, when you had a much better candidate in the form of Talemar?"

The smile and the voice dropped as one. Silence radiated outwards as people turned to watch this family drama.

"Daughter, it is not *your* business to question how I run *my* business. Even if I had consulted your Talent to Find me a suitable apprentice..."

"Which you didn't," cut in Brinnesha, suddenly hurt by this despite not having considered it before. Why hadn't she been consulted?

"Which I didn't," agreed her mother, without a trace of shame. "But even if I had, you would have been only an advisor. The final decision would always have been mine. I did get your friend's application, and I considered it seriously. I considered all the applications seriously, and I chose the best candidate."

"But, Mother...!"

Brinnesha felt a rant building up inside of her, but before she could explain exactly how *unreasonable* her mother was being, she saw two things. One was Mother herself, turning back to the gawping crowd with a fresh smile and a demure apology for the interruption. The other was Talemar, very red in the face and begging her to come away. The first only added fuel to Brinnesha's rage, but the second held her back from setting the torch to it.

As her friend dragged her away, Brinnesha faintly heard one of Mother's circle mutter something about 'a difficult age'. Only the pressure of Talemar's hand on her wrist kept that spark from landing.

—◦—

Talemar dragged Brinnesha over to one of the tall windows, where the open shutters let in some much-needed, cool evening air. Talemar stood looking out of the window, and traced the patterns in the delicate gauze that kept the night insects out. She had dropped Brinnesha's wrist, but not said anything since they left the main party. Once Talemar reached the edge of the pattern for the third time, Brinnesha couldn't bear the silence any longer.

"Why did you do that? I had an audience – Mother would've *had* to listen, and the others would have seen sense even if Mother was stubborn. I was just about to get you your dream job!"

"I didn't ask you to get the job for me! I want to get it for myself!" Talemar snapped, flinging the curtain down. "And those friends of your mother's were taking her side, not yours. All you did was make me look like a sore loser. Not to mention weak and selfish."

Brinnesha stared at Talemar. That wasn't what she had done at all.

Talemar continued, "I haven't given up, you know. There will be other chances, other masters. But not if I get a reputation for expecting preferential treatment. Your mother's new apprentice could be my colleague one day, both of us sitting in the town hall hearing official business. This is not the way I want him to remember me when we're serving as Town Elders."

Brinnesha was confused and shocked. Talemar had always seemed to like it when she had helped her in the past. She must be more affected by this disappointment than Brinnesha had realised. She felt a sudden surge of fondness for her friend and leaned in for a hug. A weaker bond might have strained under the events of this evening, but not this friendship. Not if Brinnesha Tynar had anything to say about it.

"I'm so sorry I upset you," Brinnesha said. "Perhaps we could..."

Talemar pulled back and put a hand over Brinnesha's mouth. "Hush!" she whispered. "He's right outside the window!"

From her red face and huge eyes, Talemar had to mean her long-standing crush, Samri. Any other night, Brinnesha would have called him inside the room and made him acknowledge her friend, but perhaps it wouldn't be such a good idea this evening. Talemar was in a strange mood, and it would never do to have her snap at Samri and scare him off for good.

But when Brinnesha listened to the voices outside the window, she couldn't hear her friend's crush at all. Just two voices, one belonging to her brother's master, a respectable Shopkeeper from the town centre, and the other a voice she didn't immediately recognise.

She frowned, and whispered to her friend, "It's only Murrin, Berran's boss. What's the matter?"

Talemar pulled Brinnesha into a seat behind the thick, open curtains. Once safely screened from sight and sound, she whispered back, "Not him, the other one. It's that Inker, Olvar Harreal. The new apprentice."

"Is it now?" said Brinnesha. "Let's have a look..."

"No! I mean, no. He'll see you!"

"I'm not going to stare into his eyes, Talemar – just take a quick peek. And, to make extra sure, I'll use my Talent to Find what he's looking at. So long as it's not me, I'm perfectly safe."

Talemar sounded unconvinced.

"Didn't you tell me that you can only Find one thing at a time? What if someone else sees you?"

Brinnesha just laughed. "They'll think I'm eyeing up my mother's new apprentice. It won't be the worst thing that's been said about me lately."

Casually, Brinnesha leaned against the wall beside the window, then moved the gauze curtain aside until she could see out. Her brother's boss was facing away from her, and beyond him stood the new apprentice. There was nothing remarkable about his face, but he somehow reminded her of a maid she'd once known. Cringingly polite to the family but rude to the other household staff, and positively vicious when she thought she was unobserved.

Shopkeeper Murrin was well-enough respected in the town for anyone to be polite to him, but Olvar Harreal's ingratiating tone indicated that he was after something.

"You must understand that I'm still establishing myself at the moment," said the Inker. "My apprenticeship in records and accounts will take up a lot of my time for the next five years, but this is simply too good an opportunity to miss. That's why I'm looking for partners to share the workload. And the profits, of course."

Murrin sounded unsure, but evidently not unsure enough to walk away.

"I've a pretty big workload of my own, with my shop and all. What would you be expecting me to do?" he asked.

"I hear good things about your apprentice," said the Inker. "If you could trust him with your shop one day a week, or even just half a day every fortnight or so, to go and look over the workers. Make sure the Elementals aren't slacking, the overseers are doing their job, and the crop quality stays high. I'll be using my day off each week to do the same, but it doesn't do to become too predictable about inspection visits, if you understand me."

"Just keep an eye on the place, you mean?"

"Exactly. And let me know if there's anything that needs my attention. I know that you have your own business to run, and I wouldn't dream of asking you to run mine for me on top of that. There's respecting a man's Talent for business, and then there's taking advantage, you know."

The Shopkeeper chuckled. "Young flatterer," he said. "We both know it's Ralnat Tynar with the real Talent for Trading – I'm just a Shopkeeper myself. Are you going to take this offer to my apprentice's father as well? Or am I a special case?"

Olvar Harreal gave a nervous chuckle that might have been meant for self-deprecation. "I'm sure Trader Tynar will only be interested in my little venture once it is ready to take to the Citadel. I will, of course, defer to his Talent for large-scale Trading once I get to that level myself, but this is still the humble beginnings stage of the business."

Brinnesha hesitated. Olvar was right about the scale of her father's business, but she didn't like his tone. This Inker was making Trader Tynar out to be too high and mighty to help small businesses, which couldn't be further from the truth.

Olvar Harreal was still talking, in his most flattering manner, to Murrin Durr.

"You may call yourself 'just' a Shopkeeper," he said, "but I hear you're the shrewdest man in town when it comes to keeping things on track. If you'd be so good as to join my little venture, I'd value your insight."

Flattery *and* an implied criticism of every other Talent in town. Brinnesha was disliking this Inker more with every sentence that came out of his mouth.

But apparently Murrin didn't feel the same way. "Where is this work-area of yours, then?" he asked.

"It's up in the foothills, almost due south of here," said Olvar. "Prime grape-farming country: north-facing, with excellent drainage. And unclaimed, if you can believe it! Well, previously unclaimed," he added, hastily. "I've put the paperwork through now, of course."

"Grape-farming?" said Murrin. "That takes time to establish. How will you make it pay?"

"Why do you think I need this apprenticeship?" laughed the Inker. "The workers are paid in food and shelter, and there are ways to make that cost less than nothing, of course."

"Of course," the Shopkeeper agreed. "But what about my involvement?"

"An investment, if you like. Add up your time, at a given hourly rate, and call that your buy-in. You know that there'll be profits enough for everyone once production is up and running."

Brinnesha felt Talemar tugging her arm and reluctantly pulled back from the window to sit beside her.

"You are attracting attention," said Talemar, in her ear.

"I was only standing by the window," protested Brinnesha.

"With clenched fists and stiff shoulders," observed Talemar. "Your whole body language was radiating anger. Not to mention the audible breathing."

Brinnesha tried not to resent her friend's caution. The nearest people were a dozen strides away, too far to read something as subtle as the set of her shoulders, or the state of her hands, though Talemar might have a point about the breathing. She was certainly angry.

"Did you hear what those two were saying?" she asked.

"No, I was too focused on being your lookout," said Talemar, a touch of irritation in her voice.

Brinnesha forced herself to speak quietly as she filled her friend in on the substance of the Inker's conversation with the Shopkeeper.

"And he as good as admitted that he was exploiting Elementals," she said. "Paying them a pittance to work his vineyards. They have no idea what wine is worth in Avlenia – or even in the Sidrax Empire. It's... it's immoral!"

Talemar didn't seem to share Brinnesha's entirely justified outrage.

"It's not nice of him to take advantage of the natives like that," she agreed, "but I'm not sure the sister of a Salesman should be dictating how moral another person's business plans are. Not to mention, you know, that eavesdropping isn't exactly virtuous."

"What's wrong with being a Salesman?" replied Brinnesha. "You're very anti-Talent this evening, my friend. First you abuse your own, and now you're coming down on my brother's."

Talemar's eyes went wide, and she protested so loudly that Brinnesha saw some of the nearest faces turn their way for a moment.

"I'm not abusing anyone's Talent," she said, sounding shocked and offended all at once. "There's nothing 'wrong' with being a Salesman, but surely it's just the way of business to get done things as cheaply as you can, and sell them for as much as possible. You've told me how your own father has taken you on business trips to Find him the best deals. I know you don't like this whole Olvar Harreal situation – I don't either, come to that – but you can't criticise him for following good business practice. *I'm* more annoyed that he's treating my dream job as a stepping stone to his real ambition."

Brinnesha felt her face burn, torn between anger at Talemar for comparing her father and brother to Olvar Harreal, and wonder that her own best friend couldn't understand what made the Inker's behaviour so very wrong.

She took a couple of deep, steadying breaths before explaining, as calmly as she could, the difference between being a Salesman or a Trader dealing with fellow Avlem, and exploiting Elementals for profit.

"It's like stealing from a child," she said. "When Father and Berran do business, they deal with other

Avlem or educated Sidrax. Everyone involved under-stands 'good business practice', as you put it. But this Inker – and what makes that a suitable Talent for a businessman, I wonder? – don't you see that what he's doing is completely different? He's using Elementals, and they don't understand the situation at all. He's probably made it sound like a wonderful opportunity to the point they could even be grateful to the man for giv-ing them such good jobs. You know Elementals don't really understand money – most of them can barely read, much less calculate Talent-hours. Even my own maid, who is really very clever in her own way, would rather be paid in food and clothing than in scrip. We've explained to her – to all our servants – that they can take their wages to any shop in town and buy whatever they need, not just what we have available to give them. The Sidrax servants will take it, but the Elementals all prefer to take their due in kind."

Brinnesha smiled a little at the memory of the times she'd tried to teach Alra the value of Talent scrip. Her father, truly the kindest man in town, had taken to buying up suitable clothes and well-preserved food when he went Trading, though never in such bulk as to draw attention from other merchants or from bandits. All to pay their Elementals fairly, as they understood it. When she compared her father's consideration with this... *Inker's* underhanded cunning...

Talemar's hand on her arm brought Brinnesha back to herself.

"You're seething again," murmured her best friend. "Stop it."

Brinnesha tried to use her Talent to Find inner peace. It came back with a strange blankness that Brinnesha recognised as 'not there', before making her eyes land on her best friend. She smiled – she'd always suspected her Talent of having a sense of humour. Or was it just her own sense of humour that made her interpret her Talent that way? Talents were such a serious matter that it seemed almost blasphemous to associate them with anything so trivial as laughter.

<hr>

"Remind me how I let you talk me into this?" Talemar grumbled as she pulled her boot out of yet another sucking mud puddle. "And how are you still clean on this awful road?"

Brinnesha turned to look back at her friend. "Sorry, I've been Finding the clean places to step. I always do when I come to the village after rain. Just step where I do and you'll be fine."

"And why are we going to the village at all?"

"I told you, I want to find out what's going on with Olvar Harreal's scheme. And you're coming because I want a witness."

Talemar sighed. "The things I do for friendship," she said, but she smiled as she said it. "Don't forget you promised to show me some truly beautiful weaving. It had better be worth it, after all this."

Brinnesha walked on, leading the way. A minute later, Talemar must have missed a step, and gone into the mud again to judge by the noises behind her: A squelch, a gasp, and a string of muttered curses that Brinnesha told herself she was far too well brought up to understand.

When they got to the village, the place was strangely quiet. The adults were working, of course, but Brinnesha was struck by the absence of children. They were always out and about, playing with simple toys, calling to each other in the strange, broken Sidrean of the Elementals. One of the things she loved about the village was seeing people who had so little, both materially and intellectually, managing to find true joy in life.

But today the children were nowhere to be seen. Brinnesha and Talemar walked through the village until they came to a larger-than-average hut at the far end.

"This is who I brought you to meet," Brinnesha said. "He's not the chief – his hut is over there," gesturing to the only building larger than the one they stood outside, "but he's pretty important to the villagers, all the same."

"I suppose he must be, with a house like this," Talemar said. She took hold of the door curtain and examined it critically.

"Nice work," she concluded. "Very neatly made, and the pattern is quite striking. But hardly the breathtaking wonder you made it out to be, my dear friend."

Brinnesha Tynar just laughed as she took the curtain from her friend's hands.

"I didn't bring you here to admire the door, silly," she said. "*This* is what we're here for."

With that she pushed Talemar into the hut. She fully expected the gasp of amazement that came from her friend. She did not expect to hear it echoed tenfold by the occupants of the hut.

Brinnesha entered quickly, and let her eyes adjust to the shady interior. The strategically placed openings in the roof and walls gave the perfect amount of natural light – another thing the Elementals did so cleverly. In a moment she could see quite well: the resplendent tapestries adorning every wall, the hut's owner, sitting in his crude chair, and the small crowd of children clustered around his feet. They had clearly been listening to something he was telling them, but now every eye was on Brinnesha and Talemar.

Talemar was still standing just inside the door, apparently struck motionless with awe at the weavings around her. Brinnesha preened herself on the wisdom and kindness of bringing her friend here.

"Don't mind us," she said to the children and the lone adult. "Go on with whatever you were doing."

She poked her friend gently to get her moving again. "Go on, take a proper look. I know you want to."

Slowly, Talemar moved towards the nearest tapestry. It wasn't a picture of anything, so far as Brinnesha could tell, and was comprised of only two colours for the most part, with occasional pieces of decoration attached here and there. There didn't seem to be any pattern at all, but Brinnesha would defer to her friend's judgement there. As a Weaver, patterns were Talemar's speciality.

The hut's owner was talking to the children again, but the lesson, or whatever it was, must have been nearly at an end, because the children filed out of the hut before Brinnesha had time to grow bored watching her friend's Talent at work. The children stared at the two of them as they left, something that didn't surprise Brinnesha at all. She was used to being an object of fascination amongst the villagers, and doubly so for the children. She and her friend were wearing their plainest clothes, but even so, they were better dressed than anyone in the village. And their hair was far curlier and more carefully arranged than that of the Elementals. Yes, all things considered, Brinnesha rather liked it when they stared at her.

Once the children were gone, Brinnesha approached the storyteller. He simply *had* to come over and talk to Talemar about these amazing weavings. Brinnesha wouldn't brook any refusal and briskly informed him that he mustn't mind a bit about his Sidrean not being perfect – that they were here for the tapestries, not to give a language lesson.

There was a slight delay while Talemar and Brinnesha tried to explain the word 'tapestry'. The storyteller gave them the old Elemental language word, and said that it translated into Sidrean as 'story blanket'.

Talemar's eyes lit up. "You mean, you don't write things down – you weave them? That's wonderful. I wish we did that."

Brinnesha smirked. "Much better than ink on paper, certainly," she agreed.

The storyteller shuffled his feet and seemed suddenly awkward. For a horrible moment, Brinnesha thought that he might have interpreted their enthusiasm as flirting – somewhat disturbing given that he looked older than the two of them put together.

"Is it permitted... in the way of your people... to be teaching?" He spoke carefully, sounding almost afraid of the answer.

Talemar flushed. "I don't think I could teach you anything," she said. "You already know so much more than I do."

Brinnesha approved of her tact. Elementals didn't have Talents, so they couldn't be blamed for not understanding how rude it was to ask for lessons. As if one could simply learn a Talent, and then do without the Talented person completely.

However, the storyteller seemed pleased, rather than disappointed. "Yes, good. I know more. You understand. Is it permitted to teach? No angry mother, angry father, say, 'Why give my daughter knowledge? Bad village!'?"

Brinnesha saw her best friend's eyes go wide. "Are you offering to teach me this pattern?" she asked, almost in a whisper.

"Teach story blankets, yes. Make new patterns, your stories."

Brinnesha was embarrassed for Talemar. An Elemental couldn't be expected to understand. They thought differently. Talemar must be finding it so hard to refuse the offer of apprenticeship without giving offence. But her embarrassment turned to horror the next moment.

Talemar's eyes lit up again. "Yes, please!" she said.

———◆———

It took all of Brinnesha's self-control not to drag her friend out of the hut and all the way home. With a supreme effort of will she made herself smile at the storyteller and make a polite excuse to leave.

Actually, 'I must talk to the chief before I return home,' was more than a polite excuse. The storyteller's tapestries had been the price to have Talemar's company, and Brinnesha Tynar, like the good friend she was, put her friend's interests ahead of her own. She would do it again now, since her friend clearly couldn't look after herself.

"What were you thinking?" hissed Brinnesha, as soon as they were clear of the storyteller's hut. "You can't just take on an apprenticeship like that, without telling your family."

"I'm going to tell them," Talemar replied, unabashed. "It's ever so much better than trying to learn from our Tailor. Wonderful woman with cutting and shaping cloth though she is, she can't teach me how to create. Just think, Brinnesha – record keeping on a loom! It's perfect!"

"Your family will never let you spend so much time in the village."

Talemar snorted. "Ha! Your family let you come here all the time."

"No, they don't," Brinnesha said. "I sneak out and I get in trouble for it. If they could tie me into an apprenticeship, they would – but my Talent's valuable enough to the family that they won't force the issue."

"And mine isn't?"

"I didn't say that! But, Talemar, you said yourself how important your reputation is. Think what people will say if you start visiting the same man in the village almost every day."

"Don't be so vulgar," chided Talemar, looking a little sick. "You come here often enough, and your own sist er..."

"My sister works with a mixed group, out in the fields. And I keep to public areas unless I have company. Even then, people are starting rumours about me – at least according to Eris. You can't come here alone, no matter how much you want to train your Talent on those new patterns. I'm sorry, Talemar, but that's the truth."

Talemar nodded, and they walked in silence until they were almost at the chief's hut. Suddenly, she smiled. "So, I won't come alone," she said. "You'll be my official chaperone, and I'll be yours. Let's see the gossiping old cats try to make something of that. Unless they think we're both courting the old storyteller."

Brinnesha pulled a face, and Talemar laughed. Then Brinnesha became very serious.

"We'll sort this out later," she said. "Right now, I have to find out how far along Olvar Harreal is with his plans. Life grant that the chief speaks good Sidrean."

The chief did indeed speak Sidrean. She (and not he, as Brinnesha had supposed) understood even more than Brinnesha Tynar had expected, as she proved after listening quietly to Brinnesha's impassioned rant.

"You fear this Avlem means to take advantage of my people's ignorance," she said. "Or, rather, of our desperation. We have no lands of our own where we can grow food, or hunt game. We exist here on the edges of your towns because you permit it. Different tribes, different people, looking for a way to survive. The work we get from serving in your houses and working your fields is limited by what you are willing to give. And now another Avlem offers other work. Why should we not hear him out?"

"Because he's awful!" Brinnesha said. She wanted to tell the chief about the time, two years ago, when Olvar Harreal had played a nasty trick on his cousin right in the town square on market day. But... would that be shaming Perayen's community reputation? Should she tell Elementals about such things?

Brinnesha hesitated, and the chief went on.

"Brinnesha Tynar, you have been coming to this village for many months" she said. "When your family took our sons and daughters away to be your servants, they called it a generous offer. When your neighbours take fathers and mothers away to toil in the fields that you also took, they call it an honest day's work. And now someone you don't like is taking people to live up in the hills to work on his farm. How is this different?"

Brinnesha Tynar was horrified for the second time in as many hours. She tried to remind herself, again, that Elementals saw things differently, and they couldn't be blamed for not understanding how Avlem society worked, but her indignation was too powerful for reason. How dare this Elemental accuse her family of being like Olvar Harreal? As if finding jobs for these people was anything like the selfish exploitation at the heart of this Inker's scheme. The Tynar servants had good food, comfortable accommodation, and time off every single month. It wasn't the same thing at all!

The comment about the fields rattled her a bit, though. She thought about it as she said stiff and polite farewells to the chief. She thought about it some more during her walk home. It was still on her mind when she said goodbye to Talemar, and promised to meet up the next day to discuss things.

She finally brought it up over dinner, which was just her and her parents that evening.

"Mother," she said, trying to sound casual, and only academically interested. "In your history books, does it say how the Elementals used to farm their land before we arrived here?"

Pabiran seemed pleased to be asked a question related to her Talent, but puzzled by the topic. "What makes you ask?"

Brinnesha blushed. She could hardly repeat the chief's scathing accusations, so she settled on, "Something one of the villagers said. It's not important, I just wondered."

Her parents looked at each other, but Brinnesha couldn't decipher their expressions.

Eventually, her mother said, "The natives didn't farm, not as we'd understand it. They grew plants, but it was more like gardening – little vegetable patches and the occasional tree. They didn't even have wheat until we brought it over, and they couldn't use ploughs. They didn't keep proper flocks or herds, either. I know it's hard to imagine, Daughter, but farming, real farming, arrived in this country when we Avlem did."

Her father nodded. "Just one of the many ways we improved things for everyone," he said. "Remember that. It's good that you care so much about people – even the native people – but don't forget that their lives were pretty basic and harsh before we arrived to help them, Daughter of mine. It's our responsibility to improve their lot, and teach them how to live their best life."

He smiled at her, and Brinnesha beamed. She knew it would all make sense once she had the right view of things. Of course the chief didn't understand – she was only an Elemental, after all. And so, it was up to Brinnesha to make her understand how dangerous Olvar Harreal's scheme was: how unfair to the villagers, and how the man himself was only interested in the money he could make from cheap, Elemental labour.

Words alone wouldn't prove anything, Brinnesha realised. She had to gather solid evidence to present to the Elementals. The chief might have some mistaken ideas, but she was a sensible woman at heart. Brinnesha was sure that she would listen to reason in the end. And, if she wouldn't, then Brinnesha would take the evidence round to each and every villager, and explain the matter personally.

It was the least she could do.

When Brinnesha and Talemar met the following morning, both girls were full of plans. Unfortunately, those plans were for completely different things.

"Brinnesha, my parents are absolutely fine with my apprenticeship, just so long as they come with me on my first day, and you promise to go with me after that. In fact, you can come on the first day, too, if you're free the day after tomorrow."

"Talemar, you need to help me raid Mother's office. Well, not Mother's exactly, but her new apprentice's. I need some solid evidence to persuade the village chief."

They stopped, and each processed what the other had said. Brinnesha recovered first.

"I'm really pleased for you," Brinnesha said, and meant it. "Come on, let's go into town. We'll have to do the raid today or tomorrow. You'll be a busy apprentice after that!"

Talemar glared at her friend as they walked. "I am not going to help you steal from your own mother," she said. "I intend to work there one day, and I won't have that on my conscience every time I look at Archivist Tynar."

"It's not stealing, it's investigating," Brinnesha said. "And you wouldn't have to do anything – just maybe watch out for me, show me the right rooms."

"Don't you know the rooms already?"

"No, I've never seen Mother's offices. Father has taken me on trading visits with him, but Mother's never needed my Talent – her own Archivist skills let her find any information she needs."

"Then why not ask her to get you what you want? Far simpler and safer, not to mention massively less, you know, *illegal!*"

Brinnesha tried very hard not to sound as though this was the stupidest thing she'd ever heard. She almost succeeded.

"I can't risk Olvar Harreal finding out that I'm investigating him," she explained. "He'd hide or destroy anything incriminating, and then we'd never get to the truth. I have to act now before he realises anyone's on to him."

Talemar pinched the bridge of her nose, and shook her head in defeat. When they reached the square, she gave Brinnesha directions to the correct room. Then she sat down near the entrance to the town hall, and refused to move.

"Come and Find me when you're done," she said. "I'm a disappointed candidate, and won't be trusted anywhere near the archives for months. Especially after the party. If anyone sees you going in, you're simply visiting your mother."

Somewhat disappointed, but undeterred, Brinnesha Tynar, Finder Extraordinaire, went investigating.

She returned less than half an hour later, looking furious.

"There's nothing there!" Brinnesha said, as soon as she caught sight of her friend. "My Talent told me that I was in the right office – sorry, Talemar, not that I doubted your directions, but I thought Mother might have changed the apprentice's room once it was no longer going to a trusted family friend. But no, I was in the correct room, and that room contained nothing at all about vineyards. He must be keeping the dangerous documents at home."

Talemar squeezed Brinnesha's hand. "At least you tried," she said. "I'm sure the Elementals would appreciate what you're doing for them, if they knew."

Brinnesha set her jaw and glared straight ahead.

"I haven't given up," she told her friend. "This just adds an extra challenge. Where else would a person like Olvar Harreal keep evidence of his shady dealings?"

Brinnesha walked with her friend away from the town hall, following the path around the town centre. As they walked, Brinnesha constructed the next phase of her plan. Talemar was talking, saying something about discretion and patience. Phrases like 'unnecessary risks' and 'knowing when to quit' floated in the air, but Brinnesha was barely listening. She'd decided on her next step.

"I know you're just worried for me, my friend, and that's sweet of you. But this is more important than me. More important than any individual. I have to see this through," she said. Brinnesha looked earnestly at Talemar, and tried to impress upon her the urgency and importance of this investigation. "You told me you haven't given up on your goals. Why would you expect me to give up on this? Would Appundarel have reclaimed the Faldra Throne if he'd given up at the first difficulty? Would Plyn have discovered the hidden ice routes if she'd gone home after her canoe broke?"

"Those are *stories*, Brinnesha! You can't live your life as though you were the hero of a folk tale. This is real life!" Talemar threw her hands up and seemed about to shout, until she took a deep breath and made an audible effort to speak calmly. "You're right, I haven't given up on my dreams. But there's a difference between perseverance and recklessness!"

"I don't have time for perseverance, Talemar! Once Olvar Harreal gets his claws into those poor Elementals, it will be too late. I need to expose him now, not in five years' time. That's why I need you to go and talk to Mother and her new apprentice this afternoon. Be gracious, maybe even pretend to apologise for my 'outburst' at the party – anything to keep them talking. Keep them until noon, then head home. I'm going to be busy for the rest of the day."

"Busy doing what?" asked her friend. "And where?"

"I think it's better if you can honestly say that you don't know," said Brinnesha Tynar.

Brinnesha walked down one of the wide avenues that led away from the town centre, strolling with exaggerated nonchalance to where her Talent told her Olvar Harreal's house lay. She paused by an alley, sending her Talent to Find the Inker, and then her best friend. The sensation for both was from the same direction, and similar strength. Satisfied, Brinnesha disappeared down the alley and around the back of the Harreal family house.

The gardens were neat, but drab. There were none of the bright, flowing colours that graced the Tynars' garden, nor the open elegance. Olvar Harreal's family were more given to hedges in wide lines, dividing the space into little boxes. There weren't even any water features, although Brinnesha knew that Merizat had offered her Irrigation Talent to every family in town.

Brinnesha felt a grim little smile grow on her face. This whole family was clearly as mean and as selfish as she'd suspected. People like that always had servants willing to complain about them, and what better source of information than a disgruntled footman or cook? First though, she used her Talent to identify the window of the Inker's personal study. It was facing the most boring part of the garden, which didn't surprise her at all.

Brinnesha next used her Talent to Find the nearest people. Satisfied that they were too far off to present any risk, Brinnesha peered through the window. The window was ajar, but it was risky to raid this room by daylight. It was too much to hope that Olvar would have left anything incriminating out on display, but she did note the position of the desk, and the door.

All Brinnesha allowed herself to do was to reach in and loop a thread from her dress around the window latch, leaving it to hang down against the wall. The fibre was too fine to see unless one knew it was there, and Brinnesha silently thanked her storybook heroes for the idea.

Brinnesha quickly Found her way to the kitchen door. Here, she hesitated. It was easy enough to angle for information once she had got one of the servants talking, but how was she to start? Could she just knock on the door? No, they would wonder why she hadn't gone to the front door. Perhaps she should just wait until someone came out, and then she could say... what? *"Hello, isn't it a nice day, please tell me everything you know about your master's evil schemes?"* Ridiculous. She'd have to try something else, like, *"Hello, how–"*

"Hello?"

Brinnesha nearly jumped out of her skin. She hadn't been paying attention to her Talent, nor had she heard the kitchen door open, but now there was a small person, with a mess of sticking-up hair and huge eyes on a dirty face, gazing up at her from the level of the door handle.

"Hello," she said. "Who are you?"

Brinnesha heard her voice take on the sing-song gentleness that she used when speaking to her sister's baby, and she realised she was talking to a child. An Elemental child, but still a child.

"I'm Tam," said the small person. "I'm doing the fire, but I saw you in the garden, so I came to find out. Who are you?"

Brinnesha bent down to examine the large eyes which blinked but never moved. She frowned at the thick, colourless sheen that covered them, torn between disgust and pity.

"What do you mean, you saw me here? I'm not near any windows," she said, very carefully not adding, *And you're blind.*

Tam said, "I saw your heat. Why are you standing around in the garden? Who are you?"

Brinnesha was so overwhelmed with horrified fascination that she almost forgot why she'd come. The child's questions brought her mission sharply back to mind, and she still had no idea what to say.

"I'm nobody important," she started, when a thought struck her. This child couldn't see her, so perhaps...

"I'm from the village. Someone told me that the master of this house had work for Elementals, somewhere out of town. Is that true?"

The child laughed. "You're mad. I don't know nothing about no work but my own, and you can't have that. Go home, before Cook catches me talking to you."

Brinnesha started to reply when her Talent alerted her to someone else approaching. She glanced behind her and saw a distant, blurry figure coming up the garden, through the painfully straight hedges.

"Never mind," she told the child, and darted around the house before the approaching figure could get close enough to identify her. She didn't stop until she was back on the main road. When her Talent told her that there was no-one within a hundred strides, she strolled deliberately back to the town centre and made her way home.

Brinnesha sat at her dressing table that evening, deep in thought. She was sure that Olvar Harreal had incriminating evidence hidden in his desk. If only she hadn't had her Talent seeking out danger, she could have used it to confirm that fact while outside the study window. Still, it was for the best. Her Talent had warned her to get out of there before anyone got close enough to identify her, and she'd not given her name to the blind kitchen-child.

She would have to try again, that was all. The evidence was there, and if she could show the Elemental Chief what Olvar Harreal was really up to, it would go a long way towards protecting the villagers from exploitation.

Brinnesha spent the next hour reviewing her memories of the Inker's family home, sketching the layout in her mind, and fixing details of the window rigged with a thread from her skirt. She considered the distance from her own windowsill to the floor, and practised lifting herself up on her arms. She tucked her skirt up into her sash, and was actually kneeling on the sill of her window when her maid knocked at the door. Brinnesha leapt from the window to the bed, stumbled, and landed awkwardly across her mattress just as Alra entered the room.

"Miss Brinnesha, your parents want to see... oh dear. Are you hurt, Miss Brinnesha?"

"I tripped. You startled me," Brinnesha said, flustered in spite of her perfect truthfulness. She scrambled to her feet and pulled her skirt straight. Alra stepped in to re-tie the loose sash, and Brinnesha checked her plaits.

"Did you say my parents want me?"

"Yes, Miss Brinnesha."

"Well, let's not keep them waiting. Lead the way, Alra."

Brinnesha followed her maid to the centre of the house where both her parents were, indeed, waiting for her. To Brinnesha's annoyance, so were both of her sisters.

"Quite the family council," Brinnesha observed, taking her seat. "Any particular reason why Brother Berran isn't here to complete the set?"

"Your brother is hard at work, but he is just as worried about you as the rest of us, Daughter."

Brinnesha laughed. "I don't think my dear brother needs to worry about any of us, Mother. But it's nice that he cares."

"He's not worried about us, Little Sister; he's worried about you. We all are. You're ruining–"

"–the Tynar reputation, yes. I've already heard this speech. Eris gave me a pretty thorough lecture just before the Founders' Day party. I told her, and I'll say it again: You're not going to stop me visiting the village. In fact, now that Talemar has an apprenticeship with their weaver, I'll be going every day. She's asked me to be her escort."

"We're not talking about your trips to the village," said Merizat.

"...for once," Brinnesha muttered.

"This is about your visit to Mother's new apprentice."

Brinnesha Tynar felt herself react and hated herself for it. If only she could be as cool and impassive as her heroes. They never let a blush or a grimace betray their thoughts.

"What do you mean?" she asked. She cringed inwardly at the forced tone of innocence in her voice.

"You were seen snooping around the house and gardens of the Harreal house," replied her mother. "I don't know what you're planning, but no matter how angry you are with me for not choosing your friend as my apprentice, I will not have you taking it out on an innocent party."

Brinnesha felt the heat in her face, but this time it was anger, not shame, that coloured it. Her family didn't seem to see the difference. Her father actually laughed – a gentle, affectionate laugh, but still unutterably irritating.

"Tell me, Daughter," he said, "did you have time to set up your retribution, or were you interrupted too soon?"

"Retribution?" Brinnesha didn't have to feign confusion now. She was still gathering the evidence against the Inker – retribution and redress would be for the town elders to decide, surely? Hope rose in her heart. Her family had no idea what she'd really been doing! It wasn't too late!

"I don't know what you're talking about," Brinnesha replied, coolly. It was wonderful what the moral high ground could do for a person's nerves. "What makes you think I went anywhere near that house at all?"

"As I said, apart from your own reaction when it was mentioned," said her mother, "there's the little matter of your being seen. Olvar Harreal's head gardener saw you at the side door, talking to the kitchen boy."

Brinnesha relaxed. The figure on the path had been a mere distant blur – too far off to identify.

"That's ridiculous! How could he have known me from that dist-" she said, then bit her tongue. Of all the idiotic, obvious traps! She didn't know whether to be more furious with her mother for stooping to it, or herself for getting caught out.

Fortunately, her parents seemed to think that her embarrassment was punishment enough, and let her escape to her room with nothing worse than an absolute ban on going near the Harreal family house again without an express invitation.

"I won't have you hounding innocent members of the Community with your nonsense," said her mother.

"Innocent?" Brinnesha cried. "That creep's anything but innocent! He's exploiting the Elementals, and he doesn't even care. And I can prove it!"

"Brinnesha..." Pabrian's tone was half-weariness, half-warning. But it was Ralnat Tynar who spoke next.

"No, Wife. If she has proof, let her present it. Well, Daughter?"

Brinesha hesitated. "I haven't got it yet. I heard Olvar Harreal talking about his plan, and I know it relies on exploiting the Elementals, but..."

"If there is wrongdoing in the case, it will come to light in time," her father said. "You are too sensitive when it comes to the natives, my dear child. It's your kind heart, and your sense of justice, but it makes you a little hasty sometimes. You need to let this go for now. Do you understand?"

Brinnesha understood. Her raid on Olvar Harreal's study would have to wait one more night. Just to give things time to cool down.

⸺◦⸺

The next day, Brinnesha spent the whole morning at home, in sight of at least one member of her family at all times. When she did go out, she made it clear that she was only going to visit Talemar.

But before she reached her friend's house, Talemar met her in the road and swept Brinnesha away. Only when they were out in a meadow between the town and the village did Talemar turn to her friend.

"So?" she asked, eagerly. "Did you ask your parents about tomorrow?"

"Tomorrow?" Brinnesha blanked for a moment. She was making her move on Olvar Harreal tonight, but she wasn't going to tell her parents about that.

Talemar's shoulders slumped, and her face fell.

"Did you forget about my new apprenticeship?" she asked.

Brinnesha's face burned, but she rallied.

"I didn't *forget*," she said. "But I have a lot on my mind right now. My family were busy tearing into me last night and I had to placate them this morning. That means I've got to do everything else today."

This gave Talemar pause. "What were they angry about this time?" she asked. "Was it... about me?"

"You? Oh... no. No, it wasn't about my visiting the village for once! This time, they were angry with me for going to that Inker's house. Practically accused me of house breaking, and now I'm forbidden from going near the place!"

Brinnesha's righteous indignation left her breathless, and she had to pause before going on. In the pause, Talemar said, "Well, maybe it's for the best. You were starting to get obsessed with this business, and you know how that usually goes."

Brinnesha, now with her breath back, was left momentarily speechless.

"For the best?" she finally gasped out. "What do you mean, for the best? This is only going to make it harder for us to gather proof. You're going to have to do the actual collection now, and just bring me everything. I'll Find the key pieces, and you'll trace the connections in this evil tapestry. We can still make this work, but–"

"No, Brinnesha!" Talemar cut in. "We need to stop this now. You need to stop. If you're really worried about the natives, you can check on things at the village when you're there with me."

"But his workers won't be in the village," Brinnesha objected. "He's setting up way out in the hills, where he can control and exploit his workers without any supervision. We have to stop him now!"

Talemar took her friend by the shoulders and looked earnestly into her face.

"What we need to be," she said, "is sensible. You don't even know for sure that Olvar Harreal means to exploit anyone. You're assuming the worst because you don't like him. And I get it – I don't like him either. But we have to be fair and keep our heads."

Talemar paused, but Brinnesha was too stunned to take advantage of it. Her friend seemed to interpret this silence as consent and changed the subject.

Brinnesha nodded along with her friend's talk, but didn't hear a word. Her mind was busy with thoughts of that night.

⸻⟡⸻

Olvar Harreal's house was just visible in the light of the double moon. Brinnesha Tynar was alone. This felt appropriate, she thought. The hero is always alone just before the final challenge. She moved confidently to the study window and used her Talent to Find the nearest awake person. The answering tug was faint, probably someone not even in this house. Brinnesha felt around the window and was pleased to discover that her thread was still in place. A gentle pull opened the latch, and Brinnesha climbed through the window into the enemy's study.

She moved quietly, using her Talent and her outstretched fingers to avoid obstacles until she came to the desk, then switched her Finding Talent to confirm that there were papers here to do with Olvar's private project. She debated for a moment about lighting one of the candles, but it might draw attention and so Brinnesha decided against it. Instead, she trusted her Talent to direct her to the most relevant – the most incriminating – evidence she could. It was difficult because there was so much of it. Brinnesha grinned in the darkness. She'd got him!

A Talent for Finding is a rare and wonderful thing. But, like almost all Talents, it could be used on only one thing at a time. Brinnesha Tynar, secure in her silence and heroism, had focused her Talent exclusively on taking down the nefarious Inker. She should have had it watching the house.

The door opened as Brinnesha was gathering the precious papers together. Once the blinding dazzle of the lantern wore off, she made out the figures of Olvar Harreal, the burly gardener, and the little kitchen boy.

"That's the one, sir," said the gardener. "Same as was in the garden yesterday, tying that string to the window."

"There's no way you saw anything," Brinnesha said, suddenly more angry than scared. "If you did, why didn't you stop me?"

"That's her, mister Harreal," put in the boy. "She come round the kitchen door, and talking about windows, too."

"Thank you, Tam," said the Inker, impatiently. "As for your question, Miss Tynar," he went on, "why should Sarrin have stopped you yesterday? It's not a crime to tie things to windows. Breaking in through a window in the middle of the night... well now, that *is* a crime. And a rather serious one, too."

Brinnesha Tynar arrived at the Town Hall in the company, or rather custody, of her family. Her face was red with anger, a feeling that was exacerbated by her father's approval of her 'feeling ashamed of herself'.

Shame? What had she to be ashamed of, apart from the stupidity of her family? But at least she was going to be heard now. She might not have the evidence that she'd wanted, but if she could outwit the Inker in court, then perhaps she could get him to incriminate himself.

It was all just another twist in the story. With courage, cleverness, and determination, Brinnesha knew she would win.

Heroes always did.

The 'cells' at the Town Hall were two small, upstairs rooms, with guards outside the doors. As Brinnesha was led to one room, she could hear (and smell) the drunk in the other. She made a face, and the guard looked at her with a mixture of sympathy and condescension.

"I wish it hadn't come to this either, young miss, but like the Mayor said, your family have already tried their best to help you."

"She actually said that they'd proved unable to control me," Brinnesha snapped. "I'm not even going to start on the many things wrong with that sentiment."

Brinnesha seethed. It was intolerable! The Inker had clearly been abusing his connections and riding on his privilege. The council had made up their minds before she'd entered the room, much less made her case. She hadn't even been allowed to talk about Olvar Harreal's suspicious work-village scheme. Instead, they'd kept harping on about 'criminal trespass' and 'slander' – as if those were what mattered!

The door was closed and the bolts shot home. Brinnesha turned to the window and looked out over the gentle slopes that ran down to the Great River. If it wasn't for the latticed shutters and the height-and-a-half drop, that window would make a great escape route.

She lay down on the bed and clutched the sheets in her hands, forcing herself not to give in to despair. There would be a way. It wasn't possible that her story should end here, in capitulation and quiescence.

The bed sheets were coarse compared to her fine linen at home. Rough and thick and... Brinnesha froze, then bit her cheek to keep from laughing out loud. A bedsheet rope! It was a classic, and she'd practically been handed it on a plate.

Heroes always found a way.

⸺◆⸺

Brinnesha tore the clothes from the bed before thinking that she ought to wait until after dark. Instead of trying to replace them perfectly, she wrapped herself up in the bundle and pretended to be overcome with remorse. She fell asleep like that, curled up on the plain straw mattress and woke when a guard entered with a dinner tray.

To her surprise, she was served a hearty, if simple, meal – complete with a knife and spoon.

"Don't you have rules about letting prisoners have sharp objects?" Brinnesha knew that she shouldn't criticise a mistake made in her favour, but incompetence always irritated her.

"Quite the little penologist, I see," chuckled the guard. "And you're right, really. Lonbar in the next cell there never gets anything more dangerous than a leather cup and a soft-wood spoon. But you're not a violent criminal, are you, Miss Brinnesha? That's why you can have a real hot drink and a proper plate. I don't need to worry about you throwing anything at me!"

"I see," replied Brinnesha, coolly. Would this town never take her seriously?

"I will want it all back after you've eaten," said the guard, still smiling. "So no using that knife to saw through the shutters, alright?"

"Of course."

As if she would stoop to anything so crude. Far more effective to Find a weakness in the wood, the catch, or the hinges, and break the shutters that way.

⸻◆⸻

It was dark at last. Brinnesha saw the light dim from behind the door and knew that her 'guard' was likely asleep. She had used the knife to cut her sheets at dinnertime, rather than the shutters. Little notches that would let her tear the cloth into strips. The ripping made more noise than she'd expected but was fortunately masked by the far noisier drunk in the next room. As for the shutters, they were simplicity itself for a Finder of her skill and imagination. By the time the moons rose, Brinnesha Tynar was flitting through the lamp-lit streets; a shadow amid shadows, to keep an appointment with Justice.

Luck was with Brinnesha that night. She Found her way back to the Inker's study, ready to force the window open if she had to – only to find that her thread was still in place. It must have been forgotten about in the bustle of her arrest. Brinnesha thanked Life for this piece of good luck and climbed into the room, alert this time for any movement in or near the house. Rather than waste time sorting through the evidence at the scene, Brinnesha simply took every scrap of paper she could Find. She left the study loaded down with contracts, accounts and more, surely enough to convince any fair-minded person of Olvar Harreal's guilty plot.

Safely away from the Inker house, Brinnesha went home. She crept into the darkened house and up to her room, where she spent an instructive couple of hours sorting through the evidence. She worked by the light of just one candle, heavily shaded, and trusted her Talent to Find the most important papers. Soon, she had three piles: Irrelevant, Interesting, and Incriminating. She put these last two into her best leather satchel, then went into the next room to wake her maid.

"Miss Brinnesha! What are you doing here? And in the middle of the night, too! They said you were locked up in the cells, Miss."

"Yes, I was. And now I'm here. And it's not the middle of the night, it's a couple of hours off dawn. Get up, I need you to pack a bag for me."

"If you run away, Miss Brinnesha, I'll have to tell your parents. I've got my place and my family to think of, not to mention my duty to your family. Do reconsider, Miss."

"I'm not going to run away, you silly girl. I'm going to save everyone, including your family, from the self-serving schemes of a depraved autocrat. Now stop pestering me with questions and pack that bag. Enough for a week or so."

As her maid got to work, Brinnesha allowed herself to rest for a moment. She lay down on top of her own bed, and was asleep before the first light of false dawn touched the sky.

She woke to the sound of angry voices and heavy feet. Her maid looked absolutely terrified, so Brinnesha gave her a reassuring smile and asked for her bag.

"They say they're here to arrest you, Miss Brinnesha. Your poor parents are with them now, but I don't think the guards are going to leave without you."

"I don't want them to leave without me. I have to present this evidence, and an armed guard is the best way to make sure that I get to do so. Now, hand me that bag and a fresh gown. I'm going to appeal to the Citadel."

⸻⸻◆⸻⸻

Brinnesha Tynar wasn't an Archivist's daughter for nothing. She'd learned long ago about the rights of every Avlem citizen, rights carried over from the old world to the new as inalienable. And one of those was the right to have a case heard by a higher court if there was any reason to believe that a local court would be unable to be impartial. Since the Tynar family were well-known (as they kept reminding her) and since Olvar Harreal had already approached at least one influential person to her knowledge, and likely others, it was impossible for the town council to be properly disinterested. Hence, her appeal to the Citadel.

Brinnesha patiently explained all this to the mayor and the elders. She tried very hard to hide her contempt for them, for Olvar Harreal, and for this whole process. There was a lot of talking, mostly about the Inker and his 'rights', but Brinnesha tuned it all out. She had appealed to the Citadel, and that was the end of the matter.

Finally, after what felt like days, the Mayor stood up to give the judgement. It was passive-aggressive at best, but since it got her what she needed, Brinnesha decided not to complain.

Mature and sensible as she knew she had been, this decision didn't prevent the Mayor's snide remarks from echoing in her ears all the way home.

"Out of respect for the feelings of the family, the council is minded to allow this youthful rebellion to run its course. To the Citadel you have appealed, and the Citadel's judgement shall prevail."

More was said, of course, but the only important part was Brinnesha swearing before witnesses to agree to house arrest and to travelling to the Citadel in the custody of her family. Galling, but bearable. Heroes often had to suffer to do the right thing.

II

This was only the second time Brinnesha had made the long journey to the Citadel. The first had been with her father the year before, when he had taken her to a high-level trade negotiation as part of her Talent training. On that trip, she had gazed about eagerly, glorying in the beauty and order of this monument to civilisation. This was what Avlenia had to offer the world; and the Sidrean and Elemental touches emphasised the worth of the underpinning Avlem foundation.

Brinnesha had leaned halfway out of the windows as their carriage traversed the wide, paved streets, and she had been almost overwhelmed by the colours, the scents, and the sounds.

This second trip could not have been more different. She was with her mother and brother, rather than her father, and they travelled with the curtains down almost the whole way. Her mother passed the time between reading and sleeping, and Berran watched Brinnesha as though she might try to escape at any moment. Their brief rest stops were dull, Brinnesha under close guard the whole time; a routine that didn't change even when they arrived safely in the Citadel itself. They had rooms in the inner ring, not ten minutes' walk from the Governors' Keep, and Brinnesha saw nothing beyond the four walls of her room from the hour they arrived until it was time to go to the Keep for the hearing.

⎯⎯⎯◆⎯⎯⎯

On the day of the hearing, Brinnesha dressed carefully and checked her sealed file of evidence for the twentieth time. It was intact, in the fine leather tube brought from Mother's office for this exact purpose. Direct from the Inker's desk to the Governors' court, to seal his fate.

Berran and Brinnesha arrived at the courthouse rather early and were shown into a waiting room that was as bland as it was grandiose. Dark, heavy carved furniture dominated the room, the wood worn smooth around the cracked green leather. Everything was made just a little too big, and Brinnesha felt like a child when she tried one of the armchairs. It was ridiculous and unnecessary, not to mention uncomfortable. After two minutes, Brinnesha perched on the windowsill instead, kicking her heels against the panelled wall beneath, and glancing over her shoulder at the Citadel below.

The 'courthouse' was really an upper floor of the old Inner Keep, first erected when the land was being settled and now repurposed as an official residence for the Governors. Above the courtroom level were only the guards' quarters, if she remembered the diagrams from her history lessons correctly. The windows up here were narrow, barely wider than the archer slits they had replaced, but they afforded a nice view of the Citadel: the semi-permanent street market in the middle of Crafters' Street, and the backs of some of the cheaper houses in the inner ring. The best houses were, of course, on the other side of the ring, away from the bustle of merchant life. Brinnesha considered this cheapness a bonus; when she was successful enough to live in the Citadel, she wanted a house as close to the market as possible. She wasn't going to be one of those stuck-up rare Talents who kept real life at arm's length. However rich or influential her Talent eventually made her, Brinnesha Tynar would never, ever look down on the honest workers who kept the wheels of civilisation turning.

She glanced across at her brother, who had pulled out a chair from the table to sit on, and noticed that he was only just able to rest his feet on the ground. Brinnesha felt a rush of unaccustomed protectiveness towards him. He was one of those honest workers, with his shop and his Talent with customers. Berran would never move in the world of high-level deals like Father and herself. Did he feel overshadowed by his youngest sister? Perhaps she ought to say something, just in case.

"Brother, come and see," she said, turning in her seat and tucking up her feet, the better to look out of the window. "The Citadel looks wonderful from here – you can see all the shops and the market stalls."

After a moment, her brother came and stood behind her. With a cold certainty, Brinnesha sensed a lecture coming on.

"You know, Little Sister, the Citadel is a wonderful model of civilisation."

Brinnesha fought back a smile as she nodded. A lecture, yes, but one that fitted her own thoughts so well that she couldn't resent it.

"As with the wider world, the few who rule are dependent on the many who are ruled; and the many live in peace and order, thanks to the few. You see that it must be this way, the many below and the few above?"

Brinnesha gazed out over the bustle and shimmer of the inner ring and listened to the sounds of the outer ring.

"Below, yes," she conceded. "But not crushed underfoot. This Keep isn't built on the backs of the lower classes, it stands on its own foundations. In fact, it even shelters smaller buildings from the wind and rain."

"And from the sun," put in her brother. "Order requires a hierarchy. By definition, some people must be low and others high. Little Sister, you must stop trying to elevate everyone to your own level. It damages the very fabric of our society."

"I think 'bedrock of society' would fit your analogy better, Brother dear," said Brinnesha. "But I take your point. Now, will you take mine? I don't want to bring us down to the level of the Elementals – I want us all to rise. By improving the lot of our lowest and poorest we will improve life at every level, don't you see? This Keep is the finest, tallest building in the Citadel, but the lesser structures are still clean and well-maintained. And their being so only adds to the glory of the Citadel, without diminishing the Keep one fingerbreadth."

Brinnesha lifted her chin triumphantly, but faltered in the face of Berran's laugh.

"My beautiful, blind, naïve child," he said. "Do you really think the Citadel is clean and well-maintained? Or that the Governors in the Keep care that it should be so? Can you even see the mucky urchins on the street, or do you just imagine them gazing up at us in shining adoration?"

He pointed to a fuzzy blue blur, moving quickly from one alley to the next.

"Do you see that fellow there, in the blue coat? He's perfectly at home, scuttling from shadow to shadow as he goes about his business. Do you think he'd want to come up here, to be made to look shabby and dirty next to this fine furniture and our good clothes? Trust me, Sister, he'd have to be dragged up those stairs, fighting at every step. And if you went down and made him a present of one of these beautiful cushions, or even my own coat, he wouldn't be easy in his mind until he'd torn and dirtied it, to fit it to his level. It's how we all are – happiest with what we know."

Brinnesha hmm'd noncommittally, and heroically refrained from asking why the Elementals couldn't gradually be made comfortable with a higher standard of living. Her brother was clearly in no mood to have his mind changed, and she would save her energy for the more important task of persuading the Citadel Governors.

"Don't give me 'hmm' Little Sister. You can't sound off at the Governors the way you do at the Town Elders back home. I know you want to put the world to rights, but please: be respectful."

⸺ ◆ ⸺

The prison transport lurched through yet another puddle, throwing Brinnesha against her neighbours.

48

She barely noticed anymore. The other prisoners were sullen, depressed or resentful, but not Brinnesha Tynar. She was angry.

She was furious.

From before she'd entered that courtroom, the Governors had been prejudiced against her. They'd listened to her, but in that horribly indulgent way that old people listen to children. She'd wanted to smack the insipid smiles from their faces, shake them by their chains of office, and force them to take her seriously.

Could she have done anything differently? Said anything that would have reached those age-hardened, bigoted brains?

Instead of considering her evidence, they'd sentenced her to six months' hard labour for breaking and entering, harassment, and slander. They took the facts she'd so painstakingly gathered and twisted them to make Olvar Harreal look like the victim. She shook with rage in the cart and it made her chains rattle.

"Don't be scared, it'll be alright," said someone in front of her. Brinnesha blinked, and dragged herself back to the present with difficulty.

The boy who had spoken was young and scrawny. He was bound with leather and rope rather than chain, and sat next to a burly Sidrax guard. The boy grinned at Brinnesha as if they were on their way to a day at the beach instead of six months underground.

"I'm not scared," she said.

"Good. It's not so bad, really. They don't make us kids do the really tough work – they give that to the big guys. I reckon that's why Mr. Feldspar here is so stupidly law-abiding. They'd make him dig out whole tunnels by himself!"

The huge guard growled – actually growled at the boy, who laughed. "You love me really, Feldie," he said. "We've been friends for... how many years now?"

"Six. And I'm not your friend, I'm your parole offi-cer. Taking you to the mines for a third time, because apparently the first two didn't stick."

"See?" said the boy to Brinnesha. "I'm an old hand. Stick with me; you'll be alright."

The guard looked at Brinnesha, as if seeing her for the first time.

"I hope you've got more sense than that," he said, "whatever fit of foolishness brought you here."

———◦———

As it happened, Feldspar needn't have worried. As soon as they arrived at the prison mines, the boy was singled out by the warden and sent down to 'level two, sector twelve'.

"Level two? Are you sure?" asked his parole officer. "He's not even fifteen yet."

"Not fifteen, yet here for the third time. And he's a flight risk. Well, a scamper risk," replied the warden, with a snide smile.

Feldspar frowned. "That's why you have Sidrax guards, to watch the Sidrax prisoners who are too quick for you Avlem. Would an *Avlem* minor be sent to level two?"

"If necessary," said the warden, with a significant look towards Brinnesha. "I have authority over this sector, and may send my prisoners where I see fit. That is my job. Your job, Feldspar, was to deliver your charge here without letting him escape. Your job is done. Goodbye."

"See ya, Feldie," said the boy, but his cheery smile didn't reach his eyes.

By now it was almost sunset. Brinnesha expected to get her uniform, a meal, and then go to bed. They were all given uniforms, but then the warden assigned each new prisoner to a couple of experienced ones and told them to pay attention and practise, because they'd be working at full speed come the morning.

Brinnesha tried to focus on what she was being shown, but it was late, and she was tired. Also, it was boring. As far as she could tell, they were sorting rocks into crates. She did her best to listen to the older Elemental woman who was instructing her, but it was no good.

"Look, just tell me what we're looking for," she said. "I can't remember all this detail. Sorry," she added, belatedly. "I'm just not as good with all this rock business as you Elementals. I need you to keep things simple."

The Elemental woman replied with a scornful look, but followed it up with some very basic instruction so Brinnesha forgave her. It had been a long day.

⸺⸺◆⸺⸺

Seventeen long days later, Brinnesha decided that she'd had enough.

Sorting rocks wasn't a service to any community. It wasn't teaching her anything apart from how to use her Talent on rocks, and how to survive in thoroughly uncivilised conditions. She wondered how her family would react if she returned to them with a taste for thin gruel and a habit of sleeping on the floor with a single blanket.

Her family. She'd hardly thought of them for almost three weeks. Brinnesha suddenly regretted spending her last moments with them talking about the trial and making them promise not to trust Olvar Harreal. Why hadn't she said that she was sorry for making them worry? That she'd miss them? That she loved them?

There and then, while her hands tossed rocks into crates, Brinnesha Tynar vowed to put those omissions right the moment she saw them again.

In just over five months. It felt like an eternity.

She threw the rocks harder than necessary, sending up chips and dust into the faces of the girls working around her. The Elemental who was supposed to be mentoring her used a gust of air to blow the dust back into Brinnesha's own face, making her start a coughing fit just as the other girls were mostly recovered.

"Tynar. Get back to work."

She scowled at the overseer, who ignored her. Red-faced, and only partly from lack of air, Brinnesha returned to her spot. With sarcastic care, she placed each rock into its crate as if building a piece of art. With her Talent, she didn't need to examine the rocks to know where they should go. She simply Found the rocks for a particular crate and let her hands drift towards them. Even going slowly, she was still faster than the others.

For the first few days she'd tried to be kind to the girls in her room, but it hadn't worked. There was only one other Avlem, and she'd been raised in a Sidrax orphanage so she didn't really count. The Elemental and Sidrax prisoners made fun of her voice, her manners, even how she held her spoon at mealtimes. She tried to make allowances for their low upbringing and even offered to help some of the slower ones with their quotas, but all for nothing. They didn't even want to hear her story. It was as if they didn't care that she was suffering in this horrible place because she was a defender of the Elementals. To them, she was just another Avlem.

It was so unfair!

The whistle sounded for the mid-day meal and the girls stood as one to line up by the door. There was no shoving or rushing – newcomers soon learned that misbehaviour got you held back by the overseer. In fact...

"Tynar, with me."

Great.

Brinnesha moved quickly before anyone could push her. A snigger chased her down the passageway as she followed the overseer. They stopped outside a room marked 'Warden, Sector 36'.

"In."

Brinnesha wasn't quick enough to avoid the shove this time and stumbled into the Warden's office. She turned to glare at the overseer but saw only an empty doorway.

"Ah, Brinnesha. I've been wanting a word with you," said the Warden. "Sit down."

The Kindly Smile didn't fool Brinnesha for a moment, but she did take the chair that was offered. After standing in line for hours, she wasn't going to let pride get in the way of a chance to rest.

The Warden fixed her with what was probably meant to be a fatherly look. Brinnesha sneered. Her father had never looked at her like that in his life. He had too much respect for her; and for himself.

"Brinnesha, do you know why you're here?" asked the Warden.

"I'm here because my enemies have the power to pervert justice."

"I see. Justice is very important to you, isn't it? And not just for yourself."

Brinnesha closed her eyes and took a deep breath. *I will not call this man an idiot, not while he has so much power over me*, she thought. Then said, "Surely justice is important to everyone. Sir."

"Indeed. And justice requires law, and law requires order. You are here to learn to respect law and order. Do you understand?"

"Yes. Sir." Brinnesha really did try to keep the irritation out of her voice. She was missing a meal for *this?*

"I don't think you do," the Warden said, making no effort to disguise his amusement. Brinnesha's face burned. The patronising jerk!

"I understand that your Talent is related to Finding things," the Warden said.

The abrupt change in the conversation's direction knocked Brinnesha from her train of angry thoughts.

"Yes, sir. I'm a Finder."

"A very useful and versatile Talent. You are indeed blessed. So, if I entrusted you with a message for sector eight, you'd be able to Find your way there?"

"Of course." Brinnesha didn't try so hard to conceal her irritation this time. Was this common thief-watcher really questioning her Talent? No-one back home would have dreamt of being so rude. Home suddenly felt very far away, and Brinnesha clamped down on her Talent before it tried to tell her exactly how far.

Five minutes later, Brinnesha Tynar strode through the twisting passages of the mines on the most direct path to sector eight. She was carrying a message for the warden of the sector and was technically unaccompanied. She didn't miss, however, the way that every guard watched her as she went by, nor the quite astonishing number of occasions when a guard just happened to be going her way as she crossed between sectors.

As if I were likely to escape by going deeper *into the mines*, she thought. Though she was not sorry for the company on the darker and nastier crossings. Perhaps sorting rocks on the upper levels wasn't so bad after all.

Eventually, she reached sector eight and handed her message to its warden. He – or possibly she – was a gorilla-shaped Sidrax, wearing a uniform specially tailored to the animal form. Most Sidrax in Brinnesha's experience simply shaped their skin to look like clothing, but this one presumably spent so much time in gorilla shape that it was worth getting clothes to fit. Curious. Even more curiously, the Sidrax was somehow able to speak despite being in animal form.

"There is no answer," the warden of sector eight said. "Take the prisoner back to her own sector. The long way."

"Yes, Warden. Come, you."

Brinnesha turned to see whom the warden was addressing and found herself taken by the arm and propelled from the room before she could get a proper look at her new escort. She appeared to be another Avlem – or at least, Avlem-shaped. Spotting Sidrax back home was easy, because whatever they appeared to be wearing would be the exact colour of their face, hands, and hair. But having just seen one Sidrax in clothes, she had to wonder if the guards really were all Avlem, as she'd first thought. She glanced at the fingers wrapped around her upper arm and hoped they wouldn't suddenly become claws.

"I'm not going to run away, you know," Brinnesha said. "You needn't to hold me so tightly."

The guard didn't reply right away, but eventually relaxed her hold.

"Stay close," she ordered. "We're coming up on a working area."

The ringing of tools on stone always played in the mines from breakfast to lights out, but it had been getting louder and more distinct for several passages. Now, Brinnesha heard voices between the blows, surly and unhappy. And, occasionally, something that sounded horribly like leather striking skin.

The dull thwacks were quieter than the chime of iron on stone, but by now Brinnesha's Talent told her that the working group was only one more corner away. She could hear every strike, and they turned her stomach. She set her jaw, but couldn't hide the shudder of disgust.

"Don't you fret, missy," said her attendant guard. "You're safe enough if you stay close to me." She patted her sword hilt.

Brinnesha averted her eyes.

⸺◆⸺

They rounded the corner to see the supervisor laying into a scarred, grizzled Elemental with a short whip. The man's tools lay on the ground by his feet, as helpless as their wielder. Brinnesha started forward before her guard could stop her.

"Leave him alone, you brute!"

Trusting her Talent, Brinnesha plucked the whip from the guard without looking, and used her other hand to smack him across the face. The beaten Elemental turned towards her with an unreadable expression, then closed his hand on her arm.

"No striking the guards, miss. Don't want to get ourselves in trouble now, see?"

Brinnesha could never quite understand what happened next, no matter how many times she considered it. One moment she was standing between the guard and his victim, and the next she was behind the rescued Elemental and in the hands of three others. Her attendant and the sector guard were laid out on the floor, relieved of their weapons. Someone had taken the whip from Brinnesha, and by the time a second sector guard arrived, he was too late to do anything but join his colleagues on the floor.

With an enormous effort of will, Brinnesha found her voice.

"Are they...? Did you...? Are they...?"

"Dead, dearie?" said the female prisoner who was holding Brinnesha by the shoulders. The voice sounded dry and ancient in her ears, and the breath smelled like rotten apples. "Oh no, don't you fret about that, missy. They're just having a little kip while we... discuss things."

"Indeed," said the first Elemental. "See now, I should have a name for my little defender, Miss...?"

"Brinnesha Tynar." She lifted her hand towards him out of habit, as if they were in a drawing room instead of a prison pit. One of the other Elementals grabbed her wrist to hold her back. Irritated, Brinnesha jabbed her elbow backwards into the spot her Talent told her would make him let go. She heard a groan, and the other prisoners laughed.

"Forgive Korax, Miss Tynar. He's no idea how to treat a Lady like yourself. Now, let's come away and have a comfortable chat, see, while the guards sleep it off."

The group around her seemed to relax, and Brinnesha could feel how they looked up to him. She therefore didn't object when the man put his arm around her shoulders, dislodging the rotten-apple woman's hands. It was unpardonably familiar of him, but he clearly didn't realise. Here, thought Brinnesha, was a fatherly man, used to respect. She wouldn't shame him before his people.

Proud of her insightfulness, and congratulating herself on her delicacy, Brinnesha barely noticed what he was saying or where she was being led. She gathered that the man's name was Gles, and that the half-dozen prisoners with him had been captured from their homes a few years ago and brought here to slave underground, though none of them were even Earth Elementals.

Brinnesha realised that she hadn't really understood the difference between the Elemental tribes before coming here. She was learning quite a lot after all, though not whatever it was the narrow-minded authorities had intended her to learn.

***

The gentle movement of the group came to a sudden stop, and Brinnesha felt the tension in the air as well as in the arm that was still around her shoulders.

"Which way? Which way?" muttered a voice from the front.

"Left."

Brinnesha had said it without thinking and only realised she had spoken when a dozen eyes turned on her.

"You want the best way out, yes? Then go left. Those paths are abandoned."

"See now, how do you know that, Miss Brinnesha Tynar?" asked Gles. There was an edge to his curious tone, the merest trace of suspicion.

"I'm a Finder. I asked my Talent for a way out that keeps us away from other people. Wait..."

Brinnesha tried to Find the nearest guards instead, and felt a steadily strengthening pull from behind. "There are guards after us," she said.

"Already? Impossible. I saw to 'em m'self."

The tension in the group shifted like a storm cloud, ready to break any moment.

"Enough chatter, see? We go left," said Gles, sounding for the first time more like a chief than a father. Brinnesha didn't have long to think about this change, because now the group was moving swiftly. It took her a moment to get perfectly in step, and she nearly tripped on the tangle of legs and feet around her.

There were not many junctions, but Brinnesha pointed the way each time. After the third choice, a particularly awkward spot with seven directions, the Elementals no longer hesitated to obey her. They walked on through rough and smooth until Brinnesha called a halt.

"There are people ahead on each of these paths. I can't keep us hidden any longer." Brinnesha looked around at her Elemental group and saw the worry in their craggy, work-worn faces. "I'm sorry," she told them, and meant it.

"Now, lass, don't be sorry," replied Gles. "You just find us the best way, and we won't ask for perfect, see? Surely you didn't think we'd get all the way out just by going through the deeps?"

He adjusted his hold and patted her far shoulder. Rather heavily, if she was honest, but the intent was surely to encourage.

Brinnesha smiled her acknowledgment. It took her a bit of experimenting to get a clear response from her Talent. It didn't do well with numbers, but eventually she thought she'd Found the safest path, and told Gles.

He patted her shoulder again, his big hand wrapping around most of her upper arm.

⸺◆⸺

The chosen path opened onto a cavern. Brinnesha heard voices ahead that sounded younger and fresher than any in her group. For a moment she wondered if she'd managed to come round to her own work station again, but she didn't recognise anyone. Three Elementals from the front of Brinnesha's group moved silently into the larger space.

From then on, Brinnesha was in a nightmare. The fatherly hand on her shoulder became a vice that pinned her arms to her sides. The grateful, friendly Elementals morphed into monsters, armed with weapons that must have come from the fallen guards. The three from the front returned with hostages of their own, children all. With a sick feeling of recognition, Brinnesha saw that one was the young Sidrax boy who'd befriended her on the journey from the Citadel. Her eyes swam with tears, blinding her to the chaos but leaving her ears to supply her imagination with horrors enough.

Gles laughed, harsh and mocking. "Don't cry, girlie. See, I won't let anyone hurt you. Not you, as was so kind and showed us the way here, see? Not you, girlie."

Brinnesha recoiled from the feel of his hand on her face, and then her eyes suddenly stung with dryness. Not just her eyes, but her whole face was now as dry as if she'd been walking in a strong wind. When she could see again, she saw Gles' hand, covered in a glistening film of liquid: her own tears shaped into vicious spikes.

Gles grinned and gestured sharply towards the hostages.

"Now, these brats," he said. "See, that's another thing altogether."

<hr/>

Fire and water and chaos filled the enclosed space, and Brinnesha lost track of events. Words were shouted, but she couldn't understand them. People screamed, weapons clashed, and the air was full of heat and steam. The only constant was the painful grip on her shoulder, dragging her forward.

She was dragged past guards and prisoners, lying on the ground in various states of injury. One young man was sprawled across the path, and Brinnesha almost tripped over him as she was pulled along. He wasn't dressed as a guard, but neither was he chained. A young woman came up alongside Brinnesha as they stepped over the fallen man.

"Fool," she said, to the insensible body at her feet. "Do you think they will care if you die for them? You should have chosen your loyalties more wisely, brother."

Brinnesha watched the woman pull ahead, and felt numb. They were killing indiscriminately: anyone who got in their way, or failed to join them. She suddenly knew that she was going to die, and only hoped that it would be quick. What would her parents do when they heard the news? And Talemar, what would she think?

The fact of her death filled Brinnesha with more regret than fear. So many things she would never do now. When she felt herself being lifted up, she didn't fight it. It was the end and all her own fault.

Gles lifted Brinnesha by her shoulders and threw her backwards, away from the exit. She landed hard, not on the gritty floor but against the armoured bodies of the pursuing guards... and then the floor. She took down two of the guards and tripped up three others. The noise was awful, almost as bad as the pain from where the guards' weapons had nicked her.

As Brinnesha and the guards got to their feet, the exit passage imploded. Once the dust settled there was no sign of the escaped prisoners or their hostages.

Brinnesha Tynar was sitting down, which was a welcome relief. Her wounds, minor as they were, had been dressed and she was waiting in a curtained-off alcove of the main hospital area. Everyone was rushing around, and the fixed pattern of meals and sleep seemed to have been forgotten.

And so, she thought, had Brinnesha.

She dozed, despite her aching body and heart, until she was dragged awake, quite literally, by the warden of her own sector. He looked furious but didn't say a word. He held her by the arm and walked her out towards the main entrance of the prison mines. For one surreal moment, Brinnesha thought she was going to be thrown out of the prison. But before the final turning, the warden pulled Brinnesha into a side tunnel and up a short flight of stairs. They emerged into a magnificently ornate room.

It was as foreign to Brinnesha's Avlem sensibilities as the Elemental huts in her far-off village had been. She didn't think it was Sidrax, though the military decorations certainly were. The carved stone was too ornate, and lacked the functional, geometric designs that typified the Sidrax architecture in the Citadel.

Brinnesha Tynar made herself think about the room, the decorations, even the glimmer of what looked like sunlight coming from behind the door. Anything rather than what she'd witnessed in that cavern. She'd seen dead animals before, but dead people were different. So... *wrong*.

Brinnesha fixed her eyes on the sunlight as another door opened to admit them. The blinding glare would account for her tears.

***

It was a fair punishment. Everybody said so, and Brinnesha had to agree. The six prisoners had each been condemned to twenty-five years for murder and banditry. She would serve out their sentences in their place, with an additional five years for her part in the death of the guard who had been killed, and six months for each prisoner injured in the escape.

Brinnesha wryly wondered if that included herself. Not that it mattered. She would be dead before she had served half her time. She felt as though she wouldn't mind dying right away. It would be better than living with the knowledge of her failure.

All her dreams of freeing Elementals from oppression, and all she'd managed to do was free a band of convicted killers. The fact that they were also Elementals didn't make her feel any better.

Brinnesha Tynar went to work where she was told and spoke to no-one. She lasted about a fortnight before grief and self-neglect caused her to collapse at the rockface. The next thing that Brinnesha Tynar was aware of was waking up in a rough bed and someone handing her a letter.

To Whom It May Concern:

At the request of the Tynar

family of the Avlem town Perayen, and with the approval
of the Perayen town council,
the prisoner formerly known as
Brinnesha Tynar is disowned and
utterly dismissed from the Tynar family, and from the Perayen
Community.

Said prisoner forfeits immediately all rights to the name
of Tynar, and is required to
cease all communication with
that family.

The rest of the letter, including the Mayor's elaborate signature, dissolved into a blur for the former Brinnesha Tynar.

"Harsh," said the warden, not unkindly. "But fair, I suppose. Especially if you had siblings affected by the stigma. Well, that just leaves one question. Assuming you don't want to be 'Prisoner 793' for the rest of your life, what are we to call you?"

She thought about it. Perhaps it would be alright to keep a part of her name.

"Call me Nesh," she said.

~ End of Act One ~

ACT TWO: PRISONERS & EXILES

Being the record of how one woman
crossed the New Land, in company with
two Sidrax and sundry Elementals.

I

The years passed, and slowly enough at first for Nesh. Her muscles hardened to the work, and her senses adjusted to the poor light and echoing sounds of the deep mines. She became used to the pattern of the days, and the rhythm of the work. She even got used to her new name. But she couldn't get used to the way the Avlem guards looked at her.

At first, it was anger over her part in the death of one of their own. But time passed, and those who had known the dead guard retired or moved to other service. Newer guards heard her story – she was a curiosity by then, one of the fixtures of the place – and looked at her, not with anger, but with hatred.

It was the newer guards who started the bullying, Nesh was sure. The old timers ignored her, but the younger generation could be spiteful. Herding her to the back of the line at meal times so that she never got quite enough to eat, or time to eat it. Keeping her away from the most comfortable (or the least uncomfortable) places to sleep. They seemed to be behind a string of petty accidents too, although those ended after a support beam came crashing down and nearly hit one of the Earthers assigned to the sector. Nesh heard the other Earther complaining about that to a couple of guards that evening, and the accidents stopped.

The looks didn't.

Every couple of years, Nesh would be moved to another sector. Sometimes she was used as a way for wardens to score off each other, sometimes it was because she was making friends with another prisoner, and sometimes just because. Wherever she went, the message was clear. Elemental, Sidrax, and especially Avlem wanted it known that Nesh was not one of them.

On her first transfer her escort said, "This is our resident Avlem," when handing her over. "Our collective disgrace, summed up in one wretched woman."

"An Avlem prisoner, eh?" said one of the receiving guards. "What's her Talent? Making the rest of us look bad?"

"I blame the parents," said the other guard.

"Not this time," said her escort. "She ain't got no parents."

"Orphan?"

"Outcast. Ain't ya, *Nesh*? Family had the sense to cut ties. Too bad you can't be made non-Avlem, as well."

Variations of this scene played out over and over until it almost, but not quite, lost its power to hurt her. The Avlem would say it with bile, the Sidrax with scorn, and all with hatred.

There were no Elemental guards, although Nesh got the impression that the Earth Elementals were something more than just prisoners. Young Earthers came in as older ones disappeared, but they never worked with the other prisoners. They were more often used to open up new spaces, maintain current ones, and carefully collapse old tunnels. Nesh wondered if that last was a new policy, given how the escape had been managed. She could think of the escape now without pain, but not without shame. She'd been so quick to believe, just because she wanted to see all Elementals as simple innocents. Well, Nesh told herself, she certainly knew better now.

Take those three young Fire Elementals, swaggering boys on the cusp of adulthood of her latest sector (her twelfth, Nesh thought, or maybe only her eleventh). They weren't innocent by any stretch of the imagination. They bragged about their attacks on civilisation, and how they'd be out in a few months to do it all again. And, worse in Nesh's eyes, they bullied a fellow Fire Elemental, a young boy who seemed no older than ten. He was 'only a thief', not a 'freedom fighter' like themselves, and they never let him forget it. They kept him away from the best food and sleeping places. No, Nesh wouldn't fall for any story that those young men could tell.

⋯⟡⋯

Their young victim kept on catching Nesh's attention. Even in the dim light of the mines, she could read his body language – and his being the smallest body in the sector made him unmistakeable. Sector twenty-seven, her current residence, was home to petty, but habitual, offenders. How could such a child be a habitual anything?

She watched him in the evening, sat at a distance from the central fire pit and picking at the scraps of food he'd sneaked past his tormentors. The older boys sat almost touching the flames, ready to chase off the 'little thief' if he dared to approach. But he'd stopped even trying, and Nesh watched as he made a bed for himself in a cold corner as if he had chosen it specially. She might have believed the act, if she hadn't heard his teeth chatter in the middle of the night.

The next day, Nesh placed herself between the boy and the other prisoners as they worked. The boy was diligent enough and seemed not to notice when Nesh slipped some of her own ore into his bucket. But that night he made his bed with Nesh between himself and the rest of the room, as if her shadow were fire enough for him.

⸺◦⸺

It was another three days before he spoke to her, and then only in a whisper. She woke in the night and turned over to ease her aching hip. The boy was awake and looking right at her, his face close enough for Nesh to see in detail.

"Why're you helping me, Lady?" he said, so quietly that Nesh strained to hear. "What's in it for you?"

Nesh's heart, toughened and leathery though it was, broke anew at the idea of a child not understanding kindness. Had no-one ever done anything for him without expecting some return?

"I don't like to see anyone bullied," Nesh whispered in reply. "It's..." She grimaced. She wasn't going to share her life story with this child. But he seemed to understand anyway and reached out to pat her on the arm.

"I don't mind 'em, not really. They can say what they like, it's only noise. But I wish I could get a bit of the fire. I'm a Fire Breather. I need my Element, you know?"

Nesh nodded. She'd watched the other prisoners long enough to understand that.

"The torches in the walls just ain't enough. I need something stronger. More... natural." The child hesitated, then dropped his voice as if confessing to a terrible greediness. "I need sunlight," he said.

Sunlight! Nesh's heart sank. She hadn't seen a glimpse of the sky in over twenty years. She reviewed the mental map of the sectors she'd been in and fell asleep turning the problem over and over.

It was still on her mind the next day. Their seam of ore split off into a side branch that looked so feeble as to be not worth the effort, according to the resident Earth Elemental. Nesh followed it with her Talent and saw that it might be exactly what she was looking for to help the young Fire Breather, Volnar.

Even after more than twenty years, Nesh remembered arriving at the entrance to the mines and walking in through the towering face of a great inland cliff. Since then she'd been about a dozen different sectors and realised that, although the deepest and dampest were below ground level, most were inside the cliff itself.

If only she and Volnar could work that side seam! It would be so easy to strike a little too hard and open a small hole in the cliff – just enough to allow daylight in. Nesh looked at the boy, working beside her again as was becoming usual, and she was determined to help him.

⸺◆⸺

She first felt hope when overhearing a conversation between the warden and the Earth Elemental, if it could be called 'overhearing' when the warden was loud enough to be heard in the Citadel.

"I don't expect a primitive rodent like you to understand, Earther 27, but that ore is valuable. In the hands of civilised people it is capable of great things, and we can't afford to leave any of it just lying in the ground, uselessly. You must open a path for the miners."

Nesh could almost hear 'Earther 27' scowl as he answered, though in a more measured tone than the warden's, "It's not worth it. That seam peters out in a few yards, and the surrounding rock is unstable. You'd need a team of Earthers, and maybe a couple of Marshlanders, and after a week's work you'd have barely anything to show for it."

"That's for me to judge, not you. Remember your place, Earther 27."

As the Earth Elemental and the warden argued back and forth, Nesh began to plan. She had most of it by the time the warden finished talking, and the rest fell into place when he stalked off after flat-out ordering the side-seam to be opened. As he left he made a point of kicking over Nesh's bucket. Or trying to, for it was too heavy. So instead, he hit her across the shoulders for 'blocking the path', and threatened to give her worse if she did it again.

Nesh smiled. Some sectors had unpredictable wardens, but this one was pitifully easy to read. She'd have no trouble getting him to play his part in her plan.

***

Under cover of the clatter and bustle of breakfast, Nesh told Volnar about her plans for the side seam, and how it would take them close enough to the outside wall to make a window.

"We just need to make the warden the right amount of angry," she said. "Enough to give us punishment work, but not to do anything worse."

Volnar grinned. "Leave it to me," he whispered. "I'm good at making people angry."

Before Nesh could warn him not to overdo it, Volnar had disappeared into the crowd.

The next moment, she heard a howl of pain and fury that was not Volnar's. Then a sharp shout that was. Chatter slowed and stopped as the prisoners' attention was taken from their meagre breakfast by the scuffle.

Taking this as her cue, Nesh pushed her way through the crowd and joined Volnar. With one well-placed, Talent-guided strike, she felled the largest of the Fire Elemental bullies. The other two hesitated, then drew back into the crowd. Silence fell.

They didn't seem to be looking at Nesh, but at something or someone beyond her. As she and Volnar turned, three guards laid them by the collar and dragged them to the office of the warden of Sector 27.

⊷◆⊶

Being yelled at by an Avlem with a Talent for Sound Manipulation was like being beaten by a storm wind that blew in all directions at once. Nesh felt breathless and buffeted but didn't answer back. After a few protests, Volnar followed her example.

"Since you can't play nicely with other people," roared the warden, "perhaps you should spend time working alone. Up a nice little side seam, away from the temptation to fight."

Volnar took a step towards Nesh, and trembled even as he tried to hide it.

"Not a side seam," he begged. "Please, I... I don't like small spaces. Please, mister warden..."

His voice trailed off and his eyes opened so wide that they shone in the torchlight.

The warden's booming laugh shook the room. "You should have thought of that before you made trouble," he said. "Send Earther 27 to me!"

This last instruction was so loud that Nesh wondered if it was meant for the guards outside, or if it was meant to echo through the tunnels and reach the sector's sole Earth Elemental directly.

"Earther 27, have you opened that new seam yet?" the warden demanded as the Elemental came through the door.

"It's not a solo job," the Earther replied, in the weary tones of one who's said this all before.

"Well, now you've got help," the warden told him. "These two to dig while you 'stabilise', whatever that's supposed to mean. You Earthers like to make out this whole place would fall apart without you, but I'm too clever for your games. You only do it to make yourselves feel important, and we both know it."

Earther 27 came over to Nesh and Volnar. He never sounded particularly happy, in Nesh's experience, but now he seemed downright disgusted.

"A Fire Breather and an Avlem? No offence, lad, but your Element's the one thing that can't help us down here. And what use do you think an Avlem is going to be?" He sighed and scrubbed a hand over his face.

"Can you at least obey orders?" asked the Earther, looking right at them. Nesh nodded, but the warden broke in before she could reply properly.

"You are my prisoners, in my sector, and if there's any orders to be obeyed then they'll be my orders! Is that clear?"

He waited for Nesh and Volnar to mutter, "Yes, Warden," and then waited again for the Earther to respond. It was a long wait, and eventually the warden must have seen something that satisfied him because he said, "Alright then. You two, *my* orders are that you follow the Earther's instructions. Within reason," he added. "As for you, Earther 27, I order you to open that seam and extract every last bit of ore there is. Now go, and don't let me catch any of you slacking."

———————◆———————

Digging was simple enough, and Nesh could usually let her mind wander while her body worked. But this time she needed to call on her Talent to Find the best places to strike, to open the path that Volnar needed. It felt uncomfortably familiar, asking her Talent for the best way to the outside world, and Nesh had to keep reminding herself that this was a different case. She wasn't leading a band of cut-throats to escape, she was helping one little boy. A suffering and desperate child.

Thinking about Volnar made it easier to work through the long day. Nesh was aware of her body, and her fatigue, in a way that she hadn't been since she was twenty, before she'd learned how to let her mind escape. She was discovering, too, that a body in its forties is a lot less forgiving than one in its teens. By the time the horn sounded for the evening meal, her arms were shaking with fatigue.

Nesh and Volnar set down their tools and began the depressingly short trip back to the main tunnel, only to be stopped there by a guard.

"Not you," she said. "Warden's orders. Back to work, and someone will bring you something to eat later. You sleep here, you eat here, and you work here until the seam is exhausted."

The guard was a Sidrax, with a patterned grey colouring that put Nesh in mind of horses. She certainly liked the pit donkeys better than she liked Nesh, but that wasn't very revealing. Most of the guards here liked things scraped from the bottom of their boots more than they liked Nesh.

Volnar started to protest, but Nesh led him back to their tools. The Earther was there, running his hands over the walls and pacing with bare feet over the path. Volnar sat down with his back to their working face and said, as cheerfully as if he'd just had a hot meal, "I love watching other people work."

Nesh expected the Earther to say something like, "Less watching, more digging," but he only grunted and carried on inspecting the walls. Nesh sat down next to Volnar and let herself doze, propped up between her tools and his. She woke up when a bowl of thin stew was thrust into her hands by the Sidrax guard. The guard stayed until they'd eaten, then took the empty bowls away along with their working lantern.

"Don't take the fire!" Volnar begged, but the guard only laughed. "We don't expect you to work through the night, kid. Get some rest while you can."

"You don't understand, he needs that fire," Nesh said, but the guard was already gone. Darkness closed in, and Volnar clutched at Nesh's tunic. Was the child scared of the dark, or was he simply that dependent on his Element? Nesh tried to imagine being without her Talent, unable to Find anything. Was that how it felt for Volnar to be away from fire?

She felt the child fall asleep, still holding onto her. Nesh made herself as comfortable as she could, and drifted off herself.

They worked through the whole of the next day and most of the third before Nesh's Talent indicated that they were near the surface. She started to strike with less force and more deliberation, wanting to create an opening for just enough sunlight that it might blend with the torchlight and escape notice. Unfortunately, the warden of Sector 27 chose that moment to make an inspection.

"Put your back into it, you useless excuse for an Avlem!"

The warden put all the force of his Talent behind the shout, and underscored it with his billy club. Nesh felt the force of both on her shoulders just as she was about to land a blow on the outside wall, and her control disappeared.

So did the head of her pickaxe, along with half the handle. What had been a dark grey mass streaked with ore became a flaky mess. A crack ran up from the centre of Nesh's strike, creating a cascade of dark grey snowflakes as it grew. Tiny pieces, some smaller than the nail of Nesh's smallest finger, but so many.

The Earther appeared behind Nesh and placed a hand over the crack. The loosened rock still fell like ash. The Earther moved to the left, repairing the growing crack almost as quickly as it appeared.

Almost.

The warden despatched a guard for help, then relieved his feelings by yelling at the Earther. Nesh was sure she was not the only one who was relieved when he stalked back to the main tunnel. Volnar crouched down, eyes fixed on the walls as if he could hold them up by willpower alone. The guards stood near the entrance to the side-seam, keen to abandon their post as soon as it might be forgivable. Nesh watched the Earther at work.

It was an education, seeing that short, middle-aged man race the splintering rock. His hands and feet were soon lost in dust – or maybe inside the very stone itself. There had been no Earth Elementals in her old village that Nesh knew of, and watching this one handling his Element made Nesh almost forget the danger. Then the warden returned with the promised help. And then everything went very, very badly.

The Earther and the warden argued, which delayed the repair work. The warden shouted and stamped his feet, which made more loose rock fall. Nesh watched the two men. As one grew redder, the other grew paler. Nesh thought she could see the Earther shaking with the effort of holding the tunnel open, or maybe the vibration was in the wall and floor. She heard him give the guards one last warning, and then she was inside a thundercloud.

That was the only thing she could compare it to. The world went dark, and rocks curved over her head and away into the main tunnel with a roaring sound. Nesh flinched and covered her face. When she looked again, she and Volnar and the little pit donkey who had arrived with the work crew were all on one side of the pile of rock. The warden, the guards, and the work crew themselves were on the other side.

The dust settled and the dark grey world turned red. Volnar shouted with delight. Nesh turned around and saw that the sun was sinking low through the evening mists, turning everything red-orange. They were standing on the outside of the mines, not more than two or three strides up from the ground. There was even a slope of debris that might have been made for them to climb down over.

Volnar was down it and out of sight in a moment. Nesh dropped her head into her hands. She'd somehow engineered a second escape, and no-one would ever believe it was an accident. She considered her options. The only sane thing to do was to follow young Volnar's example and run away. With her Talent she stood a good chance of evading pursuit, and now that she was no longer a Tynar, her family couldn't be shamed by her actions.

Nesh began to pick her way down the steep slope when a small voice said, "Is my Stony-Man asleep?"

It was a little girl, younger even than Volnar, and copper-coloured from head to toe. Even her simple frock was the same shade. She was leaning over the exhausted Earther and sounded as if she was about to cry.

"It's not time to sleep yet. It's supper first, then stories, then sleep." The child carried on in this vein for a while, alternately begging her 'Stony-Man' to wake up and chiding him for being asleep.

The Earther didn't respond at all, and for one horrible moment Nesh thought he might be dead. She joined the little girl at the Earther's head and laid a hand on his chest. She was relieved to feel it rise and fall as he breathed, and the slow but steady thump of a heartbeat.

"He's very tired," she told the mysterious girl. "We should let the man sleep. He'll wake up in the morning and everything will be fine. Why don't you come with me now, and we'll go for a nice walk?"

"Can my Stony-Man come, too? I'll carry him."

Nesh looked at the little girl, then at the Earther, then at the little girl again. Only she wasn't a little girl anymore, she was a donkey. The same little pit donkey who had been with the work crew. A Sidrax, then – but so young!

"How are you here, and by yourself?" Nesh asked the Sidrax. "Where are your parents?"

But the donkey only nosed at the Earther and looked miserable.

Seeing as she couldn't leave the child, and the child wouldn't leave the Earther, Nesh found herself with no choice but to heave the unconscious man onto the donkey's back. The donkey helped as much as she could, pushing her head under the Earther's body, and letting Nesh roll him over until he was draped over the donkey's back like a very lopsided bag of rocks. It was quite an effort to get him properly balanced, and he kept sliding off every time the little donkey stood up.

In the middle of this ridiculous scene, Volnar reappeared. It was fully dark by now, but a single lantern had somehow survived the upheaval.

"What are you doing?" he asked Nesh. "Never mind the old man, let's go!"

"I thought you'd gone already," she replied.

"Too dark," Volnar said. "I come back for the light."

"Well, help me with this before you go off again," Nesh said, shortly. "I'll explain later."

With Volnar's help, the donkey was finally loaded and able to get up. The first moon was just rising as donkey, woman, and boy picked their way down to ground level and set off into the night.

Nesh let her Talent guide her, setting it to Find a place where they could hide once the sun rose. She kept one hand on the neck of the donkey, trusting the sure-footed Sidrax to keep to the best paths. When the little donkey picked up her feet and stepped carefully, Nesh made sure to do the same. Volnar seemed to manage with the meagre light from the lantern.

The first Nesh knew of the trees was when a branch hit her in the face. It was a light and springy branch, fortunately, but it was still a shock. She stumbled, and put her free hand up to protect her from further surprises. The ground became uneven as they walked over tree roots. Both moons were up now, but their feeble light couldn't penetrate the leafy canopy. Nesh switched her Talent between searching for a safe place to hide and searching for a place to put her foot. It was exhausting, and when her Talent nudged her towards a rise in the ground, Nesh mistook the reason and planted her foot squarely into a hole in the soft earth.

Her stumble startled the children, and it wasn't until Volnar brought the dying lantern over that they could make sense of what had happened.

Nesh frowned. "Does this hole get bigger as you go in?" she asked Volnar, who was reaching in with both arms.

"It's big enough to stash 'im," the boy said, jerking a thumb towards the still-unconscious Earther. "And being in his Element might rouse him in time to make space for the rest of us. If he wants to, of course."

Nesh didn't really understand, but she thought the sky was getting lighter in the east. With a lot of help from Volnar and the little donkey, Nesh managed to slide the Earther feet-first into the hollow in the bank. She was sure she felt his feet hit the bottom while his shoulders were still outside, but then it felt as though the ground drew the man into itself. The boy scrambled in after the Earther, then popped his head out again a moment later to ask Nesh for twigs, grass, or anything that would burn.

"There's room for all of us, except the donkey," Volnar informed them. "Come and see. All we need is a bit of a fire, and we'll be all set."

Nesh set her Talent looking for twigs, and found a handful hanging close overhead. Grateful not to have walked into them, Nesh gathered them and tugged until she had a double handful. When she looked back, the donkey was nowhere to be seen.

"Donkey?" Nesh tried to call softly, resulting in an odd sort of whispered shout. "Little Sidrax, where are you?"

A copper-coloured girl's head poked out from the earth. "Come down, Lady! The Fire-Boy wants twigs."

Nesh lowered herself carefully into the damp, dark hole. Except it wasn't completely dark, thanks to Volnar. The boy had used the last of the lantern's fuel to soak some grass and was coaxing little flames from the mixture. When Nesh held out her twigs, he snatched them to feed to the hungry fire.

"I'll have it steady in a bit, but fire always needs a lot of feeding at the beginning. It's like a baby that way," he said, with a grin.

Nesh sat down with her back to the entrance, feeling the cold dawn air against her scalp even as the young fire warmed her face. To her left, less than an arm's length away, lay the Earther. He was still unconscious as far as she could tell, but even as she watched, the soft earth shaped itself around his body – or maybe his body sank into the soft earth. One or the other, Nesh couldn't tell. The little Sidrax girl curled up near his feet, legs and arms out to one side, as if she were still a donkey.

Volnar sat like Nesh, back against the wall and the fire in front of him. His eyes flickered closed, and Nesh expected the fire to dwindle to nothing once the child stopped feeding it. She reached out through the opening for some more grass with which to feed the fire through the day. But before the sun was warm on her hair, Nesh was asleep too.

⸺◆⸺

She woke to find Volnar and the Sidrax child already awake. The fire was doing well despite her neglect, and the girl was still hovering over the sleeping Earther. The only change in him that Nesh could see was his having sunk a little deeper into the soil.

The floor was level, and the walls curved. Nesh wondered if the Earther had woken up to neaten their temporary shelter or if he'd done all this in his sleep. Either way, it was good work. The whole space was drier too, probably thanks to Volnar's fire.

"Here, have some breakfast."

Nesh started when Volnar spoke, but was even more surprised by his producing a hand-sized piece of bread for her, seemingly from thin air.

"Pockets," he said with a grin. "Made 'em soon as I got these clothes, and always keep a bit of food from meals. You never know when you'll need it."

"Thank you, Volnar," said Nesh, faintly. She was hungry enough that even stale prison bread was appealing. "Has the little girl eaten yet?"

"The little Maddie-gal? Nah, she won't move 'til he does. I've tried telling her that all he needs is a good sleep in his Element, but she's fretting."

"Madrigal?" echoed Nesh, unsure if she'd caught the name correctly.

At the sound of her name, the little girl looked around.

"Why won't he wake up?" she asked, equal parts worry and frustration. "He's always wake up before breakfast, and it's more than breakfast. It's nearly time to go back home. Does he need to be back home to wake up?"

The child sounded on the brink of tears, and Nesh felt herself start to panic. What did one do with a crying child?

Nesh reached out and drew Madrigal into her arms. *Try soothing noises and hair stroking,* suggested her brain in a combination of instinct and memory.

"I ask him and ask him to go home, but my Stony-Man just sleeps and sleeps. He should be wake up and go home!"

Nesh patted and soothed, waiting for the next insight on child-handling from her brain – but in vain.

"Hush, Madrigal. There, there," Nesh said, trying to keep the copper-coloured hair out of her mouth. "Have you spoken to the Earther – your 'Stony-Man' before? Does he know you in this form?"

This, at least, stopped the tears. The Sidrax child pulled away from Nesh's arms and seemed almost offended. "Of course he–"

The Earther chose this moment to sit up. He got about halfway before Madrigal reached him with a flying tackle.

Even in the flickering firelight, Nesh could read the Earther's confused body language. She wanted to laugh at the puncturing of his overinflated dignity, but then Madrigal changed shape.

Nesh had to move aside quickly to avoid being pushed into the fire by the coppery hindquarters. The Earther, though, seemed to stop breathing in response. After the happy bubble of Madrigal's delight, the silence was oppressive. Nesh came closer and realised that the Earther was rigid with terror. She laid a hand on Madrigal's broad shoulder and sent her outside to graze. The child changed form again to scramble out through the hole, and Nesh turned her attention to Volnar. He was a fuzzy shape behind the heat haze of the fire, but she made sure to give him her full attention. The Earther clearly didn't handle surprises well, and it seemed only fair to give him a moment to collect himself. Nesh prepared herself to explain things to the confused and frightened Elemental, when he shocked her by calling out to Volnar,

"What are you thinking, going out alone after that thing? It's a Shifter!"

Nesh wondered if Volnar even knew what that vulgar slur meant. She herself hadn't known about it until she heard one of the more uncouth villagers use it to describe her father's Sidrax assistants.

Volnar only said, "Maddie's a little kid. You don't leave little kids out on their own," before heading out after her.

Nesh noted with pride Volnar's defence of the little girl, but was herself too angry to risk speaking in front of the boy. As soon as Volnar was out of sight, she rounded on the Earther and let him know exactly what she thought of a person who could harbour so much hatred for a child.

"Madrigal seems devoted to you – though Life alone knows why. You don't have to like her, but if you hurt her then I swear by my Talent that I will hurt you."

He didn't reply at once, and for a moment, Nesh thought she'd got through to the stubborn man, but a moment later he was on his feet and staring her down. He was almost spitting in his fury as he accused Nesh of stealing his home and family – the kind of dated rhetoric she'd heard from the village greybeards when she'd been a child in her father's arms. To hear it from someone of her own generation was more ridiculous than hurtful. Maybe his grandparents had been displaced by the arrival of the Avlem, but she knew perfectly well that her generation had focused on helping the Elementals, not harming them.

"And I thought my eyes were bad," she said, thinking of how other people always seemed to make out details at absurd distances. "Yours can't see anything closer than a hundred years ago."

Nesh was suddenly, gloriously aware of her freedom to speak her mind. She lambasted the speechless Earther with all the frustration of two and a half decades spent holding her tongue in the face of injustice. How dare this man play the victim, as if she – or little Madrigal – were in any way responsible for his life choices.

The Earther didn't reply at first, which Nesh took some pride in. It had been a long time since she'd argued someone speechless. But when he did find his voice again, it was clear that she'd made no impression on him at all. His return rant was only halted by the arrival of Volnar, who wasted no time in leaping to Nesh's defence. On the one hand, Nesh was touched; on the other, all Volnar had done was to draw the man's fire. She moved to stand between them, which seemed to confuse the Earther. As he stumbled to a halt, Nesh sent Volnar back outside. The Earther wasn't much taller than Nesh herself, but he was certainly broader, and probably stronger.

———◆◦◆———

For all her hardships in the mines, Nesh had rarely been in a fight. The mealtime scrums didn't count, though she had learned how to make good use of her elbows and knees. She looked her opponent up and down, then sat down on the floor. This had the joint advantage of defusing the atmosphere and hiding her trembling limbs. Trembling from fatigue, of course, but she didn't want the Elemental to get the wrong impression. After a tense moment, the Earther also sat down.

Not only did he sit, he even appeared to listen as she told the tale of their accidental jailbreak. Nesh took the opportunity to inform the Elemental that he owed his current situation entirely to the children. For herself, she would have been happy to let him stay in the rubble and take the blame for the whole business.

The Earther was not grateful. He told her that he hadn't asked to be 'kidnapped' and that his place was back in the mines, repairing the damage. Nesh had long suspected the Earthers of being in the mines as staff, not slaves, but it was interesting to have it confirmed. Even more interesting to be slapped for making the observation. Nesh could make neither head nor tail of what the Earther thought he was doing in the mines, but it had something to do with rebels and 'the people of the land' – farmers maybe – overthrowing the Citadel. She let him ramble on while she surreptitiously rolled her jaw to ease her stinging face.

"It's getting dark," said the Earther, suddenly. "No doubt you and your Shifter will want to be moving along. I'll take the boy back with me."

Nesh stared, too stunned by this suggestion to pick him up on his bad language.

"You can go where you please," she said, at last. "*Alone.* After all the trouble we went to getting him out in the sunlight, do you think Volnar would willingly go back there?"

But the man didn't seem to care what Volnar wanted. All that mattered to this stubborn Elemental were his own ideas of right and wrong – and letting Volnar travel with Nesh was a definite 'wrong' in his eyes.

"I can hardly leave him with you, can I? A child of the People in the company of a Shifter, and with an Avlem so bad that even her own people take against her? The Earthers and Fire Breathers were always on good terms, I won't abandon one of them to you," he said.

Before Nesh could say anything, the Earther turned away and exited their temporary shelter. She waited for him to get clear before leaving herself. Their 'door' was a hole in the bank, barely big enough to squeeze through, and about waist high when seen from within. Nesh tried not to think about the undignified scrambling she'd have to do, and wanted the Elemental to be at a distance before she tried it.

When Nesh finally climbed out onto the bank of the hill, the evening sun was turning the world red again. She blinked, trying to reduce the dazzle, and when she could see properly, she found herself once more face-to-face with the Earth Elemental.

"There," he said, and the ground trembled faintly under her feet. "Once the fire burns itself out, no-one will be able to tell you were ever here. Take your Shifter and go; I'll catch up with the boy and head home."

Nesh wanted to cheer. Good for Volnar, getting away like that. Nesh hoped he would join her again once they'd got rid of the mad Earther.

Madrigal wanted to go back to the mines too, but Nesh didn't trust the man to look after her. Also, the Earther seemed to assume that Nesh would take the Sidrax child, which made things easier. At least, at first.

The little girl cried at the thought of not going 'home', and Nesh held her until both Elementals were out of sight. The night fell fast, and Nesh guided Maddie along what felt like a path. After a while, the child became a donkey and Nesh walked beside her. The steady pace of the sure-footed creature gave Nesh confidence, and she rested her Talent for minutes at a time.

Then the path ran out. Or maybe it turned sharply up or down the hill. Nesh reached for her Talent to Find it, but noticed that Madrigal had become a child again and focused her attention there instead.

"Are you tired, Madrigal?"

"No..." she said, and promptly yawned. "But why aren't we catch him yet? And this road feels wrong. Are we lost?"

"Catch who?" Nesh asked. But she thought she knew.

"My Stony-Man."

Nesh wished there was enough moonlight to show her the child's face. She stumbled through an explanation: they were going away, somewhere nice. She didn't like being underground all the time, surely? There would be sunshine, and mushrooms, and lots of room to play, and...

"And then we go home?"

Oh dear.

Before Nesh could think of how to answer, Madrigal's hoofbeats were racing back the way they'd come.

Well, that could have gone better. Nesh wondered if she'd actually woken up at all, or if this was all one long nightmare and she was still knocked out in the mine collapse. She pinched herself. No, this was real enough. So now what?

Half a lifetime of not making one's own decisions can make a person rusty in a crisis. Nesh followed the little donkey halfway back to the mines before realising that Madrigal was likely heading 'home', and would be fine. But it was irresponsible of her to abandon the child. But it would help nothing to get herself captured, and standing in the open when the sun rose was asking for trouble. But what if Madrigal needed her? But...

Abruptly, Nesh pulled her Talent away from Madrigal. When had she turned into such a ditherer? She could feel her younger self's scorn blazing across the years. *Pick a direction and stick to it.*

Nesh turned her Talent to seeking a safe place to spend the day. She walked with a smooth gait, skimming her feet lightly just above the ground with each step. It was a trick she'd developed for navigating the uneven ground in the mines, especially where it was too dark or too bright to see properly. A hand at the level of her eyes served to protect her from anything that might overhang her path, and Nesh set off into the darkness.

At first, Nesh tried switching her Talent focus every few steps; from guiding her to a safe place to checking the area for dangers. But soon she found that she could trust her ears instead. The night was full of noises, but none that seemed to indicate pursuit. They seemed to be mostly animal sounds, layered over the wind through the trees. It was chaotic and soothing at the same time, and Nesh let herself fall into the pattern of walking as she used to let herself fall into the pattern of digging. The body took over and, despite her best intentions, her mind went to sleep.

It was the birdsong that woke her. Nesh turned her face to the east, keen to see and feel her first sunrise in decades. The light gradually increased, but brought no clarity with it. Nesh was confused for a moment, then she remembered that fog was not uncommon in the morning, especially for low lying areas.

She walked towards the fuzzy outline of a tree, and relaxed as it began to come into focus. The pre-dawn light was pleasant, and the air fresh, and Nesh sat against the tree to rest for a while. The light got brighter, painfully, blindingly bright. But the fog remained, muting the shapes and colours around her.

"Hullo, Nesh!"

Volnar's voice cut through the birdsong and the dazzling light of day. Nesh turned, and from the larger, static blurs that were (probably) trees, a smaller, red-topped blur approached with a quick, bobbing motion, until it was almost recognisable.

"Volnar? What are you doing here? And how did you know me in all this fog?"

"Got away from the old man, didn't I? But there's no fog. We need to move – standing here on the skyline like this, anyone could see us."

There was no fog.

Volnar tugged her sleeve, and Nesh stood up and half-followed, half-led him towards safety.

There was no fog.

The green shimmer of the trees deepened. Darkened.

There was no fog.

The sun was hot on her face, and the light hurt her eyes. Nesh covered them with a hand, and walked until she felt a shadow fall.

There was no fog.

"I never know'd you was blind, Lady," Volnar remarked.

"I'm not blind!"

"Yeah, you hid it well back in the mines. Smart of you. We're coming up on a cave," he added, helpfully.

"I know," Nesh said, fighting back a surge of anger and impatience that had nothing to do with the boy. "I *can* see. Just... not very well," she admitted.

He took her hand and leaned against her arm in what might, for a boy of Volnar's age, have been meant as a hug.

"Don't worry," he said. "I won't tell no-one your secret."

They headed into the cave, where the light faded from bright noon to soft twilight in a hundred paces. But although they went deeper, the light stayed about the same. Nesh used her Talent to Find openings in the roof but came up empty. Whatever was making the darkness grey rather than black, Nesh welcomed it. The pain in her eyes that had begun with the sunrise faded to a dull ache, then to nothing at all.

Volnar talked at intervals about his home in the Citadel. Nesh listened with half an ear as he told her about his friends, his gang as he called them. Quite the enterprising crew of children, it seemed, and a mix of Avlem, Sidrax, and Elemental. Volnar talked about the 'Eldest' being in charge, responsible for the others.

"But Dalran won't be Eldest long now, I reckon" he said. "She's nearly fifteen, big enough to get real work."

"Dalran? Is that an Elemental name?" Nesh asked, struggling to imagine a fourteen year-old being in charge of anything, much less a half-dozen younger children.

"Dunno about the name," said Volnar. "But Dalran's Avlem. Got some kind of magic with food, so as she can make anything taste good."

He sounded like he was remembering something delicious, and Nesh wondered where she was going to Find a meal for them that night.

But all she said was, "Avlem Talents aren't magic. Your friend has a way with food – a Talent – and she uses her Talent to help her community. That's what Avlem do. It's a gift, but it's not magic. Just like your way with Fire isn't magic."

"Dalran says it is," replied Volnar, stubbornly. "She says there's all kinds of magic, and the only thing that matters is what you do with it. She uses hers to feed us and I use mine to keep us warm. Or... I did," he added, sadly.

Nesh looked for a way back to happier topics. As sad as the idea of homeless, parent-less children was, Nesh was pleased to think that they did at least have Avlem among them, to provide a level of leadership.

"So," she said, "Dalran is fourteen, you say? And how old are you, Volnar?"

"Dunno, 'zackly," mumbled the boy. He sounded as though his mind was still away with his friends. "Twelve, prolly. Dalran said I was eleven last spring, and it's spring again now."

Nesh adjusted her mental picture of Volnar. He was small for twelve, but that was only to be expected after the hard life he'd known. Nesh promised herself that she'd do her best to make Volnar's future better than his past. He could leave that life behind him for good.

⸺◈⸺

When they were too tired to go on, Nesh lay down on the smoothest patch of stone she could Find and tried to ignore her hunger and thirst. She wasn't prepared for Volnar to start a fire, and she hissed with pain as the light hit her eyes.

"Sorry," said Volnar, "I should've warned you. Guess you ain't full blind after all, eh?"

"I told you," Nesh said, then felt a piece of stale bread being pressed into her hand.

"That's the last of it," Volnar said. "And this is the last of the water. Hold still."

He slowly poured something onto the bread, letting each drop soak in. "Eat up," he said.

Nesh's stomach growled, but she still made herself ask. "What about you?"

"I've got my share, no fear!" replied Volnar, cheerfully.

"And what about tomorrow?"

"What about it? We'll deal with tomorrow when it comes. Place like this, there's bound to be water somewhere. And probably something to hunt, come to that. Eat your bread before it dries out."

Nesh smiled at his bossiness. Volnar would have made a good 'Eldest' himself, if he'd been Avlem. Though the thought of that sort of life was poor enough, and Nesh was determined to give Volnar a better one if she could.

—◆—

Nesh fell asleep, and dreamed of home for the first time in years. What would they think if she turned up in Perayen with a gaggle of street children for a family? Volnar, and Dalran, and all their friends. She could start some kind of asylum for orphan children, let them all stay together and be brought up properly. The idea made her smile in her sleep, and she woke quite refreshed.

When Nesh opened her eyes, she was in such pitch darkness that for one horrible moment she thought she'd gone blind in earnest. She Found Volnar, curled up asleep a half-stride from her side. Rising carefully, feeling for any overhang or protruding rocks from the walls, Nesh got to her feet and swept her steps until she found a soft pile of what was, on closer inspection, some kind of ash. Whatever Volnar had been using for fuel was completely spent. As was their food and water.

Nesh closed her eyes, not that it made a difference, and sent her Talent out for fresh water. There was a faint pull in one direction, but without any points of reference she didn't know if it was pulling her back towards the surface or deeper underground. She tried feeling around their sleeping space, carefully counting her steps and letting her Talent guide her back to Volnar every few minutes. She found a few loose pebbles and tried to make marker points, but they were all too similar and too easily pushed aside by her own feet.

Volnar, who must have woken up while Nesh was exploring, whistled long and low at the darkness.

"This is blacker than the inside of Creeley's warehouse," he said. "And me without a thing left to burn, unless I start on clothes."

"Don't," said Nesh. "We might have to go deeper, and you'll want every stitch." She shivered, remembering her own stint in the lowest levels of the mines. The torches and braziers had barely helped during the day, when hard labour kept everyone warm. The nights... she refused to think about the nights.

Volnar grumbled, but didn't try to light a fire. After a minute or so, Nesh heard him cry out and fall heavily.

"Tripped on some pebbles," he admitted, sounding ashamed of himself. Nesh blushed furiously. It was careless of her to have left the pebbles lying about.

"I'm sorry, Volnar. Are you badly hurt?"

"Hurt? Me? Nah, just surprised that's all. Give me a moment to get me breath back and I'll be right as rain."

Nesh couldn't resist checking for injuries with her Talent. Relieved at Finding nothing, she allowed herself to relax. Volnar's breathing grew calmer, until the silence rang in Nesh's ears like a distant roaring. Like a distant memory of the wind on a stormy night, or the fuller's mill in the spring flood...

I can hear water, she thought. Then, aloud, "I can hear water!"

Volnar was at her side as quickly as the darkness and uneven ground would allow. "Where?"

Nesh reached out with her Talent, automatically, then stopped and listened instead.

She pointed and started to say, "It's that way," before realising. Instead, she said, "Follow me. And mind your step."

After Volnar had tripped on his third stone (not Nesh's fault that time) she taught him how to glide his steps like she did, and brush the rough ground with his toes as he walked.

After Nesh had bumped her head twice, Volnar told her how to hold her arms so that they protected her whole head, not just her face.

And so, heads down and arms up, skimming their feet like bootless skaters, Nesh and Volnar headed towards the sound of water. Before long, it was audible even over the scuffing of their soles against the ground. Nesh turned her Talent towards keeping them on the clearest paths.

Light began to return, so gradually that Nesh didn't notice at first. Not until Volnar exclaimed, "I can see – Nesh, I can see you!"

Nesh blinked, slowly, and realised that she could see faint outlines of rocks around her. And the shock of red hair that was Volnar. There was no mistaking that colour.

"Nesh, I don't know how you do it! Going around blind, or even nearly blind – you're amazing! Not to mention you saved me a broken leg. How did you learn that walk?"

Nesh shrugged. "I just worked it out, in the mines. It was never very bright in there, even with the torches, but I managed. I still do."

Volnar took a long time to reply, and when he did all he said was, "I had this friend, right, back home, who twisted her foot one time on a... an errand. Real bad, almost broke it. She 'managed', too – but she let us put her on guard duty for half a year all the same. And our

Eldest at the time said that just 'cos you can don't mean you should have to."

He paused for a bit, and then said, "We shouldn't have to live on the streets and steal to eat, either. Life is what it is, and we do what we can with what we've got. And right now, I think we've been given a supply of fresh water. Come on!"

Nesh could hear the river, and set her Talent to Find safe drinking water. With her ears and her Talent leading her in the same direction, Nesh moved confidently to the riverside. There was enough ambient light now to shine on the water, though she still didn't know what was causing the light so far below ground, nor why it came and went.

A mystery for another day. Right now, she rinsed and refilled Volnar's small flask, then drank long and deep of the icy water. The light grew stronger and brighter, which Nesh welcomed until Volnar gave a hiss of surprise and pulled her back towards the wall.

"There's a tunnel off to the side, and someone coming down it," he said, in the quiet, non-whisper of someone used to dodging notice. "I'll see if I can get a look at them, and which way they're going. Wait here."

And before Nesh could object, Volnar was gone.

⟞⟶◉⟵⟝

He returned a moment later telling Nesh to come out.

"It's only Maddie and that grumpy Earther," he said. "I thought we were done with him. Only consolation is, he don't look happy to see us, neither."

Madrigal trotted forward happily, moving from donkey to child so smoothly that Nesh was sure she'd blinked and missed the moment of change.

"Did you getted here in the dark like us?" asked the girl, as soon as she could talk. "My Stony-Man can see in the dark, you know. He's very clever. Can you see in the dark?"

"We, uh, came another way," said Volnar, awkwardly. Nesh was grateful to the boy for not mentioning her eyesight trouble. But as Madrigal drew closer, even Nesh's eyes couldn't miss the angry-looking welt on her leg.

A cold rage froze Nesh in place, and in that moment she felt as though she could have quite happily killed the wretched Earther.

"What did you do to her?" Nesh demanded. "Didn't I warn you not to hurt Madrigal?"

The Earther, far from cowed, seemed ready to pick up their fight where they'd left off.

"You're the one who let her run off," he countered. "*And* you're the one who stirred up the guards so much they were out looking for escaped prisoners to shoot on sight."

"Oi, it was you they was all scared of, not her!" Volnar broke in. "That warden didn't say nothing about Nesh, but he had a lot to say about the *'dangerous criminal, Earther 27'*. Don't talk like this is all her fault."

In his eagerness to rush to Nesh's defence, Volnar missed his footing on the uneven ground and fell heavily. Nesh felt her rage disappear, completely swallowed up by concern for Volnar.

Strangely, the Earther appeared to feel the same. She'd expected him to berate the boy for his rudeness, or mock his carelessness; but instead he knelt at his side and checked him for injuries – fortunately finding nothing worse than bruised ribs.

For some reason that she didn't want to think about, this gentle action on the part of the rude, selfish Earther annoyed Nesh. Once Volnar was established to be safe and whole, Nesh rebuffed his attempts at acting concerned for the child. She pointed out that he'd now managed to get *both* children injured, and pointed at Madrigal to drive it home.

Only, Madrigal wasn't there. Nesh's Talent drew her to an empty patch of water, where neither child nor donkey could be made out.

<hr>

The minutes they spent calling and searching felt like hours., They finally found Madrigal in the stream where she'd been holding her breath, playing at being a fish. Or maybe actually being a fish; Nesh didn't really understand Sidrax shape-shifting.

Volnar got hold of one of the fish to show Madrigal something or other, and held it out to her. The fish was carefully examined by both children, then Volnar put it back in the water.

"Swim, fish, swim," said Madrigal. She looked to the adults, standing on the other side of the stream. "Why don't it swim? Is it asleep?" she asked.

"I think it's dead," said Volnar. "How can it be dead? I only had it out for a minute."

He sounded puzzled, concerned, and very young. Or rather, he sounded exactly like the pre-adolescent boy he was. For all his survival knowledge and ability to take care of others, Nesh realised that Volnar was still a child. The thought gave her pause.

What he did next was, if possible, even more surprising. Once Madrigal was safely away, Volnar splashed towards Nesh and handed her the dead fish.

"Hold this a minute while I find a sharp stone," he said, quite in his usual manner. "The guts and scales will do for fuel, if we're careful about it."

And Volnar wasted no time getting the fish cleaned and cooked. Nesh wanted to comfort him, but this competent, practical child didn't seem to need comforting. They ate in silence.

The Earther showed a surprising degree of tact by taking the young Sidrax away to get her own dinner elsewhere. Nesh realised, a little too late, that Madrigal might not like to see one of her new friends being cooked and eaten. His unexpected kindness irritated her. Just when she thought she had him clearly defined as a bitter old man, he would do something completely out of character, just to spite her. Life blight the wretched creature!

Nesh finished her share of the fish, then prepared a corner for bed. She thought she'd rather be asleep when Madrigal and the Earther – what was his name, anyway? – got back.

It was hard to get to sleep with so many thoughts racing around her brain, but Nesh did her best. She was very nearly asleep by the time she heard Madrigal trotting through the stream, and barely noticed when the ground beneath her body softened and reshaped itself around her.

⎯⎯◦⎯⎯

The next day Nesh let the Earther take the lead, because Volnar explained that he could use his Earther senses to keep them on safe and open paths.

"It's like he's got a map of this whole area, right in his head," Volnar said. "We've only had two Earther kids in our gang in my time, but they were the best at getting around. Like they could *feel* where the quiet alleys was, just by listening to footsteps. Course, they hated heights. Especially wooden houses and ladders. They'd have loved being down here."

"Maybe you can bring them for a visit some time," said Nesh, absently.

"Nah, they was both gone before I was big enough to go out alone. Not even in the city anymore, from what I heard. People don't stick around 'less they gotta, right?"

Nesh didn't know what to say to that. She'd never known anyone to leave their home without a compelling reason, although of course people left the mines as soon as they could. Well, except for the Earthers apparently, but most people there didn't 'stick around', as Volnar said.

Their own Earther seemed rather distracted this morning and paid no attention to anyone, so far as Nesh could tell. Then, quite suddenly, he stopped in front of a dark patch on the far wall. With no explanation beyond a brusque, "Wait here," he pushed his way into the darkness.

Nesh was on the far side of the stream, and couldn't reach him before he disappeared from her view. She called after him, "Hey, you! Earther! Where are you going?"

A voice came out of the darkness, still quite near. And quite annoyed.

"Kerrig."

"What?"

"My name's Kerrig. Not 'Earther'."

Nesh made a heroic effort and kept her temper. "Noted. Now, where are you going?" she asked. She didn't attempt to repeat the awkward name, sure that she would mispronounce it and make things worse.

"I want to check this side path. Wait here, I'll be back in a moment."

Then Kerrig's voice also disappeared into the dark, and Nesh was alone with the two children.

Volnar was quite good at keeping Madrigal distracted. Despite his sore ribs and her sore leg, he found games for the two of them to play in and around the water. This worked right up to the moment that Madrigal wanted to show her 'Stony-Man' her latest achievement.

A donkey who is determined to go somewhere is difficult to dissuade. It became impossible for anyone to hold her back from following Kerrig down the narrow, pitch-black passageway. Once Nesh realised this, she concentrated her Talent on making sure the path was safe, racking her brain to think of dangers, and being relieved when she didn't Find any of them.

After five minutes, Volnar perked up. "There's a fire nearby," he said. "A cooking fire, I think. Come on!"

Five minutes after that, they met the Earther Kerrig returning. He showed no surprise at meeting them partway down the tunnel, but simply led them towards the firelight.

It was a cooking fire, just as Volnar had said. Entering the cave, Nesh was struck by the sudden change in air temperature. The chill of the tunnels was replaced by a rush of warmth, and a smell of food which took Nesh back in a flash to the Elemental village of her childhood. The memory was so sharp and vivid that Nesh unconsciously straightened up to mimic her teenage posture.

Their host was an elderly Elemental woman, and she made them very welcome. Nesh thought that the old dear must be lonely, living by herself so far from civilisation. Every inch the courteous guest, Nesh accepted the simple hospitality with grace. It was, in fact, better than anything she had eaten in almost twenty-five years, but her memories of the village were acting so strongly upon her that she felt like Brinnesha Tynar again.

After the meal had been cleared away, the old Elemental introduced herself as Zirpa. Nesh recognised her cue and rose to her feet respectfully. She addressed their host as she would the chief of a village and introduced each member of her group by name as if she had known them all her life, and not at all as if she'd only learned one of the names within the last hour.

Kerrig, of course, couldn't let Nesh have things all her own way; he jumped in with some unnecessary extra information about where they were all from. He even told her not to be alarmed if Madrigal changed shape, which Nesh thought was quite insulting to the old woman's intelligence. As if anyone didn't know what a Sidrax was! Fortunately, their host didn't seem to take offence. Even more fortunately, after another minute or so, Kerrig stopped talking. Nesh had just enjoyed a good meal and was sitting comfortably for the first time in decades. She didn't want to spoil the evening by getting into another fight with the Earther.

⸻ ◆ ⸻

Nesh sat and watched the firelight throw impossible shapes until she was almost asleep. She wondered what the flames looked like to normal eyes, then stopped that thought before it could reach self-pity. Her eyes were failing, and she would have to deal with it. Between her Talent, and Volnar's help, there was no reason that it should become an issue.

As if conjured by her thoughts, Volnar himself appeared and told her that their host wanted a word. He showed Nesh to a curtained alcove that she thought she wouldn't have seen even if her eyesight had been perfect. The curtains blended with the wall hangings so well that, even up close, the door was completely hidden. Nesh wondered how many more hidden entrances there were in this cosy cave.

Zirpa was a white-haired beacon against her amazing patterned blankets. The tiny woman filled the space with her presence, and Nesh felt young for the first time in many years. She barely remembered her grandparents, all of whom had been traditional Avlem and very conscious of their greatness. But this small Elemental looked somehow like a grandmother ought to look. Nesh smiled at her, ready for any grandmotherly wisdom the little old woman might be about to share.

"So, girl," said Zirpa, "you're one of those Avlems. Does that make you special, do you think?"

Nesh blinked and tried not to show her surprise. Zirpa spoke so harshly that Nesh's mental image of her morphed from 'sweet old lady' into something more like Kerrig on a particularly bad day.

"N-not at all, ma'am," said Nesh, cautiously.

"Good," snapped Zirpa. Then, in a slightly softer tone, "The boy speaks well of you. That's something. Now tell me, how do you plan to keep your group fed and watered when you leave here?"

"I could probably help out with my Talent," Nesh offered. "I'm a Finder," she added by way of explanation. "Though Madrigal can feed herself, and Volnar's been looking after me more than the other way around. As for our Earth Elemental, I think he'd be offended if I tried to feed him. Kerrig is... independent," she said, tactfully.

Zirpa chuckled. "Resents your leadership, does he?"

"Leadership?" Nesh hesitated. As one of only two adults and the only Avlem, she ought to be the leader; but the thought worried her. She didn't know how to lead – or where, for that matter.

"I don't think we have any actual leadership," she said at last. "We're just trying to stay alive and keep the children safe."

Zirpa gave a non-committal 'hmm', before telling Nesh, "Those children need you and your skills, so mind you keep yourself sharp. The Fire Breather youngster trusts you. Don't let him down."

"My Talent is at his service," said Nesh, seriously. "And that goes for Madrigal, as well. And Kerrig, of course."

Nesh didn't expect an Elemental to understand the seriousness of this statement, but she was unprepared for the scornful laugh that broke from the old woman's throat.

"I'm not talking about your silly Avlem talents," she said. "I mean your real skills. Volnar says you keep your head in a crisis, are good at getting around in the dark, and don't mind getting your hands dirty. That kind of thing will be more helpful than being precious about some useless, one-of-a-kind talent."

A spike of anger surged through her, but Nesh fought it down before it could come out of her mouth. *She's only an Elemental, she doesn't understand, she's an old woman, she's not being offensive on purpose...*

"Out with it." Zirpa said, breaking through Nesh's attempt at calming herself down. "Don't stand there pulling faces like you were trying to swallow a ripe cauliber whole. You want to argue with me, so what's stopping you?"

Nesh took a deep breath, making one last effort to be polite.

"I'm sure you don't mean to be insensitive," she began. Zirpa laughed again..

"I say what I mean, and mean what I say," she told Nesh. "You Avlems are so 'sensitive' about your silly talents, and you must think you have good reasons for it. So, come on then! Why is your oh-so-special talent more important than other people's lives?"

Nesh gasped. "It's not," she said, when she could speak again. "Talents aren't more important than life. The two are equal. Talents are life. Life is Talents." She stopped, at a loss for words.

For all the abuse she'd faced in the mines, no-one there had suggested that Talents were unimportant. Her personal Talent had been mocked, just like everything else about her, but there had been no hint of abusing the idea of Talents. Then again, there had always been at least one other Avlem in earshot. Was this the kind of thing all Elementals said among themselves, or was it just some crazy idea that this lonely Elemental had picked up in her long life?

It was Zirpa who broke the silence first, and she didn't sound so confident this time.

"Your talent... is as important as your life?" she asked.

She sounded almost confused, as if the concept were completely foreign to her. Nesh nodded, partly at the old Elemental's question and partly to herself. Yes, this was a misunderstanding.

"So," said Zirpa, "if someone tried to 'take' your talent in some way, you'd kill them?"

"Not if I could help it," Nesh said. "Two wrongs don't make a right, you know. But I'd certainly try to stop them. Wouldn't you? If someone tried to take your identity? Your Elemental connection? Wouldn't you try to stop them?"

"Do you even know what it is? My 'Elemental connection' as you call it?"

"Does it matter?" replied Nesh. "You Elementals have your Talents – even if they are disturbingly similar. The Sidrax have their Shape-shifting, which is even stranger in some ways. We Avlem have individual Talents. It's all part of the same thing – our connection to Life."

After a thoughtful silence, Zirpa said "Well, I still say there's more to you than your Talent. But if you're willing to use your skills – all of them, mind – to protect and help those children, then I suppose that goes some way towards... Well, never mind."

Zirpa was quiet again for a few breaths, then seemed to come to a decision and spoke in her earlier, brisk tone.

"Go along with you now," she said to Nesh. "Seems I've given you something to think about, and I didn't know thinking was a talent any Avlem ever had. And send that young Kerrig in here to me."

⋯⋖○⋗⋯

Her conversation with the old woman kept Nesh awake half the night, and plagued her dreams when she finally fell asleep. More than her Talent? How could anyone be more than their Talent? How could you be more than yourself? She wanted to dismiss Zirpa's words as the bitter ramblings of an ignorant Elemental, but every time she had almost decided to do that, some inconvenient memory would intrude of Avlem who had skills not related to their Talents.

Even if Talemar's skill with politics could be considered 'weaving relationships', Nesh couldn't find any connection between her sister's Irrigation Talent and her way with dogs. Or her neighbour's sporting prowess and Talent with metalworking. Even that wretched Olvar Harreal had shown a keen eye for profit; and that had no connection to ink.

Still, she was a Finder. She wouldn't – couldn't – abandon that side of herself. Even if it might be only a side, and not the whole.

In the morning, Zirpa generously supplied them with food, water skins, and even some basic medical supplies. The bags were made of the same stuff as the rugs, and had long straps that let them be worn comfortably either on one shoulder or across the body.

After they were all equipped, Zirpa disappeared briefly behind one of the many wall hangings and returned with something that was almost as tall as herself, and twice as big around. She called it her 'life' and tasked them with taking it somewhere safe.

When Zirpa pulled back a corner of the cover, Nesh saw only a meaningless jumble of colours. But when she leaned in to examine it properly, a memory rose up in her mind's eye.

"This is a story blanket, isn't it?" she said. "Did you make all this yourself?"

"Most of it," Zirpa replied. "Some of it is my father's work."

"It's beautiful," said Nesh, losing herself in the unreadable pattern of the closely-woven threads.

⸻ ◆ ⸻

Nesh and Kerrig ended up carrying Zirpa's life-story between them, one end each. The journey through the caverns was, if not exactly quiet, then certainly uneventful. Madrigal clung to the Earther's side like a vine to a tree, chattering away about everything and nothing. Volnar seemed to find the sedate pace impossible, and made up for it by darting into and out of every crevice and shadow. Nesh kept her Talent trained on him and hoped that the Earther would keep to smooth paths. She still skimmed the ground with each step though, just to be sure.

The soft light of the caverns began to brighten, and Volnar ran forward with a shout of excitement. Nesh heard Kerrig call him back, and then Volnar cried out again. Pain? Fear? More than simple surprise, to be sure.

Nesh set her Talent to Finding 'danger' and got a response at once, dead ahead. She felt Kerrig set down his end of Zirpa's weaving. He handed Madrigal to Nesh, then walked out of her sight, creating a short wall of stone behind him. It rose up so close to Nesh that it almost knocked her down, and the precious weaving tumbled backwards.

There was some kind of conversation happening, but Nesh stopped listening when Madrigal cried out, too. Nesh reached for the girl, only to be met with a glancing kick from a donkey's hoof. The pain was sharp and sudden, but settled to an ache within two or three breaths. Madrigal was limping and, when she got close enough again, Nesh could see why. Zirpa's strong bandages, bound snugly to support a little girl, were too tight for a donkey's leg.

Nesh instinctively wrapped the copper-coloured neck in a hug.

"Be a girl again, Madrigal. It will make the pain stop," Nesh whispered.

The child changed shape and tried to struggle from Nesh's hold. For a moment Nesh thought she might kick her again, but then something happened that shook the floor and temporarily blocked the sunlight. Nesh instinctively wrapped herself around Madrigal, trying to shield the little girl from whatever had made that awful crash. The noise and dust blotted out Nesh's senses for a moment, and she sent her Talent to Find the danger – only to come up empty.

Nesh relaxed her hold on Madrigal just as Volnar came over to them, scrambling around the edge of the stone wall. He was talking excitedly, telling a surely exaggerated tale of soldiers with crossbows, and monstrous creatures with knives, and Kerrig bringing down the hillside.

The Earther himself said nothing. Once he had checked on Madrigal he led them out of the caves and into a pleasant-smelling valley of soft greens. It was early evening, Nesh thought, or else early morning. The air was crisp, and the light soft.

Nesh helped Volnar build a cooking fire, then she Found a stream of clean water to use in making dinner. Madrigal appeared after a while with her bandages fixed, but Kerrig kept to himself. He didn't even want to eat, which worried Nesh. The last thing they needed was for their local guide to get sick. Not to mention the fact that Nesh couldn't carry Zirpa's massive history blanket by herself.

The night fell, and the children bedded down beside the fire. Volnar leaned in so close to the flames that Nesh was sure he would get burned, but he resisted her efforts to move him away. Madrigal wriggled and complained that she couldn't get comfortable in this 'wrong shape'. Nesh patted the child's hair until she fell asleep, but felt horribly wakeful herself. She tried to Find the Earther, but he seemed to have taken himself off. She dreaded the idea that he might decide not to return to them, but she dared not leave the children to chase after him. She patted Madrigal's hair again and tried to relax. Kerrig seemed attached to the child, at least. Surely he wouldn't abandon her?

Nesh stared into a sky so dark that it made no difference whether her eyes were open or closed. A shiver of fear ran through her at the thought that one day it might not take a dark night for her eyes to be completely useless. Then she shivered again and looked round to the fire. It was very low, so Nesh used her Talent to Find some more fuel, and added it.

After a troubled, but not entirely sleepless night, Nesh was woken by Madrigal limping over to see if she was awake. Between the feel of the child's footsteps, and her shouted whispers to Volnar, it was impossible for Nesh to stay asleep.

"Good morning, Madrigal," she said, through a brave attempt at a smile. "Morning, Volnar."

Nesh glanced around and didn't see anything that looked the right size to be the Earther... Kerrig, she reminded herself. She shoved the tickle of fear to the back of her brain and busied herself with breakfast. Volnar got the fire going nicely, and Madrigal had to be talked out of changing to her donkey form to eat grass.

"You'll hurt your leg again, Maddie," Volnar pointed out. "Anyway, ain't a hot meal nicer than wet grass?"

The little Sidrax explained that she wouldn't hurt her leg because she'd take off the bandages first this time, but eventually conceded that a hot meal did sound nice. She could always have grass afterwards, if she was still hungry.

If Kerrig had gone for good, at least Nesh had Volnar to help with Madrigal. Though even Volnar might have difficulty convincing the child to go anywhere without her favourite Earther. But they didn't have to find out how difficult it would be, because at that point Nesh heard someone approaching.

Volnar called out, "Hullo, Kerrig," long before the Earther arrived. Nesh suspected this was for her benefit, and thanked Life in her heart for Volnar. When the Earther got close enough to talk, he didn't. This was not exactly a surprise, but Nesh was so glad he was back at all that she didn't have room to be annoyed.

II

They took their time over breakfast, and Nesh enjoyed the sensation of not having any work waiting for her. She explored with her Talent, finding cover to the south in the form of woodlands. The relaxing atmosphere, combined with an unhurried meal, made Nesh careless enough to share her discovery with Kerrig.

"How do you know what's ahead?" the Earther demanded, rudely. He, predictably enough, wanted to get back underground. Volnar, equally predictably, objected to that idea.

The budding argument was interrupted by the arrival of a couple of strangers. They sounded nice enough, but Kerrig leapt to the conclusion that they were dangerous. For the second time in as many days, Nesh found herself behind a wall. This one, though, was only made of loose soil and was easy to push through.

She stepped carefully over the disturbed ground, using her Talent to Find safe places for her feet. As she walked she heard a young man talking. Well, babbling nonsense, really. She'd heard a young woman's voice initially, indicating at least two strangers.

As she got close enough to make out details, Nesh thought she could see two faces – both much too near to the ground to match the voices, though. Then she realised that they were standing in a pit, with only their heads and shoulders showing. Some trick of the Earther's, no doubt.

The young man's terror still seemed overdone, Nesh thought. Even if he was stuck - and that wasn't necessarily the case – why did he think that Kerrig was going to kill them?

"Is he always this incoherent?" she asked the woman.

"Only when he's nervous. Ash, breathe. We're not going to die."

Ash's response to this was to drop his voice to a mumble, without dropping the subject. Nesh caught the words 'flying mountain', and rolled her eyes.

"Don't mind him," said the woman. "We're not soldiers, not any more, and we can explain everything. We might even be able to help you."

Nesh hesitated. What did she mean, they weren't soldiers 'anymore'? Were they deserters? Nesh had no love for the army, but an oath was an oath all the same.

Kerrig, meanwhile, was getting to the point.

"Who are you, and why are you here?" he demanded, standing over his captives.

It was the young man who answered. "I'm Ash," he said, "and this is Tray, er, that is, Try-gull, and we're-"

"It's Traegl, you fumble-tongued foreigner," said his friend, with gentle laughter. "I'm Traegl, Marshlander of Westhaven, and this is Ash, Sidrax of nowhere in particular."

"Hey! I have a home," protested Ash, and Nesh smiled. It was an Elemental habit, she noticed, to include your place of birth along with your name. Perhaps because they didn't use surnames. Then again, neither did the Sidrax.

When she paid attention to the conversation again, Kerrig was voicing her own concern about trusting oath-breakers.

"Ironically, that's exactly why you *can* trust us," Ash said. "We're deserters, on the run every bit as much as you are. And we know the land – or at least, Trae does. The Western Marshes are not too far ahead, and she can lead you through them. Trust me, you do *not* want to go near that place without a Marshlander – like Trae here."

Traegl did something that Nesh couldn't make out, freeing herself and Ash from their trap.

"And, please notice," she said, "I could have done that at any time. I'm not here to hurt you, and neither is Ash."

Nesh liked the young woman immediately, and was very pleased when she and Ash indicated that they would like to join the travellers.

"We can help you," Traegl had said. "You didn't even set a guard – look how close we got before you noticed us."

Despite liking them, Nesh decided to wait and see how these newcomers behaved before trusting them completely. She wasn't afraid for herself, but didn't want to think about what might happen to the children if they were betrayed.

The young woman seemed sensible enough and Kerrig, going by his voice and manner, looked too tired to bother about anything less than an immediate threat. She smiled at him, then went to pack up the camp. Kerrig might be their local guide, but that didn't mean he should have to do everything.

Clearing up took a while, but eventually they were moving again. The history blanket hung heavy between Nesh and Kerrig, and Nesh carefully adjusted her stride to match the Earther's heavy tread. Madrigal was perched on Kerrig's other arm again, and the newcomers put themselves on the other side of Nesh. The young man seemed particularly keen to keep his distance from the Earther, while Traegl sounded more amused than afraid. She seemed less amused when Nesh said, in a mild and firm voice,

"Now, why don't you start at the beginning? Unlike some people, I'm a very good listener."

Ash said, "They told us we were tracking a criminal gang who'd kidnapped a child and stolen a donkey. But that's not true, is it? That kid wasn't treating you like captors, and the donkey is actually a Sidrax child."

He sounded slightly unsure, even now. As if doubting his superiors was a new experience, and he expected to be told off for it. Nesh half-envied, half-pitied him his naïvete. She could barely remember being that young, and yet knew that she had been, once.

All the same...

"You deserted over one bad order?" Nesh wasn't sure she wanted such flighty company. "That's rather drastic, isn't it?"

The young Marshlander woman came to her companion's defence, explaining that it had been more a question of things coming to a breaking point. She hesitated once or twice, and seemed to be choosing her words carefully, but she managed to convey her feelings about her ex-commander rather vividly.

That led to her having to justify to the Earther her decision to join the army in the first place, as if Elementals didn't have a perfect right to try for proper work. Nesh felt a lecture building up inside her about how low expectations for the next generation perpetuated the divide between the cultures, but let it go in favour of talking to the Marshlander instead.

She had the feeling that trying to argue with Kerrig would be like trying to wear down a mountain.

Nesh envied the light way the Marshlander talked about her family, and felt a pang when the young woman complained about the necessity of visiting her grandparents. It seemed likely that Nesh's own grandparents were no longer alive. Even if they still lived in their villages on the sunny hillside above Perayen, they wouldn't want her to visit them.

These thoughts occupied Nesh through the rest of the day's walk until she distracted herself with setting up the camp. The ex-soldiers had some good ideas about how and where to arrange things for the night, and Nesh was just starting to relax when her attention was drawn by everyone going to investigate something.

Nesh couldn't see what was happening, but a new voice rang out above the rest. Another for dinner? She poured some extra water into the pot, just in case. Then she went to stand by Volnar, who was holding a burning branch like a weapon. The Sidrax soldier came to stand with them, radiating anger and humiliation. Whoever this new arrival was, she was clearly unwelcome.

Nesh heard a scuffle, and then the new voice raised in a howl. It seemed someone had landed a blow on the stranger, and the stranger was hitting back hard. Nesh tried to Find a way to help, but her Talent came up empty. This dangerous newcomer seemed invincible.

The fight stopped as suddenly as it had started, and something large came floating towards Nesh out of the perpetual fog. The stranger's voice came with it, asking about dinner.

⸺◆⸺

When she had first heard the term 'Air Walker', Nesh had thought the name quaint but metaphorical. Just as Fire Breathers didn't really breathe fire, surely Air Walkers didn't actually walk on air. Only, this one clearly did.

She not only walked on air, she swam in it. This stranger flew as easily as Kerrig made the ground into a seat, or Volnar directed a flame. It was the single most terrifying thing Nesh had ever witnessed, and her mind went completely blank.

Nesh suddenly remembered the year it had been the Tynars' turn to host the Founders' Day party. Everything had been frantic in the hours leading up to the guests' arrival; but the moment they did arrive, Nesh's mother transformed into the perfect host. It had been like watching a Sidrax change forms (meaning no disrespect to her mother, of course). In the blink of an eye, she became the Lady of the House with nothing on her mind but entertaining her guests.

Nesh made herself smile at the new arrival. "Welcome," she said. "Please, join us. Dinner is almost ready."

She made polite conversation about nothing until the Air Walker, who was called Falerian, drifted away, taking her bowl of broth along. Nesh divided the remaining food among the remaining bowls, and tried to shake off the unpleasant feeling their guest gave her. Or maybe Nesh had simply been around plain-speaking Elementals for so long that normal conversation felt suspicious. She didn't want to be unfair to the first civilised person she'd talked to in decades. Even if that person was an Elemental.

⸻ ⬦ ⸻

The next morning Nesh busied herself with making breakfast and packing up the camp. There was an intense discussion going on about how they should travel and she wanted to stay out of it. She was there to look after people, not to be any kind of leader. Things always seemed to go wrong when Nesh took charge.

The Earther also seemed to have been left out of the decision-making process, and was radiating irritation in every word and movement. Nesh was close enough to see Kerrig scowl fixedly at a group that, to judge by the shape floating above, must have been the three newcomers: Ash, Trae and Falerian. Nesh tried to distract him out of the black mood that was looming but with no success. She only managed to inadvertently set the Earther off on another rant about the terrible history of his tribe, and how that explained why he was so grumpy all the time.

Nesh sometimes thought that she couldn't so much as say 'good morning' to Kerrig without reminding him of some ancient injustice perpetrated against his people.

Fortunately, Madrigal arrived before the Earther could really hit his stride. The child brought the conversation firmly back to the present, wanting to know when her bandages could come off. Kerrig was a different person around Madrigal, and was soon completely engrossed in entertaining the child. Nesh marvelled at the change in him, considering how he'd initially reacted to her. What *had* Zirpa said to him?

She took advantage of Kerrig's distraction to slip away, and even allowed Ash, the Sidrax soldier, to take her end of the history blanket. Nesh walked with Volnar, carrying only her own pack. She felt wonderfully light, as if she might float up to join the Air Walker at a moment's notice.

It didn't take much to get Volnar talking, and Nesh listened with interest as he told her more about his 'family' of fellow orphans. It sounded as though they had quite a close-knit community of their own, and Nesh wasn't surprised. It wouldn't be a community in the true Avlem sense, of course, but even the Elementals understood the importance of having a social structure and contributing towards it in different ways.

Volnar's description of the Citadel didn't sound at all like the place she remembered, but his affection for it was plain. It was home for him, and she couldn't fault him for wanting to talk about it. Still, as he chatted, Nesh found her thoughts going down some painful paths, thinking about her old family and friends as she hadn't for years. Nesh hadn't said, done, or thought more than she could help for so long now that she believed her old life to have been completely forgotten, but it was only frozen. As it thawed, it hurt.

The rain started just before sunset, and put an end to all but the most necessary conversation. They spent the night in a cave, shaped by the Earther and dried out by the Marshlander. The Air Walker stayed above ground, wrapping herself in a shield of warm air, and Traegl sat in the entrance to keep watch. She seemed to positively enjoy being soaked through, while the rest of the group huddled in the dry cave for warmth. Ash had travelled as a bird at first, letting the rain slide from his feathers, but once they were under shelter he became something more like a wolf, and curled himself around Madrigal to keep her warm.

Madrigal's leg seemed to be healing well, and in the morning, Nesh heard her beg to be allowed to be a donkey for a while. She thought that the Earther might have agreed, but the Sidrax got in first.

"Respectfully, Mr. Kerrig, we should wait," he said. "Hoof prints in the mud could make us a target for the local bandits. They'll think we're carrying enough goods to need a beast of burden. Maddie, you're going to have to travel as a girl until the ground firms up some more."

To be fair to the young man, he did sound sorry to disappoint Madrigal. Perhaps to make up for it, he taught her how to forage like a Sidrax. By the end of the day, the two of them had quite a collection of leaves and berries to add to the stewpot. Ash even managed to find a couple of eggs, though he drew the line at eating meat. Nesh wasn't the only one confused by the fine-grade distinction in Sidrax morality, and so the ex-soldier tried to explain while Madrigal grazed in donkey form nearby.

"We Sidrax don't kill animals," he said. "We study them and learn their forms, but we only take what they can spare: shed horns, fleece; excess milk, honey, eggs; even skin and bones from animals that die naturally. We never take their lives."

Nesh wondered how a Sidrax with only carnivore forms was supposed to live, and might have asked if the Earther hadn't chosen that moment to hark back to his favourite theme: the wrongs and woes of his people. Ash and Traegl both tried to put things in perspective, but that involved talking about all the good the army was doing, which did not improve the mood of anyone who'd been in the mines. Nesh made an effort to ignore the whole conversation, and bit back a few choice remarks that came into her head about how much 'good' anyone could do by sending soldiers to every problem. They might not solve everything with swords, but they still carried them.

❧

The road they were on was good, and Nesh hadn't been giving too much thought to where it might be taking them. Suddenly, she heard Falerian laugh at Kerrig.

"Hark at Mr. Grumpy-Pants Earther here! Oh, you are so going to love Trae's village," she said. "If it's anything like mine, there'll be a whole gaggle of grandparents for you to moan with. You can all get together and talk about how much better everything was a hundred years ago."

"Ugh, don't even joke about that," groaned Traegl. "I know it's the safest place for us, but I am not looking forward to my welcome."

"Are you worried about your family condemning you for bringing Evil Outsiders to the village, or about them swamping you with embarrassing displays of affection?" asked Nesh, unsympathetically. The Marshlander didn't react to her tone, but simply sighed.

"Both," she said. "And probably at the same time. And don't call it 'my village', either," she said to Falerian. "I was born and raised in Westhaven, thank you very much. It's my grandparents' village, not mine."

Nesh was interested in spite of herself. She'd heard of Westhaven once, many years ago, from her mother. She'd asked why the Elementals in the village weren't allowed to live in proper houses, and Pabiran Tynar had put her right.

"They're very welcome to have proper houses whenever they want," she'd said. "But sadly they don't want them. Unless we forcibly demolish their huts and replace them with real houses, there's nothing we can do."
Brinnesha had remonstrated with her mother for making jokes, but Pabiran Tynar said that it had worked before.
"Of course, the destruction itself was an accident," she said. "But when some brave pioneers built the town of Westhaven on the ruins of what had been a swampland village, they included the local Elementals in the project. The ones who accepted the offer are really very civilised these days."

Nesh smiled at the memory. Traegl wouldn't have been born when that conversation happened, but it would seem as though Traegl's parents were what Pabiran Tynar would call 'really rather civilised'.

⸺◆⸺

Nesh first understood what Traegl's Elemental abilities could do when they left the road to head into the marshes. Her Talent was keeping her on the path, but it was also showing her how effectively Traegl was making that safe route through the marshy land. Nesh's Talent would register no path ahead, then a way through the boggy land would appear to her Finding sense. Nesh was fascinated, and gladly surrendered her end of the history blanket to Ash for a while so that she could walk closer to the Marshlander and watch her work.

At first, Nesh thought it was her bad eyesight making the young woman so blurry, but closer inspection showed that she was covered in a layer of water.

The soldier (or ex-soldier, Nesh thought) was barefoot, drawing water from the ground as she walked. The water ran up to her shoulders and along her outstretched arms, eventually dripping back down to either side of them. Nesh only felt that last part, when she accidentally leaned too close to the Elemental's hands.

"Careful," said Traegl. "Keep on the path. This marsh is treacherous if you're not born to it."

Nesh fell back in line, gradually dropping back to resume carrying one end of the blanket. She expected Ash, relieved of his burden, to go and walk with the young Marshlander, but he stayed to talk to Madrigal. They were both Sidrax, Nesh realised with a pang. The only ones on this journey who were not alone. For she had begun to realise that, even though Kerrig, Volnar, and Traegl were all Elementals, they were not exactly the same *sort* of Elementals.

Nesh puzzled over this for a while, letting her Talent guide her feet while her mind travelled to the Elemental village she'd visited so often as a girl. Had they been different sorts of Elementals? She knew that there were Water Elementals and Fire Elementals there, because some of them were employed in the town for their abilities. Had there been Air Elementals? Earthers, like Kerrig? Nesh thought that her maid might have been an Air Elemental, but she wasn't sure. She didn't remember the girl using any Element in particular, but then she hadn't paid much attention at the time. She'd been too busy fighting for the rights of all Elementals to notice individuals. But she was sure that the villagers hadn't divided themselves along Elemental lines the way they seemed to do out here in the wilder parts of the country.

Of all the benefits the Avlem had brought to Ashanna, Nesh wondered if uniting the Elementals might not be the greatest. It was nice to think that her ancestors had done that, even if they had also exploited the Elementals. If she could help to correct the failings of her people, and allow the good they had done to remain, perhaps the Elementals would be able to come to appreciate having the Avlem around.

Nesh had never felt so miserably unwanted and out of place as when she entered the Marshlander village. She had expected it to be like the village she remembered visiting in her girlhood: the Elementals a little over-awed and awkward at having a stranger and an Avlem in their midst, but quite friendly for all that. She was not prepared for the openly hostile body language, and even words, that were directed at her. Many of the words were in a language she couldn't understand, but the tone was unmistakable.

She wondered if she would have been allowed in at all if she hadn't been helping Kerrig to carry Zirpa's life-story. Falerian made herself at home right away, chatting happily with the youngsters as if she'd known them all their lives. Ash had Traegl to speak up for him, but would anyone have spoken up for her? Not Kerrig, certainly. He'd ignored her completely since leaving the caverns, though he did at least seem to have got over his fear of Madrigal. As if anyone could be afraid of such a sweet child!

The Marshlanders were pleased to get the history blanket, but it hurt Nesh's heart to see how Traegl's family treated her.

It wasn't that they were abusive or aggressive, but they made it perfectly clear that they didn't want her around. Traegl treated it lightly, but Nesh heard the pain in her voice with every word. It was the same pain Nesh felt each time she thought about her own family, or rather the family that had disowned her. She still loved them, and it gave her a hollow ache to know they were happier pretending she didn't exist.

Nesh even tried to Find the right words to say, but her Talent came up empty. There was nothing she could say or do to make herself or Traegl acceptable to these people. It made her feel sick.

To her surprise, Nesh found that Kerrig was almost as unwelcome as herself. Some old grudge about the Earthers not helping the Marshlanders with something, back in the day. Kerrig and a village elder played a round of Who's Got the Most Tragic History, which the Earther appeared to lose. Nesh was torn between satisfaction at seeing their grumpy guide taken down a peg, and irritation that all Elementals appeared to be champion grudge-holders.

Back when she was still Brinnesha Tynar, Nesh would never have imagined that Elementals cared which Element a person wielded. Now she saw that, while the Avlem found strength in diversity, the Elementals had splintered along tribal lines. It was a shame to see it. And yet she didn't remember any inter-Elemental trouble in the old village, and Volnar's description of the Citadel included friends from different Elemental tribes.

"It's a bit hard," she said, to no-one in particular, "that we Avlem get shut out by the Elementals, when it seems we've done more than anyone to bring unity to Ashanna. People from different Elements mix freely in and around our settlements, instead of living in isolation. Why can't they just accept us?"

"Funny you should ask that."

Nesh's soliloquy was broken by a voice from her left. She turned to see a slim figure in shades of green and brown.

"The Shanzir asked the same thing," the stranger said. "They're still waiting for an answer."

Nesh smiled and tried to sound friendly. "Hello there," she said. "I'm afraid I didn't catch your name. I'm Nesh."

"Golwik," said the stranger, coming closer. Her face was indistinct against the afternoon sun, but Nesh thought she heard a hint of a challenge in the girl's voice. She forced her smile to stay in place and nodded politely.

Nesh tried her best. "Nice to meet you... Hholwi'." The strange throaty 'g' and 'k' sounds were beyond her. Golwik's derisive laughter told Nesh that her best wasn't nearly good enough.

"So that's why you call my cousin 'Trae', is it? Does the Sidrax have the same problem, or is it only you Avlem that can't handle our 'complicated Elemental names'?"

For a moment, Nesh wished that her family had kept up with old Avlenian, instead of letting it be lost with her grandparents' generation. She still had the accent, unsullied despite her years away from civilisation, but she wasn't able to demonstrate the true majesty of her ancestors' language. She remembered hearing her mother's parents use Avlenian between themselves and being struck by how light and delicate it sounded. How unlike the guttural growls of the Elementals or the flat, heavy tones of Sidrean.

Rather than get into a debate over phonetics, Nesh changed the subject.

"And who are the Shanzir?" she asked.

Golwik scowled so hard that Nesh could make out the shadows of the lines on her face.

"You don't even remember them? You Avlem wipe out so many tribes that you lose track, is that it?"

It was Nesh's turn to scowl now. "That's ridiculous, we've never 'wiped out' anyone. In fact," she said, dredging up memories of her mother's history lessons, "my grandparents originally came here to protect our culture. We're the ones that were almost wiped out!"

"Really?" Golwik sounded genuinely intrigued. "Who were you running away from?"

"The Sidrax Empire," said Nesh.

There was a pause, and the shadows changed on Golwik's face in a way that Nesh couldn't read.

"The same Sidrax Empire you invited here to help you rid the Land of the People?" she said.

Nesh could hear the sardonically crooked eyebrow, even if she couldn't see it. She raised her own in reply.

"The Sidrax are here, as you say, at the request of the Avlem. Not to rid Ashanna of anyone, but to defend our right to a home. We are equals here, living in proper, Avlem-style towns – just as you and yours live as equals in proper, Elemental-style villages."

Golwik laughed. "What would you know about 'Elemental villages', as you call them? Come to that, what would you know about Avlem towns? I bet you've never been to Avlemland in your life."

"Avlenia," corrected Nesh automatically. "Not 'Avlemland'."

"Kalgshan," echoed Trae's cousin. "Not 'Ashanna'. Means 'the Land of the People', by the way. Not 'the land of the Avlem' no matter how much you mangle it."

There was a lot Nesh wanted to say to that, most of it sarcastic and all of it angry. But she held her tongue, albeit with great difficulty. There was no reasoning with that kind of righteous victim thinking, and Nesh was tired of being blamed for the 'crimes' of her ancestors.

Golwik seemed to take Nesh's silence as conceding defeat. Having made her point to her own satisfaction, the young Marshlander warned Nesh against going too far from the village, then left. The sun was low in the afternoon sky, and Nesh turned her attention to finding a good place to spend the night. She doubted that any of the locals would offer them a bed.

The following morning was a mixed bag of emotions, with only one point of agreement: that the visitors could not leave soon enough. The Marshlanders' sheer hostility choked Nesh, and she suspected that Traegl and Kerrig felt the same. Ash seemed happy to go wherever he was sent, while Volnar sounded desperate to get back on the road. Madrigal complained about the tough grasses and muddy puddles, and switched to her donkey form around the villagers to avoid talking to them. Nesh wondered if the little Sidrax was annoyed about their being unkind to Kerrig. Madrigal could be rather protective of her 'Stony-Man'.

Falerian was nowhere to be seen at first, and they met up with her again at the point where the marsh met the main road. They all turned south to continue their journey. Walking was easier without Zirpa's life-story to carry, but Nesh almost missed it. The bulky history blanket had been a problem to solve together, as well as a constant reminder of Zirpa herself. It had given purpose beyond mere flight to their journey, and made Nesh feel useful. It felt strange to be travelling like this, with no purpose beyond some vague promise of safety for the Elementals. It felt worse to know that she wasn't needed, and might even be a greater burden than the bulky history blanket itself.

For the next few days Nesh was in a miserable, dream-like state. She walked without knowing or caring where they were going, letting herself be guided by her Talent and by Volnar. She wondered who would be the first to ask why she was still with them. Why the Avlem was where she wasn't wanted — yet again.

Nesh lost herself to dark thoughts, and trudged along in Volnar's wake.

She came to herself quite suddenly one afternoon, aware that someone had asked her a question.

"Sorry, what was that?"

"Could an Avlem with a Talent for tracking find us on Falerian's 'secret island', do you think?" asked Ash.

Nesh was about to reply with 'what island?' when her brain supplied a few pertinent memories. Even while her mind was occupied with inner turmoil and self-loathing, her ears had taken in snatches of conversation. There was supposed to be an island somewhere in the south that was an Elemental haven, and Falerian was leading them there.

Nesh considered Ash's question carefully. Her own Talent might be able to Find such a place, if she knew to look for it, but a Talent like Finding was rare enough that discovery seemed unlikely, and Nesh said as much to the ex-soldiers.

"One thing I never understood," Traegl said, "is how the whole 'Talents' thing works. The way Avlem talk, it's more than just something you're good at, right? It's like a whole... thing. Can you talk about it, or is it a sacred Avlem taboo or something?"

Nesh stifled a smile at the strange superstitions of the Elementals, then tried to find a way to explain Talents to someone who hadn't grown up with the concept.

"Your Talent is your... well, it's your whole self. Everything that you have, everything that you are. It's..." Nesh hesitated, Zirpa's words ringing in her head. She shook them off and continued. "Your Talent is as much a part of you as your name, and means more. It's your identity, and your place in the community."

Traegl looked impressed. "That's a lot to expect from an accident of birth," she said. "What if you don't like your talent?"

"I don't think that's possible," Nesh said. "Anymore than you could not like your Element. To an Avlem, our Talents are, well..."

"Everything," Traegl said. "You said. But there's more to me than being a Marshlander, just like I'm sure there's more to Kerrig and Volnar than their Elemental abilities. I play a mean game of ragball, you know, and that's nothing to do with Water. What's more, Marshlanders are meant to be good with plants, and I hate gardening. Our Elements are important, but they're hardly 'everything'. Being bound by a Talent like that? Urgh, I'd go mad."

Nesh thought about Talemar's wish for a more politically useful Talent, but couldn't imagine even Talemar actively disliking Weaving.

"Some Avlem connect with their Talent more than others," Nesh said, feeling her way along a dangerous mental path, "but even if you have other interests, you never turn your back on your Talent."

"Or try to learn another one?"

Nesh tried not to look as scandalised as she felt. This Marshlander wasn't trying to be offensive, Nesh reminded herself, she was trying to learn. All the same, Nesh had to take a deep breath before she could go on.

"A Talent isn't something you set out to learn, it's a gift that you're born with. You can't choose it, any more than you can choose your parents, or the colour of your eyes. And anyway, if you tried to develop something as a replacement Talent, there's a good chance you'd end up imitating someone else's Talent, which would be very awkward. Not to mention that your community would have to either do without your natural Talent or bring in someone else for it. No, the Talent you're given is the Talent you use."

Nesh was looking for a way to close the subject when Traegl blew it wide open again.

"Why?"

"Why what?"

"Why is it so bad if two people have the same talent? Or if a person is good at more than one thing? Aren't there times when it would be useful to have help with things, or be able to take a break by switching between tasks?"

Nesh stared. This really was pushing the boundaries of credulity. The Elemental didn't seem to be mocking her or trying to start a fight, but how could she explain something so fundamental?

"Alright, look," Nesh said. She was trying hard to keep her cool. "Have you ever had a really big task to do, and wished that there were two of you?"

"Of course. That's kind of my point."

Nesh made herself ignore the patronising tone, and continued with her lesson.

"Would you really want a double, though? Someone else with your name, your face, your place in the world? Even if it might make a single job easier, you wouldn't really want to have a clone take over your life, would you? And then turn around and tell you that it's alright, because even though you're not Traegl anymore, you can go and be Madrigal instead? It might even be fun to be a Sidrax child instead of an adult Elemental; but would you really go through with it?"

The younger woman hesitated before saying, cautiously, "Yeah, that would be super-weird. Sounds like something out of a crazy story, people swapping names and bodies and lives. But what's that got to do with your job? Being a soldier, even being a Marshlander, isn't what makes me... well, me. No matter how many other soldiers, Marshlanders, or even Marshlander soldiers there are, I'm still the only me."

Nesh sighed. "If you don't get it, you don't get it. I suppose when so many people share the same Talent, you have to find other ways to measure your value to the community. But to an Avlem, our Talent is our identity. I am a Finder. Even when I lost my name, home, and family, I never lost myself because 'myself' is being a Finder. Everything can be taken, but not a person's Talent."

Traegl didn't answer right away. When she did, she sounded almost sad.

"You lost your name? That's awful. How does that even... no, sorry. That's private." She took a deep breath, and shook her head. "About Talents, though... I still say that's a lot to expect from an accident of birth, but I think I understand how much it means to you. To all Avlem. And maybe why you don't like talking about it."

Then Traegl shed her serious voice and seemed to bounce back into her usual, cheerful self. "You know, you could have told me to mind my own business," she said. "So, thanks. I mean, thanks for explaining. My grandparents just start shouting whenever I go all 'But why?' on their weird traditions. The world needs more people like you, lady."

Nesh forced a smile, but it didn't reach her eyes. She'd love for that to be true, but really – one walking disaster was plenty.

⁕

That evening there was an impromptu storytelling session. Ash started things off with a Sidrax myth, then Traegl gave them an old Marshlander tale about where the rain comes from. Finally, Nesh had a try, the afternoon's conversation still weighing on her mind.

"This is the way Talents were explained to me when I was a child," she said and began, losing herself in the memories. The hard ground and chill night air faded away, and Nesh was Madrigal's age again, enraptured by her mother's telling of the Avlem legend, "The Origin of Talents".

"Long ago, at the dawn of time, Life exerted herself to cover the world. Animals and plants on land and water, birds in the air, and people to take care of them all.

"Life loved her little caretakers, the people she had made. She wanted to do everything for them, to see to all their needs as they grew to maturity. For they were a young people, and not ready to look after themselves much less a whole world.

"But her people needed so much! Life was exhausted by their demands, which seemed to grow greater by the day. She worked and worked until the strain finally shattered her into tiny pieces.

"Each piece settled onto a different person, and everything that they had been used to ask Life to give them was now something that one of them could do for themselves – and for each other.

"And so Life gave a piece of herself to each Avlem, in the form of a Talent."

There was a moment of silence after Nesh finished the story. Then Madrigal asked if it was a really true story or only a pretend one. Nesh smiled, and echoed her mother's words once more.

"It's a legend," she said, "which means it's more than true."

The journey to the river was rather dull considering that this was supposed to be bandit country. The ex-soldiers explained that the real danger posed by the bandits was to the villages in the southwest, but they still took the precaution of setting a watch every night.

Nesh and Kerrig took their turns at watch, and both absolutely refused to let Volnar take a shift. Madrigal seemed happy enough to be a child and let the grown-ups take the lead, but Volnar seemed desperate to be counted as a responsible adult. Nesh tried to keep him with her as much as possible, allowing Volnar to help her a little more than absolutely necessary. Though it disturbed Nesh to note how necessary most of his help was.

Nesh was impressed by the boy's discretion. Even after several days' travelling together she doubted that anyone else knew of her vision problems. Her Talent helped, of course; so long as she could look people in the face and walk unaided no-one would have any reason to look too closely at her eyes.

Crossing the river itself was nerve-racking. The Air Walker, Falerian, ferried them across in three groups. Nesh crossed with Traegl, and held onto her arm the whole way. She watched the seemingly endless expanse of white and blue water foaming beneath her feet – out of focus but clearly lethal – and wondered if it was going to be the last thing she ever saw.

As a precaution, Nesh set herself to Finding a safe landing on the river. Just in case the Air Walker got distracted, or thought it would be funny to drop them halfway across. Her Talent came up empty, which froze Nesh to her bones. She couldn't speak – she couldn't breathe until there was solid ground under her feet again.

Falerian didn't stay with them on the island. She hovered so that her feet hung at eye level. Then she moved backwards until she was nothing but a smudge in the sky. The rushing river drowned out her words, and Nesh was turning away when the Air Walker's voice sounded in her ear.

"See you around, Avlem," it said. "Unless you see me first?"

The wind swept Falerian and her laughter away.

The first person they met was a farmer, who grudgingly agreed to their sleeping in his barn. Kerrig and Volnar, though, were allowed into the house by virtue of being 'people'. Nesh wondered what that made the rest of them.

The barn was warm and the hay soft, and Traegl, Ash, and Madrigal fell asleep almost as soon as they lay down. But Nesh couldn't get comfortable. Even her Talent couldn't help her Find a good spot. After what felt like half the night, she gave up and went outside. Maybe the night air would help.

Nesh sat on a smooth part of the stone wall outside the barn and gazed up at the faint brightness of the twin moons. The air was as sharp as the shadows, and Nesh enjoyed taking in the scenery. On a night like this, she thought her eyes were almost as good as ever.

A door opened behind her, and footsteps approached from her left. Nesh set her Talent to Find danger, and it came up with nothing. Relieved, Nesh turned to see who had come to join her — and saw the distinctive outline of Kerrig.

Nesh almost wanted to scold her Talent for failing to warn her, but the Earther didn't seem to be in the mood for an argument. He sat on the ground and seemed to be taking in the view. When he did speak, it was almost kindly.

"Can't sleep either, eh?"

Nesh told Kerrig about the barn, then he enthused about the 'traditional Earther house' for a while.

"I'm sure our host would be flattered if he could hear you," Nesh said. And, in all fairness, Kerrig did make the earth-and-stone cottage sound inviting. Nesh suddenly remembered the village of her youth, and how she'd never have considered any of those dwellings 'inviting' while she still had a real house to go to. Well, of course, this cottage wasn't inviting her in, nor any other Outsider.

"Oh, don't be like that," said the Earther, and Nesh realised that she'd spoken that last thought aloud. "You can't help being an Outsider, but you're not like other Avlem."

A laugh built in Nesh's chest as she realised that the Elemental was trying to be kind by drawing a distinction between her and her people. Wasn't this what she'd wanted, as a girl: To throw off the shackles of Avlem tradition, and be different? The laugh emerged as a strangled sob and Nesh blushed furiously. She wasn't going to cry!

She forced a smile and tried to make light of her total lack of connection to her people. It didn't sound convincing, even to her own ears. The Earther seemed to notice that she was upset but didn't (thank Life!) press the issue. After a few more clumsy attempts at comfort, Kerrig reverted to talking about how happy he was to be on this island.

Nesh didn't argue. Everyone here looked down on her, but this had been true for decades and wasn't likely to change no matter how far she went. She might as well stop feeling upset about it.

⚯

The next couple of weeks were a jumble of busy-ness and boredom. Madrigal stayed in her donkey form all day, working in the farmer's fields along with Kerrig. She arrived in the barn each night with a day's worth of talking bottled up inside, ready to come pouring out.

Nesh listened patiently, but was puzzled whenever Madrigal asked them to pass something along to her 'Stony-Man' – which she did a lot. Traegl was evidently confused by this as well; on the third night, after the tenth 'message' for Kerrig, she asked,

"Maddie, why do you need us to talk to Mr. Kerrig for you? You work with him all day."

Madrigal gave the long-suffering sigh of one pointing out the obvious. "I'm being a donkey all day," she said. "Not a girl. Donkeys don't talk."

"Not in front of Farmer Balmar, no," Traegl conceded. "But why not talk to him when you're alone? I've heard him talk to you when you're a donkey, and you understand him, don't you?"

Madrigal snorted, seemed dissatisfied with the feeble sound, and changed into her donkey form to snort more powerfully. Then she brayed at Traegl.

Ash laughed.

"You tell 'er, kid," he said. To Traegl and Nesh, he explained that talking while in animal forms called for very complex and controlled shapeshifting.

"It involves blending forms, which is difficult to get right and potentially dangerous to get wrong. I've started Maddie on the basics of it, but it will be years before she can safely speak in anything but her girl form."

"But Ash," Traegl said, "you blend your forms all the time, *and* speak in them."

"And it took me years to learn," he said. "I have one blended form; it's not like I can mix and match at will."

"Oh." Nesh thought that Traegl sounded disappointed, but maybe she was just confused. It was certainly a lot to take in. Nesh had always assumed that Sidrax shape-shifting was instinctive and unlimited. Then again, she'd always been more interested in Elementals than in Sidrax – and even so she didn't know much about the actual mechanics of Elemental abilities.

———◆◇◆———

Around day five, a Fire Elemental family came forward and offered to take care of Volnar, but they didn't count on the boy's independent nature. He did his work at their house during the day, then slipped out at night to join the 'Outsiders' in the barn. After a week of this, Nesh took him aside for a word.

"Volnar, you know we like having you around, right? And I hope to see you a lot, but you can't keep on coming here to sleep. For one thing, your new family will worry about you–"

Volnar scoffed at the idea, but Nesh pressed on, "And for another, we're not going to be here after tonight. The Farmer, Balmar, wants his barn back, so Ash, Traegl, and me are moving into an abandoned barn near the middle of the island."

"Great! That's not far from where they live – I can get there easy."

Nesh sighed. "You're supposed to sleep at your new home," she said. "Haldra's family are responsible for you and they will worry – whether you believe it or not. Did you at least leave them a note to say where you'd gone?"

Volnar laughed. "I don't want them to know anything. What's a note?"

Nesh blinked. "A note. A message, you know. Something written on a piece of paper, or slate, or whatever you use."

"Writing? What's someone like me got to do with writing? First sign of trouble, that is, a bit of paper. All the kids know that – you see a bit of paper in a hand, and you run for it."

Nesh stared. "You can't write at all? Or read?" she asked, trying to imagine the concept. "Didn't your parents – what am I saying, of course... I'm sorry, Volnar. Well, I'll teach you then. You'll need to be able to read and write if you want to get anywhere in life, and it's never too late to learn. Come along!"

Nesh led Volnar over to a patch of soft earth and crouched down.

"What, are we doing this writing thing right now?" protested Volnar. "It's getting dark!"

"Light up a torch if you need it," Nesh said. "Now, watch this."

So saying, Nesh traced letters in the topsoil with her finger. The lesson lasted until moonrise, and when Nesh brushed her fingertips over their work, she could feel Volnar's misshapen efforts below her own.

She hadn't written anything in years and would have to get Traegl to help her check Volnar's work for details. But there was something satisfying about passing on the gift of literacy before she lost her ability to read completely.

⸺⸺◆⸺⸺

They said goodbye to Madrigal and Kerrig the next morning, and set out for the centre of the island. When they arrived at their new home, it felt to Nesh like the biggest space she had ever been in. Which was nonsense, of course, since she could walk across it in a dozen paces, but she couldn't see across it, and she only knew the roof was there because it cast a shadow and held off the rain.

Ash and Tragl had soon rigged up bedrolls in their own corners, and Nesh Found some moss and grasses for her bed once Traegl told her what to look for. They had a place to sleep prepared by nightfall, and they built a fire just outside the massive double doors – which were stuck open.

"Ah, this is the life," sighed Ash, pushing away his empty bowl. Traegl snorted at the ridiculous remark.

"Were you raised in a cave or something?" she said. "We're stuck in a rocky field with nothing but an abandoned barn for shelter, and you... you're happy, aren't you? I swear, you could get comfortable on an ants' nest."

Ash laughed. "I don't think the ants would like that much," he said. "And yes, we don't have much in the way of creature comforts here, but think about all the other things we don't have. No orders, no drills, no-one barking us out of our beds before sunrise. And no reports to write, ever again! I always wanted to retire to the countryside, and this could be a nice place to settle. Well, once we've fixed it up a bit."

Nesh thought that it would take rather more than a bit of 'fixing up', as Ash put it. But it was nice to go to sleep without worrying about hostile roommates for once.

⸻ ◆ ⸻

Nesh cornered Traegl the next evening and asked her about writing.

"Ash mentioned that you both wrote a lot of reports as part of your job," she said. "But, would you believe it, young Volnar can't read?"

"I don't suppose he can," replied the younger woman. "Half our recruits need a basic class in reading Sidrean as part of their training."

Nesh blinked for a moment, then asked, "Did you?"

"Nah, I grew up in Westhaven, with every modern convenience – including literacy. But not all parents are as progressive as mine."

Something about Traegl's words sat awkwardly with Nesh. Perhaps it was the dismissive tone, for surely the sentiment was sound enough? Elementals being raised as civilised people was the whole point of places like Westhaven. She herself had worked towards it in her own town back in the day. Her parents had done everything they could to teach their servants to appreciate the benefits of Avlem living, and it wasn't their fault that they'd not had much success.

Why did it feel so wrong to hear Traegl subscribing to the narrative she'd heard from Father a hundred times? Elementals need to adopt civilised ways, learn the common language, shed their barbarous past. That was true... wasn't it?

Nesh pushed the thoughts away to the back of her mind, where she'd learned to keep doubts and regrets (both equally useless) out of the way. She smiled in Traegl's direction and hoped the pause hadn't been too noticeable.

"I've been teaching Volnar to write in the dust with a finger, but he'll need to learn about pens and paper too," she said, then sighed. "Though I suppose it will take a lot of paper, and I don't know where we'd find enough."

"Not a problem," said Traegl. "Have you ever seen one of these?"

She fumbled at her belt pouch, then produced a small, shallow box about the size of two flat hands. Nesh tried to look as though she could see it clearly, but her heart sank when Traegl opened the box and the inside was a uniform blur. Nesh was afraid she'd have to confide the truth after all.

But when Traegl handed over the box, it was empty. The insides of the base and the lid were smooth and soft, but empty.

"It's lined with soft wax," Traegl said. "And the stylus..." she placed a small, thin object in Nesh's hands, "the stylus makes marks for the letters. Straight lines and dots with the chisel tip at this end, and half-circles with the curve at the other. See?"

Traegl took the stylus back and leaned over the wax tablet for a moment, pressing down lightly several times. When she was done she paused expectantly. Nesh brushed her fingers over the wax and felt the shape of letters, though she couldn't make out what they were.

Traegl seemed to want a response, so Nesh smiled and said something vague and approving.

"Oh, do you need more light to read it?" Traegl asked, sounding as though she'd been struck by an embarrassing realisation. "I know some, um, older people get that, ah, difficulty. In bad light, I mean. But that's what's so good about wax tablets, you know? With a bit of practice we can read, and even write, in complete darkness. Here..."

The stylus was pressed into Nesh's hand again, and her fingers closed around it automatically. just as if it hadn't been decades since she'd last used a pencil.

"Try writing something," Traegl said. "Or just make a few marks. You have to press, not drag, and it can be awkward to get used to at first. I won't look, you write something, and I'll tell you what you wrote."

Traegl turned her back, and Nesh felt the stylus carefully while holding the tablet in her other hand.

She hesitated, then pressed a series of letters into the soft wax.

"Finished? Great. Hand it over."

With her head turned away very deliberately, and her eyes probably closed as well, Traegl felt the letters.

"W ... L ..., no, that's an E. A ... V ... E again, and... oh, an R. Weaver. Nice!" She closed the lid with a triumphant snap, then opened it again to look at the word. "Neat trick, right? It's called touch-writing."

"Yes," said Nesh, carefully. "I can see how this would be very useful. At night, I mean. But I don't think Volnar needs to learn anything quite that... advanced."

Traegl was quiet for a moment too long. Finally, she said, "And for you? Learning something yourself, alongside Volnar, might help him to focus. Make it a challenge – can he learn the letters by sight faster than you can by touch? What do you think?"

Nesh nodded, distracted. Traegl seemed distracted as well, gazing at the wax tablet with its single word for a long time before smoothing over the marks with her thumb. They sat in silence in the twilight for some time before the Marshlander said, suddenly, "That massive blanket thing was a real hit with my grandparents' people. I wish I'd met the old lady who made it. What was she like?"

It took Nesh a moment to catch up with this sudden change in the conversation. She hadn't been thinking of Zirpa at all, but of Talemar. Traegl's odd mixture of directness and tact reminded her of her old friend. Where was she now, Nesh wondered.

But Traegl had asked about Zirpa, hadn't she? Nesh once again forced her mind into the present and talked long into the night about the strange old Elemental in her cave, surrounded by her art. And if, now and then, her depiction was more of Talemar than Zirpa, it didn't matter.

Volnar seemed unsure about allowing Traegl in on his lessons at first, but the idea of competing with Nesh soon won him over.

"Don't think I'll go easy on you just because you're..." Volnar hesitated.

"An old lady?" Nesh cut in. "Young man, I think you'll find this 'old lady' is still pretty sharp."

"Volnar, don't be rude!" said Traegl. "You talk a big game for someone who writes his 'e's upside down."

"I do not!"

"Do too. Nesh'll tell you. See?" Traegl handed Volnar's tablet over and Nesh felt the uneven letters. Vastly improved from his first dust-drawing efforts, but still...

"Yes, those are upside-down. Sorry. But your 'b's and 'd's are coming on nicely."

Traegl laughed as she took back the tablet. "You're just showing off with touch-writing now," she told Nesh. Volnar snorted, but didn't comment.

Over the following weeks Nesh, Ash, Traegl and Volnar worked on turning their dilapidated buildings into something liveable. Things went well at first, but gradually a mood of general discontent began to set in. It was the kind of feeling Nesh associated with constant bad weather, but the late spring days were so pleasant that it had to be something else.

Although Volnar was the most vocal about his discomfort, even Nesh started to feel uneasy as the days went on. She kept thinking how she ought to feel safe in this lovely camp, then getting annoyed with herself for it. And so when Volnar announced one day that he was leaving the camp, Nesh immediately said that she was going too. The surprise was that Traegl also wanted to go.

"They don't want us Outsiders here," she said, a touch of bitterness in her voice. "So let's get out of their way and find somewhere that does want us."

It hurt Nesh's heart to hear the young Marshlander describe herself as an outsider – but of course, that's what she was. Nesh supposed that, in her own way, Traegl was as much cast out from Elemental society as Nesh herself was from the Avlem.

Meanwhile Volnar's writing lessons had been going well. Within a month Traegl had declared him at basic proficiency level. Nesh was well on her way to mastering touch-writing, and had even managed to Find enough wax to make tablets of her own.

The spring passed into summer, and the old barn was as comfortable as they could make it. Nesh found herself imagining a future here after all, but Traegl and Volnar kept on coming back to the idea of leaving the island. Though it was only talk for a long time. There was always so much to do, especially with Traegl working on Marshlander farms all day.

Until one evening when Nesh found Traegl and Volnar gathering long-stemmed grasses and discussing where to get logs.

"Why do you need logs?" Nesh asked, coming up behind them. Traegl and Volnar were so startled that they almost fell over. Nesh stifled a laugh, but not her curiosity.

"For our raft," Volnar explained. "The grasses are for ropes, but we'll need logs or planks or something as well."

"Is this is about leaving Camp Freedom? Why didn't you ask me to help? Also, why a raft? A Marshlander can surely get us to the shore without that."

Traegl hesitated, so Volnar answered instead.

"We're not going to the shore, not right away. We're going down the river, and get a look at the Citadel. Trae's good, but she can't keep all four of us afloat on nothing but willpower."

"Four?"

Traegl nodded. "You, me, Volnar, and Ash."

Nesh thought for a moment. She wanted to leave, of course, but where would they go? Wasn't it better to stay here, in comfort and safety?

But the barn wasn't particularly comfortable, was it? And they were only safe until some farmer or other decided to drive off the Outsiders.

Nesh shook her head and tried to get back to the matter in hand. How best to channel her Talent into Finding suitable raft-building materials? Asking for 'wood' was too generic, as was 'log'. She didn't know enough to Find the right kind of logs, and they didn't have the tools to work the wood anyway.

While she was mulling this over, Volnar said, "Look, Trae – Ash is coming back at last!" Nesh used her Talent to 'look' in the right direction, grateful for Volnar's continued support. Without his help, Nesh was sure that she would have been found out before now. This would be bad, though just at that moment she couldn't remember why.

Ash got closer and Volnar ran up to meet him.

"Where have you been all day, then?" Volnar demanded. "Ducking out of work, were you?"

He sounded serious, but from the way Ash laughed it must have been an act.

"Cheeky youngster, isn't he?" observed the Sidrax. "I blame you two. You let this boy get away with far too much."

Ash wasn't nearly as good as Volnar at pretending to be serious.

It turned out that Ash had been busy after all. He'd managed to get hold of some axes, and he and Traegl set to work on a couple of fallen trees. Nesh listened in awe as they chopped away. Volnar tried to describe it, but quickly became so lost in wonder that he forgot to talk.

After a while, Nesh thought to ask Volnar how he was going to make rope from grasses, and if she could help. Although she was unwilling to take charge in any way, she was equally unwilling to be a mere passenger on this journey. She had her limitations, but they did not outweigh her obligations as an Avlem to contribute to her community.

Volnar explained the grass-ropes idea as well as he could, but added that it was a Marshlander technique and he didn't really understand it yet.

"It'll be better once I've seen Trae do it," he said. "Something to do with twisting, but I think there's more to it than that."

Nesh and Volnar experimented with twisting various grasses together until Traegl returned, but couldn't make anything useful.

"It's easy," Traegl said when they showed her their efforts that evening. "I watched my grandparents do it often enough. Here, I'll show you…"

But Traegl's attempts were hardly any better than Nesh's or Volnar's. No matter how she twisted and pinched the grasses, they wouldn't stay together. In the fading light, Nesh thought she could see red marks appearing on Traegl's pale palms, and suggested that they stop for the night.

"Maybe it only works with Marshland grasses," she said.

"Maybe I should have paid more attention to the 'traditional arts' when I had the chance," replied Traegl.

"Maybe we could use something else," said Ash. "Are you particularly fond of any of these blankets?"

<hr>

When Kerrig arrived for a visit a couple of days later, he found Nesh and Volnar busily plaiting strips of cloth into coils of rope. Volnar excused himself on the Earther's arrival, perhaps guessing that Kerrig wouldn't approve of his returning to the Citadel.

To Nesh's surprise, Kerrig stayed and helped with the ropes. He asked questions about the raft and seemed genuinely interested in their safety and well-being. He even returned to help out once or twice a week, all through the summer. Building a raft took longer than they'd hoped, especially as the locals expected everyone to work if they wanted to eat. Since they wanted not only to eat for themselves, but also do something to eke out the stores at the barn, this cut into their raft-building time considerably.

Traegl and Kerrig between them built a pond large enough to test the raft, and that took time. When they were done, both Elementals seemed quite pleased with their handiwork.

"I might move here myself, after you've left," Kerrig remarked one evening. "I can't live with Farmer Balmar forever, and this pond will be a lovely feature." He paused awkwardly. "Not that I want to hurry you away, mind," he added. "There's plenty to keep me busy at the farm. But it's never too soon to think about the future."

Nesh wondered if it was ever too late to do so. What kind of future awaited her? She didn't want to stay here, resented by the rest of the island, but where could she go that would be better?

She put the question out of her mind. She'd help the others first, and maybe Find her home along the way. It wasn't much of a plan, but it was better than feeling hopeless.

The hopeless feeling came creeping back when Ash returned from a scouting flight. The raft was finished, and had passed all the tests that the pond could throw at it. Belongings (such as they were) had been packed, and now it was time to pick a day for departure.

Ash had volunteered to fly to the river shore, picking out the best route for the raft. He also mentioned taking a look at the weather, but Nesh wasn't sure what that meant. Probably a Sidrax thing.

Everyone had been in high spirits that morning, full of ideas about their upcoming river journey. But Ash returned within an hour, and in a terrible state.

"Don't talk to me yet, I can't..." he said after he touched down and switched forms. Then he switched again into a wolf, and curled up beside the remnants of their fire. Nesh could hear him shivering, and pulled one of the surviving blankets from her pack to put over him.

Ash burrowed under the blanket and slowly stopped shaking. His breathing returned to normal, and he sat up, man-shaped again.

He kept hold of the blanket.

"That," Ash said, when he could speak again, "was really weird. I'm not sure how to describe it, to be honest. Something made me... afraid... of the river. More than afraid – terrified. The thought of flying over the river made me feel... I don't think I have the words, even now. I couldn't do it." Ash shuddered again, and Traegl hovered in the edge of Nesh's vision as if she wanted to offer comfort but didn't know how.

"I'm not a coward, Trae. You know that, right?"

"Of course you're not a coward!" Traegl almost shouted. "What a stupid idea!"

Ash laughed, a weak chuckle but a sincere one. "Well, I never claimed to be especially clever. So, riddle me this: Why did I lose my mind over that river? Why not the pond, if I've developed a sudden fear of flying over water? What happened out there?"

"How far did you get?" asked Volnar. "You were gone a while."

Ash shook his head. "I had a few goes at it," he said. "Never got past the treeline at the shore, and each attempt was harder than the last."

Nesh felt her blood run cold. To be hit by an irrational fear once was bad enough, but to turn and face it multiple times...

She wondered how brave she would be if given the chance to enter Avlem society again. Could she face the whispers, and then do it again the next day? And again?

Traegl got to her feet and called for Volnar.

"Come on," she said. "We're going to ask our neighbours about this."

"What?" said Volnar. "Why?"

"Because we can," Traegl told him. "They won't talk to 'Outsiders', but they might talk to us. Something's not right on this island, and we're going to find out what that something is."

Nesh listened to Volnar's grumbling grow more distant as he set off after Traegl. She went to check on Ash, but he'd turned back into a wolf and gone to sleep. Nesh sat and listened to the birdsong until she, too, drifted off to sleep.

***

"It's a dome, I tell you," Volnar said. "And we're trapped under it like bugs under a cup. Ash, you've tried every angle, right? High and low?"

"For the last time, yes!" snapped Ash. He'd been in a foul mood all week; ever since his first encounter with the terror-shield or whatever it was. Nesh tried to feel sorry for him, but he was starting to get on her nerves.

Traegl's investigations hadn't turned anything up, and Nesh was about to ask for Volnar's report when the boy dashed past her towards the open door.

"Hey, it's Maddie!" he shouted.

Ash sounded like his old self for the first time in days when he said, "Good to see you, kid."

Nesh let her Talent tug her towards joining the hug, and met Volnar going the same way.

It was nice to see Madrigal again, but even nicer to see Ash back to his old self. When Kerrig asked what they had been arguing about, however, Nesh could no longer stay smiling.

"We can't leave the island," she said. "It turns out that 'Camp Freedom' is even more of a prison than the mines. We're trapped here."

"What do you mean, 'trapped'?" the Earther replied. He sounded as coldly defensive as the day they'd broken him out of those same prison mines, and Nesh suddenly realised that he must have been warming up to them over the months for her to notice the change now.

"I mean *trapped*, Kerrig," said Nesh, then decided that an example would be more effective than a long explanation.

So she asked him if he'd been down to the river at all during the long, hot summer. As she'd thought, he'd not set foot in the water despite working near the shore at least once. The others added to the explanation, and Nesh could almost hear the Earther's blood rising.

"I'll put the word about," he said, after hearing the full story. "Another sanctuary turned into a prison! This is an outrage, and we need to break the trap. The farmers will help."

Nesh doubted how willing the locals would be to help any Outsiders, but Kerrig seemed confident that his fellow Elementals would share his outrage at being held prisoner.

That, or he could appeal to their self-interest in getting rid of the Outsiders for good.

⸺◈⸺

It was astonishing to Nesh how quickly Kerrig went from surly passenger to driven organiser. She felt she was getting a glimpse of the Earther who had worked to keep the mines safe, as Kerrig despatched Volnar and Traegl as ambassadors to their respective Elements. He then appointed himself to the task of convincing the Earthers; he declared that he would either free the island or rescue the islanders.

Nesh wondered if she'd discovered another reason for the Earther's grumpiness after being taken from the mines. He was used to being the protector, and didn't like it when other people stepped in to protect him.

Well, Nesh was happy to let Kerrig get on with it. As the only Avlem present, Nesh knew that she ought to be taking charge or at the very least supporting the Sidrax in taking charge of the situation. But bad things tended to happen when she tried to lead, so Nesh was not sorry that Kerrig had stepped in.

⸺◆⸺

Breaking the trap was easier said than done. Nesh didn't understand all the details, but it seemed to hinge on Air Elemental guards sending messages on the wind. She suddenly remembered the way Falerian had spoken clearly to her, despite being out over the river when she said goodbye.

There were soldiers somewhere, probably either side of the river, whispering away and getting the islanders to think and feel in ways that would keep them from trying to leave. Nesh could certainly believe that. How much had her own time in the mines been controlled by the whispers of those around her?

The immediate solution to this whisper control was for everyone to block their ears and communicate by means of writing on slates. Nesh had a moment of panic before Volnar 'confessed' to needing to read out loud still. He promised to be quiet about it, though. Nesh unblocked one ear to listen in as Volnar read aloud to her. It was interesting to notice how her doubts about the wisdom of leaving the island came and went with the removal and insertion of the carefully moulded earplugs that Kerrig handed out.

Nesh struggled a bit with writing on a slate, but since her role was mostly to keep out of the way and do what she was told, she managed reasonably well.

Planning the escape had taken several days, partly to wait for the double new moon, and partly so that there would be no sudden commotion that might alert the guards. With no Air Elementals on the island, there was no-one to ask about the whisper messages and their limitations. Could the soldiers hear them, as well as talk to them?

Traegl had come up with a way to use water as a temporary interference shield, just in case, and she put it up whenever they talked most openly about their escape plans. It was during one of these shielded conversations that Kerrig gave up on his idea of staying behind as defender of the island.

"We can't break this trap without finding and confronting the Air Walker soldiers," he said. "We're better off slipping away quietly and hoping they don't notice."

There was a resigned note in his voice, and Nesh wondered if he wanted to go out and fight the Air Walkers. This Earther seemed to have two moods: sullen resignation and raging anger. He was always spoiling for a fight, physical or verbal.

It seemed, however, that the Earther's real reason for not wanting to leave was that he'd become fond of the island itself. He all but admitted it when talking about the other Elementals who had elected to stay behind, most of them Earthers and Marshlanders. In his own words, "We get attached to places; leaving is always a last resort."

Nesh almost laughed at that but restrained herself. She remembered how Kerrig had needed to be 'kidnapped' before he contemplated leaving his home, even though it had become overrun with Outsiders. Sadly, mass kidnapping was not an option here. She only hoped that the ones who stayed behind wouldn't come to regret it.

***

There was a double new moon, and the night was pitch black. The logs from the disassembled raft had been turned into path markers, lining one edge of the temporary road that had been raised up by the Earthers and dried out by the Marshlanders. Nesh cautiously felt her way along, keeping one hand on the shoulder of the person in front, and one foot brushing the guiding logs with each step.

Everyone in the group had been told to wear their earplugs as a protection against the suggestions in the Air. But Nesh was so unnerved by the prospect of walking across a river that she left one ear partially unblocked. She wanted to be able to hear if the river was about to overwhelm them, to be ready to protect those nearest to her. It was only in the middle of crossing that she realised her mistake.

Her upstream ear was full of the muted rush of the water, the careful footsteps fore and aft, the creaking, rumbling wheels of Madrigal's cart, and the sound of the air. The air that was full of talk about how fine Camp Freedom was, and how leaving was madness.

The voices blended with her thoughts and filled her mind with the folly of trying to walk across a river. Then she became afraid that this thought was also from the Air Elementals, meaning that they knew about the plan and were waiting on the bank.

Someone brushed against her, running back to the island. She stumbled, but didn't fall. The shock of it seemed to help, breaking her out of her nightmare. It was a physical reminder of what might happen to her if she allowed herself to be frightened.

She used her free hand to settle her earplugs firmly in place.

Not real, not real, Nesh reminded herself. *Focus on reality*.

The path beneath her feet. The hand on her shoulder. The log at her foot. Her Talent telling her there was no danger ahead. Those things were real; not the voices in the air or even the thoughts in her head.

Nesh concentrated on her steps, one foot in front of the other, and tried to ignore the creeping dread that filled her insides and threatened to drown her from within.

It felt like a long, long way to the shore.

III

The morning after the daring escape was such an anti-climax that Nesh was torn between laughter and despair. They had moved a little way downriver before stopping for the night, and it seemed as though most of the Elementals thought that leaving the island meant they could forget all about Camp Freedom.

As if the Air Walker soldiers couldn't hear them on this side of the river. As if the army didn't use this road all the time. As if they might not be captured and returned to the empty mockery of 'Camp Freedom' at any moment.

Nesh's own feelings were mixed. To have left a place where she wasn't wanted was a good thing, of course, but she might still have been able to build a home there, if she had been left alone. And if there had been no creepy whisper trap, of course. But here she was, travelling with the bulk of those who hadn't wanted her around in the first place.

Ash and Madrigal were treated with suspicion, and Traegl suffered the same kind of rejection as Nesh herself had lived through. It was painful to witness. Then there was Kerrig. He blew hot and cold, his cool efficiency interspersed with moments of unpredictable rage. She couldn't make sense of him, and that disturbed her.

People milled around until nearly noon, some looking lost and others picking fights with anyone and everyone. Nesh thought she heard Kerrig's voice in more than one argument and drew back to avoid getting involved.

There was a general movement eastward as the day went on, so Nesh went along with it. East was as good a direction as any. She cast about with her Talent and Found Madrigal and Ash walking together a little way behind the noisiest part of the crowd. For all that Madrigal idolised the Earther, the little donkey seemed to know when it was a good idea to stay out of his way.

The trio walked on for a while, with only the rumble of cartwheels to disturb the silence, until Nesh heard Madrigal give out a full-throated donkey's laugh.

Nesh cast about for the source of the amusement, but asking her Talent to Find a joke was an exercise in futility. She got her clue when Ash's laugh joined Madrigal's, and he said, "So... I still need to work on my donkey shape. Sorry Mads, looks like I won't be taking your place in those shafts just yet."

This insight into Sidrax abilities piqued Nesh's curiosity. It was so hard to ask Elementals about their skills because they kept offering to share them. Generous, of course, but Nesh still struggled to hide her revulsion at their promiscuous ways. And they expected their offers to be reciprocated. The very idea made Nesh's skin crawl.

With the Sidrax, it was different. No Sidrax had ever offered to teach an Avlem more than the most commonplace skills – and none had ever asked to learn an Avlem's Talent. Although Sidrea was certainly less civilised than Avlenia, no-one could accuse the Empire of that particular breach of decorum.

Thinking about this gave Nesh the courage to ask Ash how Sidrax shapeshifting worked, what Madrigal called her 'shapes', and Ash his 'forms'. He seemed happy to oblige and began a short lecture on the art of becoming different animals that he addressed as much to Madrigal as to Nesh.

"So," said Ash, "as Maddie already knows, most Sidrax have two forms that come easiest to us. One is this one," he gestured at his current man-form, "and the other is the shape in which we're born. That is dictated by our mothers, by the way. We also tend to find it easier to learn any of the forms our mothers used while carrying us, but they must be learned for all that.

"All forms have to be learned, but any that we learn before the age of about twenty months seem to come easier than those learned later in life. No-one really knows why, though I've heard it suggested that babies don't understand the many ways in which shape-changing is fundamentally illogical."

Nesh's head swam with questions, most of which were far too indelicate to ask in front of Madrigal. She settled on, "Illogical? How so? I'd always thought of it being like your version of Talents, if a whole Empire's worth of people could somehow all have the same Talent."

"And are Talents logical?" asked Ash. "I've seen Avlem do some frankly inexplicable things, all rationalised as their 'Talent'. I'm not sure what yours is, but can you tell me you really understand how it works?"

"Of course I do," Nesh replied, indignantly. "I'm a Finder. When I know what I'm looking for, my Talent shows me where to look."

"But how?" insisted Ash. "Does it tug at you? Do you hear a sound? See a flashing light? Get a scent?"

Nesh smiled. "It doesn't work like that," she said. "It's my Talent. I just... know. It's a gift from Life, not a skill to be studied by anyone but another Finder."

Ash made a sound that might have been a sigh or a groan. "Yes, Avlem Talents are a gift from Life, and Sidrax shape-changing is a gift from Wisdom, and the Elementals are descended from the children of Time, if you believe in all that. But there's got to be an explanation for it somewhere, otherwise it's nonsense.

"You can't just shrug and say 'who knows?' about everything," Ash continued. "Who knows why compass needles always point south? Who knows where the world ends? Who knows how the birds time their migrations? It has to make sense on some level, even if we don't understand it yet. That's why the Sidrax Empire exists, to try to understand the world, and to spread that understanding."

The young man stopped, breathing rather hard, then started again in a smaller, almost sheepish tone of voice.

"Sorry," he said. "I get a bit carried away sometimes. It's probably a Sidrax thing; we're born curious."

"But not born logical," replied Nesh, smiling. "You were saying, about babies and learning shapes...?"

Ash plunged happily into a long explanation of the finer points of shape-shifting while Nesh and Madrigal listened – probably with about equal levels of comprehension.

Some time later, Traegl came up alongside Nesh and listened to Ash for a while.

"...make models from wood, but I always preferred clay. And some do everything in drawings, but there's something about having a solid, handleable model to learn from that... uh, hi, Trae."

Ash's lecture trailed off. When he spoke again he sounded much less definite.

"You, um, doing alright, Trae?" he asked.

Madrigal leaned her head across Nesh and blew her own hello to Traegl.

"Hello to you too, Maddie," said Traegl. "That cart looks heavy."

Nesh had one hand on Madrigal's neck, and felt her firm nod. It was hard to make out the copper-coloured head against the earth tones of the road, but Nesh felt the way the little Sidrax shook out her mane and held her head high.

She heard Ash and Traegl laugh together, all awkwardness gone for now, and it made her smile.

"I know how strong you are, Mads," said Ash. "We're all very proud of you."

Traegl reached across to pat the donkey's neck, and Nesh drew back to give her room. It was a perfectly natural, unselfconscious move on her part, but as she fell back further to walk beside the cart, Nesh had a sudden fear that this was her life now. Following behind the few who tolerated her presence, staying close to familiar things so that she wouldn't get lost in the featureless light, and always being in the way. She pushed the morbid thoughts aside and paid attention to the conversation between Ash and Traegl instead. They had moved from talking about Madrigal to discussing Volnar.

"He was with Kerrig the last time I saw him," said Ash. "Though I think it was more a question of keeping away from some of the Fire Breather families than seeking out our favourite Earther. A couple of them are still trying to adopt him, even after he kept running away from them."

"I almost wish they would," Traegl said. "You know he's dead set on going to the Citadel, especially now we're on the road for it."

Nesh felt sick. This was the road to the Citadel – of course it was. The river flowed eastward, and the Citadel was built at the river's mouth. She had no idea how far inland they were, but being anywhere near the Citadel was downright dangerous for herself and for Volnar. Not to mention Ash and Traegl, and maybe Kerrig and Madrigal as well.

"This is not good," said Ash; he so perfectly mirrored Nesh's thoughts that she wondered for a moment if she'd spoken aloud.

"We'll have to strike out to the north," Ash continued. "If we can persuade Mr. Kerrig to come along, that would be for the best. But Trae and I shouldn't get any closer to the Citadel than we must."

"Volnar certainly needs to stay away," said Traegl. "And I don't suppose you want to see the old place again, do you?"

It took Nesh a moment to realise that Traegl was talking to her, and she shook her head.

"As for you and me, though," and now Traegl seemed to be talking to Ash, "we could probably risk it. If nothing else, we could watch out for young Volnar, if he insists on going. It's not as dangerous for us as it would be for you, Nesh. Or even for Kerrig."

Nesh stared at the young Marshlander. "Traegl, do you want to go to the Citadel?" she asked, incredulous.

The hesitation was obvious, and Nesh wished she could read Traegl's expression.

"No, but I..." Traegl hesitated, but no-one interrupted. "Look, I like being beside the river, alright?" she said at last. "We're nowhere near the Citadel yet, and it's all Fire Plains to the north. I agree we shouldn't let Volnar go to the Citadel, but he's dead set on it. If he wants to travel on this road for a while..."

Traegl let the sentence fade out. For a while there was only the rumble of the wheels to break the silence.

Finally, Ash suggested they start by talking to Kerrig. "He's got influence," Ash said. "People will listen to him more readily than to any of us."

Nesh doubted the Earther would agree to any plan hatched by an 'Outsider', but didn't want to discourage Ash.

"Let's wait until we've stopped for the night," she said, by way of compromise. "Give everyone a chance to relax and think things over."

⚬

As the shadows lengthened, the ambling caravan morphed into several small camps. Nesh made out a few spots of light that must have been cooking fires, to judge by the smell. Traegl disappeared for a while, then reappeared carrying a couple of fish, already gutted and cleaned.

Ash unhitched Madrigal from the cart and told her not to go too far off while grazing. He sounded annoyed about something, and Nesh remembered (too late) about his distaste for killing. Even for killing fish, it seemed. Nesh was reminded of the fish she and Volnar had cooked in the cave so many months ago, and suddenly felt guilty. She hadn't meant to remind Madrigal of her first encounter with death, even the death of a 'swimming thing'.

So, while Traegl hung the fish over the fire to cook, Nesh suggested to Ash that they go and sort things out with Kerrig. It would give her time to decide how she felt about dinner.

Nesh had prepared herself, or so she thought, for any or all of the Earther's strange moods. What she hadn't been prepared for was a strange Elemental butting into the conversation, just as Ash was explaining how important it was for Maddie to continue her training.

"Who's Maddie?" demanded the stranger. "And why is an Earther of the People talking to a couple of Outsiders?"

Nesh bridled at this rudeness even as she tried to make allowances for him. It wasn't fair to expect an Avlem-level of politeness from an Elemental, but there were limits!

So busy was Nesh with her own thoughts that Ash's response caught her completely by surprise.

"'Who's Maddie?'" he echoed. "I'll tell you who Maddie is. Maddie is the little donkey who's been hauling your baggage around since we escaped that trap of an island. Good little worker, isn't she? She's a nice kid, too. And we had to tell her to hide herself; to not let anyone know she's Sidrax like me because jerks like you would bully her for it."

Ash was breathing hard and sounded angrier than Nesh thought possible for the easy-going young man. The stranger didn't seem to notice, or care, that he had enraged someone who could bite him in half. Not that Ash would, of course, but still...

"Then take her and go," said the stranger. "We of the People certainly don't need anything from Outsiders."

Ash became almost incoherent with rage, and it took both Nesh and Traegl to haul him back to where they'd left Madrigal.

"I'll take first watch, Trae," Ash said, once he'd calmed down. "I'll never get to sleep like this. 'Ooh, my ancestors lived here centuries ago so I know everything about wilderness survival'," he said, mockingly. "Idiot!"

Traegl punched him lightly on the shoulder.

"You shouldn't let them get to you," she said. "And if you're going to take watch, then watch. Don't get caught up in imagining long arguments."

Ash snorted. "As if I would do something like that—" he said, when Traegl interrupted him with a cough that sounded like, "Raskon Trail."

"—while on duty," Ash amended, hastily. "Go and eat your prey, then get some sleep. I'll wake you for your watch."

Traegl laughed. "Come on then, Nesh. Let's go eat our 'prey'. A couple of nicely cooked trout, waiting for us by the fire."

⸻◆⸻

As Traegl was about to lie down to sleep, she groaned.

"Ash is right, these farmers are idiots. Look at all those fires, how far they've spread themselves out. There's no way one person can watch over all this. I'll have to stay up and take a section."

Nesh had a thought, hesitated, then took a chance.

"I can cover some of it," she said. Nesh was far from confident in her abilities as a leader, but standing guard was a different matter. "How did you manage last night?"

"Ash and I split the duty, like we were planning to do tonight," Traegl said. "But last night everyone stayed close together. This sprawling camp is another thing entirely."

"Get some sleep," Nesh said. "I'll go and Find the other end of this 'sprawling camp' and watch from there."

Traegl huffed, resignedly or impatiently Nesh couldn't tell. "No, that's no good. I'll take this watch and tell Ash what I'm doing. We'll try and find you a partner for the second half of the night while we're at it."

"Oh, you leave that to me," Nesh said. If there was one thing she had worked out about Kerrig, it was that he hated being obliged to anyone. She'd guilt him into taking his share on watch simply by telling him everything Ash and Traegl had been doing to protect the group.

With a very slight feeling of malicious satisfaction, Nesh settled herself to sleep.

⸺◈⸺

Her plan worked well enough as far as getting the Earther to take his turn on watch. What she hadn't expected was that they would actually be attacked.

Nesh heard the goats crying out from their various tethers and saw the flare of fires being stoked. She quickly built up her own fire, then woke Traegl. The poor thing had only had a couple of hours' rest.

She tried to Find Ash, but Kerrig was nearer. He was holding a burning branch and seemed to be waving it like a shield at something inland. As Nesh approached, she heard the Earther ordering people to retreat to the riverbank.

"What's going on?" she asked.

"Some kind of wild animals," Kerrig told her. "We need to move people without causing a panic. Wake your lot, then find Ash and Traegl. I don't want to leave this fire – I think it's keeping them away."

Nesh did her best, but the ex-islanders were not keen on taking her orders at any time, and especially not when they had just been woken up in the middle of the night.

She herded the crowd towards Kerrig and the fire, then searched with her Talent for clues about what was going on. The problem was that she didn't know what she was looking for. Should she be helping someone? Getting out of the way? Would asking questions start a panic in the crowd? Nesh didn't even know who was standing next to her until he spoke.

"You alright there, Nesh?" said Volnar. He managed to make it sound like a casual enquiry, and not a young carer checking up on his charge, which Nesh appreciated. "This is a bit of excitement, isn't it? All those wild animals over there, and us over here behind this little moat. Nice and cosy."

Nesh smiled and patted Volnar's shoulder. "A little excitement goes a long way, I think. Let's hope the animals go away soon."

Volnar was silent for a while, his shoulders tense under Nesh's hand. When he did speak, it was in an awed whisper.

"I think that's our Ash," he said. "He's gone all wolf-shaped and scary. He's not going to fight all those animals by himself, is he?"

"No, not by himself," said Traegl quietly, from the other side of Volnar. "I've got a direct line to the river from here, and I'm just waiting for Ash to give a signal."

There was a long pause, with only the growling back and forth of Ash and the wild animals. Nesh thought furiously, trying to come up with a plan, any plan, that might help against an unknown number of dangerous animals. She was still trying to come up with something when Volnar and Traegl gave simultaneous sighs of relief.

"They're moving off," Volnar said. "Three cheers for Ash!"

Nesh sank to her knees and asked her Talent to Find the nearest wild predator. It returned a weak signal that got fainter with each passing minute. She added her own relief to that of the others, and prepared to sit out the rest of her (hopefully uneventful) watch.

The following day, Kerrig took charge again and started handing out jobs. There was plenty of opposition, but the Earther handled it without resorting to violence. Nesh's opinion of him rose slightly, even as her feelings about herself took a sharp dive. She understood from Volnar and Traegl that the whole group of Elementals planned to be a sort of travelling market, going from town to town across the Fire Plains to sell what they made on the road. The goats gave milk, which the farmers could turn into butter and cheese with the tools they'd packed onto Madrigal's cart. Many people had spindles in their pockets, which they could use to turn the goats' shed hair into a fine yarn. Volnar had teamed up with a potter and was helping her make earthenware pots and bowls.

Everyone was contributing something, it seemed. Even the resolutely anti-crafts Traegl had her role as protector of the caravan, not to mention the way she led the hunting and foraging parties. Ash would have preferred them to have been foraging-only parties but had been out-numbered on that decision.

And what could Nesh bring to the table? Her Talent, of course, but the wilderness training of the two ex-soldiers was too good for them to rarely need her. She had managed to Find water for the group exactly once – until a Marshlander had demanded to know why they were using an Outsider to deal with an Element of The People.

Nesh always heard it that way now: The People, complete with capital letters. It didn't mean all people, not Avlem, nor Sidrax, nor any other people there might be; no, it meant Elementals and only Elementals. They were The People, and this was their Land, and Life help any Outsider who suggested that perhaps being born here, to parents who were also born here, might make it partly her land, too.

Nesh wondered why 'The People' only seemed to understand Talent theft when it involved 'Outsiders' getting involved with their Elements. They'd had no compunction about imitating every Talent in sight when her grandparents had landed in Ashanna for the first time. Before it even *was* Ashanna, back when it was simply Orameshia, a beautiful Avlenian word meaning 'New Home'.

Because that's what it should have been for them. A new home, a place for them to be Avlem, away from the shadow of the Sidrax Empire. And here she was, speaking only Sidrean, cut off from her home and her people, and enjoying the grudging hospitality of a community that largely hated her.

It galled Nesh to be in, or at least with, a community and make no real contribution towards it. She took night watch duties, but it didn't feel like enough. However, there was one unexpected bonus – she could blame her headaches, fatigue, and unwillingness to socialise on her not getting enough sleep.

The truth was that her eyesight was still getting worse, and she didn't know when, or if, it would stop. She fretted late into the night over what she ought to do. Could she advertise her services as a Finder when they stopped to trade? It felt like a good idea, but Nesh decided against it for a couple of reasons. Firstly, she didn't want to encroach on any local Talents. Also, she wouldn't relish answering the questions about her community and family history that would surely follow.

So, instead of making herself known as a Finder, Nesh decided to offer to help on the stall, keeping track of sales and watching out for thieves. Well, Finding out thieves, anyway. The takings would be held in common, she was sure. At least, they would if Kerrig had anything to say about it. Nesh hoped his influence would extend this far. The last thing they needed was for people to start fighting over personal possessions on top of everything else.

Still, it might be useful to know what sold best and where. Nesh had a couple of wax tablets now, and was getting so good at touch-writing that she'd begun to develop her own shorthand. As stall-minder and log-keeper, Nesh thought that she might claim some place in this strange, mixed community at last.

All this thinking took more than one night's watch, and Nesh thanked Life for preserving her sanity by means of a growing friendship with Traegl. The two of them often took their meals together while Ash and Madrigal disappeared to forage and practise their shapes.

Traegl liked to talk about her family, and Nesh soon realised that she could do the same. This young Elemental was from a different part of the country and couldn't know any of the people Nesh remembered, so there was no chance of anyone connecting the disgraced convict Nesh with the honest and respectable Tynar family.

She was careful to avoid names, all the same.

As they talked, Traegl's crush on Ash became painfully obvious. Eventually, after making Nesh promise not to even hint to anyone, Traegl confessed to having fallen head-over-heels for him. Nesh did her best to look solemn, and even tried to sound surprised at the news.

Nesh had no romantic secret to confess in return for her friend's confidence, but she shared her ideas about record-keeping. Her desire to be useful to the group was as close to her heart as anything she could imagine.

"I think you're right: it's a good idea to keep records of our sales," Traegl said. "But be careful who you share them with. I don't like to think of the fallout if, say, Drishmel's family finds out that Balmar's goat butter is selling better than their own reed baskets, or vice-versa."

Nesh nodded. These Elemental farmers were a disorderly bunch, and she sometimes wondered how Kerrig kept them in line. Perhaps his mercurial temper confused his fellow Elementals as much as it did her.

⸻◆⸻

In the first place they traded, Nesh was ready to offer her services as stall keeper. But Kerrig decided that anyone who might be recognised from the mines should lie low until they had an idea of how 'wanted' they were. Nesh might have suspected him of merely wanting to spite her, if it were not for the fact that he sent Madrigal into town without going himself.

In fact, he more or less put Madrigal in charge. Nesh heard him tell the farmers (or ex-farmers, she supposed) to pay attention to the little donkey's moods, and tell Madrigal to be a good girl but also look out for anything suspicious.

It seemed like a lot to put onto such a youngster, but at the same time it showed a marked change in his attitude towards the Sidrax. When she heard him rebuke a fellow Earther for calling Ash 'shifter' and 'unnatural', she wondered if this could really be the same man whom she'd see recoil from Madrigal in horror on the first day of their escape.

That night, Nesh didn't spend her watch thinking about what she ought to do next. Instead, she found herself thinking about the past. She wished she could talk to her younger self, the rash teenager who'd been so certain about everything. A couple of late nights spent in serious thought would have been good for her, back then. So much pain and trouble that could have been avoided...

But that was not a helpful line of thought and, after one final pang, Nesh fixed her mind firmly on the present.

Time passed with no fallout from the towns they visited. Kerrig had reluctantly allowed Nesh to go along on the most recent trading visit. She'd stayed in the the background, but no-one had tried to arrest her. The farmers were beginning to accept the fact of her, and one or two were even civil.

She used her Talent to help a woman Find a lost spindle, and the woman had been so impressed that Nesh was embarrassed. Despite all her years surrounded by Elementals, she sometimes forgot that Talents were not part of their understanding. Watching a Fire Breather control a flame was ordinary for them, but someone who could speak to birds, or Find lost objects, was a marvel.

The praise was nice, though. Nesh couldn't remember the last time someone had been so flattering and genuine when talking to her. She felt ready to face whatever strifes or struggles lay ahead. But she wasn't at all expecting what Volnar had to say when he visited her late that night.

"Hi, Nesh," he said in a low, quiet voice. It wasn't a whisper, and it wasn't quite the treble piping of the boy she'd broken out of the prison mines half a year ago. *Young Volnar is growing up,* thought Nesh; and she didn't know whether to be glad or sorry.

"How are you keeping, in yourself?" Volnar asked, as if they were two old folks sitting together in the middle of a slow day, instead of the middle of the night. "Pretty well, I hope. Night watches not too tiring?"

Nesh aimed a look at Volnar, though it was probably too dark for him to pick up on it.

"I'm very well, thank you," she said, mildly. "I hope you're not having trouble sleeping, young man? Nothing on your mind to keep you up in the midnight watch?"

Volnar sighed. "You're right, of course. I just didn't know how to lead up to it. Thing is, Nesh... look, don't yell at me, but... I'm leaving in the morning. Going to the Citadel with Mashpa the potter. We're going to start up a business there, under her name at first, all open and legal."

Volnar spoke quickly, keen to make his case before Nesh could object. "I know there's a risk, but I can't wait any longer. They need me. And even if they don't, I need to know that. I need to know they're safe and well. You understand, don't you?"

And she did. She wasn't able to save those lost children, and Volnar... for all his youth and vulnerability, Volnar might be best placed to help them. A dozen objections sprang to mind in a moment, from Volnar's being too young, to his being needed here in the caravan. But she remembered being a child herself, and how all-consuming duties felt at that age. There was no arguing with that kind of set purpose, and Volnar's seemed less hare-brained than her own had been.

So all Nesh said was, "I understand. I'll miss you, but I understand."

Volnar brightened up, and for a moment forgot to speak quietly. "You could..." he began, then checked himself and said, in a softer voice, "You could come with us. Help us run the shop, and live with us. I already cleared it with Mashpa and she said it's alright. Do come, Nesh. Please."

"To the Citadel?" Nesh stared into the night and thought this over. Back to civilisation — even if it was a rather Sidrax kind of civilisation. A house, a job, a normal life. Among other Avlem, who would know her for Avlem at once and ask her name and her hometown and...

Nesh shook her head, then remembered that it was night and said, "No. Thank you, Volnar, but... no. I can't go back. Not yet. Maybe not ever. But knowing that you were willing to have me, that means a lot. Thank you. I mean it."

A person with a fixed purpose of their own can often tell when another person's 'no' means 'no'. Volnar said nothing for a long moment, then he took a deep breath and let it out slowly.

"In that case, I'll miss you, too," he said. Nesh heard him get up and rose to her own feet to say a final goodbye.

"Look," Volnar said, suddenly very awkward. "I don't like hugs and such as a rule. Too much like being grabbed by the guards. But just this once, do you think I could...?"

Nesh put one hand on Volnar's shoulder and gently tugged him towards her. The boy wrapped his arms around her and held her tight. She returned the hug, gently, and let him be the first to let go.

"Goodbye, Nesh," he said at last. "Don't forget me?"

"Never," she said. "Now, go get some sleep. You've got a long journey ahead of you tomorrow."

Nesh listened until she heard Volnar lie down, then set her Talent looking for dangers again until Traegl relieved her.

In the morning, Nesh tracked Volnar with her Talent as far as she could and was pleased when Traegl told her that Ash was flying at a discreet distance to watch over the pair on their journey.

⚹

The caravan would stay put until Ash returned, and everyone seemed to be very busy. After Nesh had caught up on some sleep, she tried to Find somewhere she could help out. Kerrig asked her to take Madrigal out grazing and let her have some time being different shapes if she wanted to.

"I know it's not right," he said, "but some of the farmers here still get nervous around Sidrax. Don't go far, but give her some time away from the complainers."

Nesh was more than happy to accept the job, and spent a very pleasant afternoon with Madrigal. The girl wanted to talk about her shapes, though she was careful not to do anything that Ash hadn't approved.

"Teacher Ash says shapes can hurt if you don't do them right," Madrigal informed her, seriously. "I can do donkeys right, and be a girl right, and I can be scaly all over, but not on the inside yet. And I can do this, look!"

Nesh squinted, blinked, and could just make out the copper-coloured shape of Madrigal against the green of the grasslands and the blue of the sky. She was girl-shaped still, but something was different about her head. Was she holding her arms up? No, there were her arms, out at her sides. Something stuck up either side of her head...

"Are those your donkey ears, Madrigal?" Nesh asked. "Just your ears, not all of you?"

Madrigal laughed with delight.

"My new thing I can do, all by myself!" she declared. "I can show Teacher Ash, too. Where is he?"

Nesh hesitated. Did Madrigal know about Volnar's leaving? Did she know he wasn't coming back? Nesh decided to go cautiously and be ready with reassurance if needed.

"Ash is looking after Volnar today. You know Volnar's gone to the Citadel?"

Nesh braced herself, but Madrigal merely made agreeing noises and nodded until her ears flapped.

"I know," she said. "He told me goodbye specially, and when I go to the city I see him there. But not yet."

Nesh was relieved and absently patted Madrigal on the head. Coming across the ears, she smiled.

"You really are very clever, Madrigal," she said. "I had no idea there was such a lot of work involved in making your shapes."

Madrigal lifted her head and sounded serious. "I learn a lot and a lot," she said. "It's hard work, sometimes. Not hard like pulling a cart hard, but still hard. Dif-fi-cult," she said, carefully. "I learn words, and shapes, and a lot of things!"

"That's right, you are learning lots of things," Nesh said, fighting the urge to mirror the little girl's grammar. "But you need to rest and have fun, too. What do you want to do this afternoon, while we're here?"

Madrigal tugged at her ears and sounded unsure of herself. "Do I got to rest?" she asked.

"You do have to take a break from work," Nesh said. "A rest means something that makes you feel better. You can sleep, or play, or eat, or whatever you like. What do you want to do?"

"Can I run?" suggested Madrigal, shyly. "Really fast?"

Nesh looked out across the plains.

"Don't get lost," she said. "And come back before it gets dark. And watch out for dangerous animals."

Madrigal's eyes got so big that Nesh could see the whites, bright against the rest of her face. Afraid she'd gone too far, Nesh made herself smile with all the reassurance she didn't feel and added, "Most importantly: enjoy it. Alright?"

Madrigal answered by taking on her donkey shape, kicking her heels in the air, and tearing across the grass at full speed.

Nesh used her Talent to Find Madrigal at intervals, but she could just as easily have tracked her by the sound of delighted braying.

Ash, in his bird form, had watched Volnar and Mash-pa safely to the Citadel, then reported back. Nesh was grateful to him, and said so – once he'd had a good long sleep to recover from his travels.

"I know you didn't really get to know him very well," she said, "but Volnar means a lot to me, so thank you for taking the trouble. I hope you're not too worn out, flying all that way?"

"Not now I've had my sleep out," Ash replied. Nesh could just about remember being that young, when one good night's, or day's, sleep made up for staying awake for a day and a night. These days, the ratio was very different.

"Anyway, I could hardly refuse Mr. Kerrig's orders now, could I?" said Ash. "He's not officially my captain, but he's every bit as scary. In his own way, of course. But don't tell him I said that; I don't think he likes being reminded of her, or what she made him do."

Nesh frowned, unsure what Ash meant. She remembered Volnar telling some wild story about a huge white monster and Kerrig crushing it under an even huger rock, but that was surely an exaggeration. Then again, Traegl and Ash had both referred to their troop scattering 'after what happened to the captain'. So maybe...?

If she was honest with herself, it was probably best not to think about it. She said goodnight to Ash and stood to let him take over the watch.

"Goodnight, Nesh," he replied. Then he shivered and sniffed deeply at the night air. Too deeply for him to have been using his usual, man-shaped form.

"There's something unsettling in the wind," he said. "It's standing all my fur on end. Wrap up warm and try to sleep well, Nesh. I think we might be in for some rain tomorrow."

———◆———

Ash had understated the case. Nesh was shaken awake in the pre-dawn light to help Ash, Traegl, and Kerrig build some large shelters ahead of a storm. They were more like bunkers than anything else – mostly sunk into the ground, with mouths that were wider than they were tall.

Kerrig and Traegl took care of excavating and drying out the bunkers, while Ash and Nesh were despatched to collect stones. Nesh didn't understand what they needed stones for, but in her sleep-deprived state she didn't care enough to ask. She simply used her Talent to Find all the stones she could, and employed Ash's help in digging them out and carrying them to the bunkers.

There were three bunkers in the end: large, dry, and deep enough to stand up in. Kerrig took the stones and did... something... to them. Nesh couldn't tell what exactly, but it involved covering the roofs of the shelters from the outside. When Kerrig moved to work on the second roof, Nesh examined his work on the first. The stones and pebbles had all been flattened out and interlocked into a solid dome. The finish wasn't very smooth, but solid enough for Nesh to lean against it as she thought over what this new discovery taught her about the Earther.

Short-tempered, given to holding grudges, and downright dangerous as he was on the one hand, the gruff Elemental was also fond of children, dedicated to protecting others, and a meticulous worker. Kerrig was a walking contradiction who made Nesh uneasy. She could never be sure which facet of his personality would be uppermost at any given time.

But she wasn't given long to think and worry in peace. The children began to wake up, and were curious about the new dens. Nesh explained that it was going to be a wet and windy day, so they had made these dens to keep everyone dry.

The children thought it a brilliant idea, and were soon dashing around and bringing things into the protection of the shelters. Madrigal tried to bring her cart in, and Nesh had to explain that it was too big.

"Your cart will be safe so long so it doesn't blow away," Nesh said. "Let's make sure it's empty, then tie it to a tree so it can't get lost. Does that sound good to you?"

Madrigal thought about this, then said it was alright so long as the tree wasn't going to blow away as well.

Nesh Found a suitably strong tree, secured Madrigal's cart, then led her back with her harness to the nearest den. She had to change to her child-shape to fit through the door, and she struggled a little with the donkey-sized collar around her much smaller neck. Nesh took it from her, and they entered together.

A few Fire Breathers had already got a fire going in the middle of the room, making the den warm and bright as the world outside got darker and colder. The sun was barely up before it was swallowed by storm clouds. Nesh let her eyes adjust to the firelight and listened to the noises from outside. She made out some low-grade squabbling under the howling wind but ignored it. If idiots wanted to argue in the rain, they could and welcome.

What did catch her attention were the increasingly agitated calls for 'Shebbok'. Nesh didn't know who or what 'Shebbok' might be, but she understood fear when she heard it. Cautioning Madrigal to stay put, Nesh got closer to the door and tried to Find the source of the distressed calls.

It was a family, calling for their youngest child. Shebbok had run off into the storm, and Kerrig was organising a search. Nesh decided to join at once. She had already set her Talent to work, and it was simply a matter of following it.

It took her several minutes to talk the other people in the den out of joining her, especially Madrigal. In the end, she left the adults to look after the children, with dire warnings about what would happen to any adult who let one of their charges get so much as damp. By the time Nesh reached Kerrig, he'd already sent one group of three out on the trail.

"Don't send anyone else out, Kerrig," Nesh said, raising her voice to be heard over the wind and rain. "I know where he is. Make sure no-one else gets lost, and I'll be back with young Shibo soon."

"He's called Shebbok," Kerrig said. "And if you're going out in this storm, then Traegl and I are coming with you."

Nesh wanted to argue, but the lost boy was getting further away every moment. She strode off into the storm, and could just about hear Kerrig and Traegl hurrying from behind. When the Marshlander caught up, she did something to keep the rain from hitting quite so hard. It was nice of her, but not necessary. The rain might have been blinding, but Nesh wasn't using her eyes. Her Talent drew her onward and her feet tested the ground with each step.

After what felt like far too long, they started to catch up with the child. Perhaps he'd stopped running and was trying to get back by himself? Nesh adjusted her course and slowed down a little. It would never do to run into the poor boy.

***

They were close, Nesh could tell. But she thought she could hear multiple voices and wondered how the other search party had reached Shebbok ahead of them. She knew that she'd taken the most direct route.

"I'm so glad you found him," she said to the adults. She didn't recognise them, but that didn't mean much. She hadn't met every Elemental in their group yet, and might not have known them even if she'd had perfect eyesight. So she left the adults to Kerrig and focused on the boy. He was tired and cross, but appeared unhurt.

"Thank you for finding him," the Earther said. "We have shelters nearby, if you'd like to wait out the storm with us."

"Let's get back," said Traegl. "I never thought I'd say this, but I can't wait to get back to a decent fire." She was using one hand to push the rain away from Kerrig, the boy having latched onto the other one. The two Marshlanders were seemingly torn between enjoying their Element and wanting to get warm.

Then the newcomers got nearer and the wind... stopped. It was still howling, and whipping the long grass, but the air around the six of them was as still as if a door had been closed on the storm.

Nesh was stunned by the difference it made. Even more than the rain, the wind had been chilling and deafening. It was a relief to be able to hear again, and to thank the strangers properly without having to shout. Nesh was so grateful that she didn't realise at first what it meant. Then she did: Their caravan had no Air Elementals. That had been part of the difficulty of getting off the island, not having Air Elementals to ask how the whisper trap worked. These people were strangers, then.

But Nesh reasoned that any strangers who began by rescuing a lost child couldn't be all bad.

They turned out to be a husband and wife team who made a habit of listening out for travellers in trouble whenever the weather got nasty.

Unfortunately, they couldn't do anything about the nasty tempers that flared up when their Element became clear. Not only Kerrig, but what felt like every Earther in the caravan immediately became prickly and officious.

To Nesh's disgust, Kerrig made himself thoroughly unpleasant to Erben and Sanwe. (They introduced themselves in a way that sounded like one name, but Nesh thought she had it right.) After one particularly crass comment from the Earther, Nesh pulled him out into the rain and gave him a piece of her mind.

She didn't know what had made her so bold, so willing to risk his rage, unless it was that she'd reached breaking point. She was sick of her concerns being ignored, her pain being dismissed, and her experience being overlooked. Two decades of being patient broke that night in the rain, and Nesh raged at Kerrig for his stubbornness, his insensitivity to others, his inflated sense of his own victimhood, and his one-eyed view of just about everything and everyone.

With one final shot, Nesh walked away before her nerve gave out. She turned her face up to the rain to cool down before going back inside. Part of her was ashamed for being unkind to an Elemental, but a larger part was pleased to have spoken some much-needed truth.

The next day, Nesh realised that she hadn't got through to Kerrig at all. He worked all morning in an all-Earther group to dismantle the storm shelters. Afterwards, everyone packed up to move on – but the Earth Elementals all walked together near the back of the column. Nesh only picked up scraps of what they were saying, but she was sure she overheard more than one expression meant as a slur on Air Elementals.

The Earthers pulling away into their own little clique was annoying, not just because their petty behaviour made it hard to organise the camp, but because without the Earthers to provide a buffer between them, the Fire Breathers and Marshlanders were soon at each others' throats. Nesh hadn't known how bad the clannish mentality could be between Elementals of different tribes, and was a little disappointed. It was one thing to learn from her mother's historical records that the Avlem-Sidrax alliance had claimed Ashanna all the more easily for the disunity that existed between the tribes, but it was quite another to see it still going strong a century later. Had they learned nothing from their defeat? Or, at least, nothing but a glowering resentment of more civilised, organised nations? Nesh wished she could make them understand that community makes all those involved stronger.

She thought she might have the chance to make her case when they stopped in Sanwe and Erben's village to trade. In this place, Elementals, Avlem, and Sidrax lived side-by-side in peace; each culture bringing out the best in the others, and serving as a good example to curb each others' bad traits.

Here, there should be Elementals who understood the concept of serving the community with unique abilities, and Sidrax who could be more than soldiers or labouring beasts. Maybe Nesh would even find Avlem who accepted their responsibilities towards other races, instead of always looking to exploit them. She could only hope so, in a such a wonderfully diverse village as this.

It started out well enough. The caravan was made welcome, and even invited to make camp in the town square. The people were ready enough to trade, in goods as well as in coin, and Nesh was kept busy making notes of the various transactions.

She was vaguely aware of Shebbok and his family recounting their story to everyone who'd not heard it before, and many who had, but only gave it a fraction of her attention. She knew how it ended, and never knew how she was supposed to react to hearing herself praised. But when she heard Erben and Sanwe's names being mentioned instead, Nesh took more interest. How would the community take the praise of Air Walkers? It showed foresight on the part of this village to keep storm watchers, and she said so to the first local she met.

"Well, they pay their dues like everyone," he replied, in a marked Sidrax accent. "And they get work as general helpers to anyone who needs 'em. No reason to make people live outside the walls just because they're Elementals, you know. They can be really quite decent, in their own way."

Nesh blinked, which made less of a difference than it used to, but at least gave her face something to do while her brain dealt with this change in direction.

"You mean," Nesh said, feeling her way forward with care, "that Erben and Sanwe aren't employed by the town to watch for people in danger during a storm? They do that voluntarily, and then take paid work on top of that?"

"Well, of course. Why would the town pay Elementals just to live here? They've got to work, like everyone."

Nesh didn't think she'd ever been so badly disappointed in her life. She'd been so sure that this village was her ideal come true, where Elementals lived side-by-side with Sidrax and Avlem in mutual respect. But it seemed as though this village was as segregated as the rest of Ashanna.

In the end, the two Air Elementals decided to pack up their current home and travel along with the caravan for a while. Their decision did nothing to ease the tensions in the group.

Things got so bad that Nesh couldn't get her Talent to work right when it was her turn on guard duty. Whenever she tried to Find trouble, her Talent led her to the latest in-camp spat, meaning that she had to try and imagine what dangers might be lurking in the dark, and cycle through Finding them. It was so tedious that Nesh decided to try listening instead.

Which turned out to be a good thing because it meant that Nesh heard when children began to cough in their sleep. Whether it was a result of getting cold in the storm, or something in the water, several children developed fevers within a few hours.

Nesh was impressed at how quickly the Elementals began to put up shelters, low buildings made of some kind of clay. Some would serve as active hospitals, while others were for quarantined recovery, and still others for those not yet affected.

Nesh sat on a pile of blankets in the shade of Madrigal's cart and got to work. She made a list of names, with their family connections, on her tablets. She noted who was sick, and who was caring for them. Who could cook, and who could watch over the other children. Which families were directly affected, and which were able to help with organising work.

***

There was some delay in getting the shelters ready for patients, so when Kerrig came to speak with her at the end of a long day, she was not in the mood for his usual nonsense.

"Unless you're here to tell me the quarantine dens are ready, go away," she said. "Three more children have caught this sickness, and half the others are showing early signs of going the same way. I give it a few hours before we have our first adult victim, and then it's going to be chaos."

Kerrig assured her that the dens were almost ready, and encouraged Nesh to take a break. When she stood, Nesh was hit by a wave of sick dizziness. She passed it off as fatigue and went to find a meal. She absolutely refused to be the first adult victim herself.

***

Nesh and Kerrig organised a workable rota of duties. The Earther handled things well, not allowing any of his usual prejudices to interfere with the task in hand.

Nesh had been prepared to step in if he'd assigned the Air Walkers all the nastiest jobs, but he hadn't.

Kerrig might struggle to be polite, but he could, it seemed, be professional. At least, he could until he fell sick. One minute he was noting down suggestions on his slate, and the next he was on the floor in a dead faint.

With half the adults already sick, and the other half anxiously watching over their children, it took Nesh a while to find anyone to transport the delirious Earther to a bed. Once he was safely in care, Nesh tried to walk back to her desk and continue building the rota. She made it about halfway before she had to sit down. She cast about for a seat, then gave up and sat on the floor.

Just a brief rest, then she could carry on with...

She woke up in a bed, tried to get up, and passed out before she could get even one foot on the floor. The third time this happened, Nesh decided it was probably best to stop fighting it. She fell asleep and knew nothing more for several days.

By the time Nesh was conscious again, many things had happened. Nesh was the last of the patients to be allowed out of bed, which was infuriating but did at least mean that the danger period had passed. It also gave her time to catch up on the news; many things had happened while she'd been unconscious.

The most interesting, to Nesh, was the arrangements that had been made for the children. Ash had introduced a thing from Sidrea called a 'school', and was teaching the children in groups. Nesh couldn't decide if it was more or less efficient than the traditional mix of home-training and apprenticeships that she'd grown up with, but it was certainly helpful while so many parents had been too ill to look after their own children.

Meanwhile Kerrig seemed to have made some kind of peace with the Air Elementals. The way Ash told the story, they'd bonded over other Elementals being horrible about Madrigal.

Nesh was fully aware of the irony in that, but didn't share the joke with Ash. The young Sidrax was something of an innocent and had nothing but respect for Kerrig. These two men, so vastly different in age, race, and temperament; they made for an odd friendship – but not necessarily a bad one. Nesh supposed that it was no stranger than her own friendship with Traegl, though there at least it was a young Elemental looking up to an older Avlem.

Traegl did look up to her, didn't she? Nesh thought she probably did. Traegl was always polite, and that surely counted. Once she had also recovered from the illness that swept through their camp, Traegl had been very helpful, even acting as Nesh's scribe at times. The sickness had passed, but there was still plenty of organising left to do: keeping track of the food, maintaining the water roster, and replenishing the stock for trade. Having Traegl available to take dictation was a big help, especially when it allowed Nesh to rest her eyes.

⸺◇⸺

Nesh couldn't fault the care she'd had from the Elementals while she was ill, but she'd noticed a marked worsening of her vision after she'd recovered. Not only was she barely able to make out the outline of her hand in front of her face, but her headaches had progressed from dull and throbbing to sharp and piercing. They seemed to come and go with no rhyme or reason, and Nesh withdrew from all but the most essential conversations. Focusing on her work made for a good cover story, but it left her open to observation by her keen-eyed young friend.

Traegl finally brought it up one evening as they were tallying up the day's work.

"Out with it, old lady," said the young Marshlander. "You're frowning at that desk like you're trying to set it on fire. What's bothering you?"

Nesh bit back the angry 'you are' that came to her lips, and tried to banish her frown of pain.

"Just annoyed about nothing," she said, with a forced lightness of tone. "Getting into training to be a grumpy old woman." Nesh wondered if she should risk a laugh, then decided against it.

Traegl didn't reply for a while, and when she did she sounded serious. "You don't look annoyed, though," she said. "You look like Ash did when he was marching on a sprained foot."

Nesh grimaced, and Traegl laughed.

"Now you do look annoyed," she said. "Were you being stoical? Don't, it only prolongs the agony. Where are you hurt?"

Nesh tried to smile, but it felt more like a wince. "I'm not hurt," she said. "It's just a headache. How did Ash sprain his foot?"

"It was when he– Hey! Don't try to change the subject!"

Nesh smiled, and Traegl laughed again.

"Seriously though," she said. "Don't soldier on, okay? Have a moan, if nothing else. Forbid people to talk to you. Curse the sun, anything. It helps, honest."

Nesh's smile twisted. "Back in the mines that was called showing weakness," she said. "And I'd never curse the sun after being without it for so long."

Even if daylight does hurt, she thought.

Traegl gave a low whistle. "Huh, I guess the other prisoners could be pretty brutal, eh?"

Nesh nodded. "Some of them, yes. It was mostly the guards, though. Bullies in uniform."

Traegl was quiet for a moment too long, and Nesh hurried to correct her blunder.

"I don't mean you," she said. "Sorry, I forgot you were in the army yourself. I didn't mean to say you're like that."

Traegl laughed again, but it was hollow. "Of course not. I'm not really in uniform anymore, for starters."

Nesh cast about for a way out of this painful topic, and hit on a guaranteed method. "So come on now, tell me what Ash did to his foot, and why he tried to hide it."

Nesh listened to Traegl tell the story, and thought that half the caravan must have picked up on this budding romance by now. She just wasn't sure if that half included Ash and Traegl themselves.

⊷◆⊶

The whole business came to a head a few days later. In the evening, Kerrig announced that the caravan would be moving on the following morning. Most of the farmers were happy to go along with the idea, but a handful wanted to stay put and make the temporary hospital into a permanent settlement.

Some began to talk of 'the island of the Elementals' again. The Air Walker, Erben, claimed to have been to an island in the east, not Camp Freedom, that really was home to various Elementals. When he'd first mentioned it, many had been sceptical – including Nesh herself. But Erben insisted that his island was a real place.

Nesh remembered Falerian dismissing the idea of the island being in the east as a mere fantasy, arguing that 'a new dawn in the east' was unforgivably trite and clichéd. At the time, Nesh had been in a rather depressed, detached state of mind; she remembered thinking that it all sounded a bit too much like a story to be true.

Then again, Falerian had lied to them about Camp Freedom. Maybe her debunking of the island myth had been just another lie. Life was a wonderful gift, but certainly wasn't above the occasional cliché. And she had recovered some of her faith in stories since, too. What was her life now if not the most unlikely story?

Nesh barely had time to finish this thought before she heard Traegl exploding with rage.

"Oh, not that old tale again!" she said, with un-characteristic venom. "Another legendary Island where the People can pretend the world doesn't exist? It's probably just another trap – if there even is an island."

Ash said something that sounded like an attempt at soothing her, but Traegl wasn't going to be soothed.

"No, I'm allowed to be angry about this, Ash! About being stuck, trapped, by my own people. About those Air Walker soldiers making me afraid of my own El-ement, sending words into my brain until I couldn't trust my own thoughts. I get to be angry about that, and I am!"

When Ash spoke again, he was still quiet. The silence of the spectators felt suddenly conspicuous.

"Trae. when you say 'your own people', you mean...?"

This time Traegl matched Ash's restrained tone. "I mean our people, Ash. Yours and mine." Traegl sound-ed hurt now, as well as angry. "I joined the army because I believed in it. Hunting bandits, catching criminals, protecting the weak – it was like being a professional hero. But that island..." She took a deep breath, as if trying to not start shouting again. "I trusted them, and they betrayed me."

Nesh's heart twisted in sympathy, coloured with a trace of guilt. She should have realised how the Camp Freedom situation would have affected Ash and Traegl.

"But, Trae," Ash said, "you'd left the army by then. We both had. Why did you desert in the first place, if it meant so much to you?"

Nesh winced. *Was Ash really that oblivious, or just being modest?*

Traegl laughed uneasily, seemed on the brink of a confession, then hesitated. The next thing Nesh knew, Traegl had rushed past her and away into the night. Now it was Ash's turn to hesitate. After an awkward silence, he stammered something about making sure she didn't get lost in the dark, and raced off after her.

Nesh was pleased that her friends had finally got their feelings out into the open, though perhaps rather more publicly than they might have liked.

⸻ ◆ ⸻

The caravan moved in the morning, with most of the farmers eager to sell their wares in the next town. Nesh, however, was not so pleased. In visiting Sanwe and Erben's village, she'd been able to hide in the crowd and make herself useful out of sight. But their next destination promised to be a larger settlement. Newharbour was one of the earliest Avlem towns in Ashanna. Nesh dreaded the inevitable meeting with other Avlem and the impossibility of even introducing herself.

What would her fellow Avlem make of her single name? Would they guess her disgrace, or would they think it an affectation? Either way, she would be despised. Not that being despised was a new experience, but it wasn't one that improved on acquaintance.

It seemed unfair to be so utterly cut off from her people, and yet still care so much what they thought of her.

⸺◦⸺

When they arrived, Nesh kept her mind and hands busy with setting up their stall. She took so comfortably to directing the operation that she asked one of the farmers to run an errand, as a matter of course.

"Hi, you there. Are you free?" she asked, noticing a farmer standing around and chatting with his neighbour. "We need cordage, at least twenty lengths, preferably more. Barter for it if you have to, but not too generously. We need to turn a profit on this trip if we're going to buy the supplies we need to go on."

The farmer was Balmar, and he objected loudly to being 'dictated to' by 'some Avlem'. Kerrig took him aside, and Nesh heard no more about it. She did wonder how many Elementals were giving her dirty looks, though.

Their first customers arrived soon enough, and Nesh was forced to make conversation. The early morning rush was bearable; people were mostly in a hurry to get through their business and move along. Yarn skeins, pats of butter, and other everyday items were sold to this busy crowd.

The trouble started afterwards, once the casual shoppers came by. They liked to take their time over their purchases, and made conversation while they made up their minds.

"You've got an impressive outfit here, my dear," said one such browser. "But doesn't it get difficult running all this by yourself?"

Nesh blinked, unsure how to answer for the moment. She hadn't thought how it would look, one Avlem with two Sidrax and a crowd of Elementals. Of course, people would assume she was in charge. Under normal circumstances, she probably would be. But how to explain...?

"Oh, I don't have to do very much at all," Nesh said, after slightly too long a pause. "There are several very senior Elementals to keep order, and my Sidrax friend, Ash, to keep us safe on the road."

Nesh realised her mistake too late.

"A Sidrax 'friend', indeed?" said the other woman, archly. She looked about her for a moment, then sniffed. "I think I see him. Rather young for you, don't you think? Unless they can hide that kind of thing with their... abilities."

Nesh flinched. She could almost hear the narrowed eyes, the curled lip, and the arched eyebrow. She was saved from having to reply by Traegl interrupting, sharply.

"He is, however, exactly the right age for me," she said. "Everything alright here, Nesh?"

Nesh was torn between relief and mortification. It was like Traegl to leap in when her friends were being attacked but still...

"'*Nesh*'?" It was practically a screech. "And what kind of a name is that for any self-respecting Avlem? Is that a sop to your Elementals, taking a name like theirs?"

Nesh could feel her face burning, though whether from rage or shame she could not tell.

"My name," she said, speaking carefully to prevent her emotions from spilling forth, "is Nesh. I'm here with this caravan to trade, like the rest of these people. If you don't want to do business with us, may I ask you to move along and make way for those who do?"

The Avlem woman scoffed and stalked off, leaving a "Well, I never!" in her wake.

Traegl watched her go, then clapped Nesh on the shoulder. "Good for you, Nesh. That's telling her," she said. "Who made her the name police, anyway?"

It occurred to Nesh that while she could indeed hear the sneering looks from the locals, she could also hear her friend's smile.

Not far from the town there was a good crossing to a large island, just off the east coast. According to the locals, many Elementals had settled there when the mainland got 'too civilised for them'.

As word got around, everyone had to decide whether they would travel to the island, or stay on in Newharbour. Nesh lay awake for hours and thought over her options. They weren't many, and none exactly ideal, but she had to choose.

Stay in Newharbour and try to get work as a Finder? Or some other work, that wasn't covered by a local Talent? The problem was identifying such a job, and then claiming it in a way that wouldn't offend her future neighbours. Even if she did use her Talent to Find and fill a gap in the market, wouldn't that imply that Newhaven was unable to meet its own needs? As Nesh understood it, Town Elders were in charge of organising that sort of thing. Stepping on their toes didn't seem to be the best way to start life in Newhaven.

So, if not here, where? The caravan wasn't likely to continue past this point, and she could hardly head out alone and fend for herself in the Fire Plains. The safest thing would be to stay with Ash and Traegl, except that they were almost certainly going to the island. Kerrig was going. Madrigal would follow her beloved Earther to Life's own Garden and beyond. Ash was taking his role as Madrigal's teacher seriously and would go wherever she went, and Traegl would go with Ash. All of which left Nesh no real choice but to cross the water with them and hope for the best.

Hope that there would be somewhere for 'Outsiders' to live. Hope that the resident Elementals wouldn't bar them from landing. Hope that she would be allowed to go along in the first place.

The caravan was camping outside Newharbour itself, and one evening the people interested in crossing to the island all gathered on the shore. Nesh tried to blend into the crowd, but Kerrig picked her out all the same.

"What are you doing here?" Kerrig said. "This is the last Avlem town. We're well away from anyone who could know about your... whatever happened to you."

Nesh almost smiled at this clumsy attempt at tact, but didn't interrupt or explain. Kerrig hesitated, then said,

"I don't even know if the caravan is going to exist after we reach the island, not when everyone can settle down with their own kind. This is your last chance to be with your people."

"I know all that," said Nesh. She made an effort and kept the irritation out of her voice. "You still don't understand, do you?" she said, a trace of bitterness creeping in. "I can't so much as introduce myself to another Avlem without revealing my past. It's in my name – or the lack of it. With Elementals, I can be just 'Nesh', and that's enough. Among Avlem, it will never be enough."

"So use your old name," Kerrig suggested. "You remember it, don't you? No-one here knows it was taken away, or removed, or whatever. You don't have to be just 'Nesh' if you don't want to."

Nesh felt the familiar refrain start up again... *He's only an Elemental, he doesn't understand...* before wondering if she ought to try and help him understand, instead of accepting ignorance as inevitable.

So she said, "Look, everyone knows about the Earthers' Great Sanctuary getting turned into prison mines, right? And when you tell people where you're from, they know about your life there. So, why don't you call yourself 'Kerrig of the Crystal Caverns', or even just 'Kerrig'? Every time we meet new people, you give your name as 'Kerrig, Earther of the Great Sanctuary'. Why?"

"That's my name," said the Earther, sounding confused. "I can't just decide to change my... alright, alright, I think I understand. But I'm not ashamed of my life in the mines, you know," he added.

"I'm not exactly ashamed, either," Nesh said, "but it changes how people look at you. And a person can get tired of those looks."

Kerrig and Nesh rejoined the others, who were discussing ideas for how to get to the island. The most obvious: hiring boats from Newharbour, proved too expensive even after their trading success. Those who owned boats claimed that it was peak fishing season and every hour spent as a ferry was worth four as a fishing boat. Nesh suspected that this was nonsense, and the fishing captains simply wanted to justify their outrageous prices. Still, she held back, unwilling to interfere unless absolutely necessary.

Her attempts at staying inconspicuous, however, were ruined by the woman who had lost her spindle, and been so impressed by Nesh's Finding it for her.

"Come along with me," she said. "I've got a bone to pick with that there Kerrig, and so do you – or you should have."

Nesh wanted to ask the woman what she was talking about, but it was too late. She'd been pulled to her feet and prodded forward. Presumably they were headed to where Kerrig was, so she used her Talent to Find him and walked ahead under her own power. She didn't like being poked and driven along, even if it was by her 'champion'.

"What's the big secret over here?" called out the Elemental woman, before Nesh could say anything. "Is it anything to do with getting us all to the island? And, if so, why haven't you invited any Fire Breathers to participate? There are still a few of us here, you know – we didn't all run off after that foolish dream of a new settlement."

Nesh tried to keep walking, to distance herself from the row that was about to erupt, but when Kerrig replied, it surprised her so much that she stopped dead.

"We're going over water, though," he said, sounding puzzled but not defensive. And when he asked, 'how can Fire Breathers help?' it felt like a sincere question rather than a sarcastic one.

"By reminding you that some of us were traders along the river before we got trapped in that miserable 'Camp Freedom'." said Nesh's new friend, who sounded as if she were out of poking distance this time. "The sea, in case you didn't know, *Earther*, is cold. We Fire Breathers don't just make pretty flames you know – we're experts at heat control. However you're planning to get across this bit of sea, you'll need us Fire Breathers involved if you don't want to freeze."

Surely this display of rudeness would push the man over the edge? Nesh braced herself for an explosion, but Kerrig backed down at once. He even apologised for leaving the Fire Breathers out. It seemed that the danger had passed, and Nesh had just started to relax when she felt herself being poked forward again.

"You should have asked this lady, too," insisted Nesh's new agent. "Her Talent is perfect for a situation like this."

"It is?" Kerrig said, not unkindly.

It is? thought Nesh. *How?*

Then Kerrig was asking what her Talent was, and she realised that she'd never told him. Nesh rambled for a moment as she tried to apply Finding to a sea crossing despite never having seen the sea in her life. She Found an answer just in time, and offered to use her Talent to Find the safest path for their boat (did they even have a boat?) and look out for hidden rocks or dangerous currents.

Then, because she had no idea what they were planning and didn't want to keep asking questions, she added, "The more I know about what you're looking for, the more accurately I can Find a solution."

Kerrig seemed nonplussed by this news, but not displeased. He just said, "Oh. Good to know," and made space in his circle for Nesh and a couple of Fire Breathers.

— ◆ —

The discussion lasted long into the night. The ideas tossed around ranged from the completely impractical ("Why don't the Earthers and Marshlanders make a path, like they did in the river?") to the unnecessarily complicated ("What if we take the wheels off the cart, and attach all our blankets like a big sail, and get the Fire Breathers and Air Walkers to fly it over?").

The following morning, it was decided that Madrigal's cart should be broken up into planks, the planks packed out with soil, sand, and seaweed, and the whole thing baked solid by Earthers and Fire Breathers. It was a flimsy enough platform, which had to be held together by the Earthers while the Marshlanders moved it through the water. The Air Walkers and Fire Breathers kept the children safe and warm in the middle of the make-shift raft, while Nesh was given a spot up front from which to direct the journey.

It was too noisy to attempt verbal directions, so Nesh relied mostly on pointing. Her arms ached before they were halfway to the island, and she took to holding one arm up with the other. After decades of swinging a pick, Nesh was horrified at how exhausting it was to simply hold out an arm.

Just around the time that Nesh thought she would have to beg for a break, she felt the mood change on board. The people either side of her started to murmur with curiosity, then excitement. Someone clapped Nesh on the shoulder and said, "Look! Look!" which was extremely unhelpful.

Another voice said, "I count eight. Two of each, do you think?"

"Probably. A better welcome than none, anyway."

The wind, which had never been too strong thanks to the efforts of the Air Elementals, suddenly died completely. A cheer went up, and Nesh gathered that some Air Elementals on the shore had reached out to help. Then the raft lurched forward, causing Nesh to stagger and nearly fall. Someone caught her shoulders and helped steady her. It turned out to be Ash.

"Seems we're not needed on lookout anymore," he said. "The locals are taking over."

The raft crunched up a causeway, and the water briefly flowed over it before retreating to the sea. Nesh heard cries of welcome as each Element called to its own.

"Marshlanders, over here!"

"Earthers, welcome!"

"Fire Breathers, join us!"

"Air Walkers? Excellent — this way!"

The various Elementals streamed away, each in their own direction. Eventually, Ash and Nesh were left on the beach, with Madrigal in her child form holding onto them both.

"Where do we go?" she said. "Where's my Stony-Man, and the Marshy Lady?"

Nesh's heart sank. She tried to Find them, but they were moving away from the beach at a fast pace.

"Let's find somewhere to settle," said Ash. "And when they've finished saying hello to our neighbours, they can come home to a nice dinner."

Finding. Right, yes. Nesh could Find them shelter for the night, and everything could be sorted out in the morning.

There wasn't much to Find on the island that didn't already belong to someone. Nesh tried 'abandoned house', then 'unused shelter', and finally 'complete building' before she was able to triangulate a safe place for them.

It was a cabin of sorts, something that might have been a fisherman's once, but which Ash confirmed was completely unused.

"There's weeds in the fireplace, and moss on almost every surface," he said. "We'll be weeks scrubbing it out, but the structure's sound enough."

Getting a fire started was tedious work without Volnar to help, and Nesh had to Find a water source before she could begin on dinner. Madrigal and Ash went foraging, and came back with enough for a couple of meals.

Ash had found some kind of springy branches and twigs from which he made panniers for all three of them. A broad frame to go over Madrigal's back, and two slimmer ones to fit on his and Nesh's shoulders.

"I think ours are technically 'yokes'," he said, "but the idea is to carry what we find on our trips with the minimum amount of fuss, so it all comes to the same thing in the end."

It took a lot of work for them to have something liveable by the time night fell, but they managed. In the darkness, Nesh breathed deeply and let herself relax into her makeshift bed. She had a home. It wasn't much, and would take a lot of work to make it comfortable before the winter rains arrived, but it was her place to stay.

For the first time in many, many years, Nesh thought she could see a future.

⚜

Kerrig and Traegl visited several times, separately, over the next few days. Their visits were pleasant, but neither seemed to remember that their non-Elemental friends had been forgotten on arrival and left to fend for themselves.

Nesh couldn't find, or even Find, a way to bring it up that didn't sound like whining. The more she played it over in her head, the more she thought she sounded like Kerrig at his worst, airing his people's grievances.

It was probably best to let it go. Anyway, Nesh was enduring another series of headaches, each one starting as the last began to ease off, and she didn't have the energy to start any arguments. Instead, she elected to sit with her eyes closed and listen to the others talk. It was better than dwelling on her own misfortunes.

Traegl seemed unhappy in her Marshlanders-only home. This was hardly a surprise, but it was interesting to hear the young woman's take on it. In Camp Freedom, Traegl had been rejected by the Marshlanders before she could choose; even in her grandparents' village, the decision to leave had been made for her. Here, though, she was offered a traditional-sounding home amongst her own kind. At least, Nesh assumed that 'weaving grass huts' meant living in a traditional house. Maybe it was a Water Elemental saying. Whatever it was, Traegl didn't like it.

"You've settled nicely here," she said, on her fourth visit in as many days. "I'm glad you've got somewhere. Is there... you know, plenty of space?"

Nesh gestured around at the open air, and Ash must have nodded or something because Traegl said, "Oh good. Maybe, once you're settled, it would be alright if I came here to live? I mean, I'll be with Nesh and Maddie, not... you know..."

Nesh waited for Ash to help Traegl out of her embarrassed tail-off, but he seemed to be in the same fix. After what felt like far too long, Nesh made herself say, "Of course, Traegl. You're welcome here, you know that. We don't really have bedrooms yet, but you can pitch your roll beside our fire whenever you like."

Kerrig's visits were chiefly to see Madrigal, who was always pleased to see him, of course. Kerrig seemed to genuinely like being around the little Sidrax these days. From the way he brought news, Nesh got the impression that he was trying to stay in touch with as many people as possible – which she thought was nice, but a bit unusual. The Earther had never struck her as a particularly sociable person, yet here he was going out of his way to talk to people all over this island.

He even approved of Ash, if his comments on his relationship with Traegl were anything to go by, though he knew that they would meet some people with, as he put it, 'opinions'.

"And what's your 'opinion'?" Nesh asked, amused.

Kerrig sighed, then said, "I'm happy for them. Really. Even if it does mean I'm no longer considered an Earther."

He seemed to have let that last slip without meaning to, but Nesh couldn't pretend she hadn't heard. It had been bad enough to see Traegl rejected by her family, but to be rejected by an entire tribe... Nesh shrank from the thought. No matter what she'd done, no-one had ever declared her to be not an Avlem.

"Go on," she said, as gently as she could. "Who says you're not an Earther?"

"No-one has actually declared it yet," Kerrig said. "But I've been warned about my 'un-Eartherly behaviour', and reminded that only Earthers may live in our village. That is, only people the chiefs consider to be sufficiently..."

He stopped himself abruptly. "No, that's bitterness talking. They mean well, and they've only got this far by protecting themselves on all sides. I just wish I could convince them that they don't need to protect themselves from, well, *me*."

Nesh didn't reply right away, partly horrified by Kerrig's situation and partly stunned to realise how deeply she empathised. One thing needed to be said, however, before she could let the matter drop.

"Kerrig, I'm not going to try and tell you what to do," she said. "But, your chiefs calling you 'no longer an Earther', that sounds a bit like what happened to me. And I don't want that to happen to you if I can help it. So, if you have to stop coming here, or if we 'Outsiders' have to leave this island, then that's how it will be. I know how much it means to you, being with your own people."

She expected Kerrig to either argue (out of politeness), agree and leave (out of expediency), or take offence and storm off (out of his usual practice of putting the worst possible interpretation on everything that came from an Outsider's mouth). Instead, he asked Nesh the one thing no-one had ever asked before.

"Do you regret it?"

"What?"

"Whatever it was you did that got you banished, or disowned, or whatever. Would you still have done it, knowing the consequences?"

Nesh considered the question carefully. In the long years of her imprisonment, she had often regretted helping Gles and his fellow bandits to escape from the mines. She'd also regretted her over-confidence at her trial in the Citadel, wondering if she might have won her case with different words or a different approach. But she would still have spoken up to stop the guard from beating Gles while he worked. And she had never regretted going after Olvar Harreal for his work-village scheme.

"No," she said at last. "I don't regret it. I could perhaps have been more careful, but my 'crime'? The reason I was sent to the mines in the first place? I would do it again in a heartbeat. It was the right thing to do."

"Then you understand my position," Kerrig said. "I've spent my life wishing for someone to turn back time, put things back to how they used to be, but now... the Land I've seen this year can't go any way but forward, and it's foolish to try and hide from that." He chuckled and added, "I could probably have been more careful myself, rather than calling the assembled Earther chiefs weak to their faces."

Nesh had to stop herself from gasping like a teenager. "You said that?" she asked, stunned.

"I was talking about myself really, but I suppose it sounded pretty bad," Kerrig said. "And I may have implied that I wasn't going to fix their problems for them, and they should get off their backsides and sort things out for themselves."

He dropped his head into his hands and groaned quietly. "I'm going to get banished, I just know it. Me and my big mouth. This is why I stopped talking to the guards and prisoners back in the Mines – I'd say what I really thought, and get beaten up for it."

Nesh snorted. "You've never had a problem telling me what was on your mind," she said.

Kerrig gave a small cough that might have been a laugh.

"You weren't scary enough," he said. "Just annoying."

"And right," Nesh added. "Well, mostly."

"Like I said: annoying."

The repartee caught Nesh completely unawares. She laughed out loud and punched Kerrig lightly on the arm. "Did you always have a sense of humour under that crusty shell?" she said.

But Kerrig wasn't laughing anymore. He sounded confused, and seemed to be hunched over.

"How did you do that?" he asked. "My arm's gone to sleep, and all you did was tap me on the shoulder."

Nesh quirked an eyebrow at him. "Just proving a point. I can be scary enough when I need to be; I just Find the best place to land a hit."

"Alright, you're scary," Kerrig acknowledged. "I'm glad none of the guards had that Talent, back when I was still mouthing off at them."

"You're missing the point, Kerrig. Again." Nesh gave him a wry smile. "I could have done that, and worse, at any time. You've been downright idiotic sometimes, and I've been sorely tempted to try and smack some sense into your head more than once. But I didn't, because that's not who I am. So you can go on speaking your mind without fear. And, if the worst happens, you can always come and live with us. Traegl's already as good as moved in, and one more won't make any difference."

Madrigal, who had wandered off to make shapes, came running back at that.

"Yes, stay here!" she said, reverting to her child-shape to hug Kerrig properly. "My Stony-Man, and Nesh-Lady, and Teacher-Ash, and me, all together. And the Marshy-Lady too. She's nice."

Kerrig laughed and hugged her back. "Alright, Little One, I'll stay for a while. But you know I'll always be your Stony-Man, no matter where I live."

"I know," sighed Madrigal, happily.

———◆———

Kerrig didn't move in at once but did visit daily for a fortnight. Madrigal was delighted. She split her days between lessons with Ash in the morning and showing Kerrig what she'd learned in the afternoon.

"Come early tomorrow, see my lessons?" Madrigal begged one evening. "Or, or... oh! Stay! Stay tonight, have the morning here too. Please?"

Kerrig didn't answer at first, but when he did he sounded strangely emotional.

"I have to work in the mornings, Maddie," he said. "I have jobs in the village. You don't want the chiefs to be cross with me, do you? But I always work fast, so I can come and see you as soon as possible."

Madrigal sounded unsure, but eventually replied with, "You do come tomorrow, though? Like always?"

"Like always," Kerrig agreed, sounding much happier. "Will you come and walk back with me?"

"Like always," Madrigal echoed, as if the last two weeks had been twenty years of unbroken routine. Nesh envied the child her ability to adapt so quickly. Or maybe it was a Sidrax thing – Ash never seemed to have trouble adjusting to change, either.

<hr>

The next day saw Madrigal trotting off to meet Kerrig as usual, straight after finishing her lesson with Ash. But instead of returning as usual in her girl shape, chattering away to her Stony-Man, Madrigal returned alone, sounding subdued.

"He said his chiefs wanted a word with him," Madrigal reported carefully. "And I should tell Nesh-lady, 'Nesh will understand.' Do you, Nesh?"

Her heart sank. Nesh thought she could guess what kind of 'word' Kerrig's chiefs wanted with him. Was it better to get that kind of news in a letter, as she had, or to be told to your face that you were being cut out from your community? Nesh couldn't answer that, but one thing she could do was be there for him. Remind him that he still had somewhere to call home, and people to belong to.

IV

Nesh walked as quickly as she dared, using her Talent alternately to Find her direction and to Find where to step. The noonday sun stabbed at her even through screwed-up eyes, and she struggled to hear her Talent over the pounding headache. As she entered the Earther village, Nesh took a moment to stand in the shade and breathe. She tried to ignore the pain and remember why she'd come. It would hardly be a comfort for Kerrig to be met with a scowl, after all.

Standing there, Nesh became aware of voices on the other side of the wall. She was just about to move away to avoid eavesdropping when she heard someone inside say, in a scornful voice, "...rampage through the Land, burning Outsider villages to the ground."

Nesh's breath caught in her throat. She had a sudden image of Perayen wreathed in flames, the people she'd grown up with driven like cattle by rioters...

She became aware of the voices again and listened, hoping to hear someone speak out against this terrible idea.

"...monstrosity of a Citadel. Surely you don't support the Outsiders ruling over our Land? You want to see the People free to govern themselves again, don't you?"

Nesh felt disgust, mixed with relief. Politics! Bitter, twisted bigots whipping each other up into a fervour of debate, then agreeing to meet next month to talk the whole thing out again. Nasty talk, but only talk.

Her relief lasted for less time than it takes to tell of it, because the next voice she heard was Kerrig's.

"Well, of course I do."

Kerrig agreed with them.

After everything she thought she knew about him. Nesh had really believed that the stubborn old fool had given up his mistaken ideas about 'Outsiders' and 'People'. And he had seemed so fond of Madrigal. How could he?

Nesh's fury added to the pain in her head until she thought she would split into two pieces. When she could hear again, another voice was speaking.

"We'll head to neutral ground to work out the details. Kerrig, you'll be there to represent your travelling caravan and to advise on working with multiple Elements. The best place would be where your Outsider friends have made a temporary camp. Naturally, we'll wait for them to leave. Will they be gone in a day or so, do you think?"

Kerrig, wonder of wonders, had an objection to this idea. Not to burning down the Citadel, mind. Just to this part of the plan.

"They've settled there," he said. "And I don't think they're planning to leave. When we arrived, you told me no-one was using that piece of land."

"It wasn't being used then, but now we need it. You understand that, don't you? In the interests of peace?"

Kerrig's brief moment of standing up for non-Elementals fizzled out. "I'll go and talk to them," he said.

Nesh heard him leave the hut and stood up to meet him.

"Hello, Nesh," said Kerrig. He sounded almost pleased to see her, which froze Nesh where she stood. How dare he? "Have you been waiting long?" he asked, as if nothing had happened.

"Not at all," replied the Avlem, icily. "I got here just in time to hear all about how you're going to drive out the invaders, and how you're going to talk to us about giving up our new home because your leaders need a place to discuss the best way to go to war with our leaders."

Kerrig protested, but Nesh knew what she'd heard.

"I suppose I should congratulate you on still being an Earther," she said. "Don't worry about talking to us, we'll be leaving this island as soon as I can Find a way." She turned and walked off, then looked back over her shoulder. "I'll tell Madrigal you said goodbye. Traegl will probably come with us, so give her any messages you have for Ash or Madrigal."

"Nesh, wait – I'll come and talk to them myself."

Kerrig started after her, but the Avlem held up her fists. "Don't make me stop you, Earther," she said. "You people put us 'Outsiders' aside because we're not welcome in your homes. And now, you're not welcome in ours. Go back to your war, Kerrig of the Last Sanctuary. You never really left it."

<hr>

"Pack up, we're leaving."

Nesh didn't have the energy to argue and was in no mood to deal with questions.

"What? Leaving? Why?"

"We've been kicked out."

"But where are we going to go?"

"Somewhere else."

"But where?"

"Is Kerrig coming too?"

"No!" The ice-cold fury in Nesh's voice gave them all pause – including Nesh herself.

"I mean, no," she said, deliberately calm. "No, he's not coming. As for where... I'll Find a place. But we have to go tonight. Believe me, you don't want to be here when the chiefs arrive."

Nesh wanted to sink to the ground and weep, with pain, with frustration, with sheer exhaustion. How was she going to do this by herself? She couldn't keep Madrigal from running off after Kerrig when they left the mines, how was she going to–"

"You're not Finding, or doing anything else, until you've eaten something," said Traegl.

Nesh hadn't even known she was there. She thought she could still make out the shapes of people, even if they did all look like stumpy trees these days. Sooner or later, she might not even be able to see that much. She allowed Traegl to usher her to a seat and tried to look as though she was relaxing even while her mind was racing.

Nesh ate without once being aware of the taste. She tried to come up with ways to not be surprised like that again. This time, it had been a friend; next time, she might not be so lucky.

They left their cabin and spent that night on the beach where they'd landed – the beach where Kerrig had first abandoned them. It felt appropriate, though Nesh recognised the bitterness even as she thought it.

While Ash and Traegl made a campsite in the shelter of some dunes, Madrigal and Nesh went beachcombing. For a moment, Nesh thought that their original raft might still get them to the mainland, with Traegl to steer and herself to direct. But all that remained were a handful of rotten planks that gave way under Madrigal's hooves.

So much for that idea.

Nesh knew that they had to get off the island, but she couldn't think how. She lay awake long into the night, trying to Find solutions to her various problems, but the problems were all too abstract. 'Get to the mainland' wasn't a lost sock; she couldn't expect an answer to appear in her mind just like that. And as for 'know who is around me', well... short of trying to Find every individual that might be in the area, Nesh could think of nothing.

She appeared to have reached the limits of her Talent, and she had no idea what else to try.

"You are more than your Talent." That's what Zirpa had told her, all those many months ago. She'd struggled with the concept at the time, and still had trouble with it now, but it gave her the faintest glimmer of hope that a solution existed. If she couldn't Find it with her Talent, perhaps she could come up with answers in a different way.

It wasn't much, but it was enough to let Nesh get a few hours of sleep before dawn.

<hr>

"Bad night?" Traegl asked her the following morning.

She sat herself down beside Nesh, both of them facing out towards the sea.

"Sleeping on sand can be hard at first. You have to dig down a bit to make sure you're not putting your bedroll on something sharp-edged – or even just an uneven layer of pebbles. Oh, and definitely make sure there's nothing alive under the bed before going to sleep. And nothing dead, either. Trust me, not an experience you want twice."

Nesh almost smiled. Despite everything, Traegl was still Traegl. Chatty and cheerful, and completely, honestly, kind.

"It's more than a bad bed though, isn't it?" Traegl went on. "You've got something on your mind. Can I help at all?"

Oh, yes. Observant, too. Nesh didn't know how to even start explaining, but she wanted to try. It wasn't fair to dismiss her young friend's offer even though Nesh was sure that Traegl couldn't help. Not by herself. How could one Water Elemental hold back the sea?

Nesh took one deep, slow breath in and out, to make sure she wouldn't lose it as soon as she opened her mouth. Neither shouting nor crying would be helpful. Nesh had lost a lot in the last day, but she still had her dignity.

"I do have a lot on my mind," she admitted, speaking carefully and with deliberate control. "We need a way over to the mainland, somewhere to live, a way to support ourselves, and to keep away from attention at the same time. There's Madrigal to consider, and I don't know how I'm going to explain all this to her. And on top of all that, there's my... headaches," Nesh said.

She'd forgotten for a moment that she was talking to Traegl, and not just thinking aloud. She'd almost said, "There's my eyesight."

Traegl didn't answer right away. For a moment Nesh wondered if perhaps she had been talking to herself after all. She reached instinctively for her Talent to check if the other woman was still there, then changed her mind and used her ears instead.

Calming her own body, she listened for movements beside her. There! Breathing, and hands on the sand. Nesh was so pleased with this experiment in situational awareness that she was startled when Traegl spoke at last.

"That's a lot to do and no mistake," Traegl said, and it took Nesh a moment to remember what they were talking about. "I'm not surprised you had trouble sleeping, not if you spent the night trying to solve all our current problems. But why does it have to be you doing it all?"

Nesh hesitated. She didn't want to be in charge but, well...

"I'm the oldest," she said. *And the only Avlem*, she thought, but she could hardly say that to Traegl's face. "I feel responsible. After all, I'm the one who made the decision to leave our home here."

"As for that, I see you more as the messenger than the decision maker," said Traegl. "It was the local chiefs who kicked us out, not you." Traegl yawned and stretched. "I don't think age matters that much, either," she said. "Not among adults. There are three adults here; we can stand to share a bit of responsibility between us. Stops there being too much pressure on any one set of shoulders."

Nesh blushed. "I'm sorry," she said. "I should have realised that Ash – that you – might have experience with taking command. I didn't mean to talk over you."

"Command?!" Traegl sounded horrified. "I've never commanded anyone. I don't want to start now."

Traegl raised her voice and called, "Ash – Ash? Come here a minute. Do you want to be in charge of our little group? Take command, as it were?"

Footsteps approached, dull thuds in dry sand. "Do I what?" said Ash.

Traegl repeated the question.

"Command? Me? No, thank you. Nesh, please keep on doing what you're doing. You tell us what to do, and we'll do it. Right, Trae?"

"Exactly."

"But I don't know what to tell you!" Nesh said, forgetting to sound calm and controlled.

"Of course you do," Traegl replied. "You said it before: Get to the mainland, set up a base, organise supplies, take good care of Maddie. So that's what we'll do next."

"But how? I don't know where to start," Nesh said, then bit her lips hard to prevent further whining. She sounded like a sulky child, not a grown woman!

"Oh, Ash and I'll deal with the how," Traegl assured her. "Commanders think about what needs doing, and we grunts get it done. Though, if I might make a suggestion – let's have something to eat before doing anything else."

Nesh was thoughtful over breakfast, but she wasn't dwelling on the future. She was trying to remember what her parents had done to run their house and work. They gave orders about outcomes, not about every step. Even when dealing with other Avlem, you asked a person to use their Talent to make or do what you needed. No Avlem had ever tried to tell her how to Find, only what they wanted her to Find for them.

So it was right, she supposed, to say to Ash and Traegl, "Get us to the mainland," without having to know how they would do it. She trusted them to tell her if what she asked for was impossible. Perhaps it was best to think of these youngsters as having a talent for survival and transport. Not quite like a real Talent, of course, but close enough.

Nesh finished eating and decided to practise listening again. She heard the distant but distinctive sound of Madrigal grazing, and the muted murmur of Ash and Traegl's conversation. The sea pushed against the shore away to her left and made it harder to make out details from that direction. Nesh didn't know how much time she would spend near the sea, but it might be good practice to get used to the sounds.

She got up and used her Talent to guide her steps along the beach. The sounds were interesting, and she could see enough to notice the sun, bright on the water. What struck Nesh the most, however, were the smells. She breathed deeply and tried to pick them out one by one. Salt water, seaweed, and many more things that she didn't have a name for. Well, she didn't need names so long as she could remember the scent. All these things were the smell of the sea, and she tried to fix the sense memory in her mind.

Nesh walked and walked, trusting her footsteps to her Talent. Then it occurred to her that she might try how much information she could get just through the soles of her feet. Beyond her usual skimming step, feeling for obstacles, could she learn about her path on touch and sound alone?

Experimenting in this way took up the whole morning, and Nesh only realised how much time had passed when she became aware of the sun beating hot on the top of her head, rather than coming sideways into her eyes. The sea was still at her side, meaning that getting back would be simple enough. But that didn't change the fact that, right now, Nesh had no idea where she was.

She used her Talent to Find a place to rest before heading back and listened to her surroundings. There was the sea, the wind in the grass, and... someone breathing.

This was no time for experimenting. Nesh asked her Talent to Find the nearest person and got confirmation immediately. There was someone close enough to speak to, though they hadn't spoken yet. Perhaps they wanted to be left alone? Or perhaps it looked as though she was ignoring them?

Nesh decided to nod politely and leave it at that. If the other person wanted to talk, they could. If they wanted peace and quiet, then she'd been polite.

Nesh nodded politely. The person spoke.

———◆———

"I thought you'd left," said Kerrig. "I'm glad you're still here."

"Really?" Nesh said, coolly, while her thoughts raced. "I didn't know you cared. We Found a place to stay, for now. Until someone comes to move us along, at least."

Kerrig's temper, which Nesh thought she'd seen the last of, suddenly reappeared.

"Yes, I imagine it wasn't too nice to be kicked out of your home for someone else's convenience," he said, nastily. "Not that the People would know anything about that, of course. What a unique and distressing experience that must have been!"

Nesh felt a tiny stab of guilt, but quashed it hurriedly. Two wrongs didn't make a right, she reminded herself, and let all of her tiredness and frustration fill her answer.

"Not this again," she said. "Don't you ever get tired of hearing yourself complain? And what are you doing out here, anyway? Shouldn't you be at the War Council meeting? Sitting on Madrigal's old bed and working out how you're going to destroy her family?"

"Oh, for the love of... We're not going to destroy anyone's family," Kerrig said. "This is about the Citadel, the ruling elite. We're just taking back what's ours, and showing the Governors they can't push the People around any longer!"

"So, you only want to take down the Citadel?"

"Yes!"

"The Citadel where Volnar lives?"

"Yes! I mean, no – not Volnar's home, of course. This isn't about the ordinary citizens, it's about justice. You need to see the bigger picture!"

"The 'bigger picture' gets people killed," Nesh retorted, and they argued back and forth in this manner until Kerrig upped and left – fortunately not in the same direction as Nesh wanted to go.

She got up and walked away slowly, worried by this latest development. If she couldn't convince the one Earther she really knew to give up on the idea of fighting the Citadel, how could she hope to convince anyone else?

But if she didn't, there was going to be a fight. And no-one would come out of that well, no matter how noble their intentions.

⊸◆⊷

Nesh hurried back to their temporary camp, using her Talent freely and not stopping to experiment with her other senses. She switched between Finding a safe path to walk and Finding Ash and Traegl. Traegl seemed to get closer much faster than Ash did, though. Nesh might have been puzzled by this if she'd had time to think about it. As it was, she simply stopped Finding Ash and concentrated on Traegl.

"Where have you been?"

Traegl sounded equal parts angry and concerned. Nesh was confused, then embarrassed.

"Did I not say before I went for a walk?" she said, then answered herself at once. "No, I remember now. I didn't mean to go far, but... I'm sorry. But, there's no real danger around at the moment, is there? Why were you so worried?"

"'No danger'? Of course there's danger!" Traegl was almost shouting now. "Members of all four tribes are in one place, talking about how to wage some kind of war – do you have any idea how easily that could get dangerous? What if they fall out and start fighting amongst themselves? What if one of them happened across you and decided to make an example of the Outsider? Even just a bit of showing off might have hurt you if you didn't see it coming, or they didn't know you were there. I've been staying close to Maddie all day, for this exact reason. Maybe I should have been watching you, too."

Nesh wanted to be angry herself at this lecture, but she had to admit that there was some truth to what Traegl was saying. She thought about trying to explain or justify her behaviour, but decided to simply apologise instead. After all, she had news for them.

They needed to know that the attack on the Citadel was likely to go ahead, and that Kerrig would likely be part of it. Getting to the mainland was more important than ever, as was finding a way to explain the situation to Madrigal. It hurt Nesh's heart to even think about it. How do you tell a trusting, happy child that their hero had become a monster?

⸻ ◆ ⸻

Traegl and Nesh worked on dinner together, as they had the night before. Madrigal came over while they were working, and showed Traegl some berries.

"Are these good for eating?" she asked.

Traegl examined them carefully, then declared them safe.

"Well done for checking before you ate them," she told Madrigal. "Very sensible of you."

"Teacher Ash says always ask," Madrigal replied, between berries. "And he's not here, so I ask you. He says you know what's good."

"He said that?" Traegl asked, sounding pleased but unsure. "Wow, that's really nice of him. And a big compliment, if you knew him back in training. That guy takes foraging very seriously."

"It's very important," Madrigal said, sounding serious as only a child can. "If you get it wrong, you go dead. Better to go hungry than go dead. That's what he says."

"Very right too," said Nesh.

"Where is Ash, anyway?" she asked, moving her head as if looking around. He couldn't have simply wandered off, otherwise Traegl wouldn't be so calm.

"He flew over to the mainland to see about getting us a boat," Traegl told her. "We don't think word's out yet about the trouble here, so he should be able to get someone from Newharbour to come out to us."

Nesh could have kicked herself. Why hadn't she thought of that? Ash, and maybe Traegl too, could get themselves to the mainland just fine. It was transporting herself and Madrigal that posed the real difficulty. Then she thought of another problem.

"How are we going to pay, though? I might be able to get some Finding jobs once we're in Newharbour, but would a promise of payment be enough?"

Traegl laughed. "Haven't you noticed I'm not wearing my sword?" she said. "Ash took it over to trade. He was going to take his as well, but two swords with their belts and all was too heavy. So it'll be a down payment now, and the second sword for whoever comes and gets us."

"That was... very good thinking," Nesh said, humbled by how organised and sensible these young people were. It was one thing for Traegl to assure her that they could figure out the details of her orders, but it was another to see clear proof of it. For the first time since she'd left their island home (was it only two days?) Nesh felt herself truly relax.

Ash returned late that evening, saying that their boat would come for them at dawn. There was nothing else they could do in the way of preparation, so the four of them spent a pleasant evening making their camp tidy and ready to leave in the morning. Once Madrigal was asleep, Nesh told the others what she'd learned that day from her conversation with Kerrig.

"Could we stay here then, out of the way?" asked Ash. "Once the most aggressive of the locals head off to do battle, perhaps the others won't be so unhappy about our being here?"

Traegl snorted. "Did you sleep through *all* your lessons on martial politics?" she asked. "The ones who stay behind will be those who aren't able to join the fighting, not those who oppose the fight. They'll be itching for a chance to show how loyal they are, and hunting down 'traitors' would suit them no end. No, Nesh is right. We need to get away and stay away from everyone until this is well and truly over."

The next morning Nesh woke up shortly before sunrise to a strange sound coming from the direction of the sea. Something creaking, and the sound of splashing. She didn't recognise it, but thought that it must be the boat coming to pick them up.

As much as she intended to rely more upon her other senses, Nesh was forced to use her Talent for getting into the boat. She could make out vague outlines as the sun rose, but the sailor's, 'You sit there, ma'am,' and, 'Step here,' instructions were no help at all.

Why can't she describe things properly? thought Nesh, scowling through a fresh headache. Would it be so hard to say, 'There's a seat to your left,' or, 'Step up'?

But, aside from the difficulties of embarking, the journey was a pleasant one. Since she wasn't being called on for directions, Nesh could sit back and enjoy the sounds and smells of the sea. She could even make out the changing colours of the sky as the sun rose through a cloudy dawn.

After a while, the steady creaking of the oars halted and Nesh looked around for the shore. She couldn't feel anything beneath the boat's keel, and the air felt wild and open still.

"Why stop here?" Nesh heard Traegl ask. "What's the matter?"

The sailor gave a short, harsh laugh.

"There's a matter," she said. "Of payment."

Nesh Found the other woman's eyes simply so that she could be sure of glaring into them.

"Alright," said Ash, with deliberate calm. "You've had one half, and here's my sword for the rest – once we're ashore."

"No, I'll have it now," said the sailor. "And your boots while you're at it. And anything else you'd care to donate to my restoration fund."

"Your what?"

"The way I see it," said the sailor, "you Outsiders owe us one country. Anything I take from you is nothing more nor less than my due, so hand over everything you've got – if you ever want to see land again."

Madrigal slipped her hand into Nesh's and leaned against her. "Are they going to shout?" she whispered. "I don't like shouting."

Nesh squeezed the little hand gently. "I don't think there's any need for shouting," she said, smiling directly at their treacherous sailor. From the sounds of it, Traegl and Ash were getting ready to make a stand and Nesh cast about with her Finding Talent for a way to help.

Suddenly, the whole boat tipped backwards and Nesh was thrown off her feet. She fell against something solid, and covered in short hair. Madrigal brayed in her ear, and then Nesh put two and two together. A young Sidrax will tend to retreat into their birth shape when they feel nervous or threatened. And no small boat, however sturdy or well-made, can comfortably withstand the sudden addition of a donkey to its stern.

The lurching of the boat underneath her hooves must have startled Madrigal as much as anyone because she was still making distressed noises. Nesh regained her feet and patted Madrigal until the child quietened down. This left her with little attention to spare for whatever drama might have been going on at the other end of the boat. But she didn't expect to hear Traegl's voice coming from somewhere behind Madrigal – outside of the boat completely.

"Don't try anything," she advised. "I'm in my Element, and can put a stop to anything you start."

"Traitor!" The sailor spat the word out with venom. "The only thing worse than a thief is a traitor."

But between Madrigal at one end, Traegl in the water, and whatever Ash was doing (Nesh couldn't tell, but she doubted he was just sitting on his hands) the sailor chose to back down. Nesh Found the other woman's eyes again, just so she could glare at her for the rest of the trip. She didn't know if it had any effect on the sailor, but it certainly made Nesh feel better.

They pulled up on a sandy shore, and Traegl helped Nesh and Madrigal (still in her donkey-shape) out of the boat. Ash surprised everyone by handing over his sword – once the whole group were ashore.

"We had an agreement," he said. "Two swords to ferry four people. A fair price, and the one witnessed at the docks last night. In fact, here's one of the witnesses now."

"That's true," said an unfamiliar voice. "Though why she landed you here instead I don't know. All duly paid and witnessed."

"Paid and witnessed," said yet another voice. There was an expectant pause before the sailor repeated, "Paid and witnessed, Time rot you. Now get out of my sight."

Nesh and the others were happy to oblige.

<hr>

"What does 'pay Dan witless' mean?" asked Madrigal, once she was girl-shaped again. Nesh was grateful that she had asked, because it sounded like something she herself ought to know, but didn't.

"It's how we do business in Sidrea and the wider Empire," Ash said after a moment. "If we can't write things down for some reason then we get at least two other people – not ones in the agreement, you know, but two or more people from outside – to listen in and agree that things are fair."

"And those people pay Dan?" Madrigal asked again.

"Not a person called Dan," Ash said. "The expression is 'paid, and, witnessed'. Meaning 'everything is fair' – paid – and 'I saw it settled' – witnessed."

Madrigal seemed happy with this explanation, and Nesh filed it away under 'good to know' Even though she doubted that anyone would call her to witness anything.

They walked on until the sounds of Newharbour were faded and gone. Only then did Ash bring up the question of where they were going to sleep that night.

"We could go back and find somewhere in Newharbour, though we don't have much left to trade with," he said.

"No way," said Traegl. "That hot-headed sailor probably isn't the only person in the place with a grudge. We're better off alone, I reckon."

Nesh agreed with Traegl. Madrigal's only contribution to the discussion was an enormous yawn, but it convinced Ash to make camp on the road for that night at least.

⸻ ◆ ⸻

After they'd settled, eaten, and put Madrigal to sleep, Nesh, Ash, and Traegl sat around the fire. Nesh watched the bright blaze out of the corner of her eye, enjoying the warmth and the colour, but not the painful stab of the unfocused light.

"The stars are so beautiful tonight," Ash said. "That's one good thing about a clear night. And it's a double new moon, too. The sky just goes on forever."

Traegl gave a happy sigh. "I never used to bother about the stars when I lived in Westhaven. Now, I wish I knew them better. It would be nice to be the sort of person who had a favourite star. Hey, Nesh – do you have a favourite star?"

"A what?" Nesh was genuinely confused. She knew about the moons, the sun, and clouds, but had always assumed that 'the stars' was another term for 'night sky'. How could a person have a favourite night sky?

"A favourite star. You know, the little twinkly lights in the sky?" Traegl's tone was playful, but she clearly expected Nesh to understand what she was talking about.

This was it. Nesh could keep on bluffing, pretend she hadn't heard properly, and then say that no, she had no particular favourites. Or... or she could tell the truth.

"I don't have a favourite star," Nesh said. "I don't think I've ever seen stars in my life. My eyes were never that good, even when I was younger. And now... well, now I'm almost completely blind."

Nesh waited for the burst of sympathy, the torrent of questions, perhaps even some disbelief. She wasn't sure even now if she'd done the right thing, but she couldn't take it back. The silence was starting to ache, until it was broken unexpectedly.

"What's *blind?*" asked Madrigal.

"Maddie, I thought you were asleep!" said Ash. "Are you alright?"

"I'm alright," said the child. "What's blind mean?"

Nesh took a deep breath. "It means my eyes don't work," she said. "I can't see very much at all... maybe one day, nothing."

Saying it out loud was just as hard the second time around. Nesh wondered if she would ever get used to it. And Madrigal would certainly have a lot of questions, which meant that Nesh could be talking – and thinking

– about this for hours, and she'd definitely made the wrong choice and should just have kept quiet and...

"So, it's like when me and Kerrig was walking in the dark, and I couldn't see anything," said Madrigal. "I open my eyes really big, but it was all dark. And my Stony-Man couldn't see either but he's clever so he still walked us to you all safe."

She stopped, and thought for a moment. "And you walk about in the dark all the time. You're as clever as my Kerrig-man," Madrigal declared. Then she yawned and curled up next to the fire. "Goodnight, clever Nesh-lady."

Madrigal's matter-of-fact acceptance of her disability seemed to set the tone for Traegl and Ash, and there were no further questions.

⸻ ⋙◆⋘ ⸻

In the morning, conversation turned to what they should do next.

"We're in a good enough spot here, if we want to carry on camping out. Could become a problem in the winter, though."

"Let's hope things will be settled before that," said Nesh. "But I take your point. If we're going to stay here – or anywhere out in the open like this – we'll want to make a shelter."

She started to Find building materials, then remembered what Traegl had said about taking command. Not that she wanted to be in charge, but...

"Ash? Traegl? What would you make a shelter from, in this wilderness? Given that we don't have any Earth or Fire Elementals with us this time."

There was a thoughtful silence; then Traegl cleared her throat. "We'll need water," she said. Then added,

228

reluctantly, "And, if it comes to it, I might be able to do something with hedges. If you can find some established plants, I can hurry up their growth and train them into shape."

Traegl didn't sound enthusiastic about this plan but admitted that it was possible. "Tedious and complicated, but possible."

It took a week to find the right plants for Traegl to work with, and the right place to grow them. The young woman didn't really enjoy the work, but she was good at it. As the hedge walls rose, Ash, Nesh, and Madrigal all pitched in to help; and by the end of the week they had a decent wall, with staggered entrances to beat even the most insidious winter winds. Training the branches into a roof would take longer, but Traegl said that normal growth rate should be enough for that.

"If it's not doing well enough by late summer, I'll give it another boost. But, honestly, I'm happy with this place if you are. I thought I'd left all that plant-tending nonsense back west..."

Nesh heard Traegl's grumbles fade away as the young Marshlander walked off to catch up with Ash. He'd been talking her down from her grumbles all week, and Nesh hoped that it was the last time he'd need to do that.

"She's not really cross, you know," Ash had told Madrigal and Nesh on the second night, after Traegl had gone to lie down in the stream. "It's bad memories, I think. It seems as though she didn't like the person who taught her how to work with plants... or perhaps she did like them, but doesn't like remembering them?

I don't know, and I don't want to ask. I just know it's a sensitive topic."

"So we don't talk to Marshy-Lady about plants." Madrigal said.

"Not about growing them, anyway," Ash confirmed.

Madrigal seemed to file this away without complaint. Nesh sometimes wondered what the world looked like to this curious child. Did she accept what she was told because she didn't know how to ask questions, or because she trusted people to always tell the truth? Or was she working out the answers for herself, behind those wide, copper-coloured eyes?

She'd been upset when they left the island without Kerrig, but had believed Nesh completely when told she'd see him again. And Nesh intended to make sure she did.

<hr>

"So," Nesh said, that evening. "With the question of shelter, food, and water sorted – thanks to your hard work and skills, Ash and Traegl–"

"And Maddie," said Ash. "She's becoming a first-rate forager in her own right, and not just for grasses."

"And Maddie," Nesh corrected herself. "Now that we're safe and supplied, what are we going to do about the... situation with the Citadel?"

In the following pause Nesh imagined the other two adults exchanging glances. Eventually, Ash said, "I'm not sure we should do anything. I thought we were going to stop here, well out of the way. After all, it's really not our fight."

Traegl snorted, and Nesh thought that she was going to argue. But what she said was, "Too right it's not our fight. I want no part in it, for either side. Let the idiots sort it out among themselves – I don't care either way."

"Traegl! How can you say that?" Nesh was shocked. She tried to make allowances for the girl's difficult week, but even so... "Those are your people involved – on both sides, too. You can't really want to sit back and let them get hurt?"

Traegl made a low sound in her throat that Nesh might have called a growl – if she hadn't heard real growls from Ash in the past. Even so, Nesh was almost glad not to be able to see Traegl's face at that moment.

"If anyone gets hurt, it'll be because they were being stupid," she said. "The Avlem, the Sidrax, and The People have had over fifty years to play out this fight, and it's over. I'm not going to get dragged into my grandparents' quarrels just because a bunch of sheltered chiefs and angry idiots want to turn back the clock."

Traegl stopped, breathing hard. Nesh wanted to say something soothing, but couldn't Find the words. She hoped Ash would come to the rescue again.

"I hear you, Trae," said Ash.

Nesh started to relax.

"But, well... Kerrig and the chiefs, you know. They're not in the wrong, exactly."

Nesh fought very hard not to groan aloud.

"I mean, I know the Sidrax Empire came out here to spread knowledge and all," said Ash, "but the more I see of life here, the more I realise we took something too. Not just land, but... I can't explain it, exactly. Something that made this place belong to the Elementals. The Empire is a great thing, but I wonder sometimes if we were wrong to bring it here. Or, at least, to bring it in the way we did."

Ash's voice took on a softer tone, as if he were no longer speaking to Traegl, or anyone there. He sounded as though he were talking himself through a difficult problem.

"No-one likes violence, but sometimes it's the only way to make people see your point. At least, that's what I was taught. As the martial arm of Wisdom, our goal is minimal force with maximal efficacy." Now Ash sounded like he was quoting someone. "That is right, isn't it?" he went on. "It must be. The guiding principle of Sidrea, of being Sidrax, it must be..."

He trailed off, sounding disturbed. Nesh now wished that she could see Traegl's face. Was she going to press her argument home or offer comfort? Nesh decided not to risk it, and spoke up herself.

"I think you've got a good point there, Ash," Nesh said. "As you said, no-one likes violence. If it comes to a fight, then we've already lost. But I think we can make it so that it doesn't come to violence in the first place."

An idea had begun to form in Nesh's mind and, although she would have preferred to have fully thought it out first, she decided to share it.

"We need to get the Citadel to listen to what the Elementals have to say. If they would just hear them out, I'm sure there'd be no need for fighting," she said.

"That would be favourite," agreed Ash. "But how do you propose to make that happen? Kerrig wasn't very approachable when you last spoke."

"I wasn't thinking of starting with Kerrig," said Nesh. "Better to prepare the way for the Elementals by going directly to the Citadel. Take things to the top right away, that's how to get things done when you're on a tight deadline."

"Are we on a deadline?" asked Traegl.

"Of course we are," Nesh replied. "If they were still at the 'arguing among themselves' stage, we might hope for it to blow over, but the last time I tried to Find Kerrig, he wasn't in the right direction for still being on the island. If they have crossed to the mainland, they won't stop until they've marched on the Citadel. All we can do is make sure that they are met peacefully."

"Your Talent works at such a distance as that?" said Ash, then immediately interrupted himself to add, "No, that's not important right now, sorry. What I meant to ask was how will you contact the Citadel – never mind convince them to meet the Elemental chiefs?"

"I'm going to send them a letter," she said.

There was more arguing, especially after Madrigal had gone to sleep. Traegl still held out against getting involved at all, but Nesh managed to bring Ash around to the idea that those with the ability to help were obliged to exercise it.

"You write that letter, Nesh," he said. "You write it, and I'll deliver it. I've never seen the Citadel up close – it'll be interesting." He sounded like an eager child. "But I promise to hurry back, Trae," he added, quickly.

"You'd better," Traegl told him. "And, Nesh? I'll be your scribe if you dictate. No need to struggle with ink and parchment. That said... do we have any parchment?"

"Not yet," said Ash. "I'll take Maddie for a quick run into Newharbour, sell a few odds and ends, and get a few things we can't forage for."

After Ash had gone to collect Madrigal, Nesh asked Traegl what he was going to sell.

"I don't know," said the Marshlander. "It's not as if we've been able to make anything out here, aside from this hedge wall. Perhaps he came across something valuable while foraging."

"Perhaps," said Nesh, absently.

<hr>

But when Ash returned, Traegl noticed he was barefoot.

"Ash! Your boots! Why didn't you say? You could have sold mine, or..."

"Trae, I mostly go barefoot anyway. Easier for shapeshifting. Don't worry about it. Here, for the letter." And he handed over a parcel that Nesh couldn't make out in detail.

Traegl opened it, set out the writing materials on a convenient stone, then gave a small squeak of surprise.

"Ash, you shouldn't have!"

"Nonsense. Here, let me..."

Nesh looked away and asked Madrigal how she had enjoyed her day. Even if she couldn't see, it felt too much like spying to watch Ash and Traegl at that moment.

Madrigal, it turned out, had had a lovely day, and she was happy to tell Nesh all about it. Her childish enthusiasm was slightly dampened by the absence of her 'Stony-Man', but Madrigal seemed to accept that Kerrig was working for his chiefs and couldn't come 'home' yet.

Nesh had no idea when — or even if — Kerrig would ever return, but couldn't bring herself to break the news to the child. As and when she needed to do that, Nesh would Find a way. She hoped.

Madrigal's recital of her adventures gave Traegl time to set up the paper and ink, and they spent the rest of the evening on the letter. After two false starts and some scraping of the ink from the parchment, the group agreed to draft the letter on a wax tablet and only commit it to ink once it was complete.

Nesh agonised over that letter. It had to be direct, but not threatening. The tone needed to be respectful, but not flattering. The warning had to be clear, but without provoking the Citadel to take any action against the Elementals. It called for peaceful negotiations, but without mentioning war.

They wrote well into the night, Nesh writing and rewriting sentence after sentence on her wax tablets. She fell asleep over them at last, and woke in the pre-dawn mist to Traegl pulling them out of her hands.

"I'll get it copied out as soon as the dewfall is off my 'desk'," said Traegl.

"I'm not sure," said Nesh, sleepily. "I think the last paragraph still needs..."

"I think you need a proper sleep," Traegl told her. "The letter is as ready as it's ever going to be."

***

By mid-morning, the letter was written. Ash changed to his hawk-form, and took the rolled-up letter in his talons. Then, brushing a wing against Traegl's cheek in parting, he flew towards the Citadel.

Nesh kept her Talent fixed on him until he stopped moving. She checked, and both "Find Ash" and "Find the Citadel" gave the same response. Nesh went to Traegl to tell her, and found her still at the edge of their site, staring at the sky.

"He's arrived, Traegl," said Nesh. "It's alright."

"He's coming right back, isn't he?" Traegl said. "So he shouldn't be long. I'll wait here for him."

Nesh took Madrigal to graze, and occasionally used her Talent to Find Ash. The sun began to set, and he was still in the Citadel. Traegl built up their fire into a beacon, only leaving to fetch wood. She was sitting beside it when Nesh fell asleep, and didn't seem to have moved when she got up in the early hours of the morning.

"Didn't you sleep at all?" Nesh asked the young woman. "You should have woken me for watch – I'm sorry, we've fallen out of the habit a bit since you grew this shelter. Let me take over now. Get some rest."

"But what if...?" Traegl began, but Nesh interrupted her.

"He's still in the Citadel," she said. "As soon as he's nearby, I'll wake you. Get some rest now."

Reluctantly, Traegl lay down beside the fire. Nesh had no idea if she would actually sleep, but she was at least getting some rest.

Some time later, Nesh noticed that Ash had left the Citadel. She began trying to track him with her Talent, and wondered if her senses were misleading her because he seemed to be moving slowly, and not in exactly the right direction. Then, all at once, he stopped again. Nesh roused Traegl and set her Talent to Find Ash again. He was on the ground, but no longer still. Walking towards them, then?

"Stay here with Madrigal," Nesh told Traegl. "I won't be long."

Nesh fixed her Talent upon Ash and walked until she could hear footsteps – heavier than usual for Ash, but in line with her Talent that was still tracking him. Then the approaching figure called Nesh's name, and she froze.

It was Kerrig's voice.

"You've got a nerve, coming here," she told him. Then her Talent showed her Ash, in his smallest form, lying in Kerrig's open hands. The Sidrax wouldn't let himself be moved, so Nesh reluctantly allowed Kerrig to follow her back to their temporary home.

Madrigal and Traegl both reacted predictably to the appearance of Kerrig and Ash, and it took some time to answer all the questions and get everyone settled. Nesh heard Ash talking, and was relieved that he was well enough to change forms at least.

Then she paid attention to what he was saying. Someone must have mentioned the letter...

"It was sort of a... request for an interview with the Governors," Ash said. "Nesh thought, I mean, we all thought, we all agreed that if we could just talk to them..."

Ash trailed off, and Nesh could imagine the glare that Kerrig was giving him. Sure enough, it was in the Elemental's voice when he spoke. Rage and sarcasm – exactly as he'd spoken to her on their first night out of the mines, more than a year ago.

"So," he said to Nesh, "you thought you'd go and have a quiet word with the Governors. Maybe give them a warning? Tell them the natives are getting ideas again, and they should act now to stop us?"

"Don't be ridiculous," said Nesh. "And I wasn't asking them to talk to me, I was asking them to talk to you. I mentioned that, as a fellow Avlem, I believed the grievances to be legitimate, and that being Governors meant ruling for all the people of this land, not just the privileged few."

"And you sent Ash to deliver your diplomatic message, brokering peace in a war that is not yours." Kerrig gestured towards the injured Sidrax, where he lay. "What did you expect?"

"Hey, I volunteered," Ash said. "Don't get angry with Nesh, she was only trying to help. I was the one who messed up."

Nesh had steeled herself for a blazing row, when Traegl saved the situation by asking Ash to relate his adventures. This certainly changed the subject, but didn't lighten the mood. Poor Ash had been attacked by his old comrades, and the letter destroyed. He'd managed to escape, and hidden himself overnight with young Volnar. That was the only piece of good news in the whole story, to hear of Volnar and his potter friend doing so well.

The other good, or at least notable, thing was that seeing the Citadel had convinced Ash to agree with Nesh about the risks of a battle.

"I'm sorry, Kerrig," he said, "but Nesh is right. I've seen the Citadel, and trying to take it by force will only get people killed. And it won't be the Governors who suffer."

⸻◆⸻

The four adults talked and argued all afternoon. Madrigal wandered around, alternately practising her 'shapes' and sitting beside her 'Stony-Man'. Her innocent presence helped keep things civil, but the sun was setting before they came to any kind of agreement.

"Talking to the Governors is a good idea," the Earther conceded. "But I still say you had no right to speak for the People without asking."

Nesh's first instinct was for an angry denial. She'd devoted her entire life to the welfare of the Elementals. Then she hesitated. How much had her devotion accomplished?

"Agreed," she said. "I... I apologise. Shall we take this to the chiefs, or do you think they would rather come here?"

"Why not meet halfway?" said Traegl. "That way, we both get to keep our 'secret locations' secret. Even though I think it's all a bit silly: Ash has already been near yours, and you've seen ours."

"Sometimes we need to be a bit silly," Ash told her. "But for now, I think it's time to try being sensible."

A familiar, and unwelcome, voice broke in from overhead.

"Now then, where's the fun in being sensible?" said Falerian.

⸻◈⸻

The Air Walker stayed above them, and Nesh felt a faint tickle of air movement as Falerian floated overhead.

Nesh ignored Falerian's words in favour of feeling the air. After a few minutes, she thought she could take a guess at where the Elemental was even without Finding her. She was about to test herself when she heard the 'river' being talked about, and took an interest in the conversation.

"So what did happen with the river island then, if it wasn't you leading us into a trap?" demanded Kerrig.

"Well, I didn't know it was a trap, did I?" Falerian's voice dripped with overblown innocence. "It was supposed to be an island paradise for anyone unhappy with modern life." She sighed, dramatically. "And then, when I report back in, the high-ups are all, 'Oh, Falerian, you shouldn't act without orders,' and 'That's Citadel business, soldier,' and the stinky, dirt-for-brains Colonel wouldn't even see me! The nerve of it – serve them all right if I pull their silly old Citadel down around their ears."

And Nesh suddenly saw the reason for Falerian's over-friendly reappearance. The pieces fell into place so suddenly that it felt almost like Finding the answer.

"You can't though, can you?" she said. "And so you want us to do it for you. Well, too bad – we're not your personal attack force."

"You?" said Falerian, all friendliness gone from her voice. "Maybe not..."

"But we could be allies," said Kerrig. "Falerian, you should come and talk to the chiefs. Nesh, you've made it clear that you want no part in this. But it seems that Falerian does."

Nesh listened to the two Elementals leave, one on foot and the other by air. The clearing stilled, leaving Nesh to wonder what Ash and Traegl were thinking about. Were they as worried as she was about what lay ahead, or were they more concerned with the present? With their background in the army, they must be aware of the dangers of battle – but perhaps they also had more experience with handling the concerns.

Madrigal was excited to have seen her beloved Kerrig, even if only for a short visit. Her cheerfulness helped to distract Nesh from her fears. It also seemed to help Ash during his recovery, which took longer than anyone had expected.

<hr>

Uneasy weeks passed with no word from Kerrig, or anyone else. Madrigal continued her lessons with Ash, while Nesh swallowed her pride and asked Traegl for help in developing situational awareness exercises.

"You asked the right person!" Traegl said with enthusiasm. "I was top of my class in training, and that's without using my Water sense."

Nesh frowned. "Why didn't you use all your senses, though? Why block one of them?"

"Oh, it wasn't a choice," said Traegl, carelessly. "The instructor was creative about making sure I wasn't using my 'unfair advantage' to outdo the Sidrax and Avlem recruits."

"It must have been difficult to make sure that no Avlem was using a Talent," Nesh mused aloud. "Some Talents, like mine, are almost impossible to see, or circumvent."

I can understand a teacher wanting to create a standard, testable level for all students, but it seems disingenuous to teach practical skills and ignore the effect of each student's personal abilities. Nesh thought. *As if the instructor wanted to ignore Talents completely.*

She dragged her mind back to the matter at hand.

"One good thing to come out of that class, then, is your ability to teach people who don't have a connection to water," she said. "Perhaps that is what your instructor had in mind for you after all."

"I doubt it," said Ash. (When had he joined them? Nesh really needed to get to grips with this training!) "I think if Trae hadn't been beating class records left and right, that particular instructor might have ignored her entirely. But she just couldn't bear a new recruit being head and shoulders above her pet students. So, she came up with that 'no special abilities' rule."

"Which you undermined right away, if I recall correctly," Traegl added. "Something about not letting Sidrax students use animal senses either?"

"Hey, if a rule exists then it has to apply to everyone. That's what rules are for."

Traegl was silent for a long moment. Only the sound of her breathing told Nesh that she hadn't walked away.

"You actually believe that, don't you?" Traegl said at last.

"I... of course. What–?"

Ash seemed bemused by Traegl's wrapping him up in an embrace, but Nesh didn't hear him resist. She averted her face out of politeness. If these two were going to make a habit of these public displays of affection, then Nesh might encourage Traegl to grow an interior wall or two just for decency's sake.

⸺◆⸺

It took the better part of the next day to arrange the meeting, and another day after that to work through all the explanations and objections. Eventually, however, a new plan emerged, one that limited the violence to taking down the Citadel's walls – and even then only if the Governors refused to talk to them.

Once the altered plan was explained to everyone, there was a lot more enthusiasm for the fight. Messages were passed back to the island, and some who had previously held back were now willing to take part in the campaign. Everyone practised disabling, non-lethal attacks, and all weapons were discarded in favour of pure Elemental strength.

Months passed without any further news from Kerrig, Falerian, or anyone else. Ash recovered from his adventure in the Citadel, Nesh put in some deliberate work to improve her grasp of her surroundings using her physical senses, and Traegl helped them both. She even joined in to help with some of Madrigal's lessons.

"You're a great teacher, Traegl," said Nesh, one day. "If you were Avlem, I'd call it a Talent. Did you ever think of making a job out of training people?"

Traegl made a thoughtful noise. "You know what? I might just do that. 'Instructor Traegl'," she said, meditatively. "Sounds pretty good."

***

Eventually, it arrived. A message on the wind, in San-we's voice.

"It will be tomorrow. If you will join us, come. If not, you should be safely away from it. It will be tomorrow ..."

The message sounded three times, then again from a slightly different direction in Erben's voice. Nesh paid attention to the air. There was a subtle difference between the normal movement of the breeze and the directed movement of the message-air.

The last echoes of Erben's voice died away, leaving the air still again. The silence stretched out. And out. And out.

Nesh couldn't think of anything to say, and after what felt like three days she gave up and went to Find Madrigal. As she walked away, Ash and Traegl began to talk at the same time.

"So, I was thinking..."

"Look, I know this might..."

"No, sorry, you go."

Nesh smiled and kept walking; when Ash and Traegl came over later, to tell her that they'd both decided to join the battle, she tried to look surprised, instead of worried.

⬥

They all set off together in the morning. Nesh aimed to settle herself and Madrigal at a distance from the Elemental camp, within earshot of the battle. It was a delicate balance to Find a place that would allow her to hear when it was safe, but keep Madrigal from understanding what the noises were.

Before she could fix on a place, however, Ash said, "Who's that coming out to meet us?"

Nesh nearly asked, "Where?" but stopped herself just in time. She tried to Find Danger, and got nothing, but still...

"They're coming in quickly, whoever they are," Traegl said. "Air Walker, flying probably."

"You don't think it's...?"

"Falerian? I hope not."

And it wasn't. Instead, a young woman landed in front of them.

"Are you here for the fight? Hi, Traegl!" she said.

She sounded very young, and Nesh thought that she remembered that bubbly voice from the sea crossing.

"Hi, Prakka," said Traegl, with something uncertain in her tone. "Don't tell me you're going to be part of... all this."

"I wish, but no. Uncle brought me to the mainland to 'watch over me'. But while he joins in the fun, all I get to do is listen out for danger and stay with the babies."

"Babies?" said Nesh. "Are there so many children here? I expected that people with small children would have stayed behind on the island!"

"Oh, they did. Mostly," said Prakka. "Or left them with family. I don't mean they're actual babies, but still..."

There was a silence, which went on a bit too long. Then Ash said, "So, Prakka, was it? Were you looking for us, or just out for a quick flight before your babysitting duties started?"

"Oh! I nearly forgot. The battle camp is this way. And... is your donkey going to fight too? Cos, if not, she can come back with me to the childr- the *other* children," she amended, as Madrigal switched to her girl form.

Nesh felt Madrigal grasp her hand and tug her forward.

"Come on, Nesh-lady," she said. "You can meet my friends." And it struck Nesh for the first time that Madrigal had left friends behind when she followed Kerrig to the island and then followed Ash back to the mainland again. And that even uncomplaining children might not like being moved about so much without any choice.

⸻⬥⸻

Ash and Traegl stayed just long enough to say goodbye to Nesh and Madrigal.

"Where are you going?" asked one of the other children,

"We're going to the Citadel to talk to the Governors," said Ash.

"Oh. Grown-up stuff," said the child, dismissively "Tell Mum and Dad hello from me."

"Come back soon," added Madrigal, before following her friend.

"Yes, come back soon," echoed Nesh. *Come back safe.*

The place Prakka led them to felt sheltered from the wind without feeling or sounding like an indoor space. An awning? The lee of a cliff? Nesh tried to make sense of this, while Madrigal chattered excitedly with her friends.

Only a few of them sounded younger than Madrigal herself. So much for Prakka's 'babies', Nesh thought. She wanted more information, but couldn't think of questions she could ask without leading to a lot of questions from others. So she Found a place to sit down, and eavesdropped on the children to see what she could learn.

This gave Nesh so much information that she had to take a moment to work it all out. The children talked about how busy their families were, and how boring it was when the grown-ups were always arguing and never doing anything fun. Then they showed Madrigal some game that Nesh couldn't make sense of, and played until they sounded tired out.

None of them seemed aware that their grown-ups were in any danger. Nesh didn't know whether to be glad about this or not; on the one hand, they weren't worried, but they were also unprepared for what might happen.

Then again, Nesh was trying not to think about it herself. Was it better to know and worry, or to be unaware and at risk of a terrible shock?

Prakka wasn't amongst the children, so Nesh expected to hear her approach any minute. The teenager hadn't seemed shy, but still stayed away. Eventually, Nesh resorted to her Talent, and discovered that Prakka was patrolling non-stop around the edge of their space.

Could she be keeping watch? Nesh wondered if she ought to help. Then again, perhaps she could help best by watching – so to speak – the children.

Sure enough, the children soon went from 'happily tired' to cross, hungry, and bored. Nesh broke up a couple of not-quite fights, and awkwardly comforted a particularly tearful little boy, before fitting herself in to walk beside Prakka and ask the girl where the food and water were kept.

"Hmm? Oh, over there," said the youngster. "They told me not to let the babies stuff themselves, but honestly, if it keeps their minds off what's going on..."

Nesh hesitated. Prakka's directions, though not helpful as a description, served as permission to Find whatever she could. Meanwhile...

"Is that why you're pacing?" she asked, trying to sound tactful. "To take your mind off things?"

"What? No!"

Prakka's response sounded surprised rather than defensive.

"I'm on guard," she said, and the unspoken '*obviously*' came through loud and clear. "No noise to get out, and no attention allowed in."

The Air Walker suddenly stopped walking, then began to whisper *go away, run away, danger,* several times over. After a moment she stopped whispering and resumed her walk.

"False alarm," she said. "Must be just a normal rabbit after all."

"Were you...?" Nesh faltered. How did you ask someone if they were engaging in casual mind control?

"It's an Air Walker thing," Prakka said, with a trace of condescension in her voice. "I'm not sure how to explain it to a–"

"An Outsider?" suggested Nesh, coolly.

"Well, yes. Non-Air Walkers just don't understand. Sound is a property of Air, after all."

Nesh thought of how well sound travelled through the stone fabric of the prison mines, and found herself doubting that very much. But rather than argue, she merely said, "Is that so?"

"Of course," said Prakka. "Between our mastery of sound, and Air being the Element of the Mind it's possible for Air Walkers to make suggestions to people on a subconscious level."

"Really," said Nesh, so flatly that even Prakka seemed to notice.

"But we only do it for really important things. Like this," she assured Nesh. "As the most powerful Element, we have to be responsible." Prakka's innocent tone made it hard to take offence at her words. All the same, Nesh was glad that there were no adult Elementals around to hear them.

⸺◦⸺

Nesh returned to the children, Found them a meal, and settled them down as the day wore on. And on. And on. Eventually, the air changed. A light breeze blew in, followed by Prakka.

"It's over," she said. "And it sounds like things are alright. We can go and find our families now."

Madrigal raced off at once, and Nesh would have lost her if not for Prakka. The girl sent Nesh's *"slow down, you'll get lost"* right into the donkey's large, coppery ears, and kept on doing it until Madrigal changed shape – a result that the young Air Walker reported with undisguised pride.

"I may not like babysitting," she said, "but I'm dirt good at it all the same. Pardon my language," she added.

Nesh said nothing, but wondered how Kerrig would feel about his Element being used as a swear word.

They caught up with Madrigal and walked together towards the Citadel. The other children kept together and peeled off from the group as they caught sight of their families. Finally Prakka said goodbye herself, leaving Nesh and a very tired Madrigal to keep walking.

The little girl stumbled and yawned, and Nesh offered to carry her. Madrigal made no objection, so Nesh gathered her up onto her hip. With an effort, Nesh walked on. But before she'd gone more than a few paces, she was hailed by a familiar voice. A shock of red hair emerged from the misty kaleidoscope, and then Volnar was at her side. Taller, and with the occasional break in his voice, but still Volnar.

"You look exhausted," he told Nesh. "Both of you. Come with me, and I'll get you somewhere to sit for a bit."

He took hold of her elbow and steered her towards the smell of hot stew.

"Bench by your right leg," said Volnar. "Sit yourself down, and I'll fetch a blanket for Maddie."

Nesh Found the bench and almost collapsed onto it. She'd been more tired than she realised. Madrigal was sound asleep, and didn't react at all when Volnar and Nesh laid her down on a blanket.

"There," said Volnar. "And here's a bowl of stew for you, and one for me. Poor little Maddie looks like she needs sleep more'n food right now, so her bowl can wait a while."

They ate in silence, then Volnar asked,

"Were you out there? In the fighting, l mean."

He didn't sound like a child, eager for tales of adventure. He sounded more worried than anything.

"No, I was away from the fighting," said Nesh, trying to keep her tone neutral. "So was Madrigal. And the other children."

"That makes sense," said Volnar. "And so, you don't know what happened here. Well, I can tell you what it looked like from behind the walls, and we'll get the rest from the others later. They were there, right? Mr. Kerrig, and Traegl, and Ash, and the rest?"

Nesh's lips tightened, but all she said was, "Yes, Kerrig was there. And the others."

And I hope they're alright, she thought.

Volnar huffed in an 'I thought as much' way, then said,

"Well, I don't know what it was like out here, but in the Citadel it was pure madness. There were two attacks, you know? One in the morning, well that was bad enough. Soldiers on every part of the walls, pushing and shoving. Lost a week's worth of pots we did, me and Mashpa. You remember Mashpa?"

Nesh nodded, unwilling to interrupt.

"She was furious, was Mashpa. I was annoyed too, but, well... these things happen. I kept Mashpa from going out and telling the soldiers what she thought of them, but it was close. If the fight had gone on much longer, she'd have gone out into it there and then."

Volnar sounded torn between exasperation and pride.

"But the morning fighting didn't last long, Like I said. The soldiers held off the attackers, and we thought that was it. And I was sorry, in a way, because Ash told me what you were trying to do, and I think you're right."

Volnar paused, and Nesh heard him take a drink.

"Huh, I'm getting parched," he said. "Can't remember when I last talked so much. Where was I?"

"The fighting was over, and we'd lost," said Nesh, quietly. Had all this been for nothing?

"The *first* fight was over," said Volnar. "The second one started a few hours later, and made the morning look like a kids' game."

Volnar paused again, then said, "Do you know why the soldiers on the wall caused so much damage to our stock? It's because our little shop is built right up against the wall. All the tramping about and launching rocks shook us to pieces."

"That's awful," said Nesh. "Will it take very long to repair the damage?"

Volnar laughed. "There's nothing left to repair," he said. "The second attack brought down a big chunk of the wall – and a whole row of shops and houses with it."

He spoke so lightly that it took Nesh a moment to understand. Then she said, "You don't mean to tell me you've lost everything? Oh, Volnar, how terrible!"

"Of course not," he replied. "I'm alive and unhurt for one thing, and Mashpa's the same. There's plenty we can salvage from the wreckage, too. We're alright. But when the shop came down around our ears, there was no stopping Mashpa."

Volnar grinned so widely that Nesh could make out a flash of white teeth.

"When she's making her pots, Mashpa's the most patient and gentle person I know," he said. "But when she gets angry, she gets *really* angry. And having her home and work destroyed because the army was too stubborn to listen when asked nicely... Well she was proper raging."

Volnar chuckled at the memory. "Mashpa strode out into the street, went right up to the biggest, fanciest uniform she could find, and told him off. Just like that, in front of everybody.

"I thought he was going to hit her, he looked so outraged. But then one of our neighbours joins in, and soon we're all having a go at the soldiers – making them help with clearing debris and the like. And someone shouts, 'They only wanted to talk. They said so. If you lot had just opened the gates this morning, none of this would be happening now'."

Nesh lifted an eyebrow at Volnar.

"And this 'someone' wouldn't be you, would it?"

Volnar tried to sound nonchalant, but Nesh heard the spark of pride in his voice.

"Well, as it happens..." he said. "But they really *did* send a message, you know. Not just Ash's letter. There was a big message in the air, just after sunrise, calling for a meeting. The first attack wasn't until mid-morning, so..."

Volnar let the sentence hang in the air, and Nesh smiled.

"So it might have been anyone, is your point," she said.

"Exactly," said Volnar. "Anyway, once the crowd got hold of the idea, it didn't matter. We swarmed the soldiers until they agreed to stop the fighting. After that, it was just a matter of time, and clean-up."

Volnar took the empty bowl from Nesh's hands, and stood up.

"All this out here," he said, "The stew stations, and the healers' tents, and everything? That's everyone working together, mostly. Some of the uniforms got stroppy and went to sulk in the old keep, but most of us here are just trying to look out for each other."

He broke off, suddenly, with an eager shout.

"Lim! Rasser! Over here! Rasser!"

Turning back to Nesh, he said, "It's my friends! I've been looking for them ever since I got back to the Citadel."

Volnar hesitated, sounding torn.

"Um, they might be a bit... shy of strangers," he said, apologetically. "I might have to go to them. Are you and Maddie alright here?"

"I'll take Madrigal to Kerrig," Nesh assured the boy. "You go ahead."

Volnar raced away without another word, and Nesh heard him calling out to his friends to wait. She smiled and picked Madrigal up before resuming her Talent-guided walk towards a collection of large white blobs.

⸺◦⸺

The white blobs turned out to be more tents, and Nesh had to pick her way carefully around the ropes to make her way to the one that housed her friends. Fortunately, Ash, Traegl, and Kerrig were all in the same place. Unfortunately, that place was a healer's tent.

Nesh adjusted her hold of Madrigal, and the child didn't stir. *The poor little thing's had an exhausting day*, Nesh thought. She focused her Talent on Kerrig, for Madrigal's sake, and Found him just the other side of the tent flap.

Entering the tent, Nesh felt a seat right beside her. She sank into it gratefully, and let the girl's weight rest on her lap.

"Here, let me take her–" said Kerrig, then broke off with a sharp intake of breath. "I forgot about my ribs," he explained as he pulled back. "The healer told me to rest them for a few weeks, so no carrying Maddie around just yet."

Nesh smiled at the sleeping girl. "She'll be glad to see you," she warned him. "Be ready to fend off hugs when she wakes up."

Then she sighed and Found Traegl with Ash on the far side of the tent.

"I'm glad to see you all, too. I know I had no part in this fight, but it still made me feel helpless to be sitting with the children while you were risking your lives."

"I didn't know you wanted to be involved," said Kerrig. "You were against the idea from the start, as I remember. In fact," he said, speaking quietly but sadly, "I thought you'd come here to say 'I told you so', and remind me that all this pain and suffering is because I pushed for a fight."

Nesh heard the quiet anger in Kerrig's voice, but for once it didn't seem to be directed at her. It sounded almost like regret. Unsure of what to say, she could only reach out carefully and Find his arm, which she patted awkwardly. Madrigal stirred as Nesh adjusted her hold, then quickly settled back to sleep. Nesh cast about for the right thing to say, but her Talent came up empty.

The awkward silence was disrupted by the entrance of Sanwe hurrying in and asking after her husband.

"San? Over here, love." Erban sounded tired, but not in pain. Nesh felt the draught as Sanwe shot past, and Kerrig coughed.

"Let's give them some space, shall we?" he said, and stood up to leave. Nesh followed, with Madrigal still asleep in her arms.

There was a low bank of earth outside the healer's tent, and Nesh rested against it with Madrigal. She didn't sit, but leaning against the wall helped her tired arms. Kerrig was nearby, but seemed not in the mood for any more talking. Nesh stood still and listened. She heard people moving around, the air moving gently between the tents, the quiet hum of distant conversations, and the occasional shout of delighted laughter as friends or family found each other alive and unhurt.

After a while, Erben and Sanwe came out of the tent together. They sounded happy and relaxed, and said the healer had told them that all they needed now was fresh air.

Kerrig's greeting sounded subdued, and Nesh wondered if his old prejudice against Air Elementals was returning. Then Sanwe said, "Yes, there's a space where my hand used to be. It's going to take a while to get used to using Air to pick things up, but when I think of what I could have lost..."

Sanwe leaned towards her husband and sighed into his chest.

"No contest," she said.

Erben laughed, but Nesh heard the affection and relief in his voice. Then he suddenly called out in a loud voice, "Hello! You must be Volnar! I've heard about you."

Nesh used her Talent to look towards the young Fire Elemental, and felt Madrigal move in her arms –

though whether woken by Nesh's sudden movements or by Erben's booming voice she couldn't tell.

"Hey there, Little One," said Kerrig, so gently that Nesh struggled to hide her smile. "I think it's time we got you to a proper bed."

Madrigal yawned and stretched before answering.

"The Marshy-Lady was asleep in a pond," she said, sleepily. Nesh blinked, trying to work this one out. She barely registered the child wriggle out of her arms, focusing instead on what Kerrig was saying about Water Elementals needing to be in water to heal. Had Traegl been injured in the battle? It was always a possibility, of course, but she'd hoped...

Madrigal chattered happily about being a flower girl – or possibly a flower donkey – at Ash and Traegl's wedding. Nesh wasn't aware that things had got that far, but was pleased for her friends.

Sanwe and Erben joked together about love and marriage. Nesh tried to think of a tactful way to ask how Traegl had been injured, and when she would recover. Then she heard Ash let out such a cry of agony from inside the tent that she wondered why no-one had mentioned his injuries. By the sound of it, they were serious.

And a stranger's voice said "I'm sorry. I couldn't save her."

And a bird screamed high above.

And Nesh sank down onto the low wall, dazed. Surely not. It couldn't be. Couldn't be *Traegl* whom the stranger was talking about. Not her friend Traegl. She was going to get married, and become a tutor, and do so much with her life. How could Traegl be dead?

After a sleepless night, Nesh went out to watch the sunrise. She Found Kerrig, a craggy shadow against the clear sky, apparently looking out over the empty space between the healers' tents and the Citadel walls. The place where the fighting had been, she realised.

"It's not your fault, you know," Nesh said, impulsively. "I know you didn't really want to fight; you just wanted justice. I can understand that." She sighed, and added, "Honestly, I'd hoped my people were more civilised than this."

"They are," Kerrig said, softly. "But it's an Avlem and Sidrax civilisation, and that doesn't fit onto the Land or its People. We don't have cities and academies, but we have our ways. Or we did, when the Shanzir still roamed."

Nesh still didn't really understand who the Shanzir had been, but she knew enough to realise that they were important to the Elementals. Also nomadic, apparently.

"The old ways are still there, we've just added some new routes," she offered. "But I agree, it's no use trying to make this land into a second Avlenia or Sidria. The Land is its own place, and needs its own rules."

"And its own rulers," Kerrig added. "Though Time only knows how that's going to work out. The chiefs still argue over the smallest things."

"That we do," said a new voice. Nesh didn't recognise it, beyond thinking that it sounded like an older man. She stiffened. Kerrig, however, was so surprised and embarrassed that he almost squeaked – though he covered it with a passable attempt at a cough.

"Being a chief is about respect," said the stranger. "Not just getting respect from the tribe, but showing them respect, too. And the other chiefs, and even other tribes. I'm still struggling with that one, but you seem pretty good at it. Don't forget that, when you meet the Governors."

"Yessir," said Kerrig. It sounded like a reflexive response, followed by a much more natural-sounding, "Wait, what do you mean 'meet the Governors'? Why am I going to meet the Governors?"

"The Citadel sent a message," said the old man – *the chief?* "They will see exactly four representatives to discuss terms. Trying to pick one chief from each tribe is an exercise in futility, but it seems that most of them respect you. Even the Air Walker chiefs thought you could be trusted to carry their demands without 'accidentally' forgetting about them. So, Kerrig, you and three others are going to see the Governors. Do you have any recommendations for who those three should be?"

Kerrig took his time answering, and Nesh wondered who she would choose.

I'd want Traegl there, she thought, and lost what Kerrig and his chief were saying as she fought through the numb feeling.

She was brought back by the chief raising his voice in disbelief. "You want to take the Sidrax? Kerrig, I don't think you've thought this through," he said. "You can only take three companions, and whether you pick a Fire Breather or a Marshlander for your third, the other tribe is going to feel slighted."

Kerrig didn't sound upset or embarrassed. "I know," he said. "That's why I'd like Nesh to be the fourth."

Me? thought Nesh. *What's he thinking? Things go badly when I'm in charge. Plus, I'd rather not return to the place where I was sentenced.*

But all she said was, "I thought I was an Outsider. You said this fight was none of my business. Why do you want me with you now?"

The Earther hesitated, and Nesh used her Talent to lock onto his eyes. Eventually, he said, "I... I was wrong. This is about justice for the People of the Land, and that has to mean all people, not just the Peopl- the Elementals.

"You don't have to come," he assured her. "It's just that you know the Land as well as anyone, and better than most. And you know about Avlem manners, too, so we can avoid any accidental rudeness. We don't want any more... misunderstandings."

The understatement made Nesh lose her fight against her smile. "A misunderstanding? That's an interesting way to describe the last century," she said. Then she remembered how difficult the Governors had been on her last visit to the Citadel, and the smile became a smirk. "If I'm there, we shan't have any *accidental* rudeness," she promised.

⸻ ❧ ⸻

Hours later Nesh Found a window seat in the corridor and dropped into it. She tucked herself in behind the curtain, and wished she could go back to being seventeen and having her brother lecture her on manners. Not just because she thought she'd scream if she heard the words 'as per the agenda' one more time, but because, as dull as Berran's lectures could be, they were much more interesting than anything that the Governors had said all morning.

Nesh wondered where Berran was now. Had he realised his ambition of a shop in the Citadel, or had he been held back by his association with her? Not

259

that he was associated with her, in the eyes of the law. That's what her being disowned meant, after all – the Tynar name could go free and clear, without her stain. But the law wasn't everything; especially among the tight-knit and interlocking communities of the Avlem. Nesh hoped he hadn't suffered because of her.

There had been talk of issuing a blanket pardon to everyone involved in the attack on the Citadel, which would certainly make her life easier. But her parents' decision to set her outside the family was a personal matter, as well as a legal one. Nesh might no longer be a wanted criminal, but that didn't make her a Tynar again. Only her parents could do that, if they even wanted to.

If they were even still alive – No. Nesh shut that thought down at once. She was only in her forties, there was no reason to suppose her parents dead. There was no need to add imagined stress to her already stressful day.

———◆———

The bargaining sessions dragged on, through myriad subjects. One particularly sensitive topic was that of the prison island in the middle of the Great River.

"Why is Camp Freedom on the agenda?" asked one of the Governors. "Do the Elemental guards have a complaint to bring?"

"Guards? So you admit that it is a prison, then?" Nesh said, her voice tight with fury. "One operating with the knowledge and approval of this Citadel?"

"Well, of course," said the Governor. "Did you think otherwise?"

The voice sounded oily and self-satisfied, and Nesh fought to keep her lip from curling in contempt.

"What crimes had the prisoners committed, to be kept there?" she asked. "When are their sentences to end? How were they arrested, tried, and condemned?"

Nesh's own anger was echoed in Kerrig's voice when he added, "Why was it presented to us as a haven for Elementals? What becomes of the goods stolen from the farmers? Who approved this... this travesty?"

For the first time since she'd met him, Nesh found herself in complete agreement with Kerrig's anger. She had to work to keep herself from exploding right alongside him.

An awkward silence followed Kerrig's outburst. Then Ash said,

"It's a betrayal of everything the Empire is meant to stand for."

He spoke quietly, in sharp contrast to the raised voices of the other two, but the sorrowful reproach in his words spoke volumes.

Sanwe spoke next, after a delay that seemed perfectly natural, but which Nesh thought timed to a nicety.

"Speaking as an Air Walker myself, I must say that the concept of this 'Camp Freedom' seems dubious at best. While not one of its victims myself, I can't help feeling tainted by its association with my Element. Our ability to communicate on the winds is our gift from Time, to be used in ways that help our People. To see it perverted into a method of control and mental torture..."

Sanwe let her sentence trail off, and the awkward silence returned for an encore.

The three Governors seemed surprised at the levels of outrage coming from the representatives.

"But Camp Freedom is an Elemental-led project," said one Governor. "A humane way to discourage rebellion, and give the traditionalists somewhere to live.

Why, the Air Walker who proposed the scheme was quite brilliant – and very enthusiastic."

"Really, now?" said Sanwe, dry as a desert wind.

"Oh yes," said one of the other Governors. "And she was from a traditional little village somewhere up in the Peaks, so she knew what she was talking about. What was her name? Val'rn? Something very traditional, I remember that much."

There was a rustling of papers as the Governors' clerks sorted through the stacks to find the correct documents. Nesh heard Kerrig and Ash matching her own sharp intake of breath. It couldn't be, could it?

"Here we are," said the first Governor, happily. "Proposal for a reservation on the island in the Great River, by Falerian of the Clear Ice Peaks. I don't see how any of you can object to that; it was suggested by one of your own."

"Exactly," snapped Sanwe. "One of us. Not all, not most, not even some. *One.* Was she an appointed representative? A village chief? Even a family head? No. One crazy Air Walker with a plan, and you think that's an example of 'Elemental-led'? Perhaps Nesh would like to come up with an idea off the top of her head right now, and we'll call that the official Avlem position on things, shall we?"

Nesh wanted to protest at being used as an example, but before she could say anything, Ash spoke.

"Falerian's not crazy," he said. "She's selfish, and vicious, and easily bored, but she's not crazy. Of course Camp 'Freedom' was her idea. And she took us straight there. Curse the little fiend."

Nesh suddenly realised something. "Has anyone seen Falerian since the fighting stopped?" she asked. "I couldn't Find her in any of the healers' tents, and she wasn't among the fallen, either. Oh... Ash... sorry."

"She probably cleared off once the fun was over," said Ash, with a forced, faltering lightness in his voice. "She must have known we'd find out about her clever little idea once we started talking instead of fighting. Ha! 'Nobody likes you, Falerian.' That's what Trae always used to tell her. You were right, my love. More right than you knew."

One of the Governors cleared her throat noisily.

"Getting back to the topic in hand," she said, "we can't just give up on dissidents. If we allow rebellion to grow unchecked, there will be chaos."

Nesh glowered at them. "The whole point of this meeting is to correct the injustices that cause rebellions in the first place. We need to solve the problems, not just react to them."

And there must be a better way to react than sending in the army, she thought, but did not say. That was for a question for another time.

The talks dragged on, day after day. The days stretched into weeks. There seemed no end to the things they needed to decide, from the state of the roads to the rate of taxation, from provision for disaster relief to incorporating Elementals into the apprenticeship system. And, once everything had been written down, there was still the problem of spreading and enforcing these new laws.

Nesh wondered how well some of the smaller communities would manage to enforce the laws. And yet it hardly seemed right to call in the army over such civil matters.

After a month the four ad-hoc council advisors had been offered full-time positions. It seemed ludicrous to Nesh that she should go from wanted criminal to high-ranking official in one step, but after enduring the recent negotiations she wasn't in the mood to argue for logic in government.

Which raised the point: Did she want to be a high-ranking official if it meant more days like these? But, if she turned the offer down, what would she do instead? What did she even want to do?

Perhaps she needed to listen to some other opinions, and see if there was any insight to be had there. She went looking for Sanwe, and soon Found her and Erben together. The two of them were seldom apart, and Nesh had often been unsure how to enter into conversation with them. It was like talking to one person with two heads and four arms.

And three hands, she remembered. Sanwe made light of her newly-acquired disability, but Nesh was sure that it wasn't the small matter she'd made it sound.

"Hello, Nesh!" boomed Erben, as if she were fifty strides off rather than only five. "Or should that be, *Governor* Nesh?"

"Hush you," chided his wife, affectionately. "She might still be thinking it over. And not everyone appreciates your sense of humour."

"Not like you do, you mean, Governor Sanwe," replied her husband.

"Governor?" said Nesh. "You've decided to take them up on the offer?"

"Why not?" said Sanwe. "Erben will tell you I can boss with the best; and it's about time there was a bit of common sense in our government."

Nesh smiled, and wished she'd spent more time with this clever, funny woman. Of course, if she took up a position here in the Citadel, she and Sanwe would be working together. That was something, but not enough on its own.

"And Miss Nesh here is smiling... is it because she thinks you lack sense, love, or because she wants to say that, sense or no sense, we're common enough?" remarked Erben.

Nesh could hear the laughter hiding behind his words, but she still hastened to deny thinking any such thing. After all, Nesh had the deepest respect for all Elementals, and for Erben and Sanwe personally, no matter how humble their origins.

"Yes, well," said Sanwe briskly, after an awkwardly long silence, "in all seriousness, I think you should consider staying on here. Between us, you and I could do a lot of good for the Land."

Or a lot of harm, thought Nesh, but pulled her attention back to listen to Sanwe.

"And don't tell me you're not tempted by the idea of living here in the Citadel. Proper buildings, hot meals, everything conveniently at hand? Why spend your time on just surviving, when you could be using your experience and intelligence on other things."

Nesh was tempted. Surely she could serve the Community better if she had more time each day? She could Find the best course for the whole of Ashanna, not just for individuals. Then again, living in the Citadel full-time would cut her off from ordinary people almost as much as being in the mines. Could she depend on what she was told about what people needed?

—◆—

Well, Nesh thought; she'd heard from someone who had decided to accept the role, and Sanwe had made some good points. Now she wanted to talk things over with someone who had probably already turned it down. Ash, or Kerrig? Ash's reasons would likely be a sensitive subject for some time. Kerrig, then. Nesh set her Talent to Find him, and her feet took her towards a window seat in the next room. She could make out the brightness of the window and a large shadow at the sill, but needed the tug of her Talent to confirm that it was, in fact, Kerrig.

"Have you decided yet?" she said by way of a greeting.

Nesh expected a long speech about why the mere suggestion was offensive to the People, and was surprised when Kerrig's frustrated groan was followed by, "No, not yet."

As Nesh listened to Kerrig's dilemma, which stemmed mainly from trying to prioritise what he felt he owed to various different people, the right question sprang to mind.

"Never mind what other people want from you for a moment," she said. "What do you want?"

After he confessed to wanting to restart the caravan, and eventually return to the north to work on restoring the traditional Elemental homes there, another obvious question suggested itself to Nesh.

"So, why don't you? Gather up the caravan and head north."

Kerrig didn't respond for a while, and Nesh let him have the space to think.

"Could I, though?" he said at last. "There's so much still to do here."

"And there always will be. You're allowed to be a little selfish sometimes, you know."

That provoked a small chuckle at least, and Nesh counted that as a major achievement. She was feeling quite pleased with herself until Kerrig turned the question around and asked her what she was going to do next. Suddenly, all the obvious responses disappeared.

"I... no, I haven't decided yet. There's a lot to consider. Right now, I'm not even sure what I want." *Or what I ought to want,* Nesh thought.

Being 'Governor Nesh' would go a long way towards repairing her status amongst the Avlem. If she did a good job, and gained recognition beyond the fact of her appointment, perhaps she could eventually reconnect with her family.

But if – when – she made a mistake, the fallout would be much larger than just shaming her family.

"Let's think about it tomorrow," suggested Kerrig, and Nesh appreciated the idea. The two of them enjoyed the sunshine at the window for a while.

⸻◆⸻

This left Nesh to think over her next step. There was plenty of work, and her pardon gave her a free hand in most things. Even if she finally decided that she didn't want a permanent seat on the board of governors, she still wanted to do something to improve the system of laws and their enforcement.

So she attended the next meeting, and was surprised to find Kerrig there too.

"Maddie's helping Ash with something for a few weeks," Kerrig said. "Might as well make myself useful while I wait."

Nesh nodded and carefully didn't smile. She marvelled at how much the grumpy Earther had changed in the past year, and wished she could say that she had too. In many ways, Nesh felt as though she'd been frozen in time, from the moment she'd realised the full impact of what she'd done in helping Gles and his band of criminals escape from the mines.

Only her aching joints and failing eyesight convinced her that any time had passed at all. That it should be some twenty-odd years seemed frankly ridiculous.

The meeting was dull, as such meetings are. The new laws had been mostly agreed on, and what remained on the table were matters of minutiae and administration, such as how to deliver news of these changes to the various parts of the Land.

Erben and Sanwe had some contacts in the Eastern Peaks still. Kerrig, much to everyone's surprise, offered to go to the Clear Ice Peaks in the far south.

"Who better than an Earther to head into the mountains?" he said, with such a challenge in his voice that Nesh knew better than to argue.

One of the Avlem Governors drew up a tour of the Fire Plains, and then surprised Nesh by appointing the task to himself. Then someone mentioned the towns south of the river, and Nesh could almost feel the way that the room turned to look at her.

"Nish, why don't you take that area?" suggested the Sidrax Governor. "It's largely Avlem, and the roads are in good condition. You should be able to cover the major population centres in half the time it will take my colleague to travel the Fire Plains."

Objections lined up in Nesh's head, but they all boiled down to not wanting to go anywhere near her old home. She tried to Find a sensible-sounding excuse, and almost missed Kerrig correcting the Governor about her name. It wasn't her name though, was it? That was the problem. She had no name. How was a nameless convict, even a pardoned one, supposed to have any authority among law-abiding citizens?

Nesh dropped her head in defeat, then scolded herself for her self-pity and lifted it again to sit tall and calm. Only then did she realise that it looked like a delayed but firm nod.

"Excellent! That's settled then. I think there's only the far west still to be covered. Any takers?"

Too late to back out now.

"I'll go," said Kerrig. "After I've been to the Peaks, I'll come back here, pick up Maddie, and go to Westhaven. I've got to go there anyway, so might as well split two rocks with one line."

Nesh knew that Kerrig's casual tone was likely forced, but it hurt all the same. Westhaven, and beyond, was where Traegl's family lived. Then her mind went back to her own assignment, and she frowned.

⎯⎯◆⎯⎯

In the end, Nesh asked to speak to the Governors privately before the next meeting.

"I have some concerns about the Avlem towns south of the river," she said. "The elders there will want to know where these laws are coming from, and how they will be enforced. What can I tell them?"

"The laws come from the Citadel, of course," said the Sidrax Governor. "And army enforces them, just as they do throughout the whole Empire."

Nesh hesitated. She had an idea about that, and it felt like a good idea – but sending Ash with a letter to the

Citadel had also felt like a good idea at the time. What made this 'good idea' any different? *Because this time, it won't be just me deciding things*, Nesh realised. *This time, I'm asking for assistance.*

"I'm going to need some help," Nesh said, and explained her idea. The Governors listened, and then assigned her a couple of clerks and a dozen low-ranking soldiers, along with the official title of Commissioner, and permission to expand her staff as needed.

With the help of her new clerks, Nesh drew up plans for a formal law enforcement system, separate from the army.

"We'll move it out over the rest of Ashanna in time, but this will satisfy the Avlem south of the river," she told the Governors, at her next meeting with them. We... *they* like things to be official and interconnected there."

"Very well, Commissioner. The Citadel wishes you every success in your new career."

Feeling slightly giddy, Commissioner Nesh let her Talent guide her from the room and towards her new life.

~ End of Act Two ~

JUSTICE

I

Nesh's journey upriver to her new headquarters was long and slow. As well as a fully furnished office, Nesh had been given a small budget for 'personal effects'. For the first time in nearly twenty-five years, she had luggage: clothes, shoes, cutlery, washing cloths. She was torn between delight at being able to be clean whenever she wanted, and annoyance at the tendency of personal effects to get misplaced.

After the river journey came a day and a night of travelling south on roads that started off well, but soon became mere sheep tracks. Madrigal walked in her donkey form most of the way, and Nesh sometimes leaned against her on the more difficult paths.

The morning sun was barely warm when the newly made Commissioner Nesh arrived at her newly restored base of operations. She smelt the pitch-and-lime that had been used to patch up the walls. The scent of fresh timber was more reassuring, so long as the woodworkers could be trusted.

She made out the dark shape of a door in the white wall, and ran a hand along the door post, feeling for the door itself. The movement of the air, and the sound of

271

shuffling feet, told Nesh that the door was open. She let her Talent guide her, though she carried on touching the door post as she entered.

The foot-shuffling sounds intensified, and Nesh wondered how many people were watching her and why they didn't say anything. It was intimidating, but Commissioner Nesh was not about to let herself be intimidated. She drew back her shoulders, fixed a stern look in the direction of the worst of the shufflers, and spoke.

"Good morning. I am Commissioner Nesh. Who are you?"

After a tense silence, a hesitant male voice said, "My name's Jerrip, your Honour... Commissioner. Ma'am. Head Carpenter and foreman of the recent repairs, Ma'am. Commissioner."

Nesh relaxed slightly, but tried to keep it from her face.

"Very good, Jerrip." Thank Life that some people at least had pronounceable names! "Talk me through what you've done here, and what remains to be finished."

⸻ ◆ ⸻

Jerrip gave a detailed, if rather nervous, description of the entire building layout: from the open plan reception, to the large back rooms, to the stairs ("Freshly cut, Ma'am, mindful of splinters") that led up to Nesh's office.

Nesh walked around as Jerrip talked, noting all the doors, walls, and furniture. The back area was divided into two, with three private rooms on the right, and a large open space on the left. Nesh used her Talent to Find Madrigal in the group.

"What do you think?" she asked the girl. "If we put a bed in one of these rooms, and some nice hay in this open space, would you like to stay here?"

Madrigal sounded interested, but unsure. "Not forever?" she said, in the manner of someone double-checking the fine print.

"No, not forever," Nesh assured her. "Just for as long as you like. Until Kerrig gets back from his trip, maybe? Would you like that?"

Madrigal took her time answering. She seemed to be conducting her own inspection, and Nesh heard hooves more than once.

"I like it," she declared, coming back to Nesh's side. "And the other rooms for Ash, and... oh. *Not* the Marshy-Lady." The little girl was quiet again for a moment. Then she said, "That's sad, isn't it?"

Nesh reached out to hug Madrigal. "Yes," she said. "It is sad. But when Ash arrives, we'll have a nice room ready for him. Which one do you think he'd like?"

Madrigal inspected the three rooms again, and the main space leading to them, before choosing one for herself and another for Ash. Then she asked Nesh about her room.

"Jerrip?" said the Commissioner, standing straight and business-like again. "My office. Will you lead the way?"

There was a moment of hesitation before Jerrip said, "O-of course, Ma'am."

⸻◆⸻

Nesh took careful note of the route through her new... what? Office? Headquarters? Home? Whatever it was, she wanted to be able to move through it with confidence and without needing to rely too much on her Talent.

It was twenty-one paces from the guest quarters' door to the desk. Twenty-seven more from the desk to the stairs. Fourteen steps in the staircase, then a door on her right into her office.

Nesh listened to the sounds of the building, trying to learn the creak of each step and the feel of the air. She supposed that she would need to let her clerks know about her sight trouble, and get their help with certain matters, but Commissioner Nesh refused to feel lost and helpless in her own office.

She listened as Jerrip described the little work that remained to be finished. As before, she walked around and inspected every piece by touch. Her bedroom led off from her office by a discreet door in the panelling. It opened with a key, which Jerrip handed over along with a bunch of others on a leather loop.

"They're all labelled, Ma'a– Commissioner," he said.

Nesh frowned. She would have to talk to her clerks as soon as possible.

One week into her new job, Nesh was beginning to despair of ever getting this idea to work. There were so many things to consider, so many questions to answer 'immediately, if not sooner' that Nesh couldn't remember the last time she'd had a good night's sleep.

The first thing Nesh had done, though, had turned out to be the wisest yet. She'd consulted with her assigned clerks, and they had been marvellous. On their advice, Nesh had interviewed among the locals and ended up with a clerical team that could have given Pabiran Tynar a good run for her money.

Not that it was a large team: only a Chief Clerk and four assistants, but it was a very efficient one. And composed entirely of Elementals, a fact in which Nesh took great pride: two Air Elementals, including chief clerk Tarbry himself; then a Marshlander, though he was nothing like Traegl, unfortunately; finally, two Fire Elementals, a couple of siblings called Hadil and Rask.

Within half an hour of a message delivery, the clerks would have read everything, put the messages in order of urgency and importance, and be ready to report them to Commissioner Nesh.

Tarbry served as her eyes on these occasions, and she soon learned to identify the chief clerk by his step and knock. He was always accompanied by either Megram, the Marshlander, or Stard, the other Air Elemental. Stard sounded young, and a little in awe whenever she was required to read something aloud to Nesh... though Nesh was still unsure whether she was more in awe of Commissioner Nesh or of Chief Clerk Tarbry.

<hr>

The days quickly fell into a pattern as they waited for Kerrig and Ash to arrive. But, as it turned out, Nesh's first visitor was Volnar. He arrived one morning, just as she was settling to hear the first of the day's messages.

"Volnar?" said Nesh, delighted but puzzled. "How good to see you! I thought you were in the Citadel, though. What brings you out here?"

"My own feet brung me to you, and I brung you a little welcome gift. It should've been ready a week ago, but Mashpa wanted to watch it a bit longer to make sure it wouldn't crack. I reckon she just wanted to show it off in the shop though – not that I blame her. Best thing either of us ever did, I say."

Two figures eased through the door, and set something large and heavy onto Nesh's desk. It sounded hollow, but Nesh couldn't begin to think what it might be.

"Feel it, Nesh. It's for you."

Carefully, using her Talent to avoid hurting either the gift or her own fingers, Nesh ran her hand across the nearest side. It felt rough and oddly shaped. The lowest parts were also the smoothest, and seemed to be connected. One smooth surface on the left, then a thin band of smooth texture running in a strange, narrowing ribbon all the way to the right-hand side. Nesh walked around the table to explore more, caught her forearm on a raised part, and jerked away, more surprised than hurt.

"Oops, sorry. Guess the Peaks are a bit sharp if you're not ready for them. Oh grosk, I've given it away now, ain't I?"

The Peaks? Nesh felt again, more slowly this time. Beside the large smooth patch was a slightly raised and roughened area with occasional clusters of... tiny boxes? Further still, the surface rose again, then became suddenly vertical, creating a wall along the edge. Could it be...

"It's Ashanna, isn't it?" Nesh said. "The whole country, from the prison mines in the north, to the Peaks in the south. How on earth did you... you said that you made this? It's amazing."

Volnar's grin was so wide that Nesh thought she could see it. She could certainly hear it in his voice when he replied, along with some poorly-hidden pride.

"It took all three of us to make it happen, me an' Mashpa an' Ash, but I thought of it. Ash got these map things from his old bosses, and then went flying all over and making sure they was all correct. Then Mashpa made the main shape, and then she showed me how to help and we both put in all the details. Then I baked it all up, and we painted it, and I baked it again, and then it was done. And Mashpa says she can add things when new towns and stuff go up, but not to let anyone else mess with it because it's her masterpiece. But I expect you can put markers and stuff on it to help you make plans. It's for your work, you know, not just for looking at."

Nesh was speechless. She ran her fingers along the western marshes, and felt a sudden pang at the thought of Traegl. Nesh lifted her hand from the marshes with a gentle action and fought back tears.

"You do like it, don't you?" Volnar said, anxiously. "You don't have to use it if you don't want to, but please say you like it. Ash has taken himself off somewhere, and Mashpa's minding the shop, or they'd be here with me. And it took longer to make than I thought, but–"

"Volnar, it's wonderful," Nesh said, as soon as she could trust her voice. "I can't even begin to tell you how useful this is going to be – I'm already getting over-whelmed trying to remember all the different towns around here. But, Volnar, the amount of work that you – all of you... I can't think how I'll ever repay you."

"Naw, Nesh, you don't repay a gift. If you like it, and it's useful, that's all any of us want."

<hr>

Ash and Kerrig arrived nearly a week later. Nesh greeted them warmly, but she had nothing on Madrigal.

"Teacher Ash! Stony-Man! I missed you lots and lots and lots. Are you staying here now? There's rooms for you. Come and see!"

Nesh listened to the excited girl drag the two men around by the hand, and smiled to hear Madrigal's running commentary on every room. Nesh let the fingers of her left hand skim over the notes she'd made from her morning briefing, while she jotted down follow-up instructions with her right. Writing with a pencil wasn't easy, but Nesh was determined to keep as much of her skill as possible.

She had just completed her list, and was about to summon Tarbry to take it, when there was a knock at her door.

"It's me," said Kerrig's voice. "Do you have a moment?"

"As a matter of fact, I do," Nesh said. "What's on your mind?"

Kerrig took a slow breath, then said, "It's about young Ash. I know it's a lot to ask, but can he stay here with you and Maddie? I gather from her tour that you have space for him."

"More than that, we have a room for him," Nesh said. "Ash is always welcome here – as are you, if you'd like to stay."

"Thanks," said Kerrig. "I might stay for one night. But I'm meant to be heading west, taking the new Proclamation of the Citadel to the towns and villages out there. The Governors, especially our own 'Governor Sanwe', want the word to spread as quickly as possible, and with official paperwork attached. A few of us have volunteered to be messengers."

"I remember you went to the Peaks," Nesh said. "And now you're going to the Western Marshes, too?"

As soon as she'd said it, Nesh wanted to bite her tongue. She remembered the news he would be carrying to one particular village, and didn't want to talk about it.

"It's something to do," said Kerrig.

Nesh relaxed. Apparently he didn't want to talk about it either.

"I want Maddie to get her proper training with Ash, and I don't want to go back north without her," Kerrig added. "I might even sign on for that governor gig, if I run out of other work."

Nesh laughed out loud at the casual way Kerrig spoke of the highest-ranking job in Ashanna as if it were a tedious task he would do in the absence of something better.

"I'm sure you can keep busy if you put your mind to it," Nesh said, still smiling. "But you haven't said why you want to leave Ash and Madrigal here. They're welcome, of course, but shouldn't they be in here, if we're deciding where they're going to stay?"

Kerrig didn't answer at first, and when he did finally speak he sounded embarrassed.

"I don't think Ash should come with me," he said. "And I certainly don't think he should be left on his own. He's taking Traegl's death hard – not that I say he's wrong to do that, mind. And I don't know much about it, but from what Aratal tells me, Ash needs to be with people and he needs to stay busy."

Nesh didn't know what to make of this new, strangely sympathetic Kerrig. What had happened to the entitled victim, who hated all things non-Earther? Still, she could hardly comment on that without being rude, so Nesh latched onto the one thing she thought she could ask.

"Who's Aratal?"

"Oh, just someone I met in the Peaks," Kerrig said. "Talked a lot of sense, once they stopped having conniptions about the state of their mountainside."

There's a story there, thought Nesh, but didn't mean to get any further off-topic than they had already.

"Yes; going west, seeing where Traegl grew up, I can see how that might be too much for him right now. But what can I get him to do here? Aside from teaching Madrigal, of course."

"Won't that be enough?" asked Kerrig. "Teaching sounds like a full-time job to me."

Nesh shook her head. "For a group, maybe, like we had in the caravan. But with just one student... there will be times when Madrigal needs to practise, or rest, and then Ash has nothing to do but think. And that's not good when there are things you don't want to think about."

And I should know, thought Nesh, but didn't say it out loud.

Then she shook off the past and stood up. "Leave it with me," she said. "We'll find something for Ash to help with around here."

—·—

Nesh listened to Kerrig leave, and caught Madrigal's happy chatter go up a notch at the reappearance of her favourite Earther. The child had missed both Kerrig and Ash terribly, and had asked about them repeatedly while they'd been apart. It was good to hear Madrigal so happy again, and Nesh wondered how she would cope with the news that Kerrig wasn't staying.

The more Nesh thought about it, the more she worried. Madrigal would have Ash, but not her 'Stony-Man' – and there was no telling how long Kerrig would be away. Nesh's Talent could give her a direction, and even a general sense of distance. But that wouldn't tell them how he was getting on, or when he expected to return.

A knock at the door broke her train of thought. The clerk who entered at her knock identified himself promptly, though she was starting to recognise each of them from their tread on the stairs.

"Clerk Megram, Commissioner. Messages from the Citadel."

Nesh shook off her reverie. "Of course. Let me get my stylus, then you can read me..."

She trailed off, struck by a sudden thought.

"When did the messages arrive, Megram?" she asked.

"With the supply cart, Commissioner. We sorted them quickly, but seeing as you had visitors, Ma'am..."

"What? Oh, that's fine," Nesh said. "Um, good job. Right. As you were."

Commissioner Nesh diligently took notes on the letters, and tried to push other thoughts to the back of her mind.

A request for time off next month? Very good. Do we have enough people to cover? Approved.

An escort wanted for a week? What terms? Fair. Who do we have available? Excellent. Approved.

What supplies do we have in the consignment? Any more needed? Put the word out locally, use your judgement for where and who to ask.

And so it went on, responding to questions with questions, until the last point was dealt with. Until the next messages arrived, of course.

Nesh set aside her wax tablet for a moment and thought again about messages. The Citadel had scouts looking out for trouble, and there were enough supply carts to carry important messages from outposts to the Citadel. But there was no easy way for these outposts to communicate with each other.

While she'd been an escaped convict, this poor communication network had been no bad thing; now that she was supposed to be overseeing things herself, it was a problem. What other ways were there to send messages, though? Could Air Walkers communicate at any measurable distance? Perhaps, but one could hardly send confidential messages like that, where they might be heard by anyone along the way.

Couriers seemed to be the most obvious answer, but there was the issue of speed there, as well as security. A lone courier might be robbed or hurt, but sending an armed guard with every message was hardly feasible. It was a puzzle.

Ash would make an excellent courier, of course, but he was only one person. If only there were more like him. Unless...?

Nesh had always assumed that Sidrax forms were as personal as Avlem Talents, but perhaps that wasn't quite the case. Hadn't Ash and Madrigal both been learning that lizard shape? Maybe each Sidrax had a unique repertoire of forms? In which case, there might be other Sidrax with fast animal forms who could be their own protectors.

Nesh went to find Ash.

He was downstairs, having apparently just finished unpacking. Nesh met him coming out of the newly-furnished guest quarters, and asked if he had a moment.

"Nothing but moments, I think," Ash said. "Mr. Kerrig is going off by himself, and leaving Maddie and me behind with nothing to do except get under your feet."

Nesh was stunned. She'd never heard Ash so... angry? No, that wasn't the right word exactly. More ... disappointed, perhaps. She could see why Kerrig thought that Ash shouldn't be left on his own.

"I was coming to talk to you about that," Nesh said, deciding to act as if she hadn't noticed his mood. "If you have time inbetween Madrigal's lessons, I'd like your help with a project. Though I warn you, it's an ambitious one."

Nesh outlined her vision to Ash, feeling a sense of surreal delight at putting the whole thing into words for the first time.

"I've been given a fairly free hand here, south of the river. Being Commissioner gives me the right to appoint officers and conduct business out here with minimal interference from the Citadel. Unfortunately, there is a similarly minimal budget, but we do what we can.

"I want this Office to be a non-military law enforcement organisation. Calling in the army for law breakers should be a last resort, not standard practice; I want to be the next step after internal affairs for the towns here, so that things don't have to go directly to the Citadel just because local town councils can't handle a matter."

"Where do I come in?" Ash asked. "Do you want me to be one of your officers?"

"Actually, I was thinking more of 'consultant'," Nesh said, and told him about her idea for couriers.

"If we're going to be effective, we need to keep up with what's going on around us," Nesh said, by way of conclusion. "So, do you think you can help?"

Ash didn't reply at first, and Nesh was afraid that she'd overwhelmed him. When he finally spoke, it was halting and hesitant.

"That's... wow. Nesh, that's quite the vision you've got there. What made you want to be a soldier all of a sudden?"

"Not a soldier," said Nesh. "Something... different. Not a warrior, or a chief, or a mayor, or even a governor.

I want us to be an authority that exists to help first, rather than jumping directly to the use of force."

"But that's just like what the army does," said Ash. "Or at least, what it's meant to do."

He paused again, and Nesh bit her tongue to give him time to think. He was generally so mature and competent that Nesh occasionally forgot how young this young man really was.

"I want to help," Ash declared. "You're talking about being what Tr–" His voice caught in his throat, but he pushed on. "What Trae thought the army was always meant to be: professional heroes. It might be an impossible dream, but if there's any chance this could work, I want to be a part of it."

Nesh felt as though she should say something, but didn't know what. So she just made the most sympathetic face she could and let Ash have the time he needed.

"The first thing is recruitment," Ash said, after a pause. "There are still a few old friends who might talk to me, even after all the bridge-burning I've done over the last year. Those of us who learned scouting forms at the Academy weren't always the most popular, so we had to stick together. I don't know where they are now, but a message to the Citadel records department should solve that."

Nesh nodded. It was odd how she had to remember to do that more, the less she saw others doing it. "Good idea," she said.

It was only later that Nesh realised what had happened: Ash had needed to find people, and had taken matters into his own hands rather than asking her to use her Talent. And yet, she wasn't offended – not at the time, nor now.

Of course, one couldn't expect non-Avlem to follow Avlem rules, but it was more than that. Nesh realised that she was pleased not to have been given the task; it allowed her more time to study her map and decide how far apart the messenger outposts needed to be.

And that thought – about Ash's initiative, not the outposts – kept her up half the night. It was one thing for non-Avlem to forget about her Talent, but what did it mean for an Avlem to forget about her own Talent? After so long in non-Avlem company, was she losing herself?

⸻ ⟡ ⸻

Setting up a message network took longer than Nesh had hoped, and before the first message could come through from an outpost, she had another communication from the Citadel. It was short and to the point.

BANDIT ACTIVITY INCREASING. SEND REINFORCEMENTS.

Bandits? Nesh shuddered. It had been bad enough when she was avoiding them on the road. Now she was actively supposed to stop them. Her shoulders ached under the remembered weight of heavy hands.

> *"Now, lass, don't be sorry," said Gles. "You just find us the best way, and we won't ask for perfect, see? Surely you didn't think we'd get all the way out just by going through the deeps?"*
> *He adjusted his hold, and patted her far shoulder heavily.*

And then...

*Fire and water and chaos filled the en-
closed space, and Brinnesha lost track
of events. Words were shouted, but
she couldn't understand them. People
screamed, weapons clashed, and the air
was full of heat and steam. The only
constant was the painful grip on her
shoulder, dragging her forward.*

That man, Gles, was supposed to be in prison even
now for his murder and banditry. But he had been out
here somewhere, instead, thanks to her naïveté. Even
if he was dead by now, bandits were still a problem for
Ashanna.

"We have to take action on this," Nesh said. "Where
is this message from? How many people do we have
available?"

Nesh took full advantage of her growing messenger
network to plan her campaign against banditry in the
south. Her relief map of the area acquired several tex-
tured markers, and Nesh turned her Talent to Finding
the best line of attack.

There was not one bandit group active in the area,
but rather several small gangs. Nesh planned for her
officers to strike the smallest and closest of these, and
was keen to stress that their goal was to capture, not to
kill.

"We are there to protect the people, and uphold the
law," she said. "Punishment, redress, even vengeance:
these are all matters for the Citadel. Our part is to
bring the criminals in. We're not soldiers, we are civilian law enforcers. Is that understood?"

"Yes, Commissioner," came the reply from dozens of Elementals, along with a handful of Sidrax. How had she ended up with so many people? It was daunting, but gave her heart, too. Her dream of a peaceful, unified Ashanna was finally becoming possible.

———◦———

Nesh attended the first raid, partly to supervise but mostly to understand what worked and what needed to be improved.

"Chief Clerk Tarbry, you'll be my eyes out there," she said. "You have a knack for clear, concise reports; can you translate that into clear and concise description, do you think?"

"Yes, Commissioner."

"Excellent. And already I know you can be discreet. When you're telling me where people are, can you be sure others won't overhear?"

Tarbry hesitated, then said, "May I demonstrate, Ma'am?"

Nesh nodded, then jumped as Tarbry's voice sounded in her ear. He briefly described the layout of her office, the objects on each desk, and the view from the window. He sounded close enough to touch, but when Nesh asked her Talent to Find him, it revealed that he hadn't moved from the middle of the room.

Curious, Nesh touched her ear. There was a faint movement of air around her fingers. She smiled and nodded to her chief clerk.

"Thank you, Chief Clerk Tarbry," she said. "That is exactly what's needed. Hand over any outstanding duties to Clerks Stard and Megram – you're coming on the raid tomorrow."

The raid went smoothly, thanks in no small part to the experience of her Sidrax officers. They set up the Elementals all around the camp as the sun rose, which Nesh confirmed with her Talent even as Tarbry whispered the fact into her ear. She gave the order to attack as soon as the morning mist was burned off. The organised ex-soldiers quickly overpowered the tired watchmen, and then it was simply a matter of rounding up the sleeping bandits.

A couple of the sleepers fought back, and one even tried to slip away in the confusion, but between Elemental abilities, Sidrax animal forms, and Nesh's own Finding, all of the bandits were rounded up.

Professionally, it was a resounding success. Nesh tried to ignore the voice from her childhood that was disappointed by the lack of excitement. It didn't make for a very satisfying story, true – but Commissioner Nesh would take 'narratively unsatisfying' over 'danger of serious injury' any day. Especially when that danger would fall on her people.

The bandits were a sorry lot, especially once deprived of their weapons. Nesh sent them under guard to be tried in the nearest towns, aside from the two oldest, whom she took for questioning herself. Her Talent was a gift, but Life's gifts always worked best when you put in a share of the work yourself. In this case, that meant gathering information.

The interrogations were not nearly as productive as Nesh had hoped. She'd gone in prepared to deal with aggressive, confident thieves, and had her glare ready to go. She was even ready to land some blows, if that was what it took to make them talk.

What she hadn't expected was for the prisoners to become incoherent with terror as soon as she walked through the door. Nesh quickly realised that the answers she was getting were guesses at what she wanted to hear, rather than what she actually wanted to know. After ten minutes she gave up and left the questions to Officer Hill, a rather shy Sidrax.

Perhaps Hill's gentle manner would get the answers she was after, Nesh thought. Then she heard Hill bellowing at the bandits, and sighed.

Perhaps not.

The next couple of strikes against the bandit groups were equally swift and successful. Most surrendered quickly; others tried to run and were caught just as quickly. But when it came time to question the prisoners, they all seemed utterly terrified of Commissioner Nesh personally. Nesh found this baffling, and brought the matter up with Ash the next time he was passing through with messages.

"Surely they aren't afraid of Avlem, not if they raid so near to our towns," she said. "And *I'm* not a warrior, even if several of my officers are ex-soldiers. So why do these hardened criminals break down at the sight of me?"

Ash shuffled his feet, and Nesh sighed.

"I can hear you trying to be tactful," she said. "Don't. Just tell me. It might be useful to have my prisoners unnerved at times, but mostly it's a liability. Frightened people are unpredictable and more inclined to take stupid risks. If I know why I'm so terrifying, I can do something about it."

Ash coughed, politely. "I'm not sure you can, though," he said. "It's... well, I heard a few of them talking, and I think it's, um, your eyes."

"My... eyes." Nesh blinked, holding back her pain and disappointment. Of all the things they might legitimately have against her, they were scared of her blindness? For she truly was blind now; the headaches had gone, and taken the last of her sight with them. She could still track the sun, but that was as much from the warmth on her face as the light hitting her eyes.

"Well, if my blindness is what scares them, then you're right – I can't do anything about it." she said. "I'm surprised, though. I can't be the only person in the country with eye trouble. Are these bandits really so backward as to fear me for it?"

There came a quiet knock at the door, and a diffident cough before Clerk Stard introduced herself. "Begging your pardon, Commissioner, but I don't think those rascals know about your being blind. Neither do half your officers, to tell the truth. Mr. Ash is right when he says they're afraid of your eyes, though. They think you can see through walls."

Nesh forgot herself so far as to laugh out loud. "How did they ever come to think such a thing?" she asked.

"You do have a way of looking through people, rather," said Ash, carefully. "I know why, now, but before you told us about your... trouble, I had no idea.

You sort of... fix a look on the person you're talking to, and it doesn't waver. It can be a bit unnerving, if you're not used to it. Sorry," he added.

Clerk Stard coughed again. "Some of the officers were talking about the way camouflage has no effect on you, Commissioner," she said. "They say some of the leaders on your last raid were dressed up in the local flora, and almost invisible against the trees. But you looked right at them."

"They were making so much noise, I barely even needed to use my Talent," said Nesh. "As for the other thing, well... Thank you for telling me. I can make an effort to move my eyes more when I want to put people at their ease. Tedious, but worth it to get answers instead of mindless whimpering."

Ash made a thoughtful sound, then said, "You might want to encourage the rumour that you can see through anything, all the same. CLEO is an unknown quantity at the moment, and that goes double—"

"I'm sorry: what-O?" interrupted Nesh.

"CLEO. Civilian Law Enforcement Office," said Ash. "Sorry, old army habit, making acronyms. You should be glad your name is so short, otherwise you'd probably have a nickname by now. Maybe that's why my parents went with 'Ash'."

Nesh let the comment on her name pass. Ash didn't know the history of it, she was sure.

"As I was saying, that goes double for you personally," said Ash. "The unknown quantity factor, I mean. No-one knows what you're capable of, and you can use that to your advantage."

Nesh lifted an eyebrow at Ash, then remembered to look away again. Moving her face so deliberately felt strange and unnatural, but Nesh decided to think about that later.

"Like how people think we Sidrax can be anything, even though it takes months and months to learn a single form," said Ash, warming to his theme. "Because most non-Sidrax don't understand what we can and can't do, they assume we're more powerful than we are. And the more unsure people are, the less likely they are to risk an uprising."

Nesh tried to find an answer that wasn't rude. The young man was trying to help, but she wasn't sure she wanted to try anything so... cold. It felt manipulative, too much like how Gles had used Nesh's own inexperience against her all those years ago.

But, if it made bandits more likely to give up without a fight, was it really such a bad strategy? For now, while there were still dishonest people to deal with? Nesh's dream was for everyone to deal honestly with everyone else, but perhaps there had to be... well, sideways steps here and there.

⸻◦○◦⸻

The months passed, and the reports of bandit activity tailed off in most parts of the south. There was something big over in the far west of the Peaks that Nesh was trying to make sense of, but the majority of the land between the mountains and the Great River was clear of trouble. The Citadel was pleased with Nesh's progress, and had increased CLEO's funding. Nesh was hoping to employ a few more Sidrax, as well as another dozen or so Elementals – though she still hadn't managed to attract any Avlem officers.

The model of Ashanna in Nesh's office had far fewer markers on it now, and all but one of those were in the southwest. The one outlier was large, not because it represented a great number of bandits, but because the location was so vague. Reports were coming in of vicious raids, with more emphasis on destruction than on stealing. Things were taken, but the vandalism was by far the worst part.

Ash arrived one morning with a message from the Hassalt Woods, which lay between the Avlem settlements and the lower slopes of the Peaks. He came straight up to Nesh's office, followed by a protesting Megram.

"All messages for the Commissioner must go through the proper channels," Nesh heard the clerk say, over the rapid clatter of two pairs of feet.

Ash and Clerk Megram arrived at the door together, and there was a brief scuffle before it opened.

"Courier Ash to see you, Commissioner," said the clerk before Ash slipped past him. The low-backed chair scraped the floor as Ash sat down, and before she could ask him anything he dropped what sounded like a heavy letter on her desk.

"It's Falerian," he said, without preamble.

"What is?" Nesh asked, taking up the paper and holding it out to Megram.

"These destructive bandit raids. Falerian's behind them, along with the odds and ends of the crews we've been rounding up."

"Well, we never did find out what had become of her after... well..." Nesh wanted to kick herself. Ash had been doing so well, the last thing he needed was a reminder of that awful day.

"No, she disappeared after the battle," Ash said, deliberately. "I suppose things stopped being interesting for her once people started dying. Or perhaps when they stopped dying."

Nesh was torn. She wanted to help, to do or say something that would ease the desperate pain in Ash's voice. But she didn't know where to start. Perhaps it would be best to keep things focused on business for now.

"Clerk Megram, whenever you're ready?" Nesh said, but was met with silence.

"He left as soon as you handed him my letter," Ash said. "Stupid of me, I forgot you wouldn't be able to read it."

"Never mind, it will be included in the next briefing. Which should be soon, in fact. Until then, why don't you–"

"Tell you what was in the letter? No problem."

Nesh gasped. "Courier Ash," she said, "did you read a letter that you were trusted with delivering?"

"Oh, it's worse than that," said Ash. "I wrote it. All the evidence of Falerian's involvement: names, dates, places – the works."

Nesh gasped again, then forced herself to stop and settled for blinking instead. "Ash, that sort of information gathering is dangerous! What were you thinking? You recognised Falerian easily enough; if she'd recognised you, who knows what she might have done."

"Killed me, I expect," Ash said, with a shrug. "But I sent a copy of my report with the standard round, so it would only have delayed things by a couple of days. You see, I'm not as careless as all that."

"I'm more worried about how careless you're being with yourself than your information." Nesh forced herself not to shout. "Ash, no-one doubts your courage or your cleverness, but that... that was recklessness. Promise me you won't do it again."

"If we get Falerian, I won't need to," Ash said. Nesh thought that she could hear a shred of embarrassment in his voice, but it might have been wishful thinking.

The Commissioner took a deep breath, and again tried to calm her voice before replying. *He's only a few years older than Volnar*, she thought. *Be gentle.*

"Ash," she said, "you've done amazing work these past few weeks. If you need to step back then that can be arranged. I had the advantage of some downtime while this office was being prepared, but you've been working without a break. Take some time off."

"No!" The sound of the chair tipping over backwards was almost as loud as Ash's shout. There was a pause, and a scraping sound as Ash put the chair back. "I'm sorry," he said. "But I need to stay busy. I can't..."

Footsteps crossed to the window, and Nesh wished that she could make out his face. She got up quietly and made her way to the door, where she slid the bolt across.

"What are you doing?" Ash asked, sounding curious and perhaps... nervous?

"I can't give you as much privacy as an Air Elemental could, but that bolt means something here. It means that I'm in a private consultation, and anyone who eavesdrops will be on latrine duty for a month."

Nesh fetched her chair out from behind her desk, and sat down next to the window. "I know it's not the same," she said. "But I miss Traegl, too."

There was a long silence, then a stifled sob. Ash sat down heavily on the floor, and Nesh let herself cry with him until neither of them had any more tears.

⟤⟥

Commissioner Nesh went with her officers to arrest Falerian's gang. This was usual. Ash was also invited, which was not. They were using his reports to plan the approach, and he was at pains to make everyone understand just how dangerous and unpredictable Falerian could be.

"She's out of control," he said, as they assembled on the morning of the attack. "Don't waste time trying to threaten or reason with her. She's dangerous."

"She's a bandit, Courier Ash," said Officer Birch, from somewhere near the back of the room. "We've handled bandits before. Plenty of times. She's one Air Walker – we've got Air Walkers of our own, as well as a dozen other Elementals. You've got nothing to be afraid of."

"I'm not afraid," said Ash, bristling. "I'm worried you'll underestimate our target, and mess up this whole operation."

There was a crackling silence before the officer spoke again. "We know what we're doing. We've been mopping up these bandits right across the country while you've been delivering our messages. You're only here on the Commissioner's say-so, and–"

"Indeed, I do say so," Nesh said, deciding that this had gone on long enough. She fixed Birch with a glare, and didn't blink. She heard feet shuffling, and imagined people moving out of the path of her eyes.

"Now, let's have a bit less in-fighting, and a bit more looking out," she said, still keeping her Talent-guided gaze locked on to Officer Birch. "I know Falerian, though not as well as Courier Ash does, and she is not an opponent to be taken lightly. I want everyone on high alert."

"Yes, Commissioner."

⸺◈⸺

Nesh was with them as they approached the bandit camp, and Found the lookouts long before they were seen. CLEO's own Air Elementals took care of making their approach silent. One by one, Nesh pointed out the

296

remaining bandits, all still asleep. Finally, only Falerian remained. It was quiet, efficient, and seamless. All their precautions and concerns appeared to have been unnecessary.

Nesh hung back, while her officers went forward.

Tarbry stayed with her, to provide a running commentary. He'd become quite adept at this over the course of recent raids, and Nesh generally found him brief, accurate, and factual. Which was why Nesh was surprised to hear him wince while describing the moment of arrest.

"Her tent is down, but she doesn't appear to be inside it. She's... she's standing right in the middle of our people. And now she's above them – flown up as they tried to take hold of her. Except for Courier Ash – he must have been expecting this. He's diving her in his hawk shape. He's... oh no! Where are our Air Walkers? Why don't they do something? Oh, they are."

At this point, Tarbry broke off abruptly. "Excuse me, Commissioner, but I think I'm needed."

Without another word, he disappeared in the direction of the melee. Nesh tried to Find him, and then to Find Falerian, but she couldn't get a fix on the moving mass of bodies. She felt suddenly very exposed and vulnerable.

Then Falerian's voice spoke in her ear, and Nesh froze.

"You know, Nesh," she said, as cool and casual as ever, "I don't think it's very sporting of you to have all your players in the game after you've tied up all mine. I think I ought to balance things out a bit. Shall I kill Ash, or one of your Elementals? Your choi–"

The voice was abruptly cut off, and Nesh leapt forward.

"Falerian, that's enough," she said. "You're under arrest."

To Nesh's surprise, Falerian laughed.

"I'm under a lot more than that," she said. "And you still can't stop me from doing exactly what I want."

"Falerian, you need to stop now," said Ash. He sounded hoarse and weary. "You've had your fun, but it's over. Just surrend-urk"

"Ashie, darling," said Falerian, with a vicious sweetness, "you need to stop talking. Stop talking, or stop breathing."

Nesh saw a patch of darkness against the bright white of the sky, and realised that Falerian was flying, and making Ash fly about as well. She remembered something Kerrig had once said about Air Elementals 'pulling air from our lungs'. It sounded as if he hadn't been exaggerating.

"Falerian, this is your last warning," she said. "Surrender now or be killed."

Nesh felt something heavy land at her feet. Ash groaned. He was alive, then.

Falerian laughed again. "You can't kill me," she said. "You can't even hold me, unless you mean to keep a crew of four to do nothing night and day but sit on me. And two or three Air Walkers, to stop me from simply suffocating my captors. Is that what you want, Nesh? Really?"

It was time. She'd discussed this possibility with her officers but had hoped it wouldn't be needed.

"Firing squad," she said. Nesh heard them line up, all those not holding Falerian, or using their Elemental abilities to dampen hers.

She felt as though she could hear each click on each ratchet of each crossbow. The hairs rose on her neck, and her nerves were tighter than any bowstring.

"Find your mark."

Nesh set her jaw and briefly closed her eyes.

"Aim."

A dozen crossbows went off at once on the word 'aim', just as Nesh had instructed.

Nesh heard Falerian's body hit the ground. She felt sick.

Part of her knew it was bad form, to surprise Falerian with a move like that. But she also knew Falerian would block as many bolts as she could, and deflect them into the people holding her. There were things other than fairness to think of right now.

"Tarbry?" she said when she was sure her voice was steady. Tarbry was at her side in a moment. "Round up the prisoners and bring them to the camp. Make a list of the injured. Is anyone too hurt to walk?"

"Courier Ash had the worst of it, Commissioner," he said. "Everyone else is either unhurt or walking wounded."

"I can walk," said Ash. There was a pause, then a thump.

"I can walk if I'm in wolf shape," he amended. "I think."

Nesh wondered what it looked like when Ash changed forms. If she thought about that hard enough, perhaps she'd be able to stop thinking about what Falerian must look like right now.

"Take the... body and bury it according to the customs of her people," Nesh said. She set off in the direction of the camp without waiting to hear her order obeyed. After a few strides, she felt the warm pressure of a furry body against her legs. Nesh stumbled to a stop and put out her hands for balance, only to feel the tree that she'd nearly walked into.

"Thanks," she murmured, and Ash nudged her with his head. Nesh focused her Talent on the way ahead, and walked more carefully. The faint but constant warmth from her left told her that Ash walked beside her the whole trip.

Nesh and her CLEOs struck camp that afternoon. They left a few prisoners to be tried in each of the villages and towns that had been raided, for the people to see their own justice done. In the last town, they stayed overnight, and returned to base the following morning.

On arrival Nesh went directly to her office. She wanted to immerse herself in admin and mundanity, and not think about how the prisoners had screamed obscenities at her, the officers, the town elders, and anyone who'd got too close.

Should the raided towns be dealing with these bandits? Perhaps she should have taken them directly to the Citadel. The other bandit gangs had been sullen and violent, but Falerian seemed to have collected all the worst of them – men and women who enjoyed destruction and misery for their own sakes.

A knock at her door pulled Nesh from her thoughts, and Clerk Stard announced herself. "A trader wants to talk to you, Commissioner. Shall I show him up?"

Nesh blinked, hesitated, then said, "Of course. Send him in."

She couldn't think of anything more blissfully mundane than stores and supplies.

The Commissioner quickly completed her business with the young trader (so very young, to someone who had grown up with a Trader for a father) and went to check on Ash.

Madrigal was asleep in her room, so Nesh and Ash sat down in the communal area to talk. One of the Sidrax officers had some training as a field medic: They'd examined him and declared Ash to be in no immediate danger, but had also forbidden sleep for twelve hours in case there was any lingering damage from his ordeal.

Which made this, Nesh thought, as good a time as any for a chat.

"How are you holding up?" she asked Ash.

"I'm going to be fine," he said. "I feel like I should be the one asking you that. It was chaos out there and you had to give the orders. You did well."

"Thanks mostly to you," Nesh said, awkwardly. "It was your idea to have so many plans worked out in advance. I'm sorry we didn't take your warnings more seriously from the start. Falerian nearly got the better of us, even with your advice, and mostly because I underestimated her. If she'd killed you, I don't think I could ever have forgiven myself."

"Well, she didn't kill me – though I was fool enough to give her the chance," said Ash. Then added, in a more serious voice, "And, thanks to your decision, she will never kill anyone again – directly or indirectly."

Ash reached over and squeezed Nesh's hand. The sudden gesture caught her by surprise, but she only hesitated for a second before returning the squeeze.

"That must have been a difficult order to give," Ash said. "I'm sorry you had to do that – and without even the benefit of army training or officers' school. I expect you've been replaying the scene over and over in your head ever since it happened, haven't you?"

Nesh nodded, not sure how to feel about someone half her age being able to talk so calmly about orders that got people killed.

"I keep on thinking that there should have been another way," she admitted. "The sounds when she was hit, and then when she fell... I could feel it." Nesh shuddered, and Ash patted her hand before letting go again.

"You did the right thing," Ash said. "And even if you didn't – I said 'if'! Even if it was the wrong call, you still made it. That's the mark of a good commander. You didn't hesitate, or try to pass the decision to someone else. I can tell you that I agree with you until we're both old and grey, but what really matters is that *you* agree with you."

Ash's voice changed very slightly, as if he was recalling a lesson from years before. "Never second-guess yourself. When you're in command you must have confidence in yourself and your orders, otherwise how can your people have confidence in you? You must own your decisions."

Nesh smiled, partly at his earnest tone, and partly because he was so kind.

"Well, here's a decision for you," she said. "I'm sending you and Madrigal away for a bit. Go to Westhaven and meet up with Kerrig. I'm sure I can trust you to take care of yourself if you're also taking care of Madrigal."

Ash didn't reply right away, and Nesh wondered if she'd upset him. But when he did speak, it was with a laugh.

"You don't need to worry," he said. "When Falerian almost killed me, I realised that, while I might not be all that keen on living, I'm not quite ready to die yet either."

⸺⬦⸺

In the two days that Nesh had been away from her office, messages had continued to arrive. The afternoon briefing was long and tedious, as Nesh worked through dozens of minor requests. She had to ask her clerks to check files and records for most of them, so that it was getting dark by the time they moved on to the last items.

"This one is rather... unusual, Commissioner. It's from a message station in the far southwest, and seems to be a summary of messages received by them from various villages. It's farming country out there, Commissioner, mostly places founded by retired Sidrax."

Nesh felt her map and located the area. It was almost due south of the marshes, to the west of the mountains. The Great River was narrower there, and split into tributaries that cut the land up into irregularly-shaped pieces. Nesh could feel the little shapes that indicated settlements, some larger and some smaller, but none even half the size of Westhaven.

"Go on," she said to Tarbry. "I'm listening."

Her fingers continued to explore and measure the area, paying particular attention to the marker that indicated the message station.

"The villages have heard rumours of our existence, Commissioner, and that we've had, in their words, 'some success against the bandits in the south'. And they are wondering if we could provide them with, again in their own words, 'a measure of protection' against the local bandits."

Tarbry shuffled the papers and sniffed with disapproval.

"The rest of the messages are more of the same. Hmph! As if you couldn't get rid of their bandits entirely, and just as easily as you handled all the rest. The nerve!"

Nesh smiled to hear such a loyal defence but felt she had to point out that their last arrest hadn't exactly been an easy victory.

"You had to step into the fray yourself," she said. "Something for which I have yet to thank you. It was going above and beyond your duties, and I want you to know that I appreciate it. In fact, everyone did well. I must think of a way to commend them."

"Just doing our duty, Commissioner," said Tarbry, but Nesh thought that she heard a tinge of pride and pleasure underlying the words.

"As for bandit problems in the west, we shall certainly respond. However, it might be just as well if I stayed here. The paperwork builds up every time I leave, and going that far will mean being away for weeks rather than days. I'm going to need notes on all the people we have available. Then you and your assistants must help me decide who to send west, and who to keep here to manage the local work."

"Very good, Commissioner," said Tarbry, sounding resigned to a long night. Nesh glanced towards the window and noticed the lack of daylight.

"It must be getting hard for you to read in this light," she said. "Make sure to bring some candles along with those notes."

"Yes, Commissioner." This time, the resignation was loud and clear. Nesh held back her smile until she heard Tarbry leave. This job wasn't all exciting take-downs of bandit gangs. And for that, Nesh was extremely grateful.

It took half the night, but eventually Nesh had a list of who to send, and a packet of detailed orders for them. They were to make a base camp and move against the bandit gangs with the same techniques that had worked so well against the others.

Nesh sent two of her remaining four Sidrax officers to lead. She still had no Avlem in the office, and very much regretted the fact, but the Sidrax were organised and reliable. Nesh made sure to go over the plan one last time before they set out in the morning.

"You have plenty of Elementals to help you," she reminded the Sidrax officers. "Play to their strengths, and they'll be an asset. Expect them to be Sidrax, and they'll be a liability."

"Yes, Commissioner," said Officer Grace, patiently. "We have Elementals in the army too. We know how to work with non-Sidrax."

"Well, that's good," said Nesh, fighting back the urge to apologise. "You know the plan?"

"Yes, Commissioner." The patient tone was wearing thin. Nesh wondered if she ought to press the point and insist on proper respect. Would it bolster, or undermine, her authority? Traegl would have known.

Nesh decided to let it go. She dismissed her Sidrax officers and withdrew into her private chambers. But before she could get too comfortable in her regrets, she was informed of a new visitor.

"It's the trader's cart, Ma'am, but not the same man. Says he's brought part of the order, and wants a word about the rest."

Commissioner Nesh sighed. This was why she had chosen to stay behind, she supposed. To be on hand to deal with the day-to-day running of the place.

"Send him in, Stard. Let's see what he wants."

"Yes, Commissioner."

The assistant clerk left the room, and her light footsteps were soon joined by the heavier tread of the Trader. He sounded like a large man: not young, but not elderly either. His pace was slow, but regular – like a man considering each move, and not like someone who was struggling to climb the stairs.

The footsteps stopped outside the door, and Clerk Stard dutifully announced the new arrival.

"Trader Tynar, Commissioner."

Back when Commissioner Nesh had been young Brinnesha Tynar, lover of stories, she had encountered such fanciful exaggerations as time standing still, or characters being struck dumb by shock. Brinnesha Tynar had been politely sceptical about these poetic fictions. Commissioner Nesh now discovered that they were quite literal and correct.

There was surely not enough time in a day for all the thoughts that poured through her head at the sound of her father's name. Years of her life replayed themselves before her eyes, and she saw her father standing there – not the vague smudge against the white walls that her eyes saw, but the man as he was, projected from her memories.

Only long, hard years of hiding her emotions kept the Commissioner of the Civilian Law Enforcement Office from breaking into tears on the spot.

"Greetings, Trader," she said, forcing herself to speak. "Is everything in order?"

"Quite, Commissioner," replied Trader Tynar in that voice, the one Nesh hadn't heard in decades. "There's no difficulty with your order, but as you have only dealt with my apprentice so far, and as there are large quantities involved, I wanted to double-check the details."

Nesh murmured something vague and polite, and fought to stay in the present.

"And, well, I'll admit to being curious about a new client," said the Trader. "What exactly is 'civilian law enforcement', and what do you commission, Commissioner? If you don't mind my being nosey, of course."

Nesh smiled, and it was quite genuine. As a rule, Nesh had no patience for small talk, but her father had always made a point of being friendly and chatty with clients. Now she understood why. It was quite something to be on the receiving end of all that charm. She tried to remember that for him this was just a routine call, and to not fall for the patter.

As Commissioner Nesh explained her job and how civilian law enforcement worked, she decided to try a sales pitch of her own. It felt daring and slightly taboo to try and sell to a Trader without having a sales-related Talent, but Nesh reminded herself that she was a Commissioner as well as a Finder, and both roles required her to Find every opportunity for her officers.

"We offer very competitive rates on security escorts," she said. "And, if you were transporting anything valuable on our behalf, that would reduce the fee further. Just something for you to consider – there is no obligation to use our services just because we'll be using yours."

Nesh winced inwardly. That was not subtle, but then again, she wasn't a Trader or a Shopkeeper.

But Trader Tynar didn't sound offended. "I'll be sure to bear that in mind. Do you have any Avlem on the books? Or are your people all Sidrax?"

Nesh relaxed slightly. "I'm the only Avlem in the Civilian Law Enforcement Office at the moment," she said, "though we are signing new officers in all the time. Most of my officiers are Elementals, but we have several Sidrax as well."

The pause before Nesh's father's reply was slightly too long.

"You have Elementals in Law Enforcement?" Nesh couldn't tell if he was impressed or appalled. "You make sure that they're properly directed, though?"

"Of course," Nesh replied, half indignantly. "But some of them show great initiative, you know. All of my people are intelligent and trustworthy."

"I don't doubt it," said Trader Tynar, with such warmth that Nesh wondered if he had recognised her after all.

"All under my supervision of course."

"Of course."

Nesh frowned. Why had she added that last bit? It was true, but why had she... No, she knew why. It was to hear that approving look again. Her memory supplied what her eyes lacked, and she wanted Trader Tynar to– *No.* She wanted her *father* to approve of her. Which he wouldn't, if she revealed herself as Brinnesha.

⎯⎯⎯◆⎯⎯⎯

It was some time before Commissioner Nesh heard from her team in the west. And when she did, it was not good news.

No actual deaths, but several serious injuries. Officer Birch might never walk again, and Galrah's whole right side would be covered in splints for weeks. Plus, the bandits were still at large. The CLEOs had taken a couple of bandits prisoner, but they had escaped. The message concluded with 'Returning to the office with full report in two days' time.'

It was dated yesterday.

Good work on the message network, Ash, she thought. Important to focus on the positive. Let them return. She'd get details of what had gone wrong in person.

II

In the time it took Officer Grace's wounded and demoralised crew to make their way back to the main base, Nesh fretted over the failure despite telling herself she wouldn't. She took it personally, sure that her people would have followed her instructions to the letter. Which meant the lack of success was down to poor instruction, Or, if they *had* ignored her plan, then her people had no confidence in her as a leader.

Either way, this was a black mark on her record as Ashanna's first Commissioner of CLEO. So when Trader Tynar's apprentice arrived with a large delivery, Nesh welcomed the distraction.

She was pleased to recognise the voices of some of the workers he'd brought along, loyal men and women who had been her father's assistants when she herself was a little girl. She was less pleased with the way the apprentice Trader spoke to them. He instructed them how to carry delicate items, heavy items, even how to pick up and set down.

But it was the last straw when Nesh heard, "You there, you see that largest box? Not a crate, the box? That one. Right. Take that one out last, do you understand? It's balancing the load."

They know how to unload a cart, you idiot, she thought. *Some of my father's workers have been doing this since before you were born.* And she might have said it out loud, if not for the arrival of another thought – or rather, a memory.

Nesh was at her desk, listening to the morning report. Several requests had arrived that day, and she was at her wits' end sorting them all out. It didn't help that she had to get the details from her clerks before she could begin assigning names to duties. And she was still catching up with things that had fallen behind while she was out with the Falerian campaign.

"Get me the names and availabilities by noon," Nesh told Tarbry. "I'll have my decisions ready for dictation by mid-afternoon."

"Yes, Commissioner."

Another memory intruded.

"You have Elementals to help you," Nesh reminded the Sidrax officers. "Play to their strengths, and they'll be an asset."

"Yes, Commissioner," said Officer Grace, patiently. "We know how to work with non-Sidrax."

Commissioner Nesh left the apprentice Trader to organise the rest of the unloading and made her way back up to her office, deep in thought.

She sat at her desk and got a wax tablet out of a drawer, along with a wooden ruler to act as a line guide and hand rest.

Strengths, she wrote in the top corner.

What strengths did she have in her crew? Nesh quickly wrote down each of the Elementals and their Element. Then she added 'administration' beside Tarbry and each member of his team. The others probably had additional skills as well, she realised. *As their leader, I should probably know what those are.*

She wasn't even sure what her Sidrax officers could do, which was embarrassing. She'd simply accepted the people assigned to her, and not thought to ask more about them than their name and nationality.

Nesh felt her face burn, and was glad to be alone.

At the morning briefing the next day, a tired but determined Nesh laid her tablet in front of Tarbry.

"This goes on the agenda," she said. "But at the end. Let's get the daily business finished first."

"...Yes, Commissioner."

If Nesh had been less worried, she might have smiled at the hesitant agreement. As Tarbry read out the letters received, she imagined him keeping one eye on the wax tablet.

After her routine decisions, Nesh explained what she needed in rather awkward and stiff phrases, but between her halting explanations and the notes on her tablet, Tarbry seemed to get the gist.

"Any of our people who've served in the army will have skill records – including the, uh, forms of the Sidrax. I can read them to you, or make notes in wax if you prefer."

"Read me the relevant sections, if you please. I prefer to make my own notes."

Ever since Nesh had begun to develop a shorthand for her notes it was simpler for her to read her own writing than others'. But first she needed to address something she'd noticed in Tarbry's manner.

"Do Sidrax make you uncomfortable, Tarbry?" she asked her chief clerk.

"Not in themselves, Ma'am," came the careful answer. "Very fine people, as people go. It's just... well, when they... change, Ma'am. It feels, well it just feels all wrong, Ma'am, if you'll forgive me for saying so."

Nesh frowned. She thought she'd seen the last of this attitude when Kerrig had confronted Farmer Balmar about it. Coldly, Nesh asked Tarbry, "Wrong? In what way?"

"I'm not sure how to explain it to a non-Air Walker," he began.

Here we go, thought Nesh. Aloud, she said, "Try."

"When people move, the Air moves," Tarbry said. "And that's fine. But when someone suddenly changes size, the Air moves in a... no, I can't explain it. It just feels... wrong. Sorry, Commissioner."

Nesh blushed, and -silently berated herself for jumping to conclusions. In an attempt to recover some of her ground, she told Tarbry that she understood about one's Talent being hard to put into words.

"I don't suppose I could describe Finding, either," she said. "Courier Ash asked me to try, once, and it was almost impossible."

There was another awkward silence. Finally, Tarbry said, "About your Talent for Finding, Commissioner..."

"Yes?" Nesh hoped he wasn't going to ask for a 'small favour'. So many people did, when they felt a certain level of friendship had been reached.

"Well, Ma'am,"

That didn't sound like someone about to presume on a friendship, but you couldn't always tell.

"Commissioner, I couldn't help but notice that you haven't put yourself or your Finding on this list of strengths."

Nesh hesitated. She'd made the list for herself, and so of course didn't need to add her own name. But, as an office resource, she ought to be on there.

"Good catch, Tarbry," she said. "I'll add myself in."

Nesh's fingers felt for the tablet, stylus, and end of the list. She wrote: *COM. NESH. AV. FINDER.*

"While we're talking about Talents – or the Elemental equivalent," said Nesh, "is there anything that makes it easier for you to use your Air Walking? Any change in the office that could be helpful?"

Tarbry made a sound of respectful confusion, clearly trying not to ask the Commissioner what she was talking about. Nesh really wanted to ask, *"Please tell me how to stop taking my Elemental officers for granted, and how to let them do their work without my interfering,"* but was a bit embarrassed to say so directly.

"Take my Finding, for example," she said at last. "I can't explain how it works, or what it feels like, but I do know that some things make it easier. Clear goals, for example. Detailed information. The more precise I am about what I'm looking for, the better my results. So, what I was wondering was, is there anything that makes it easier for you... to..."

Nesh trailed off, suddenly lost in her thoughts. *Detailed information. I need more information*, she realised. Not just about her own people, but about the local situation with those bandits. She had already asked the message outposts for reports. Where else could she get the information she required? Nesh realised that she didn't even know what questions to ask. She would have to go out there herself, learn more about the whole area, talk to–

"Commissioner? Ma'am?" The polite confusion in her chief clerk's voice brought Nesh back to the present.

"Chief Clerk Tarbry, would you and Stard be able to run this office without me for as long as three months?

Making decisions about assignments, and handling the day-to-day running of the base?"

———————————

Commissioner Nesh missed Tarbry's skill with describing surroundings, and it took her several days to learn her way around the base camp. It had been established just below the western foothills. To the north and the west were small farmsteads, some of which had grown to become villages. And somewhere nearby was a bandit stronghold unlike any of the little camps she'd cleared away in the east.

The camp itself was a testament to Sidrax military efficiency. Although Nesh wanted to emphasise the civilian nature of their efforts, she appreciated the skills that her Sidrax – and even some Elemental – officers had learned during their time in the army. They had a wooden palisade up, complete with gates and guard towers, inside a day. The central compound was also a wooden building, divided into rooms by wicker 'walls' that could be moved as needed. There was even a second storey running around the inside edge of the building, supported on the only fixed walls in the place.

"Holding cells, Commissioner," Officer Hill explained while showing her over the base. "Even some on the ground floor, if we take a big haul."

"We'll need to take all the bandits at once, I think," Nesh said, trying to memorise a mental map of the area as she walked around. "If we only take a few, the others will raid to rescue them."

She thought she heard the Sidrax officer shudder and took it for agreement.

"What can you tell me about the local people here? Not the bandits, but the ordinary farmers and villagers?"

Hill made a sound that might have meant disgust, resignation, or indifference. "There's some token resistance," he said, "but they mostly leave tribute out in the open, then hide in their huts until the bandits have gone. Spineless, if you ask me."

Nesh frowned at the attitude, but reflected that she *had* asked so couldn't really complain. Still, if this was the degree of interest that her officers were taking in the local population, it was no wonder that their reports were sparse.

"I'd like to meet some of the village leaders, to learn what they know," said Commissioner Nesh. "How long will that take to set up?"

"Commissioner, we have reports on the situation. We don't need to waste time with–"

Nesh swung around to face Officer Hill. He quickly changed tack.

"As you wish, of course, Commissioner," he said, sounding half-resentful and half-abashed. "I'll have the first of them here by this evening."

———◆———

"Why have you brought us here, Commander?" asked a woman called Mellow, who seemed to be the speaker for the group.

"Commissioner," Nesh corrected. "This is a civilian operation. And you've been invited here to discuss the bandit situation."

"There are no bandits in our village," called someone from the back.

"Nor ours!" said the others, quickly.

Nesh tried to read their voices, which seemed to convey mostly fear. But was there a hint of defiance there, too?

"I never thought there were any bandits in your villages," Nesh said, carefully Finding each face in turn and looking directly at it. "You were invited here in the hopes that you had something useful to tell us before we move in to arrest them. There is no question of your being arrested yourselves – unless, of course, you have been helping the bandits? Would you rather they weren't removed?"

A chorus of furious denials burst forth, and this time Nesh heard no defiance at all. But the fear was still there and increased, in fact, when she'd expected to hear at least some amount of relief.

"If you are against the bandits, and not acting against the Citadel, then you have nothing to fear," she said.

"Not from you, perhaps," muttered someone. Nesh looked right at the source of the sound, and heard shuffling awkwardness in the silence.

"Go on," she prompted. "If not me, who are you afraid of?"

⸺◆⸺

Nesh listened and fought to keep her face impassive at the recital of horrors. These bandits were not at all like the opportunistic scavengers in the south-east, easily cowed and rounded up. The bandits in the west were organised and vicious. Their leader called himself Ragneir, which Clerk Megram told her meant 'the closed fist'.

Even Falerian might have hesitated before burning an entire village to the ground 'as an example to the others'. And she certainly never...

"What do you mean, 'the children were gone'? Surely, once a place is burned down, everyone has gone, one way or another."

Nesh realised that, in an effort to hold off the horror, she'd become flippant. She almost apologised, but Mellow, who came from the ruined village of Renwell, replied:

"We looked for the bodies. All the adults were there, though not always in one piece. But the children were not. No bodies, no survivors. We searched the woods, hoping they'd been sent away before the fighting began, but no sign of them. The bandits stole them, along with the food, the animals, and everything else."

Another woman took up the tale. "Not just from Renwell, either. Anyone, anywhere, who held out has been destroyed. They've stolen our children. Six years later, we see what for."

She stopped, and Nesh waited. She Found the speaker, looked at her briefly, then deliberately blinked and moved her eyes away. After a while she looked towards her again and gave a gentle nod for the woman to go on.

"A few months ago, the raiders come in, take their tribute, and I see him" she said. "No more'n twelve years old, running with the others, cheering, and smashing, and grabbing everything his young hands could get. I'd seen that face plenty of times, before he got stolen. He used to help his mother sell butter, and I remember his bright yellow hair. Same colour as the butter, and twice as shiny."

She stopped, lost in the memory. Nesh waited, horrified.

"He was so angry. They took that sweet little boy and made him into one of them." Her voice broke as she added, "I wonder what they've turned my girl into. I've not seen her in years."

Nesh heard stifled sobs, some of them coming from the normally stoical officers behind her. She had to blink back tears of her own, and she stared very hard at nothing. This was a new level of villainy.

"Thank you for telling me," said Nesh. "We need every bit of information we can get if we are going to rid the hills of this menace."

The village leaders made sounds of shock that seemed to overcome their grief.

"You can't! We didn't tell you this to help you fight Ragneir. We told you so you would understand why you have to leave them alone! We can make allowances for losses to the raids, and we know now to hide the children and not argue. If you stir things up again, how many more Renwells will there be? If you wage war on Ragneir, he'll take it out on us."

A new voice suddenly cried out from the middle of the assembly. "It's too late! We should never have come here, and now it's too late! His scouts will have seen us come in, and when the soldiers attack – he'll know we talked. Oh, you stupid, wicked woman," he said to Nesh. "How could you condemn us all to death as you have? And our children! What have you done to our children? They'll be–"

The man broke off with an agonised howl, overcome by the mere thought of what the future held.

Chaos was threatening to overwhelm the room, and Nesh heard the sound of swords being loosened in their sheathes behind her.

"Enough!" Nesh stood up and cut across the hubbub. "There will be no war. No retaliation. No-one is coming for you or your children."

"But he will," insisted the speaker. "You can't promise us our safety, no matter how many of his people you kill. He'll have more, and some of them will be our own children!"

"Then we'll have to stop this Ragneir at the source. We're not here to wage war on these bandits – we're here to arrest them. All of them; including their leader. They will face justice at the Citadel itself and be made to pay for their crimes." In a softer voice, she added, "Only the adults will be tried as criminals. Any children we find will be rescued, not punished. You have my word."

⸺◆⸺

The first children to be rescued from the bandits actually brought themselves to Nesh. They had tried their hand at being a scouting party, come to spy out the compound. Most of them ran away, but one girl was caught by the guards and brought in to Nesh. She sounded defiant and scared, and spoke Sidrean with a heavy Elemental accent, when she spoke at all. She wouldn't say much, not even to give her name, but every word she did say was loaded with a hatred of 'Outsiders' that made Kerrig's angriest rants sound like mild complaining.

That evening, one of the girl's friends attempted a rescue. Nesh was pleased about this, because it showed that this angry child-soldier did at least *have* friends. Also, the children used each others' names. Suri was annoyed with Jos for trying to rescue her, confident that their 'Leader' was coming soon.

Nesh settled the children in one of the upper rooms. Keeping them safe and alive would do for now. Freeing them from their leader would be a task for another day.

She had hoped for more time to formulate a proper plan, but the day after the children arrived. her guards intercepted a raid on the nearest farm. They returned with several prisoners.

The Air Walkers (and Sidrax with small, discreet forms) were kept busy, listening in to all the conversations between the bandits. Within three days, Nesh was confident enough in her information to lead her officers on a raid of their own, right into the bandits' own camp.

⬥

One of the first things Commissioner Nesh had done when she'd arrived in the west was to request a double armful of clay from which to make a sketch-map of the area. She took her touch-memory of the model map from her office and used it to sculpt a rough layout of the local area from the descriptions given by her people. It wasn't as well-made as the one crafted by Mashpa and Volnar, but it served its purpose.

"Are you sure that Ragneir's entire camp is in inside this mountain?" she asked Officer Hill. The clay mountain took up about a quarter of the map table, and had taken as long to finish as the rest of the terrain put together.

"All his fighters are there," Hill replied with confidence. "The prisoners were bragging to each other about how far in they'd be allowed to live once they destroyed us. Ma'am."

"Meaning that those nearest the outside of the mountain are furthest from their leader's favour?"

"That's how it seems, Commissioner."

"And probably all the more fanatical for that," said Nesh, half to herself. She was remembering Traegl's words about those left behind on the island:

"The ones who stay behind will be those who aren't able to join the fighting, not those who oppose it. They'll be itching for a chance to show how loyal they are."

Aloud she added, "Don't underestimate the devotion of these bandits to their leader. Capture and subdue where you can, wound if you must, but our goal is to get to Ragneir and rescue the children he has taken. Kill only when there is no other option."

"Yes, Commissioner."

Nesh felt sick as she authorised even the chance of killing, but knew that she had to be realistic about the up-coming fight. She trusted her officers not to abuse their power, but even so....

"I expect every drop of blood spilled by my people's weapons to be justifiable. Be sure that it is. Defend yourselves, and each other with every other resource before you draw your swords."

This time the "Yes, Commissioner" was less routine, and perhaps a shade less keen.

"For your own sakes, avoid death as much as you can," she said, more quietly. "It leaves its mark."

———◆———

Nesh missed Tarbry on this raid. Megram was an excellent assistant, but lacked Tarbry's skill at concise description.

It was just before dawn, and Nesh's officers were stationed all around the mountain. Air Walkers kept them in communication, while Earthers and Fire Breathers tracked the movements of all the bandits remaining in the mountain. Capturing the raiding party had left Ragneir's forces stretched thin, but Commissioner Nesh was still depending on the element of surprise to give her people the edge they needed.

The officers of CLEO moved as one, in response to a whispered command. Nesh prompted Megram to begin describing the action.

"Oh, right," he said, sounding flustered. "Um, they're going in – where our Earthers thought the openings were, only there's houses over the tunnels. Well, sort of houses. Shacks, really. Leaning up against the mountainside. People are mostly asleep, though. I mean, I think they are. The first prisoners are being brought out, hands tied. I only see a few but..."

"Outer layer clear," came the whisper of an Air Walker officer. "Move in, Commissioner?"

"Move in," Nesh confirmed. "Thank you, Megram. The rest will be happening out of sight, inside the mountain."

Nesh took a moment to Find her people, one by one. They were all moving towards the centre of the mountain, from a half-dozen different directions. She tried to Find Ragneir, and noticed that he was on the move himself. Coming towards her, she thought.

She turned her attention to the nearby waterfall. She'd chosen this place so that the noise of the water would mask Megram's commentary. Perhaps she could gain an extra advantage by having a Marshlander so close to water.

"Clerk Megram," she said, quietly. "Can you, without revealing yourself, tell if anyone is getting near to that waterfall? From inside the mountain, I mean?"

"Not from here, Commissioner," said Megram. "Sorry. But if I went and touched the pool beneath the falls..."

"Go with him," she said to one of the two officers who had stayed back to guard her. "Megram, be careful. Don't try anything heroic, just tell me if there's anyone coming."

Nesh waited, and listened. There was silence for a moment, then a terrible cracking sound, that reminded her of leaving the Crystal Caverns. She remembered wrapping herself around Madrigal, trying to protect her from the swords and arrows of the soldiers at the mouth of their tunnel.

It sounded as though a piece of the mountain had fallen off.

Clerk Megram arrived as the cacophony died down, sounding rather sheepish.

"Um, Commissioner?" he said. "We've got another prisoner."

The prisoner was none other than the leader of the bandits himself, according to Officer Lerrik.

On hearing this, Nesh immediately set herself to Finding injuries. She was relieved to get no response from either Clerk Megram or Officer Lerrik - but their prisoner was badly bruised and scratched, and shivering so badly that Nesh could hear his teeth chattering when he breathed.

"What happened here?" she asked, looking hard at both of her people. "How did this man come by these injuries? Is he even conscious?"

"Not... right now, Commissioner," admitted Officer Lerrik. "But, it was an accident?"

He said this last as if it were a mere suggestion. Clerk Megram took up the tale.

"We were at the waterfall, Commissioner. Most of the exits are on the north side of the mountain, but there's one tunnel that comes out by the waterfall, you know. Then Lerrik sees someone, and so I reach into the water and push the waterfall back. To block the tunnel, and trap the bandit. Only..."

Officer Lerrik coughed.

"Only, I also tried to block the tunnel, by drawing the heat out of the water and turning it to ice," he said. "And so..."

"And so," said Nesh, "You pelted the prisoner with ice, in a display of what would have been some impressive teamwork, if you done it on purpose. Very well. Then what happened?"

"He fell into the pool at the base of the waterfall, Commissioner. I think we accidentally knocked him out," said Clerk Megram.

"And Clerk Megram fished him out in no time, before he could drown," said Officer Lerrik, loyally.

"And then we got a good look at him, and he matched the descriptions we got from the villagers, and we knew we'd caught Ragneir himself," Clark Megram finished, with more confidence.

⊰⊙⊱

They loaded him, and all of the other prisoners who were unable to walk, onto a cart brought for the purpose. The rest of the captives were roped together and driven alongside the cart all the way back to the temporary camp.

Nesh sent a message to the villages, inviting them to watch the bandits brought in. The mountain had been swept clean, and the fighters swept up into custody. In a second cart, the old and infirm were brought in.

They were roped together rather more gently than the fighters, but didn't seem to appreciate the consideration. They spat, and screeched abuse at the CLEOs, who roundly ignored them, and at the villagers, who shrank from them.

Some distance behind, the last of Nesh's officers came into view, and the villagers started to run to meet them. The three officers were each carrying at least two children, and leading others by the hand, Clerk Megram told Nesh gently.

<hr>

The wicker cells were reorganised into multiple small rooms and the warriors left in their bonds. The children, those who hadn't been immediately claimed, went into the larger upstairs rooms to join their young friends, the would-be spies.

Once she had debriefed her officers, Commissioner Nesh made her way into the large room in the middle of the building. That was where Ragneir had been taken, and Nesh paused just outside the door to get a report from Officer Hill.

"He's in there, Commissioner. No trouble as yet, but watch him."

Nesh resisted the urge to sigh. "I'm going to need more than that, Hill," she reminded her officer.

"How...? Oh, right."

Hill sounded embarrassed, but Nesh thought it was more because of his own gaffe than her disability. Some among her people were still unaware of their Commissioner's blindness but most treated it as a minor difference, like her Avlem accent.

"His hands are chained, and his feet, and he's been searched for weapons," said Hill. "I recommend you stay on the other side of the desk, all the same. He's an old man, but a strong one – and clever, too. Keeps on trying to talk to the guards, get us to trust him."

Nesh nodded her understanding, and moved to the door. She took a moment to make sure that she could stride into the room confidently. She Found the desk and chair and went to them before even trying to Find the bandit leader. Which meant that she had her back to him when he started to speak.

"See now, here's the Commissioner. Now we can talk properly, see? Leader to leader."

Nesh froze. Twenty-five-year-old memories woke in Brinnesha Tynar's head as fresh as yesterday.

> *"Now, let's come away and have a comfortable chat, see, while the guards sleep it off. ... We only want our freedom now. Our rights, see? ... Don't cry, girlie. See, I won't let anyone hurt you. Not you, as was so kind and showed us the way here, see? Not you, girlie."*

The voice was older, but unmistakable. It brought with it memories of a leering smile, cold eyes, and heavy hands.

"You." Nesh forced the words out. "You should be dead."

"Oh? Met before have we, my... dear lady?"

The pause was slight, but unmissable. He recognised her, even if he might not know from where. Nesh sat down and fixed her sightless gaze on his eyes.

"Just once," she said. "Long ago. I'm sure you'll know the place when I send you back to it. *Gles.*"

Nesh heard the old man's breathing hitch at the use of his old name. He blustered, bargained, and finally begged to be taken into custody rather than spend another minute in that room.

⸻◆⸻

The return journey to the central office was slow and exhausting; everyone was needed to keep the prisoners under close watch. Between the capture of Gles and his bandits, the recovery of the lost children, and the travelling, Commissioner Nesh had been away from her office for over two months.

Tarbry had been sending messages, and everything seemed under control. Still, Nesh didn't like leaving everything to her clerks. They were able to fill in for her, but she felt bad for leaving them to do so for so long. And it wasn't over yet.

"Welcome back, Commissioner!" Chief Clerk Tarbry greeted Nesh from his own desk as she walked into the office. "We received the news of your success, and have told the Citadel to prepare for the arrival of your prisoners. Will you be going with them yourself?"

"If you can manage without me a while longer, then yes. I need to look up some birth records, and I'm hoping the Citadel will have copies."

Briefly, Nesh filled Tarbry in on the situation with the kidnapped children.

"Some of them are from places that have been completely destroyed," she told him. They're being looked after by volunteers at the moment, but if any living family can be found, then I'd like to reunite them."

"I wish you success, Commissioner," said Tarbry, sincerely. "We have a little mystery here that needs the Citadel records, too. It might be nothing, or it might need your attention. I'll send Clerk Stard with you, and she can explain the situation as you go."

"Very good, Tarbry," Nesh said. Stard was an excellent organiser, and probably a good researcher as well. "I hope to return within the fortnight. Keep up the good work."

◆

Clerk Stard was a little shy at first, to be travelling in a private carriage with the Commissioner. But once she had become used to the idea – and the movement of the vehicle – she was able to tell Nesh what the clerical team had discovered.

"Things were quiet in the office, so Chief Clerk Tarbry had us going through a lot of existing paperwork, to make sure it was all correctly filed and labelled," she explained. "The Citadel sent over a lot of information about the towns we're responsible for, and the Chief thought we should be able to immediately lay our hands on anything you might ask about."

Nesh nodded, and Clerk Stard went on.

"Most of it was as expected, but a few things stood out. One was a settlement in the south, a vineyard reporting good profits but that seemed to be employing more people than could be accounted for by our records. Could have been a clerical error, but since the whole point of the audit was to correct clerical errors, we investigated.

"I hope we haven't overstepped, Commissioner, but Chief Clerk Tarbry sent Dawn and Carver to take a look at the place. They've both got small, unobtrusive animal forms, you know."

Nesh nodded again, thinking that the idea of listing everyone's abilities had been a good one, and privately commending Chief Clerk Tarbry for overcoming his discomfort around Sidrax enough to trust two of them with important work.

"Sensible decision," she said. "Go on."

"Well, Commissioner, I don't have all the details yet – that's why I need to come to the Citadel – but it seems as though the owner of this vineyard has been less than honest in his dealings with his employees. They're mostly of the People, and even under the old laws he was skirting the edge of legal behaviour. With the new legislation, he's straight-up breaking the law."

Nesh felt her temper flare at the idea of Elementals being exploited, but she tried to be fair.

"Perhaps news of the changes hadn't reached him yet. Not that ignorance is an excuse, of course, but..."

Stard waited politely for Nesh to finish, then said, "You're right, of course. So, Chief Clerk Tarbry sent a letter to Mr. Harrell – the owner – to inform him of the new laws, and to advise him to make changes. And I'm off to the Citadel to double-check the information we have, and to ask an expert to take a look at the financial records. It might all come to nothing in the end. I hope you approve, Commissioner."

"I certainly do," said Nesh. "More than that, I'm impressed. When we reach the Citadel, tell me how I can support your investigation."

The name sounds familiar, too, Nesh thought. She racked her brain for a while before letting it go. It would come to her.

The Citadel visit was a partial success so far as birth records went; Nesh thought that she would be able to reconnect a few more families at least. The vineyard investigation, meanwhile, was an unqualified triumph.

What had at first looked like a bit of commercial skulduggery turned out to be more illegal the more they investigated. The Citadel informed them that, as a business owner, Olvar Harreal had been sent a copy of the new laws many months ago. The letter had been sent by courier, and had included a detailed explanation of his new responsibilities.

Olvar Harreal? thought Nesh. *I haven't heard that name in...* she didn't care to calculate exactly how long it had been since she was seventeen and trying to expose the Inker's plans. She felt her lip curl from just thinking about the slimy wretch, and made an effort to hide the expression. She didn't know who might see her, and didn't feel like explaining her anger at that moment.

Having received approval from the Citadel to investigate Olvar Harreal more extensively, Clerk Stard and Commissioner Nesh returned to headquarters.

It took several weeks, and more than one official visit to the vineyard, but eventually they were able to gather evidence to take Olvar Harreal and his partners to trial. Commissioner Nesh didn't need to attend the trial in person, for all her evidence could be given just as well, if not better, by the clerks and officers themselves. She was persuaded to attend the first day, however, by the Governors. Sanwe was the only one who knew Nesh well enough to notice that she was at all uncertain about going.

"You don't have to attend the trial if you'd rather not," Governor Sanwe assured Commissioner Nesh. They'd left the old Inner Keep together, and were walking through the busy, noisy privacy of the inner ring markets.

"I don't mind, exactly," said Nesh. "In fact, I think I'd like to be there when Olvar Harreal gets justice. And that's why I'm not sure if I ought to go."

There was a pause, then Sanwe said, "Go on. Why shouldn't you be there, if you want to be?"

Nesh took a moment to gather her thoughts, and Sanwe didn't interrupt. Life bless the woman! Finally, Nesh said,

"I've been dealing with bandits a lot recently. Most of them are just scavengers, happy enough to take what they could get and not think about the harm they were doing. But the leaders, the really vicious ones, they enjoyed inflicting harm. It made them feel powerful, and they liked to watch other people squirm."

She stopped again, for so long that Sanwe said, "And you stopped them. That's a good thing, isn't it?"

"Of course," said Nesh. "And I'm glad I did. The first time I came face-to-face with evil like that, I was shaken. The second time, I was glad that CLEO gave me enough power to put the monster down for good. And this time, I'm afraid I might..."

"You're afraid you might enjoy it." Sanwe finished the thought when it became clear Nesh could not.

Nesh nodded, minutely. Her face burned from the shame, and she didn't know whether to be glad or sorry that she couldn't see Sanwe's expression.

"Well, why shouldn't you?" Sanwe asked, bluntly. "You're doing a good thing, protecting innocent people from bandits. Why do you care how these 'monsters' feel?"

Because I'm not *a monster*, Nesh thought. Then realised she'd said it out loud.

"Quite right," said Governor Sanwe. "And so long as you're worried about that, you never will be."

Nesh chose not to stay in the Citadel beyond what was required of her in court. She gave her evidence, and returned to her office to await the outcome of the trials.

It came soon enough. Gles and his cronies were returned to the Mines under heavy guard. Olvar Harreal was found guilty on several counts of fraud, not to mention his flagrant violations of the new Elementals' Rights act.

Commissioner Nesh tried to focus on the wins rather than allow herself to brood over the fate of the children rescued from Gles and his bandits, or the extended harm suffered by Olvar Harreal's employees. These were things that would take many years to recover from; lasting reminders of all those who couldn't be saved.

Happy endings are for stories, Nesh decided. *In real life, all we can do is try to make each day a little better than the one before.*

One morning, about a month after the Harreal affair had been wound up, an invitation arrived on her desk to have dinner with a family in the nearest town.

"Read that again," said Commissioner Nesh. And, when she'd heard it again, wondered what in the world it was about.

The town was close by, and Nesh walked over to it that afternoon to follow up on this strange enquiry. With a bit of assistance from her Talent, she located the house from which the invitation had come.

After an awkward conversation, with several false starts, Nesh discovered that people were talking about the Commissioner, and about the Civilian Law Enforcement Office, and that half-a-dozen families were vying for the honour of a personal visit.

Commissioner Nesh just about resisted the urge to say that she mostly paid personal visits to criminals, and that they didn't consider it an honour at all. Instead, she politely thanked them for the kind thought, and said that she was likely to be much too busy for social calls.

"But please do get in touch if you need our help with anything," she said as she left.

Her journey back to her office was spent in trying to factor in this new, unforeseen aspect of being 'Commissioner Nesh'. She should have guessed that her new neighbours would be curious about CLEO, but wading through paperwork and hunting down bandits was infinitely preferable to spending even one night at a party where she would have to make polite, empty conversation with inquisitive strangers.

The invitations kept on arriving. Nesh was tempted to ask her clerks to simply refuse them all with a blanket statement, but felt that might be taking professional detachment into the realm of rudeness. She might not want to socialise with her neighbours, but there was no need to be antagonistic. So she dictated polite and personal refusals to each one, whether they were for a meal, a party, or anything else. They really were busy, besides, as big investigations such as bandit-hunting gave way to myriad smaller problems.

Which was another reason for not accepting favours locally – she never knew when her office might need to deal professionally with these same people. She didn't want anyone to be able to accuse her of personal bias, either for or against anyone. It was this, in the main, that drove Nesh to resolve to turn down all future invitations.

Then two things happened at once to attack this resolution.

The first was yet another invitation, which Nesh was preparing to refuse when she noticed the address. It was from Perayen, Nesh's old hometown.

She hesitated. On the one hand, Perayen was full of people who might recognise her – not to mention all the painful memories. On the other hand, there was a chance to see her home again, and perhaps learn what had become of her friends and family.

Nesh set the invitation aside, to answer later.

The second thing that happened was a message that arrived later the same day. It was a request from one P. Tynar, Archivist, for an interview about the Harreal business. The letter explained that Archivist Tynar acted as record-keeper for Perayen and its five surrounding communities, which included the places affected by the misconduct of the Inker, Olvar Harreal.

It was a professional matter, and needed to be dealt with, Nesh told herself. And yet it was also a personal matter that she would rather avoid. Commissioner Nesh hesitated, then told Clerk Megram to set up the interview.

⁂

"Archivist Tynar is here, Commissioner."

Nesh tried to keep her face and voice impassive as she said, "Very good, Tarbry. Give her any information she asks for about the current status of Olvar Harreal's company." She took a deep breath, and said, "And please tell her I would like to talk to her before she leaves."

There was a slight hesitation before Tarbry said, "Yes, Commissioner." Nesh wondered at it, then it hit her. He was probably wondering how Nesh knew that the Archivist was a woman. That was the problem with employing clever people and encouraging them to pay attention to details, Nesh thought. Sometimes, they picked up on details you hoped would pass unnoticed.

———◆———

Commissioner Nesh sat alone in her office and thought. From below came the faint murmur of voices as her clerks handled Pabiran Tynar's requests for information. Should she reveal herself to her mother? Why had she asked to see her, if not to do that?

Nesh shook her head, impatiently. Of course she wanted to tell the truth. The question was, how to do it? What would be the most tactful, the most appropriate way to lead up to it? She was still mulling over her options when someone knocked on her door. Commissioner Nesh took a moment to compose herself, then called out, "Come in!"

"Archivist Tynar to see you, Commissioner," said a voice, and Nesh tried to smile. Her face felt rigid and ridiculous. Her stomach, meanwhile, was making up for the stillness of her face by turning cartwheels and trying to climb into her throat.

The door closed, and the visitor said nothing for a long moment. Then, just as Nesh was trying to think of what to say, Pabiran Tynar beat her to it.

"...Brinnesha?"

⸻◈⸻

"Hello, Mother," said Nesh, sheepishly. "I'm called 'Nesh' these days. And I know you can't call me 'Daughter' before consulting with the family, but..."

The end of her sentence was muffled by her mother's embrace.

"You *are* my daughter," Pabiran Tynar declared, as if she didn't care who might hear her. "My long lost baby, come home again. Even if I can't acknowledge you publicly yet, I can speak the truth in here. Just you and me, Daughter."

The tears stung her eyes, and Nesh let them fall. But when she spoke, it was brisk and matter-of-fact. She had some important decisions to make, and she couldn't allow herself to wallow in sentiment. Not yet.

"Well, speaking of doing things publicly, I could use your advice. Here," and Nesh plucked the Perayen Founders' Day event invitation from the desk and held it out towards her mother.

"My work has attracted some attention – and cautious approval – south of the River. I've turned down most of the invitations already, but this one is from Perayen. They've invited me to their Founders' Day party."

Nesh listened hard, but could make out no sound of surprise or distress from her visitor. "So the question is, do I accept? And do I reveal my old name now, or hide it and risk exposure later?"

"Which would worry you more, Daughter?"

"I'm most worried about which would reflect worse on you and the family."

Pabiran Tynar held Nesh's shoulders and seemed to be looking her daughter up and down.

"You accept that invitation, my girl," she said. "And you come as yourself, with nothing to be ashamed of."

⸻

Commissioner Nesh disliked parties. Especially ones where she would be the centre of attention, and have to spend the entire evening Finding the right thing to say, the right way to look, and the right place to put her feet, hands, arms, and eyes.

At least finding the right things to wear hadn't tasked her Talent at all. She'd simply asked her mother and been assured that one of the Tynar maids would be sent to help out.

There was a knock on the door frame of her borrowed office-cum-bedroom at the Perayen Inn. It was surreal to be back in her old hometown, and in the inn which she had never visited before. The strangeness of the inn was comforting in a way. It would have been much stranger to enter her old home again, even if it could have been managed without causing a scandal.

Nesh called out to the visitor to enter. The door opened, and someone stepped through so lightly that Nesh could hardly hear them.

A silence followed, and Commissioner Nesh frowned. All of her people knew to introduce themselves at once – though not all of them knew why, even now. Nesh Found the visitor's eyes and looked a question at them. Finally, she said, "And you are..."

"Here from Mrs. Tynar, Ma'am."

Nesh blinked. The accent was familiar. Memories of her old life kept on creeping up on her unexpectedly. To cover her confusion, Nesh babbled something about 'too kind' and 'much appreciated'.

"It's been... some time since I attended anything formal," Nesh explained. "Mo– Mrs. Tynar has offered help, and I put myself entirely in your hands. Please, style my hair and dress in a way that will be appropriate."

"Yes, Miss Bri– I mean, Commissioner," replied the maid and now it wasn't just the accent that sounded familiar. Nesh forgot to move her eyes and stared, uselessly enough, at the dark shape against the white walls. She asked her Talent to Find her old maid, the Elemental girl from the village of so long ago.

It indicated the woman who stood before her.

"Alra?" Nesh could barely bring herself to believe it, even with the evidence of her Talent.

"Yes, Miss Brinnesha," said the maid, sounding as if she might cry. Then, in a more business-like tone she added, "Let's get you dressed, if you're ready."

Nesh felt the tears on her own face, and didn't wipe them away.

"Did my mother send you? I mean, did she tell you...?"

"I heard Mr. and Mrs. Tynar discussing who to send," confessed Alra, "and I volunteered, Miss Brinnesha."

Nesh smiled a little sadly. "You know that's not my name anymore, don't you?" she said.

"Not at the moment, perhaps," said Alra.

Nesh filed that away to think about later. Meanwhile, she allowed Alra to sit her down and begin work on her hair.

"And how has life been treating you, Alra?" Nesh asked, as efficient hands brushed out her simple plaits.

"Me? Oh, not badly, thank you, Miss," said the maid. "Of course, Uncle's the one with the really interesting story."

"Your uncle?"

"Oh yes, ever since he started teaching your friend Miss Talemar how to weave, he's become very popular with the town. So many young ladies and gentlemen coming to learn from the People these days, but Uncle was the first." The pride in Alra's voice was unmistakable.

"He tells that story as often as any legend, now. He says that making the weaving of it was his apprentice's masterpiece, but that might be just the story talking. And Miss Talemar, or rather Webber Rystal, I should say, well, she doesn't just weave blankets these days."

Nesh felt like a child again, waiting for the next line in a story. The fact that this was a true story, and one about her oldest friend, almost failed to register. It was a story, and she wanted to know more.

"Webber Rystal?" Nesh asked. "Not Weaver?"

"Oh, she's still a Weaver," Alra assured her. "Just like you're still a Finder, Commissioner."

More than your Talent, Zirpa had said. Perhaps Talemar was more than her Talent, too.

"I heard she invented the title of Webber," said Alra, now chatting as freely as anyone Nesh had ever heard. "Says she connects to every Avlem Community in the Land, even that odd little one out in the west, all by itself. Got a handful of in-laws in the Citadel, and her children are all out in different places as well, making connections themselves. Very influential, so they say, and doing some good for the People along the way."

Nesh started so suddenly that Alra nearly stabbed her in the ear with the final hairpin.

"For the Elementals?" asked Nesh. "Really?"

"So they say," Alra told her, calmly. "Uncle's very proud. Now, this shirt I reckon, and then the gown. No, let me..."

Nesh moved to put on the shirt – it felt ridiculously soft compared to her everyday wear – but Alra took it from her. "I should have left your hair for last, but the shirt will go over if we're careful," she said.

The soft shirt settled on Nesh's shoulders like a cloud, and she slipped her arms into the sleeves while Alra tied the lace the neck. The gown was heavier than Nesh was used to, and felt oddly stiff to wear. Alra wrapped it around her, and closed it up at the back, as well.

The shoes fastened with wide, soft laces that went around her ankles, but the shoes themselves were thankfully normal enough to walk in.

"I have a feeling I'll need almost as much help getting out of this outfit as I did getting into it," she remarked, once Alra declared her ready.

"I'll be here." promised the maid.

"Will you? That's kind," said Nesh. "I'll introduce you to Stard and Megram, two of my clerks. They've come with me to Perayen to help with some paperwork, but have strict orders to take this evening off."

"I'll make sure they spend the evening doing nothing but eating, resting, and gossiping," promised Alra.

⸺◆⸺

The room was too loud, of course. What surprised her was that it was too bright, even now. Nesh hesitated in the doorway, unsure whom she could even try to Find. Would it look suspicious if she made straight for her parents? Then again, when her true identity inevitably came to light, would it look bad if she hadn't immediately greeted her parents?

She had waited too long, and been laid hold of by her host. Nesh couldn't place the loud, enthusiastic man's voice which hopefully meant that he didn't recognise her either.

"Commissioner Nesh, we've all been hearing so much about you," he boomed. "Your marvellous new CLEO initiative has been a great boost for the entire Avlem community in Ashanna. Rooting out dangerous criminals without fear or favour, in the finest tradition of Avlem courage and integrity..."

Nesh felt as though he were speaking for the benefit of the crowd and did not expect her to answer. Which was probably for the best, given what she wanted to say about Avlem traditions. It was only after being introduced to a circle of people whose names Nesh knew she would never be able to remember, and who once again praised her 'Avlem-led enterprise' that she thought of an appropriate response.

"The Civilian Law Enforcement Office was founded by the Citadel," she said, "and is, in fact, made up mostly of Elementals, with a handful of Sidrax. I'm the only Avlem working in it at the moment. Though I expect we'll be recruiting again soon, if the Citadel likes the results we've been getting."

The excited chatter dipped slightly at this but soon recovered enough for someone to say, "But you're in charge, aren't you? You tell the others what to do, and how, and all that."

Nesh couldn't let that pass unchallenged.

"As a matter of fact," she said, "none of the recent successes would have been possible without the intelligence, courage, and initiative of the Sidrax and Elemental officers involved. We must be particularly grateful to Chief Clerk Tarbry and his team for uncovering evidence of crimes that went undetected for many years."

The awkward silence was broken by her host returning to introduce her to yet more people.

"Though I expect you already know Webber Rystal, at least by reputation," he said. "Her influence extends to all Avlem communities, so you could hardly avoid hearing about her or meeting those who know her."

Oh, I know Talemar, Nesh thought. *The question is, will she know me?*

— ❖ —

Nesh tried to tune out the boisterous introductions from their host and focus on what, if anything, she could get from her old friend.

"Commissioner Nesh, how nice to see you again," said Talemar. She sounded unnaturally calm, but Nesh couldn't tell what she was masking, or why.

"Ah, you two have met before," said their host happily, while Nesh tried to Find the best place to look.

"Not for many years," said Webber Rystal, still unnaturally calm. "If Commissioner Nesh can be spared, I would appreciate the chance to catch up."

"That would be lovely," said Nesh, sincerely. She didn't know why Talemar was being so reserved, but she saw no reason to be the same.

"Lovely," echoed Talemar, flatly.

Nesh used her Talent to follow Talemar through the noise and glare of the party. They finally stopped in a quiet corner, and Nesh sank onto a seat beside her friend.

"Talemar, it's so good to see you again. And you knew me at once! I'm touched – and impressed. There never was any fooling you, though."

"I don't know about that," said Talemar, coolly. "You did a good job of fooling me into thinking we were friends back in the day."

Nesh was stunned. She'd been thinking about this reunion a lot since deciding to attend the party, and her conversation with Alra had only given her more to think about, and more to want to say to her closest friend.

"Talemar... I... What are you talking about? We were always good friends, weren't we? I mean, I know I let you down sometimes, but..."

"You forgot about me," said Talemar, her cold voice gaining some heat, but no warmth. "You went away and forgot about me, just like you always did when something more exciting came along. What thrilling adventures kept you away this time, Brinnesha? What's been keeping you too busy to write to your so-called best friend?"

Nesh forgot to breathe while Talemar was talking. When silence hung between them again, Nesh finally took a deep breath and answered.

"I was disowned, Talemar! Ejected from the family and the community. In case you hadn't heard, my name isn't Brinnesha anymore. This time last year, I wasn't a Commissioner, or even a free citizen. I was just 'Nesh', nameless and unwanted."

Talemar sniffed. "How wonderfully tragic," she remarked. "You always did like to see yourself as the lone hero. And here you are, having single-handedly saved the Elementals and won the praise of the whole of Ashanna. So now, at last, you have time for me."

Nesh opened her mouth to argue, but Talemar went on, her voice cracking.

"Did you really think I would let a little thing like you losing your name make a difference to our friendship? Why didn't you write to me? You could have given me a way to reach you, at least. I hadn't moved away; my name hadn't changed. You could have sent me a message somehow, surely? But the truth is that you forgot."

Nesh closed her mouth again and thought. Could she have sent a letter? It would probably have been turned away at the door by Talemar's parents, but could she have tried?

"Do you know why I was disowned, Talemar? Where I was for most of the last twenty-five years?"

"I don't know, and I don't care," said Talemar. A trace of petulance coloured her anger now. "You could have tried."

Nesh had a lot that she might say to that, and many reasons to offer, but she could hear the pain in her friend's voice now, and that was what mattered.

"You're right, Talemar," she said, as gently as she could. "I shouldn't have assumed that you didn't want to hear from me. I should have tried. And I'm sorry."

Talemar sniffed again, but this time it sounded as if she was crying.

"And I didn't single-handedly do anything, you know," said Nesh. "None of my so-called achievements would have been possible without a lot of help from a lot of people. Including you, as I found out earlier today. My amazing friend, the quiet revolutionary."

"The what?" cried Talemar, shocked.

"According to the niece of your old Weaving master, you've become quite the champion of the People's rights. And all while acting in the best traditions of Avlenia by connecting communities and respecting Talents. Without your influence, working away in the background, I doubt the Citadel would have listened to us at all. And without the new powers granted to me by the Citadel, there'd be no Civilian Law Enforcement Office."

Talemar said nothing for a long moment, then took Nesh completely by surprise by sweeping her up into a hug.

"It is good to see you again, Brinnesha," she said. "And I have to confess something. I didn't recognise you as soon as you walked in – I heard about you from your parents. They told me about meeting you again, and that you'd be here as 'Commissioner Nesh'."

"They did?"

"I think your family has been feeling out the community, trying to see what sort of reception you'd get. Brinnesha, I think they want to take you back – officially, I mean. And I'm sorry if it was meant to be a surprise, but as I remember you don't always do well with surprises. I thought you might want a chance to get used to the idea."

Nesh nodded, and thanked her friend. Alra had hinted at something similar, hadn't she? Did everyone know by now?

"So this is Commissioner Nesh, is it?"

The unpleasant voice cut across Nesh's thoughts, and she used her Talent to locate the face.

"So, 'Commissioner', or should I say Miss Tynar, how does it feel to have achieved your life-long ambition?"

Nesh didn't recognise the voice at all, but the sneering tone was clear enough. She decided not to rise to the bait.

"I'd hardly say achieved," Nesh replied, modestly. "Promoting justice across Ashanna is more of an ongoing project. But it does feel good to be involved in that, certainly."

The sneer rose to a shriek.

"Promoting justice? Is that what you call ruining a man's fortune and reputation? Let's face it, you've devoted your whole life to destroying my nephew, and now you've finally achieved it. I hope you're proud of yourself, that's all."

Nesh frowned. "Your nephew?" she said. "Who is that?"

The accuser spluttered a torrent of slurs, insults, and accusations for a full minute before Nesh could make out the name 'Olvar Harreal'.

Nesh's face cleared. "Oh, *him,*" she said. "You know, I'd honestly forgotten all about him. If he'd not been breaking about a dozen laws, I might never have re-membered him at all. And now that he's been caught, I'm going to forget about him again."

Nesh lifted her head and smiled at her accuser. "Finding bandits is part of my job now," she said. "And as far as I'm concerned, Olvar Harreal is just another bandit."

***

Nesh and Talemar talked a little longer, and Nesh got to hear about Talemar's work, family, and Weaving.

"My modified story blankets are all the rage in some places – and rare enough to command a high price. I'm still a Weaver, after all, even if I do spend most of my time Weaving networks these days."

"We could use a Talent like yours in our office," Nesh observed.

"You couldn't afford me," joked Talemar. "But you Find me an apprentice, and who knows? Oh, I think your... that is, I think Trader Tynar wants to talk to you."

Nesh Found her father coming up at her side, and turned to smile at him.

"Good evening, Webber Rystal," he said, not sound-ing at all like his usual, smooth-talking self.

"And, ah, good evening to you as well, Commissioner Nesh," he added. "I think that my wife would like to talk to you, if you have a moment."

Nesh could hear Talemar's grin as her friend replied for her.

"Yes, go on, Commissioner Nesh. Go and have a quiet talk with the Tynars."

Nesh followed her father to a small room, curtained off from the rest of the party. She breathed a sigh of relief that she didn't have to do this too publicly.

Pabiran and Ralnat Tynar did, in fact, offer Nesh her name and status back. It would be announced in the town hall, and she would be officially Brinnesha Tynar again.

Nesh smiled, putting as much love and gratitude into her face and voice as she could. And said no.

Ralnat Tynar coughed, then hesitated, then managed to say, "Are you still angry with us for how we reacted? Looking back, we could have been more supportive. And not just after you were... in trouble."

"I was arrested, Father," Nesh said, with a small smile. "You can say it. And no, I'm not angry, not with you. Most of what I went through was my own fault, or at least made worse by my refusing to listen to advice."

Nesh shook her head and dismissed the memories. There was no point lamenting what was gone.

"I really do want to reconnect with the family," she assured her parents. "But I don't want to change my name. 'Brinnesha Tynar' isn't who I am anymore, and I achieved a lot as 'Nesh', even before I got the title of Commissioner to go with it. I like who I've become, and that is 'Commissioner Nesh'. It's my name, and I want to keep it."

"But you are our daughter, all the same," said Pabiran Tynar.

Nesh felt the tears on her eyelashes and blinked them away.

"Mother. Father." She held out her hands towards them and allowed herself to be pulled into a hug.

There was still much to do, but in that moment there was nothing more important than these two people.

~~ The End ~~

ACKNOWLEDGEMENTS

Writing *The Avlem Burden* began back in 2013, right alongside writing *Earther 27*, because for the first few years they were two narratives in one book. Once I'd split them apart, they revealed many other stories and became the basis for the *Fragments* cycle. Big thanks to everyone involved in helping me to untangle the two stories, especially Kerry Young and Christopher Wakling.

Deanne Adams and Hazel Hitchins have continued to be amazing coaches. Without their encouraging and constructive feedback, this would have taken a lot longer. And without Deanne's editing magic, it would have contained a lot more errors. She went through my work meticulously, and any typos are things I put in after she sent the manuscript back to me.

I remain forever grateful to my family and friends for more than I can say. Also, a big thanks to everyone on the 2022 Arvon course for your continued support. Would you believe it, I finally finished this book!

And thank you, too. Thank you for reading, for coming with me on this journey around the land of Ashanna, and for sticking around right to the end. Well, the end so far. The next book is coming in late 2025.

About the Author

Kell Willsen is a storyteller of no fixed medium, who has always asked 'why'?

A child of two cultures, and a long-standing visitor to a third, Kell loves learning about other people's 'normal' and exploring different points of view.

Her education is ongoing.

EARTHER 27

Is it betraying the dead to forgive their killers?

Kerrig, Earther 27, is an angry middle-aged man who has lived his whole life under foreign rule. He knows that one day, the People will rise up against the Outsiders; and on the day he will stand with them. Until then, he works at his job in the mines and holds himself apart from the Outsiders there.

Then his life is uprooted and he finds himself on the run with those he despises. One by one, all his certainties are destroyed; until he starts to question everything he thought he knew. Kerrig must make his peace with the past before he can change the future, but it's not so easy to forgive and forget when you're on the losing side.

Marshlander's Betrayal

What does loyalty mean to a liar?

Suri's childhood has been happy and normal... or as normal as anyone's could be with a large, extended family of freedom fighters. She can't wait to be old enough to join them, and become a champion of the People.

But when the life Suri knows is torn away, an alternative truth about her past is presented to her. Will her loyalty to her family hold out, or will she turn traitor?